KAT MARTIN

RULE'S BRIDE

THE BRIDE TRILOGY

First published in Great Britain 2013
Mills & Boon, an imprint of Harlequin (UK) Limited,
Eton House, 18-24 Paradise Road, Richmond, Surrey TW9 1SR

© Kat Martin 2010

ISBN: 978 0 263 90716 2

12-0713

Harlequin (UK) policy is to use papers that are natural, renewable and recyclable products and made from wood grown in sustainable forests. The logging and manufacturing processes conform to the legal environmental regulations of the country of origin.

Printed and bound
by CPI Group (UK) Ltd, Croydon, CR0 4YY

To my editor, Susan Swinwood, for her help
with this series. It's a pleasure to work with you

Prologue

Boston, 1857

They say good things come to those who wait, but Rule Dewar wasn't so sure. Standing in the long marble hallway at Griffin Heights, his employer's palatial estate on the outskirts of Boston, Rule waited nervously while the stone-faced butler rapped on the study door.

Ignoring the urge to adjust the knot on his cravat and smooth his hair, he straightened at the sound of muffled footsteps approaching from the opposite side of the door. The door swung open and the man inside the study smiled, clearly anticipating his visitor's arrival.

"Rule! Come in, my boy. I appreciate your stopping by on such short notice." Howard Griffin, head of Griffin Manufacturing, makers of high-quality armaments, welcomed him into the study, a vast, book-lined chamber that took up a goodly portion of the west wing of his mansion.

Rule walked past him into the room. "It wasn't any trouble. I was just going over some of the design change proposals you asked me to look at."

Griffin, in his early forties and nearly as tall as Rule, had a solid build and reddish-brown hair. He walked over to a pair of polished mahogany doors and slid them open. Hidden within was a sideboard lined with bottles of expensive liquor and cut-crystal decanters on gleaming silver trays.

"So what did you think of the new designs?" Griffin asked as he took down a pair of crystal glasses and set them on the sideboard.

"I agree with your assessment. I believe eventually the smooth bore will be replaced entirely by the rifled barrel. Which means we should consider changing the percentages of each kind of musket now being produced."

Griffin smiled, clearly pleased, though Rule had the impression business was not what the man had asked him there to discuss.

"Care for a whiskey?" The older man held up a decanter filled with golden-brown liquid. "Or perhaps you would rather have something else."

Rule preferred brandy, a slightly less potent beverage, but the Americans seemed to like the stronger liquor and he had grown accustomed to the taste. "Whiskey is fine."

Griffin poured both of them a drink and handed one of the glasses to Rule, who took a sip, the burn of the alcohol easing a little of his tension. Not all, though. Giving in to the urge, he ran a hand over his wavy black hair to smooth the windblown strands back into place. It wasn't every day his boss, the wealthy owner of the company, invited him into his home.

Griffin didn't ask him to sit down but guided him toward a window overlooking the garden. Though early in the year, spring blossoms had begun to peek through the soil, and the winding brick pathways were meticulously maintained.

Griffin swirled the liquor in his glass. "In the time

you've worked for me, Rule, you've done an excellent job. I made a wise decision in hiring you."

"Thank you, sir." In spite of the fact he was only four-and-twenty, he had been given an impressive amount of responsibility, mostly a result of his Oxford education, which seemed to impress the Americans, but also because of his pedigree.

Rule wasn't stupid. Being an English aristocrat gave him entry into the top levels of society on both sides of the ocean. Being the brother of a duke opened an amazing number of doors and Rule was willing to use every advantage to further his career.

Griffin turned to stare out the window. In the distance a marble fountain sprayed water into the bright spring sunshine. There was something in his manner that seemed in contrast to his usually dynamic nature.

"I believe you've met my daughter, Violet."

"Yes, sir, on several occasions. Lovely girl."

"She is young yet, only sixteen, and a bit of a tomboy. My fault, that. I never had a son, so I indulged her."

Rule's gaze followed Griffin's to a huge sycamore on the right side of the fountain. Beneath the branches, Violet Griffin sat in a rope swing, laughing as she pushed herself higher and higher into the air, her full skirt and petticoats billowing out around her stocking-clad ankles. She had a heart-shaped face, a boyish figure and hair the color of new copper pennies.

"As I was saying, she is young yet, but she looks a great deal like her mother—God rest her soul—and in time I believe she'll turn into quite a beauty."

"I'm sure she will." Rule sipped his drink, having no idea how the gangly young girl would look when she grew up and wondering where the conversation was leading.

Griffin turned. His gaze zeroed in on Rule's face. "Unfortunately, I won't be around to watch that transformation."

Rule's head came up. "Sir?"

"I'm dying, Rule. There is no easy way to say it. I've been to a number of physicians, all of whom agree. I'm dying and there is no way to keep it from happening."

The breath lodged in Rule's lungs. For the first time he noticed the slightly yellow cast to Griffin's skin, the faint purple hollows beneath his eyes.

He swallowed. "What…what is it, sir? What sort of illness has afflicted you?"

Griffin's eyes looked bleak. He shook his head. "Some kind of liver malfunction. Nothing they can do to stop it."

Rule's chest was squeezing, making it difficult to breathe. Howard Griffin was one of the most vital men he had ever met. An aura of power and authority seemed to follow him wherever he went. They didn't know each other well, and yet Rule had enormous respect for him.

"I'm sorry, sir. I find myself utterly at a loss for words. You say these doctors are certain?"

"I'm afraid so, yes, and as much as I would like to pretend otherwise, it is time I accepted the fact and made plans accordingly."

Rule steeled himself. "Whatever you need, you know you can count on me."

Griffin's lips faintly curved with something that looked like satisfaction. "That is what I'd hoped you would say." He turned back to the window. "Though I doubt what I am going to ask will remotely resemble what you might be thinking."

Rule made no comment.

"Whatever fate holds in store for me, my foremost concern is the welfare of my daughter. I need to know her future will be secure. I need to be certain she will be well cared for and that she'll have the sort of home a woman wants. In short, I need to find her a husband."

Rule's stomach knotted. Surely Howard Griffin wasn't thinking of him as a candidate for his daughter's hand in marriage?

"She likes you, Rule. In fact, I believe she even harbors some sort of schoolgirl crush on you."

"You are not thinking—"

"Actually, I am, but don't look so horrified. What I am about to propose isn't quite what you think."

"I understand your fears, Mr. Griffin, but as you said, your daughter is only sixteen."

"And yet it is my duty as her father to arrange for her future, to ensure she marries well and is happy and well cared for. If there were more time, of course, I would do things differently. Unfortunately, time isn't something I have."

Rule could only imagine how the man must feel. He had a daughter he loved and now he would never see her grow into a woman. "I see your dilemma, sir, but I'm afraid…"

"My choices are limited, Rule. I need to make arrangements for her future, though in some ways she is still a child. Which is the reason I would require her future husband to wait until she has reached her maturity before the marriage is consummated. She would have to be at least eighteen."

Rule found himself shaking his head. "I'm sorry, sir. As much as I respect you, if you are asking me to marry your daughter, I'm afraid I'll have to—"

"Before you give me your answer, at least hear me out."

The man was dying. The least Rule could do was be polite enough to listen. He gave a curt nod of his head. One thing was sure. No matter how much he admired Howard

Griffin, he wasn't about to get married and especially not to a sixteen-year-old girl.

"Why don't we sit down and I'll tell you what I am proposing. Perhaps when I am finished, you will no longer look at me as if I have already lost my wits."

Rule managed a smile. Damn, he bloody well liked this man. He hated the thought of him dying so many years before his time.

It was a shame he would have to refuse him.

Seated on an ornate gold velvet settee in her bedroom, Violet Griffin sat next to her cousin and best friend, Caroline Lockhart. Eyes red rimmed from crying, Violet blew her nose into a lace-trimmed handkerchief and wiped the tears from her cheeks.

"I still can't believe it."

"It isn't fair," Caroline said. "You've already lost your mother. You don't deserve to lose your father, too."

Violet sniffed, wiped away fresh tears. She had been crying for days, ever since her father had called her into his study and told her the terrible truth—that in less than a year, he would be dead. "Father says life is never fair."

"I suppose not, but it certainly should be."

Violet looked up at her friend. "F-Father wants me to marry. He says it's the only way he can die in peace."

Caroline's pale blue eyes widened. Blonde and fair and an inch taller than Violet, she shifted on the sofa, the skirt of her pink taffeta tea gown making a rustling sound as she moved. "Dear Lord, you are only sixteen!"

"It doesn't matter."

Caroline bit her lip. "So whom does he want you to marry?"

"The Englishman, Rule Dewar. You remember him. He

came here for supper several times and on another day came to luncheon. You met him at luncheon."

Caroline's expression turned dreamy. "It isn't as if I would forget. I have never seen a more beautiful man."

Violet just nodded. "That is what I thought the first time I saw him. He has the most amazing blue eyes and his hair is so black it looks blue." She glanced down at her lap then back at her friend. "Do you think I should marry him? Father wants to make sure my future is secure before—before…"

"Your father loves you very much," Caroline said softly.

"I know he does." Violet dabbed at a tear escaping down her cheek. "So should I? Papa has always asked so little of me and it would please him so greatly."

"Do you think… Does Rule want to marry you?"

"I don't know. Father says he does."

"It's an odd name—Rule. Where do you suppose it came from?"

"Father says it was his great-grandfather's name, inherited from the mother's side of the family or some such thing. He says the two of them have already come to a financial arrangement that would take care of both of us. He says Rule wouldn't actually…he wouldn't actually become my husband until I turned eighteen."

Caroline nodded. "You mean he won't demand his husbandly rights before you are old enough."

"I suppose." Violet twisted the damp handkerchief in her hands. "Until then, he is going back to London to manage the plant we own there."

Caroline smoothed her pink taffeta gown. "So do you want to marry him?"

Violet shook her head. "I don't want to marry anyone. Not yet, at any rate. But if I have to get married…well, then, I guess I would choose Rule."

Caroline grinned. "Can you imagine? The man is the brother of a duke! If you marry him, you'll be the envy of every girl at Broadmoor."

Mrs. Broadmoor's Academy for Young Ladies, which both girls currently attended, was the most exclusive finishing school in Boston. Violet didn't particularly like the place. She preferred a different sort of education, the kind her father had already provided: math and history, science and geography, French, Latin and Greek.

But she was determined to be the lady her father always wanted her to be, so she applied herself with equal purpose to her studies at the academy.

Tears welled. Now it wouldn't matter if she graduated at the top of her class. Her father would never know.

She took a shaky breath. Whether he knew or not didn't matter. Violet would know, and pleasing him now was more important than ever.

There and then, she made her decision.

"I'm going to do it, Carrie. I'm going to marry Rule Dewar."

Caroline let out a girlish squeal, slid over and hugged her. "You're going to be a bride! I can hardly believe it!"

Violet stared down at the handkerchief in her lap and swallowed past the lump in her throat. "Neither can I."

Two weeks passed. It seemed the blink of an eye to Rule. It was Saturday, a warm spring day he tried to see as a positive omen for the monumental decision he had made. Standing in the vast gardens at the rear of the Griffin mansion in front of a flower-covered arch above the altar, Rule stared up the aisle at the future Mrs. Rule Dewar.

She looked exactly like what she was, a naive young girl barely out of the schoolroom. Even in an elaborate wedding gown fashioned of endless rows of white Belgian lace, she was a gangly, boyish young woman. Hardly ready for marriage and certainly not the sort Rule would choose if she were.

In truth, marriage was the last thing he wanted.

But Howard Griffin was beyond persuasive, and the deal he had offered was more than anything Rule could have dreamed. After Griffin's death, once the marriage was consummated, he would inherit half of Griffin's fortune and become half owner of Griffin Manufacturing. The other half would belong to Violet, the woman soon to become his wife.

The laws were different in America and his bride's fortune would remain her own, but together they would be a powerful force in the financial world.

And there was an added benefit. Aside from the money and ownership of an extremely successful company, Rule would be fulfilling his father's greatest wish. The late Duke of Bransford was convinced that an alliance with the Americans would carry the Dewar family securely into the next century, and Rule had promised to see it done.

Marriage and a business that spanned the Atlantic would certainly be a satisfactory means of making that happen.

His gaze ran over the few rows of seats filled by Griffin's friends and family, an intimate gathering that would have been a spectacular affair if Violet were older and the wedding not a hurried event that was only a means to an end.

He wondered how many people in attendance knew the circumstances of the wedding and thought that Griff, as Rule was now supposed to call him, had probably spoken to most of them and explained the situation. Rule thought the majority would sympathize with a dying father's desire to ensure his only child's future and agree with his decision.

At the top of the steps leading down from the terrace, Griffin extended his arm and Violet rested a white-gloved hand on the sleeve of his satin-lapelled, black broadcloth tailcoat. She was even more petite than he had realized, and earlier he had noticed that her eyes were a pretty leaf-green. There was a sprinkling of freckles on her nose, he had observed as he had proposed, very gallantly, on bended knee in the drawing room in front of her father.

She was little more than a child and part of him rebelled at the notion of making her his wife, even in name only. He fought an urge to turn and run, board the fastest ship he could find back to England. But the die had been cast, the future laid out for him like a juicy piece of meat, and he had been unable to resist.

By the end of the ceremony, he would be on his way to becoming an extremely wealthy man. In the meantime, until the dismal occasion of his father-in-law's passing, Rule would be employed at a lavish salary as head of the London branch of Griffin Manufacturing and live in high style in the city.

The organ began to play the wedding march, returning his attention to the moment. Walking next to her father, Violet managed a half-hearted smile and started down the aisle to where he stood waiting. Rule reminded himself he wouldn't truly be a husband for at least several years, wouldn't have to face that sort of responsibility until he was ready.

Pasting on a smile he hoped looked sincere, he thought of the future he was securing for himself, the fulfillment of the promise he had made his father, and prepared to greet his bride.

* * *

Violet kept the smile fixed on her face as she made her way down the aisle. Only close family and a few intimate friends were in attendance. Quite enough for Violet, who just wanted this day to end. On the morrow, Rule would sail for London and her life would return to normal. At least for a while.

She refused to think of the months ahead and the terrible fate awaiting her father. Instead, she focused her attention on the man she would marry. Rule gave her an encouraging smile and her heartbeat quickened, began a steady thrumming inside her chest. Good heavens, he was handsome! She had never seen a man with eyes so blue and fringed with a double row of thick black lashes. She had never seen more beautiful lips, full and pleasingly curved. Winged black brows formed a faultless arch over each of his magnificent eyes, his nose was straight, and his smile flashed an even row of perfect white teeth.

When she reached his side, he took her trembling hand in his larger, warmer one, and his smile widened, carving dimples into his cheeks. Goodness, she had never seen a face assembled with such perfection.

And he was going to be her husband!

The thought made her knees start to tremble. As her father handed her into Rule's care, she stiffened her spine and told herself she was doing this because her father wished it, but deep down she wasn't completely sure.

For long minutes she stood there rigidly as the minister performed the marriage ceremony. Rule repeated his vows and she hers, and then it was over and he bent and kissed her cheek.

Violet suppressed a flicker of disappointment. She had never been kissed. She thought she deserved at least that much from the man who was now her husband.

"Well, Mrs. Dewar," he whispered softly, his warm breath feathering goose bumps across her skin, "how does it feel to be married?"

She looked up at him. "So far I have no idea. What about you?"

Rule laughed, a deep, rich, musical baritone. Of course his laughter would be perfect, just like the rest of him.

"You're exactly right—I haven't a clue, either. I don't feel the slightest bit different."

"Maybe it takes a while."

He smiled, seemed to relax. "Perhaps." She loved his accent. It fit so well with his immaculately tailored clothes, expensive leather shoes and snowy cravat.

"I believe your family has planned a wedding celebration. Perhaps now that the worst is over, we'll be able to actually eat."

Violet laughed. She hadn't expected that. That he would be able to make her laugh. It made him seem less formidable, more approachable. "I'm starving. I was afraid to eat anything earlier. I wasn't sure I would be able to keep it down."

He smiled. "Exactly so." He continued to smile, and she thought, *Could this beautiful man actually be my husband?* But as he took her hand and placed it on the sleeve of his coat, she knew that it was so.

Weaving their way through a small barrage of well-wishers, they made their way from the garden back inside the house. Rule kept her close at his side and she appreciated his effort to play the role of dutiful husband. As the afternoon progressed, she told herself that everything would work out. That her father's judgment had never proved wrong before and she should trust that judgment now.

The hours seemed to have no end but finally the guests departed, all except Rule, her father and Aunt Harriet, her mother's sister and one of Violet's few close relatives. As she stood next to Rule and the small group who remained, a wave of exhaustion hit her and she swayed on her feet.

"Are you all right?" Rule asked, his hand going to her waist to steady her.

Violet managed to smile. "I'm fine. A little tired, perhaps."

He glanced at the clock above the marble mantel in the drawing room. "The others have mostly gone and I'm afraid it's time for me to leave, as well. I have some packing to finish before I head down to the ship."

Violet felt torn.

She was married, but her husband was leaving. She wasn't sure when she would see him again.

On the other hand, she wasn't ready to be a wife and she wasn't sure how long it would take before she would be.

"We'll walk you out to your carriage," her father said, and the group made its way in that direction, ending up outside on the wide front veranda.

"Have a safe voyage," Violet said, not sure what sort of farewell was appropriate under the circumstances.

Rule bowed over her hand, lightly pressed his lips against the back, and she could feel his warm breath through her glove. "Goodbye, Violet."

She watched him descend the steps and climb into his carriage, then, as if he had never been there, he was gone.

Her father's hand settled gently on her shoulder. "He'll be good to you, dearest. He has given me his word he will see to your every need."

She only nodded. *What about love?* she thought. The word had never entered her mind until that very moment and certainly wasn't part of any conversation she'd had with her father. Love wasn't a necessary part of marriage, she knew, and yet…

For some strange reason, as she watched Rule's carriage depart, a lump formed in her throat.

"Rule will make you a very good husband," her father confirmed. "When the time is right."

"I'm—I'm sure he will." She watched Rule's carriage disappear through the massive iron gates that bore the tall, golden image of a griffin—the body of a lion and the wings of an eagle—and felt oddly depressed.

"Come inside, sweetheart," said her aunt Harriet, a silver-haired woman in her fifties with an unshakable loyalty to her and her father. "You must be tired after such a trying day."

Violet just nodded. She felt drained and strangely bereft. She had a husband who wasn't there and soon her father would also be gone.

As they crossed the front porch and went inside the house, Violet clung to Griff's arm, wishing things could be different and fighting not to weep.

One

~~~~~~~~~∽◊◊◊∽~~~~~~~~~

London, England
Three years later

"Rule, how good of you to come!" His hostess for the evening, Lady Annabelle Greer, floated toward him across the elaborately decorated ballroom in the London mansion she shared with her husband, Travis. "And I see you have brought Lucas with you."

Her gaze shifted across the room to where his best friend, Lucas Barclay, made conversation with a delectable young widow he had only just recently met. Rule and Luke had attended Oxford together. Beyond that, they were shirt-sleeve relatives of a sort. Rule's oldest brother, Royal, the Duke of Bransford, was married to a cousin of Luke's brother's wife.

Rule returned his attention to his hostess. "It's good to see you, my lady." With her light brown hair and clear blue eyes, Annabelle Townsend Greer was nearing thirty and the mother of three children, yet she was still a beautiful woman.

"I'm surprised you came. You are usually too busy working." She tapped her painted fan against his shoulder. "Don't you know it is highly improper for a member of the aristocracy to labor for money like a commoner?" She grinned. "But then, none of you Dewars have ever given a fig for propriety."

Rule grinned back. "I might say the same for you, my lady." He could still recall rumors he had heard of the torrid affair that had resulted in Annabelle's marriage to Travis Greer, a former lieutenant in the British cavalry, confirmed bachelor and his brother Reese's best friend.

Anna just laughed. "I admit to being a bit outrageous at times. Not recently, though."

Rule smiled. "No, not since your husband had the courage to take you in hand."

Anna grinned at the ridiculous remark. If anything, it was the other way round. Travis walked up just then, a well-built man with sandy-brown hair and small, gold-rimmed spectacles who was clearly in love with his wife. A respected journalist with the *London Times,* he wrote articles about whatever war the country might be fighting at the moment.

The empty sleeve of his coat bore testimony to the price he had paid when he was in the cavalry with Reese.

"Good to see you, Rule." Travis glanced around the ballroom, the mirrored walls reflecting images of dozens of elegantly dressed men and women. "So which of these lovely ladies has managed to capture your attention? I heard you ended your…association with the beautiful and intriguing Lady St. Ives."

Rule took a sip of his champagne. "News travels fast."

"I assume you're on the prowl again."

He was indeed on the lookout for a new, more interesting mistress. He had grown tired of Evelyn Dreyer, Viscountess St. Ives, and several weeks back had ended the affair. It wasn't Evie's fault, he knew. For some time now, he had been feeling restless and bored, in search of something but not quite certain what it was.

Travis's gaze shifted away from him and moved around the ballroom. "Or could it be that you are finally on the hunt for a wife?"

The sip of champagne Rule had taken nearly spewed from his mouth. He shook his head. "I'm definitely not looking for a wife. At least not at the moment."

No one in London knew he was married. Not even his family. He would have to tell them, of course, and soon. Should have done it long ago. But telling them would make it real. It would force him to admit it was past time he did his duty, went to Boston and retrieved his wife.

The thought had him excusing himself and heading for the liquor table for something stronger than champagne.

Luke caught up with him there. "The crowd is beginning to thin. How about we head over to the club? Or we could go to Crockfords, do a little gambling." Luke was nearly as tall as Rule, with dark brown hair and keen brown eyes. He had a scar through his right eyebrow that gave him a rakish, dangerous appearance women seemed to find attractive.

"Or if you are *up to it,* we could stop by Madame Lafon's." Luke grinned lasciviously at the pun, but Rule shook his head.

There was a time the elegant bordello had been one of his favorite ways to spend an evening. Lately, the notion of bedding one of the house's beautiful harlots held little appeal.

"How about Crockfords?" he said. "I've been on a bit of a lucky streak lately. Perhaps it will hold."

Luke smiled. "Crockfords it is."

The one thing Rule wasn't ready to do was go home. If he did, his conscience would nag him. He would think about the money Griff had left him when he died, the profitable investments from his lavish salary and the promise he had made. Though he had kept track of Violet through her aunt, Harriet Ardmore, he hadn't been back to see the girl since the day they were wed.

He had planned to be there when her father died, but Griff had passed with very little warning, leaving Rule no time to make the monthlong crossing from London to Boston. He'd sent a letter to Violet, of course, expressing his condolences, then was careful to write her a short note at least every other month.

But it wasn't the same as assuming his role of husband.

As he made his way out of the ballroom and stepped into the cool night air, he told himself it was time he kept his word. In the next week or two, he vowed, he would book a trip to Boston.

It was past time he went to collect his bride.

Rule ignored the sinking in the pit of his stomach.

Violet stepped off the clipper ship *Courageous,* grateful to once again be standing on dry land. At last, she was in London. She tightened her hold on the reticule hanging from her wrist and glanced at her surroundings. The docks buzzed with activity: stevedores unloading cargo, passengers disembarking from an endless line of ships along the quay, merchants hawking their wares to a herd of newly arrived, unsuspecting prey.

Gulls screeched overhead, their raucous cries mingled with the clatter and clank of ships' rigging, sounds Violet had grown so accustomed to she barely noticed.

"Isn't this exciting?" Her cousin, Caroline Lockhart, hurried along beside her, next to Mrs. Cummins, a lady of impeccable credentials who had been paid to act as their traveling companion.

"It is quite a bit different than I imagined," Violet said, peering up at the skyline marked by tall church spires and a haphazard array of roofs dotted with chimney pots. "Everything looks older than I thought but that only seems to make it more charming."

Though the area around the docks was certainly not the best. The buildings here were dilapidated and in need of repair, and aside from the travelers, most of the people on the streets were dressed in shabby clothes.

"I'll hire us a carriage," offered Mrs. Cummins, a big-boned, sturdy woman with iron-gray hair. They would be parting company soon, once Violet arrived at the residence belonging to her husband.

Husband. The word left a bad taste in her mouth. She hadn't seen Rule Dewar since their wedding day three years ago.

Oh, he had sent an occasional note but clearly he had no intention of fulfilling his duties to his wife.

And Violet was extremely glad.

She had been so young when she had met him. Young and impressed with his extravagant good looks. And she'd been grieving for the father she would soon have to bury. Griff wanted her to marry and she would have done anything to please him—even wed a man she didn't know.

"All right, girls, here we are." Mrs. Cummins led them toward a ramshackle coach pulled by two tired-looking bay horses. The driver tipped his hat as he jumped down from the box and began hefting their steamer trunks into the boot at the rear of the vehicle.

Mrs. Cummins, very conscientious in her duties, watched the proceedings with a discerning eye. She had taken the job as companion in Aunt Harriet's place since Aunt Harry turned green at the mere thought of four long weeks at sea.

The substitution was fine by Violet, who had been living mostly on her own since her father died. Desperate to fill her days with something more than sadness and grief, she had begun taking an interest in her father's Boston munitions factory.

Growing up, she had spent a great deal of time there, learning about the business of making muskets and pistols, enjoying the hours with her father, playing the role of surrogate son.

"Come, girls," Mrs. Cummins called out to them. "Let us get ourselves inside. This isn't a good place to dawdle."

The coachman held open the door and waited for each of them to climb into the worn leather interior. Violet settled herself in the seat, adjusted her conservative navy-blue traveling gown and tightened the strings of the matching bonnet beneath her chin, but her thoughts remained on her father.

In the beginning, he had been concerned that an interest in business might not be wise for a young lady, but soon it became apparent she was far more excited about making money than she was about playing the role of wealthy, pampered young lady.

Then, six months after Griff had died, Mr. Haskell, head of the Boston branch of the company, had suddenly taken ill and been forced to retire. Aunt Harry had nearly suffered an apoplexy when Violet told her she planned to take over Mr. Haskell's duties, but Violet assured her that she would keep her role completely secret, and eventually her aunt had bent to Violet's very strong will.

Mrs. Cummins's worried voice drew her attention. "Dear me, what has happened to that address?" Her chubby hands dug frantically through her reticule. "I can't seem to find the paper it was written on."

"Number six Portman Square," Violet told her, knowing the address by heart. It was printed at the top of Rule's gold-embossed personal stationery, there on each of the very few letters she had received in the past three years.

Mrs. Cummins rapped on the roof of the carriage. "Driver, did you hear that?"

"Aye, madam. Number six Portman. 'Tis a bit o' a ride, but I'll get ye there safe and sound."

"I hope it doesn't take too long," Caroline said with a weary sigh. "I am beyond ready to take off my shoes and put my feet up for a while." Like Violet, Caroline was also nineteen. The two were alike in other ways, as well. Each was a bit too outspoken and unfashionably wont to do as she pleased, but Violet was better at disguising her nature than Caroline, who didn't much care what other people thought of her.

She glanced outside the window, checking the angle of the sun. The afternoon was waning and all of them were tired. Echoing Caroline's sentiments, Violet could hardly wait to reach their destination.

Her thoughts returned to the man she had wed and a tendril of anger slipped through her. Rule Dewar had the gall to marry her, then completely abandon her. He had given her father his word, had promised that he would provide for her, and though she had plenty of money and servants enough to staff a large part of Boston, it was hardly what her father had intended.

And it certainly wasn't what Violet wanted. She wanted a husband who loved her, a man she could count on. She wanted a family and children. She had played the fool once for Rule Dewar. Not again.

A faint, bitter smile lifted her lips. Rule was about to get his comeuppance. He would retain whatever sum her father had left him, but he was about to lose his half interest in Griffin Manufacturing.

Violet couldn't wait to see the look on his handsome face when she told him she was there to obtain an annulment.

It seemed to take forever, but eventually Violet and her party arrived at Rule's London residence, a narrow, four-story brick structure with a gabled slate roof. It sat among a row of similar residences, all of them situated around a small park planted with bright spring flowers enclosed by an ornate wrought-iron fence. Clearly, it was a very exclusive neighborhood, befitting Rule's station as the brother of a duke.

The thought stirred a trickle of irritation. How ridiculous it was to marry a man for his noble bloodlines. Why, Rule Dewar hadn't even had the integrity to keep his word!

Not like Jeffrey, she thought, his handsome image popping into her head. Blond hair and warm brown eyes, a nice, sincere smile. Jeffrey Burnett was twenty-eight, nine years Violet's senior, a man of some means she had met six months ago at a party given by a friend of Aunt Harriet's. Jeffrey was an attorney who worked a great deal in the shipping business. Since Griffin shipped armaments around the world, they had something in common.

They had become friends of a sort, and eventually Violet had confided the truth of her hasty, ill-considered marriage. A few weeks later, Jeffrey had revealed his very strong attraction to her and his interest in making her his wife.

Of course all of that was moot at the moment.

First she had to obtain an annulment, which would make possible her second reason for coming on such a long journey.

She wanted to sell Griffin Manufacturing.

The driver jumped down and pulled open the carriage door, jarring her back to the present.

"We're 'ere, ladies."

Mrs. Cummins gave the man one of her imperious looks. "You'll need to wait, sir, while I make certain this is the correct address. If so, I shall be needing your services again."

"Aye, madam."

Mrs. Cummins would be leaving Violet and Caroline there, though there was a chance they would be turned away. She had no idea what Rule Dewar would do when she appeared uninvited on his doorstep.

As they reached the top of the brick stairs, Violet stood anxiously next to Caroline while Mrs. Cummins knocked on the ornate front door. A wispy, gray-haired man, apparently the butler, pulled it open. He looked down his long beak of a nose as if he couldn't imagine what three women would be doing on his employer's front porch.

"May I help you?"

Violet spoke up—she was, after all, Rule's wife. "I am Mrs. Rule Dewar. I am here to see my husband."

The butler was frowning, his bushy white eyebrows drawn nearly together. "I'm sorry, I'm afraid I don't understand."

"Then allow me to explain," Mrs. Cummins said, thrusting her big bosom forward as she made her way closer to the door.

"This is Mrs. Dewar. She has crossed the ocean to see her husband. Now please go and find him and tell him that we are here."

The man was shaking his head, opening and closing his

mouth like a fish on dry land, when Violet stepped past him into the foyer.

"Where is he?" she asked firmly.

The butler looked helplessly around for assistance as the other two women followed her inside.

"I am afraid...I am sorry, but his lordship is not at home."

His lordship? She thought his brother was the one with the title.

"When is he expected to return?" Caroline asked, speaking up for the first time.

"Sometime after supper. It could be quite late. Lord Rule rarely keeps me informed of his whereabouts."

Violet shared a glance with Caroline, whose eyes had rounded at the reference to Rule as a lord. "My cousin and I will each need a room," Violet said. "Please show us upstairs to our quarters, if you would."

"B-but I can't do that!"

Violet drilled him with a glare. "Why not?"

"Because I...because I..."

"Keep in mind that as *his lordship's* wife, from now on you will also be answering to me. I hope you don't mean for us to get off on a wrong foot."

The old man's pale eyes widened. For several long moments, he just stood there.

Caroline leaned toward her. "He doesn't seem to know Dewar has a wife," she whispered. This had not gone unnoticed by Violet.

"Which shall make an annulment all the easier," she whispered back. "I am waiting," Violet pressed.

The butler cleared his throat. "I'll have Mrs. Digby, the housekeeper, show you both upstairs."

Violet just smiled. She turned to their traveling companion. "You have done a very fine job, Mrs. Cummins. Caroline and I have both arrived safely, just as you promised. Which means your duties are ended."

Reaching into her reticule, Violet pulled out the bank draft she'd had prepared to be given as final payment once they reached London.

The older woman looked uncertain. "I don't know... You haven't even spoken to your husband yet. And this man doesn't seem to know who you are."

Violet forced a smile. "My husband has always been a very private person. But you may rest assured he will be delighted to see me." Now that was a bald-faced lie.

Mrs. Cummins reached out and tentatively took the bank draft Violet held out to her. "I could stay with you a few more days if you like."

"No! I mean, that won't be necessary. Caroline will be staying for the next several days until I am settled. Go and enjoy your family. That is the reason you traveled all the way to London, is it not?"

Mrs. Cummins smiled. "Well, if you're certain..."

"I am quite certain. Thank you again for everything."

"You have the address where I can be found, should you need me."

Violet patted her reticule. "The information is right in here."

"All right, then. I believe I shall do as you suggest. I am eager to see my mother and the rest of my family." With a wave and a final farewell, Mrs. Cummins trundled out of the foyer. A footman was sent to bring in their luggage, and a few minutes later a woman appeared who looked very much like Mrs. Cummins—gray hair, big bosom, rounded hips.

"I'm Mrs. Digby, my lady. I'll show you and your cousin upstairs to your rooms."

My lady? It appeared marriage to the brother of a duke

gave her a title, as well. Goodness, she had no idea. "Thank you."

Their luggage was brought up to their rooms and as soon as Violet closed the door, a quick rap sounded and Caroline rushed in.

"My lady! I can hardly believe it. I thought Rule's brother was the one with the title."

"He is. I don't know how it works. Rule never mentioned anything when he was in Boston."

"Probably because Americans don't use titles."

"I suppose."

"I wonder where he is."

"I have no idea." A faint smile touched her lips. "But he is certainly in for a surprise when he gets home."

Caroline grinned. "Oh, my, yes—he certainly is."

Two

Rule drained his brandy glass and set it on the table in front of him. He and Luke had made the social rounds, then ended the evening playing cards at White's, his gentleman's club. It was late and tomorrow he had work to do.

Rule slid back his chair. "I'm afraid I am out, gentlemen." He shoved his cards into the center of the table. "Looks as though I wound up even—which, with Luke playing, I consider a win."

Luke just laughed. "You're headed home, then?"

"I'm done in. I'll see you at the end of the week." The Marchioness of Wyhurst was holding a ball in honor of her daughter Sabrina's birthday. Rumor was the marchioness was determined to find the girl a husband, but so far the elegant blonde had refused every suitor who had dared knock at her door.

Rule blew out a breath, wishing he had sent his regrets, though he couldn't quite say why. But Lady Sabrina had been a good friend to the Dewars, and it was, after all, the lady's birthday.

He released a sigh, still uncertain why it was that

staying at home was beginning to hold such a strange appeal.

Making his way to the door of the club, he called for his carriage and left the building. As he settled himself inside, he pulled the bow of his cravat, letting it drape around his neck, removed his collar and unbuttoned the top few buttons on his shirt. Leaning back against the squabs, he closed his eyes and drifted off for a bit.

The next sound he heard was the latch snapping open and the door swinging wide.

"We're 'ere, guv'nor," said the coachman, a burly man with a short brown beard who stepped back so that he might depart the carriage. "Good night, milord."

He climbed to the street. "Good night, Bellows." Leaving the coachman to his late-night duties, he headed for the door. Light spilled from a window in the drawing room and he thought that Hatfield must have accidentally left a lamp burning. The old man was getting quite old, but Rule wouldn't fire him. Hat had been a loyal employee of the family for too many years.

He reached the door and was surprised when it swung open. Hatfield stood in the entry, gray hair standing on end, his eyes red from lack of sleep.

"What is it, Hat? I told you not to wait up."

The butler straightened, looking more like his old self again. "You've a guest, my lord. Two of them, actually."

Rule frowned. "A guest? I'm not expecting anyone. Who is it?"

"Your wife, sir."

Silence fell in the entry. "My…my wife is here?"

Hat nodded, moving the strands of hair hanging over his wrinkled forehead. "Yes, my lord. She arrived from America late this afternoon with her cousin, a Miss Caroline Lockhart."

"I see." Of course he didn't see at all and all he could think was, *Bloody hell, what am I going to do now?*

"Your wife, sir…she's waiting for you."

"Violet is… My wife is waiting for me? She is up at this hour?"

"Yes, sir, in the drawing room."

His mind was spinning, trying to sort things out. Violet was in London, had crossed the Atlantic to reach him. He started walking toward the drawing room, wide awake now, no longer feeling the least effects of the alcohol he had consumed.

As he strode into the room, she sat bolt upright, her eyes bright and blinking, glanced around for an instant as if to recall where she was, straightened and shoved to her feet. She was smaller than he remembered was his first impression, petite but shapely. In truth, she was different in every way than he recalled.

Except for her glorious copper hair, the likes of which he had never seen.

He groped for something to say. "Violet. I cannot believe you are here."

She gave him a chilling smile. "It took a while to reach London. But at last, here I am."

He couldn't seem to make himself move. "So you are."

He did move then, closing the distance between them, reaching out to take both of her hands. She wore no gloves, he noticed, and realized that aside from the bridal kiss on her cheek, he had never actually touched her without the barrier of some sort of clothing.

"Welcome to London," he said. "If I had known you were coming, I would have prepared a more proper greeting."

Violet drew her hands from his and looked him over, head to foot. For the first time, it occurred to him that his cravat was undone and dangling round his neck; his collar was missing, shirt unbuttoned and his hair slightly mussed.

Violet, on the other hand, looked...well...

Violet Griffin Dewar was beautiful.

"It must have been quite an evening," she said, those leaf-green eyes he remembered taking in his dishevel.

He flushed like a schoolboy. "Not really. I stopped by to see friends and wound up playing cards at my club."

"You were gambling? I didn't realize you were a gambler."

His embarrassment faded, replaced by a hint of irritation. "I rarely gamble. I was simply passing time."

"Yes, well, you certainly managed to do that." She glanced up at the clock over the mantel, the hands pointing to the lateness of the hour, condemning him.

"I am certain you are tired," she continued. "I shall leave you to find your bed. I just wanted you to know I was here and to say that I would like to speak to you first thing in the morning."

"Yes, of course." His gaze ran over her. In the yellow glow of the lamp on the table, he saw that in the past three years her features had softened, the sharp angles smoothed into feminine lines and curves. Her cheeks were as pale as cream and heightened by a touch of rose. A full bosom swelled above her tiny waist, her neck was slender and as graceful as her hands. Her lips were fuller than he recalled, beautifully curved and a lush shade of pink.

No longer the boyish young girl she had been at sixteen, Violet had matured into a woman. She was everything her father had predicted and more, the sort of female any red-blooded male would want in his bed.

And she was his wife.

A trickle of desire filtered through him, tightening his

groin. He cleared his throat, ignored the thickening in his loins. It was merely that the hour was late and he hadn't had a woman in weeks.

"My condolences on the loss of your father. He was a very great man."

"Thank you."

"I am truly sorry I wasn't here when you arrived. If only you had sent word ahead—"

"My decision was made somewhat quickly. Any letter would have arrived at the same time I did." She gave him a sharp-edged smile. "Besides, I thought it would be nice to surprise you."

His return smile was weak. "Well, you certainly accomplished that." He should have left for Boston months ago. He hadn't considered it a breach of his word until that very moment. The notion did not sit well.

Violet lifted her chin. "I shall see you in the morning, then."

Rule nodded. "I'll have Hat rouse one of the chambermaids and send her in to help you undress."

"Hat, I presume, is your butler?"

"It's Hatfield, actually. I've always called him Hat."

"Of course."

Rule stood by as she collected her skirts and swept gracefully from the drawing room. As she disappeared through the door, a rush of air escaped his lungs.

God's blood, his wife had come to London! He still couldn't believe it. He would have to tell his family, try to explain why he had kept his marriage a secret.

Rule thought of facing his two brothers and their wives—worse yet, his aunt Agatha, the matriarch of the family—and inwardly he groaned.

* * *

Violet pushed through the door of her bedroom to find Caroline still fully dressed and asleep on top of the bed. Her cousin jerked awake as Violet stepped into the room and quietly closed the door.

Caroline blinked owlishly then grinned. "Tell me what happened. I won't be able to sleep a wink until I know."

Violet released a weary breath. She had only slept in fits and starts on the sofa and jousting with Rule had left her edgy and drained.

"He was quite the gentleman. But then he always was."

Rule had accepted her arrival more graciously than she had expected. Oh, he had been surprised to see her—wildly so. But he had recovered his composure quickly and played the willing host.

Which perhaps she should have expected. His smooth, sophisticated manner had been one of the things her father had admired.

"What does he look like? Is he still so very handsome?"

Handsome was a very pale word to describe a man who looked like Rule. "He is handsome. Beyond handsome, to be truthful. He is even taller than I remember."

"With those lovely blue eyes and those wonderful dimples?"

"That would be him—though I didn't see the dimples tonight. I don't think he found anything the least bit humorous about my unexpected arrival."

Caroline grinned. "Well, then, if you are still set on tossing him over, maybe you should give him to me."

Violet laughed. "Once I am rid of him, I don't care what he does."

Caroline arched a golden eyebrow. "On second thought,

I don't want your leftovers. I think I shall find a man of my own."

Violet bit back a smile. "Good idea." Their tastes in men had always been different and even though Rule was quite a beautiful specimen, he was merely a man. Violet had learned the hard way there was more to a relationship than physical beauty.

"Did you tell him?" Caroline asked, sliding over to sit on the edge of the bed. "Did you say you wanted an annulment?" Both of them were still fully dressed. And both were exhausted.

"I would rather have a good night's sleep and face him in the morning."

"Yes, I see what you mean."

A soft knock sounded at the door.

"That will be the chambermaid, here to help me undress. I didn't know you were still awake."

"I'm glad someone is here. She can help us both."

And so a full-figured, brown-haired woman in her late twenties walked into the bedroom, hiding a yawn behind her hand.

"Me name's Mary. Mr. 'Atfield, sent me ta 'elp ye."

"Thank you, Mary." Violet turned, presenting her back so that Mary could unfasten the buttons. In minutes, she was rid of her clothes, dressed in a long white nightgown and neatly tucked beneath the covers. Caroline waved farewell as she departed the room, and Mary followed her down the hall to help her undress and get settled for the remainder of the night.

The door softly closed and Violet stared up at the blue silk canopy above the bed, certain she wouldn't be able to sleep. Instead, exhausted from the tension of the day, in minutes she drifted into a deep, all-consuming slumber.

* * *

Rule lay awake, staring into the darkness. His wife was there—Violet was in London.

Now that he was over the shock, and the notion had begun to settle in, he felt an odd sort of relief. His decision was made. He could start living up to the promise he had made to Howard Griffin.

And Griffin had certainly lived up to his.

Violet was as beautiful as her father had envisioned, though not in the typical sense. She was petite, but not slim, her green eyes a little too large for her lovely heart-shaped face. Her flame-colored hair was amazing, but not in the current vogue, and there was a confidence about her that hadn't been there when she was sixteen.

It shone in the way she moved, the firm set of her chin, the way her eyes flashed, revealing a hint of stubbornness she couldn't quite hide. And there was something more, a sensuality that hid beneath the surface, a deeply rooted passion, he suspected. He was drawn to it, intrigued by the thought of exploring it.

He couldn't remember the last time a woman had piqued his interest as Violet had, or stirred his lust in quite the same manner.

Perhaps it was the fact that she was his wife, the woman who would bear his sons and comfort him in his December years. Perhaps it was that he had married her, but never tasted the fruits of that marriage. She'd been a child back then. She wasn't a child anymore.

Her image returned, Violet elegantly gowned in pale blue silk and charmingly asleep on his sofa. As he lay awake in the darkness, he imagined carrying her upstairs and undressing her, discovering, inch by inch, the treasure hidden beneath her clothes.

His body clenched and blood began to pool in his groin. He wanted her, this woman he had married.

He wasn't ready to look beyond that. He was still trying to grasp the fact that he was a husband and in time might even become a father.

First things first, he thought, and found himself smiling. Violet was there and she was his wife. He had been searching for a woman and one had magically appeared on his doorstep.

Rule smiled into the darkness. It was only a matter of time before he could claim his husbandly rights.

Three

Violet came awake slowly and sat up rubbing her eyes. She glanced at the canopy above her head, at the robin's-egg-blue walls, and tried to remember where she was.

Then it all came thundering back. London. A bedroom in Rule Dewar's town house. Their conversation last night.

She spotted Caroline standing at the foot of the bed and jerked her gaze to the clock on the wall. "Oh, my goodness. I hadn't intended sleeping so late."

"You were exhausted. The trip was long and so was the evening, waiting for your husband to arrive."

Violet made a sound of irritation in her throat. "I hate it when you call him that."

Caroline laughed. "Well, he is—at least for the moment. Up with you, now. Mary will be here any moment to help you dress—and you had better do it swiftly. There is an army of servants waiting downstairs to greet the new Lady Rule."

"Lady Rule? You're jesting. That is who I am?"

"Apparently so."

"That sounds ridiculous."

Caroline grinned. "It does, rather. But still…"

For the next half hour, Caroline and Mary helped Violet prepare to greet her husband and his staff. After that, she planned to deliver the news she had traveled so far to give him.

She and Caroline left the bedroom arm in arm, heading for the stairs.

"I have already seen him," Caroline admitted. "I spoke to him this morning. I awakened earlier than you. I was hungry so I went downstairs. I passed him on the way to the breakfast room. I introduced myself and I think he actually remembered who I was."

"You're a woman. A man who looks like that must be used to having dozens of women fawning over him. He probably remembers every one."

"I was only a girl when we met. At any rate, he was very polite."

"He would be. It was another of the things my father liked about him."

"Your father liked him a very good deal."

"Yes, and look where that got me."

Caroline said no more and as they reached the bottom of the stairs, Rule walked out of the hallway. He smiled, perfectly groomed head to foot, even after his late-night ca-rousing.

"Good morning, ladies. I hope you slept well."

"Well enough," Violet said.

Servants began arriving, surrounding them where they stood at the bottom of the sweeping staircase. Awaiting Rule's return last evening, Violet had acquainted herself a bit with the residence, noting that the interior was done with exquisite taste. Each of several drawing rooms and all of the guest rooms were elegantly furnished, as was the dining room. She'd had an odd sense that each piece had been personally selected to fit its surroundings.

The number of servants swelled by two more and Rule turned to face them. "Now that all of you are here, I would like to introduce you to my wife. I hope you will serve her as well as you have always served me."

The servants all clapped and smiled. "Welcome, my lady," said the housekeeper—Mrs. Digby, Violet recalled—speaking for the group. "Please let us know if there is anything you need."

"Thank you, Mrs. Digby, I shall."

"This is Miss Lockhart," Rule said, "my wife's cousin. Please make her comfortable during her visit."

"Of course, my lord." The housekeeper smiled broadly, clearly pleased her employer had taken a wife.

Violet ignored a twinge of guilt. She wished she could have avoided any pretense they were actually married, but after her arrival yesterday, there was simply no way around it.

"I believe Miss Lockhart has already eaten," Rule said to Violet. "Perhaps you would allow me to join you in the breakfast room."

She managed to smile. "Of course."

"I noticed you've quite a collection of books," Caroline said. "If you wouldn't mind, I would love to find myself something to read."

"Please do. Books are meant to be enjoyed. Most of my collection is in the study. You'll find other volumes scattered here and there. Feel free to borrow anything you wish."

"Thank you." Caroline floated off down the hall and Rule presented his arm.

"Shall we?"

Violet tried not to notice that he looked even better this

morning than he had last night, his eyes no longer sleepy, but an alert, brilliant blue. His cravat was perfectly tied, his navy-blue tailcoat tailored to fit his very wide shoulders. The faint shadow of beard was gone, which had given him an attractive roguish look, and she rather missed the sight of his suntanned throat above the open *V* of his shirt.

"My lady?"

It took her a moment to realize he was waiting for her to accept his escort down the hall to the breakfast room. From the corner of her eye, she caught Caroline's grin the instant before she disappeared into the study.

She returned her attention to Rule. "I would rather you call me Violet. I am not used to your English forms of address."

He gave a brief nod of his head. His wavy black hair was a little longer than she remembered and she had the oddest urge to run her fingers through it.

Rule smiled. "Then Violet it shall be—as long as you call me Rule."

She wasn't about to address him as his lordship, so conceding was easy. "All right." She took the arm he offered and let him guide her along the hallway to a sunny room at the rear of the house that overlooked the garden. It was done in shades of moss-green accented with rose.

Rule seated her at an ornate rosewood table, then went over to the sideboard and filled two porcelain plates from a row of steaming silver chafing dishes.

Awaiting his return, she draped her linen napkin over the skirt of her peach silk gown, then watched as he set the plates down on the table. The aroma of eggs and sausage drifted up from where they nestled next to several pieces of buttered toast.

She glanced at the servant hovering at her shoulder holding two silver pots, one of tea, the other of coffee.

"I prefer coffee," she said, and the man poured each of them a cup. "Thank you." Violet added sugar and cream and carefully stirred them into the strong, aromatic blend.

"While I was in Boston, I came to prefer coffee myself," Rule said, taking a sip from his own porcelain cup.

"My father taught me to enjoy the taste."

He set his cup back down in its saucer. "I'm sure you miss him."

Violet felt a familiar stab of loss. "More than you could ever know."

Rule's thick black eyelashes swept down, hiding whatever he was thinking. He launched into his meal and they ate in silence for a while. It occurred to her that she hadn't had supper last night and she was ravenously hungry.

When she looked up from the bite she had taken, Rule was watching her and smiling. He had the whitest teeth and there was a sensual curve to his mouth Violet hadn't understood at sixteen. She felt the impact of that smile and for an instant, her breathing stalled.

Rule didn't seem to notice. "I'm delighted to see that, unlike most Englishwomen, you actually eat as if you enjoy it."

Her fork remained poised in the air. She forced herself to spear a bite of sausage. "Everything is quite delicious. The meals aboard ship were mostly just filling."

She took another sip of her coffee as silence descended again. She finished the last of her breakfast, wiped her mouth and set the linen napkin aside. Rule was already finished, which meant the time had come to divulge the reason for her journey.

"Now that we're done and I am feeling human again, I would like to discuss the reason I am here."

He frowned. "The reason you are here? I assumed the

reason you were here was to begin the marriage we started three years ago."

This was it. The moment she had been looking forward to, the reason she had traveled thousands of miles.

To confront a husband who had married her for his own selfish purposes and had no interest in keeping the promise he had made to her father. She thought of Jeffrey and the plans they had made, straightened in her seat and looked at him squarely.

"Actually, the reason I am here is to end our farce of a marriage and obtain an annulment."

The stricken look on Rule Dewar's too-handsome face was worth every torturous mile.

For a moment, Rule just sat there. "Excuse me? I must have heard you wrong. What did you just say?"

"You heard me quite clearly. I came here to get our marriage annulled."

Silence descended. He finally found his voice. "That is absurd."

"It seems quite reasonable to me. We've spent only a few days in each other's company. You never returned to Boston. Clearly, you weren't expecting to see me here. It is time we ended the charade before it goes any further. Then both of us can get on with our lives."

Rule forced himself to stay calm. His wife had finally arrived and now that she was here, she wanted nothing more than to be rid of him. "Aren't you forgetting something?"

She gave him a sugary smile. "I don't think so, no."

"What you are forgetting, Violet, is the reason your father wanted you to marry me in the first place. He was looking out for your future—your personal welfare as well as that of the company."

"The future of the company is another matter entirely. At the moment, what I wish to discuss is this ridiculous marriage we've entered into. Be honest, wouldn't you prefer to continue living your life as you have been? Staying out till all hours of the night, gambling, spending time with any number of women—doing anything you please?"

Rule couldn't seem to make his voice work. He straightened in his chair. "I told you, I rarely gamble. As for women—I remind you, Violet, thus far we are married in name only. There is a difference, I assure you—which I am very much looking forward to showing you."

She blushed. Which told him she remained as innocent as she was the day he had married her. He felt an unexpected stirring at that.

"You don't want to be married," she argued, surprising him with her stubbornness. She had acquiesced so easily before. But then, he reminded himself, this woman was not the sweet little girl he had left in Boston. "If you had wanted a wife," she went on, "you would have come to retrieve the one you married."

"I planned to come." *Eventually.* "I wanted to give you time to prepare yourself to become my wife. Your father insisted on that, if you recall."

"He didn't expect you to ignore me forever."

It was true, and guilt assailed him. "Perhaps I should have come sooner. The fact is, you are here now and clearly you are a woman instead of a girl." His gaze ran over her, settled on the swell of her breasts, and the blood pooled low in his groin. "You have reached your nineteenth year. It is time you had a husband and as I have already acquired that role, we shall proceed just as your father wished."

Violet shoved back her chair and stood up. "You do not

seem to understand. I am not asking—I am demanding. I won't be your wife so you might as well resign yourself."

Standing there in the sunlight streaming in through the window, head held high, small hands propped on her tiny waist, fiery hair gleaming against the perfection of her heart-shaped face, she was magnificent.

He had been searching for a mistress. No woman in London had caught his interest as she had, nor physically attracted him so greatly. His shaft began to harden. Violet was his wife and he wanted her in his bed.

He gentled his tone, suddenly determined to convince her. "Please…will you not at least hear me out? This is an extremely important decision for both of us."

For several seconds she made no move.

Giving up a sigh, she eased back down in her chair.

"Your father had faith in me," Rule began. "He believed he was looking out for your future when he convinced you to marry me. Before my own father died, he asked something similar of me."

Her expression subtly altered and he knew he'd caught her interest.

"My father believed the Dewar family's destiny lay in building an alliance between England and America. When your father approached me, I saw a way to fulfill my own father's greatest wish."

"You are saying it wasn't merely greed."

He frowned. "I have money of my own, Violet. I admit I have made a great deal more due to my association with your father and the success of the company, but I wouldn't have agreed if I hadn't intended to uphold my part of the bargain."

"I've seen the quarterly reports. You've done a very good job with Griffin."

"Thank you. The thing of it is, we are married. We have spoken vows in front of God and made promises to our fathers. I meant to come for you sooner and I should have. I can see that now. But the point is, we owe our families and we owe each other the chance to see if this will work."

And, of course, there was the provision in the wedding settlement that should the marriage not be consummated, he would lose his half of the business.

She was shaking her head, stirring fine tendrils of flame-colored hair against her cheeks. Desire slipped through him. He forced himself not to think of her in his bed.

"Give me a chance, Violet. Stay with me for the next thirty days and if, at the end of that time, you are still convinced it won't work out between us, I'll agree to the annulment."

But in order for that to happen, she would have to remain a virgin, as he was certain she was now. Rule was determined that would not be the case. Violet was his wife and he meant to have her—soon and often.

He looked at her sitting there, her cheeks still a little flushed from his blatant perusal. Where women were concerned, he wasn't a fool. He knew she felt at least some of the same attraction for him that he felt for her. He had a month to seduce her into accepting him.

Rule was sure a month would be more than enough.

"Will you do it? Will you stay long enough for us to get acquainted? I don't think it's too much to ask."

She took a deep breath, making her breasts rise tantalizingly, and he realized how fiercely he was aroused.

"I have already given this a great deal of thought and my answer is no."

A thread of irritation filtered through him. He wasn't used to being nay-sayed by a woman, and to think that this little slip of a girl— He amended that. Violet was no longer a child. In fact, he saw a lot of Howard Griffin in the implacable way she held her ground.

It made him all the more determined. She was his, dammit. Whether she realized it or not.

"I won't agree to an annulment, Violet. Not unless you meet my terms. That means you will have to hire a lawyer. It will take months to settle the matter in court—to say nothing of the scandal it will cause our families. It's 1860, Violet. Boston and London aren't nearly as far apart as they once were."

Her pretty lips thinned. "You are that determined? How can that be when you had no intention of returning to Boston?"

"I told you I planned to come—" Inspiration struck and he shot to his feet. "Don't move. I'll be right back."

Racing down the hall, he rushed into his study, drawing a swift look from Cousin Caroline, who sat reading in front of the fire. Searching through the top drawer of his desk, he drew out the ship's passage to Boston he had purchased last week—though at the time, he wasn't truly certain he would use it. Turning, he raced back to the breakfast room.

"I was coming," he said, holding up the ticket. "I bought this five days ago. The date is printed on the top."

He handed her the ticket and for the first time she looked uncertain. Clearly, she'd believed he'd never meant to live up to the bargain he had made.

There were times he wasn't sure himself.

"Stay for the next four weeks," he urged. "Give us a chance to get to know each other. If you won't do it for me, do it for your father." It was hitting below the belt, but for some strange reason he was growing desperate.

Violet stared down at the ticket, then looked up at him. Her chin tilted up. "All right, thirty days. Then I expect you to stand by your word."

Rule grinned, gouging grooves into his cheeks, and Violet glanced shyly down at her lap. She wasn't immune to him, he could tell, and he certainly wasn't immune to her.

Thirty days, he told himself, praying he wouldn't have to wait nearly that long to have her in his bed.

All of a sudden, being married didn't seem like such a bad idea after all.

"Good heavens, what did he say?" Caroline shot through the door of Violet's bedroom, where she had retreated to consider what she had just done.

"He wants me to stay for a month. He says if I do, he'll agree to the annulment."

Caroline's fine blond eyebrows drew together. "He wants to stay married?"

"That's what he says." She glanced up. "He was coming to get me. He showed me the ticket he bought."

"But you want to marry Jeffrey! The two of you have already discussed it!"

"I told you, Rule said he would agree in thirty days. It's either that or hire a lawyer, or barrister, or whatever they call them here. In the moment, it seemed the best solution."

"And now?"

Violet sighed. "I should have pressed him harder, I suppose, but…"

"You have that funny look on your face…the one I saw three years ago when you told me you had decided to marry him. It was there when you walked down the aisle and Rule took your hand."

"You're mad. I don't have a funny look on my face. I am merely trying to be sensible. I want an annulment. Rule wants thirty days to convince me we should stay married."

"He loses his half of the company if the marriage goes unconsummated. Didn't you tell me that?"

She nodded. "That is probably the reason he is so determined. Half ownership of Griffin is worth a lot of money. But people marry for money all the time."

"Yes, but you said you wanted to marry someone who loves you."

"I know. It's just…"

"Just what?"

"Well, I promised my father and we *are* actually married, you know. What could it hurt to at least get to know him?"

Caroline chewed her bottom lip. "Maybe you're right. But we were supposed to spend the next few weeks with my grandmother—after you got him to agree. She hasn't seen me since I was a little girl and she has been so looking forward to my visit. I have to go, Violet. That means you and Rule will be living in the house together alone."

She hadn't thought of that. Or if she had, she hadn't realized exactly what it would mean.

She shrugged her shoulders, though she wasn't feeling exactly nonchalant. "We're married. It will hardly cause a scandal."

"I'm not talking about a scandal and you know it. The man is utterly delicious. Are you certain you can resist him?"

Violet rolled her eyes. "Don't be ridiculous. Jeffrey loves me and he is expecting us to wed. I am trying to do this the easy way. And I feel as though I owe it to my father."

Caroline sighed. "I can stay another few days, but that's all."

"I'll be fine. Rule works during the day and he is

probably out most every evening." A thought that disturbed her more than it should have.

"I hope you're right…*my lady.*"

Violet laughed and so did Caroline.

It would all work out, she was sure.

Besides, she had never been to London, which appeared to be a fascinating city.

And a month wasn't really so very long.

Four

At the sound of heavy footsteps pounding down the hall, Rule looked up from the paperwork spread open on his desk to see his brothers, Royal and Reese, striding through his open study door.

"You are married!" Royal, the oldest and current Duke of Bransford, bore down on him like a big golden lion descending on its prey. He was tall and blond, the opposite of Rule and Reese, his eyes not blue but a tawny golden-brown. "I cannot believe it!"

"Who is she?" Reese, the middle brother, demanded, his jaw as hard as steel. He was once a soldier and it showed in his commanding tone and the hard lines of his face. His coloring was the same as Rule's, his hair jet-black, and his eyes an intense shade of blue. "How long have you been married and why the bloody hell didn't you tell us?"

"I intended to tell you this morning," Rule said, trying not to be intimidated, which, being the youngest, wasn't that easy to do. "That is the reason I asked you to come."

He had known his brothers were in London, in town on brewery business. Royal owned Swansdowne Ale, the most popular beer in England. Reese grew a large percentage of the barley used in the brewing process. Both of them had grown wealthy from the profits over the years.

And both were happily married.

Which, at the moment, didn't bode well.

"So how did you find out?" Rule asked.

"My wife told me," they both said in unison. Reese glared at Rule, leaving Royal to explain.

"Lily's maid heard it from one of the servants, who heard it from another of the servants, who heard it from one of yours."

"Which is exactly how Beth got the news," Reese added darkly. "I think you owe us an explanation, little brother."

Rule blew out a breath. He was twenty-seven years old, the head of a huge manufacturing firm, and they still saw him as a boy.

"I married Violet Griffin in Boston three years ago. It was arranged by her father, who had discovered he was dying. She was only sixteen at the time, so—"

"Sixteen!" Royal nearly shouted.

"You married a sixteen-year-old girl?" Reese's fierce gaze bored into him.

"In point of fact, the marriage was never consummated—since she was too young at the time we were wed."

Reese sat down in a chair across from him and Royal did the same.

"I think you had better start at the beginning," Royal said while Reese just sat there glaring.

For the next half hour, he tried to make his brothers understand what had transpired in Boston. How much he had to gain from the arrangement, how he had done it partly to fulfill the vow he had made to their father. He wasn't sure they accepted his reasons.

He was even less certain they understood his rationale when he sent for Violet and she walked into the study.

Royal looked at Reese. Reese stared back at Royal, then both of them smiled.

"It's nice to meet you, my lady," Royal said.

It was obvious his brothers believed he had married Violet because of her beauty. They thought the marriage was motivated by desire more than money.

It wasn't true then.

It was more than accurate now.

Walking toward her, Royal reached out and warmly took her hand. "Welcome to the family."

Violet looked to Rule for help, clearly hoping he would explain their arrangement, but Rule made no comment. As far as he was concerned, they were married and that was that.

Violet mustered a smile. "Good morning…my lord."

"He's a duke," Rule said, fighting not to grin. "You address him as His Grace."

"I hope you will address me as Royal," his brother said smoothly. "We are all family now."

For the first time since her arrival, Violet seemed flustered. "I am sorry. I am unused to proper English forms of address. Please…I hope you will call me Violet."

Royal seemed pleased.

"And this is my brother, Reese." Rule waited as his middle brother made a very formal bow.

"A pleasure to meet you, my—"

"Violet, if you would."

Reese's mouth twitched. For a man who never used to smile, he certainly seemed amused. "It's a pleasure to meet you, Violet."

"You, as well…Reese."

"I'm sorry my wife isn't here," Reese said. "Elizabeth is eager to meet you."

"As is Lily," Royal added. "Once you are properly settled, we'll have supper so we can all get to know each other." Royal flicked Rule a warning glance. *You have a wife now,* those golden eyes said. *You had better treat her well.*

Rule turned to Violet. "There is a ball tomorrow night. It's being given by the Marchioness of Wyhurst in honor of her daughter, Sabrina. I am expected to attend. I believe my brothers and their wives will also be going. It would give me a chance to introduce you. I would be pleased if you and your cousin would accompany me."

Violet flashed him a look of entreaty. She didn't want their marriage known, he could see. And yet she had agreed to give him the next thirty days.

"All right," she reluctantly agreed.

Royal and Reese both rose, taking their cue to leave. "Then we shall see you at the ball," Royal said.

The men left the study and the minute the door was closed, Violet turned on Rule. "You shouldn't have done that."

"Why not?"

"Once we are out in Society, all of London will believe we are truly wed when, thirty days from now, I will be returning to Boston."

Rule moved closer, so near he caught a whiff of her floral perfume. Violets, he thought, finding the idea charming. "You don't know that for certain."

"I do."

He only shook his head. "No, you don't," he said softly. Reaching out, he cupped her face between his hands, bent his head and captured her lips. It was a soft, gentle kiss, meant to coax and not frighten. But when she didn't resist, he lingered a few seconds more, tasting the corners of her mouth, feeling her bottom lip tremble.

Violet swayed toward him, set her hands on his shoulders, and desire surged through his blood. When her soft lips parted under his, his tongue slipped inside and he bit back a groan of pure pleasure.

Violet trembled and an instant later, broke away.

"That…that was not part of our agreement."

He cocked a brow, his shaft still hard and pulsing. "Wasn't it? I don't believe kissing my wife is a breach of contract."

"That was…that was…more than a kiss."

"Violet, love, it was merely a tasting. When the time is right, I will show you what is more than a kiss."

Her eyes widened. She stood there an instant, then whirled away from him and rushed to the door of the study.

Rule chuckled softly, a feeling of triumph rising inside him.

A single kiss was only the beginning of what he had planned.

Caroline was excited, but Violet dressed for the evening with dread. Tonight she would meet the rest of Rule's family, as well as his friends. He would introduce her as his wife.

She wasn't truly his wife and never would be. Their sham of a marriage would be over in a single month. She would return to Boston and marry Jeffrey, just as she had planned.

"You look like your favorite cat just died," Caroline said as she walked into Violet's bedroom. "For heaven's sake, Vi, we are going to a fabulous ball hosted by a marchioness! And we are going in company with a duke, a duchess, a countess and two lords! How can you look so glum?"

"I have to spend the evening pretending to be Rule's wife, that is how I can look so glum."

"You *are* Rule's wife—at least for a little while longer. You might as well enjoy it."

Violet closed her eyes, trying to block the image of Rule leaning toward her, his mouth settling softly, possessively over hers. She tried not to remember the rush of sensation, the incredible pleasure that had poured through every part of her body.

"There are definitely advantages to being married to a member of the aristocracy," Caroline went on.

Violet rolled her eyes. "I am deceiving his family and his friends. I am not really his wife and I don't ever intend to be."

"So what? He embarrassed you by not returning to Boston. If you embarrass him by ending the marriage he clearly did not want, he deserves it."

It was true. Rule had treated her badly. He deserved whatever he got.

"Come on." Caroline reached out and caught her hand, tugging her forward. "His family is probably downstairs by now." Rule wanted Violet to meet his brothers' wives before the ball. Maybe he thought it would be easier if she was surrounded by family when they arrived.

Violet halted before they reached the door. "Do you think this dress is all right? It isn't cut too low?" It was fashioned of topaz silk with a full, gold-shot overskirt ruched up on the sides. The same gold-shot fabric draped over her bosom, which was low enough to expose a glimpse of her cleavage. She was a married woman, no longer a child, and she had decided to dress accordingly.

"Are you joking? The gown is delicious. I like it even better than my own." A deep blue velvet that set off Caroline's pretty blue eyes. "Now let's go. We have kept them waiting too long already."

Violet took a shaky breath and followed her cousin out

the door. When she reached the top of the stairs, she spotted Rule waiting for her at the bottom. Her breath caught. Dear Lord, it ought to be a sin for a man to look that good. Dressed head to foot in black except for a silver waistcoat, white shirt and cravat, he was the handsomest man she had ever seen. She might have called him beautiful if it weren't for his solid jaw and the slight indentation in his chin.

He looked up at her, his blue cyes so intense she felt as if he reached out and touched her.

"You are staring at him like a schoolgirl," Caroline whispered, making Violet blush. "Go on down and join him."

Violet took a deep breath, squared her shoulders and started down the stairs, thinking how ridiculous it was to let a man's appearance make her feel light-headed. She was back in control by the time she reached the bottom of the staircase, Caroline a step behind.

"You ladies look lovely," Rule said, his eyes running over her but never once straying toward Caroline as a lot of men's did. Her cousin was blonde and lovely and far more the coquette than Violet.

Rule offered an arm to each of them. "Come. I want you to meet my brothers' wives, Elizabeth and Lily."

Violet ignored a sweep of nerves. She wouldn't be Rule's wife for long, but still she wanted his family to like her. Her heart raced as he led them into his elegant drawing room. The brothers rose at their entrance.

Violet looked past them to the women at their sides. Gowned in sea-green silk, Royal's wife, Lily, was as blonde and fair as he. Reese's wife, the Countess of Aldridge, was a petite woman dressed in sapphire-blue with alert gray eyes and her husband's same black hair.

Introductions were made, both women watching her

with undisguised fascination. When Caroline was introduced to the group, all of them were friendly, yet the women's attention remained focused on the newest member of the Dewar family.

"It's wonderful to meet you at last," the duchess said graciously. "Though I am still coming to grips with the notion that Rule has finally taken a wife. We were afraid he would remain a bachelor for the rest of his life."

Violet managed a smile. "Actually, he has been married for the past three years."

"So we gathered," Elizabeth said darkly. Rule had said she preferred not to use the title she retained as her former husband's widow, insisting Violet address her merely as Elizabeth or Beth. "Rule should have told us, of course, but he has always been a man of surprises." She flicked him a reproving glance.

Clearly the Dewar women spoke their minds, which Violet found strangely comforting.

Lily asked about her sea voyage, and Caroline asked the two women about their children—the nieces and nephews Rule proudly claimed.

"They are growing up far too quickly," Elizabeth said. "My son Jared will soon be thirteen and off to boarding school. Fortunately, his younger brother, Marcus, will be home, keeping me busy for a few more years." She laughed. "He has always been more of a handful than his brother."

"Girls are just as bad," Lily said with a smile. "Marybeth can't sit still for a minute."

"I'm afraid I wasn't the easiest child to raise," Caroline put in. "According to my mother, I got into everything I could get my hands on. And Violet was quite the tomboy, being raised by her father."

Violet flushed. She wished her cousin would simply

keep silent. These women were English aristocrats. In their eyes, behaving like a boy was probably quite shocking.

"At least your Alex is always well behaved," Elizabeth said of the duke's son and heir.

Lily laughed, a sound that rang like fine crystal. "Not always, I promise you." She smiled kindly at Violet. "Still, they are worth every moment of trouble. You will see once you have a child of your own."

Violet made no reply. If she had a child it would not be Rule's, but Jeffrey's.

"Once you are settled," Elizabeth said, "we shall have a ball to properly announce your marriage. Lily and I will make all the arrangements."

Violet's heart sank. She wished Rule had told them the truth. "I appreciate that, truly I do, but I think you should know that Rule and I may not be—"

"It's getting late," her soon-to-be-former husband interrupted before she could tell them that in thirty days, the two of them would be dissolving the marriage. "We had better be going. You'll have plenty of time to talk once we get to the ball."

As the women collected their reticules, straightened their voluminous skirts, collected their wraps and walked beside their husbands toward the door, Rule leaned close and whispered in her ear.

"You promised to give me thirty days. During that time, I expect you to behave as my wife. If things don't work out, we can inform my family then."

It wasn't an unfair request. Besides, whatever consequences he and his family might suffer wouldn't matter, since she would be on her way home to Boston.

"Are we agreed?" he pressed.

"As you wish."

Rule seemed relieved. They went out to the carriages, which were parked in a row out front. His brothers and their wives would be following in their own vehicles. Caroline traveled with Lily and Royal, excited to be riding in the magnificent, gilded, four-horse ducal coach.

Rule assisted Violet into his elegant black carriage and followed her inside. Instead of taking a seat across from her, he settled himself beside her, his wide shoulders brushing against her, sending a little curl of heat into the pit of her stomach.

"You look beautiful, Violet. Your father would be very happy tonight."

Guilt trickled through her. Griff had wanted her to marry Rule. It meant a great deal to him to believe he had secured her future. But her happiness was the thing he wanted most.

She wasn't about to throw that happiness away on Rule Dewar.

Five

The birthday ball, given by the Marquess and Marchioness of Wyhurst, was an extravagant affair unmatched by any of the events Violet had attended in Boston.

The mansion itself was palatial—three stories high, built in a U shape, the exterior faced with gleaming white marble. Torches lined the drive up to the house, which was entirely enclosed by ornate wrought-iron fencing.

Inside, the magnificent entry was the full three stories tall and capped by an amber glass ceiling. Columns and reflecting pools had been painted on the walls, making it look like the entrance to a villa in Rome.

The marquess, an older man with snow-white hair, stood in the receiving line next to his petite, dark-haired wife and beautiful, willowy blonde daughter, Sabrina.

Rule made the introductions. "Good evening, Lord Wyhurst. My ladies. I would like to present my wife, Violet. She is just arrived from Boston."

The blonde's gorgeous blue eyes widened. "Your wife?" she repeated as if she couldn't quite believe her ears.

Rule just smiled. "That is correct, my lady, and this

is her cousin, Miss Caroline Lockhart, also here from America."

"A pleasure to meet you both," Lady Wyhurst said with a smile that looked a little forced. Violet wondered if the marchioness had designs on Rule as a son-in-law. Being the son of a duke, he was undoubtedly considered quite a catch.

"Congratulations, my boy," the marquess said with a smile that appeared sincere. He turned that warm smile on Violet. "Welcome to England, my lady."

She opened her mouth at the use of the title, then felt Rule's gentle nudge in the ribs.

"Thank you," she said sweetly.

The marquess returned his attention to Rule. "About time you settled down, my boy." A chuckle rumbled in his chest. "Even if it took an American girl to bring you to heel." He winked at Violet and she managed to smile.

Unfortunately, she'd had little to do with the marriage. It was her father's money that had brought Rule Dewar to the altar.

The formalities were finally at an end. The group moved on, the Dewar family surrounding her as they made their way up the stairs. Crossing a false-stone arched bridge, they walked into a ballroom that had been transformed into a magnificent villa complete with gardens and a beautiful ocean view.

The conversation in the entry announcing Rule's marriage must have been overheard because the room was buzzing by the time they walked in, the entire assembly of several hundred guests whispering and staring in their direction.

For an instant, Violet's feet refused to move. She felt Rule's hand reach for hers. He laced their fingers together and gave them a gentle squeeze.

"They're just curious," he whispered. "Don't pay them the least attention. You know how people love to gossip."

She knew, all right. She just wasn't used to being the center of that gossip. Thank God, she would be on her way back to Boston by the time the marriage became known to be invalid.

Rule rested her trembling hand on the sleeve of his coat and led her farther into the ballroom, winding his way among the guests.

"Can you believe it?" one of the matrons whispered. "Rule Dewar. I can hardly credit that handsome scoundrel has finally been leg-shackled. And by an American, no less."

"Probably had no choice," a second woman said tartly. "I'll be counting the months. Won't be long before the truth is known."

"Dewar is an utter rogue," another woman said. "That isn't going to change. If she *is* with child, it won't be long before he'll have the poor chit shipped off to the country."

Violet took a fortifying breath and fought to ignore the women's words, but no matter which way she turned, the same conversation swirled around her. Rule and his libertine ways and the matter of his hasty marriage. None of them knew, of course, that he had been married for the past three years.

A thought that galled her.

And embarrassed her.

She was his wife—at least in name. He should have had the decency to own up to the vows he had made. It took all of her will not to turn and march out of the ballroom.

Ever supportive, Caroline hurried up beside her. "They're all just jealous. Rule married you, not one of their prissy daughters."

"Your cousin is right." Black-haired and beautiful, Elizabeth Dewar floated toward her. "They'll have their fun for a bit, but in the end, you are Rule's wife. That is all that matters."

"Both Beth and I faced the same sort of gossip when we were first married," Lily added. "In time, your marriage will be old news, just as ours is."

Violet glanced to where her husband stood in conversation with a group of men and women. "Apparently Rule is quite popular with the ladies."

"Yes, well, that is all in the past," Elizabeth said. "Your marriage was not yet official, not the way Rule saw it. Now that you are here, you won't have to worry about that sort of thing again."

But Violet didn't believe it. A leopard didn't change its spots, and a scoundrel didn't cleave to just one woman.

It didn't matter. In a month, he would be free to live as he chose, and she would be on her way back home.

"I appreciate your kindness and support," she said to the women. "Truly I do."

Lily smiled. "We're sisters now. Sisters take care of each other."

Violet felt an unexpected thickness in her throat. She had never had siblings, though she had wanted a brother and sister very badly. "Thank you." She felt a renewed shot of guilt. The Dewars were willing to accept her into their family, while she had no intention of living up to their expectations of her as Rule's wife.

A little shiver of awareness went through her as he returned to her side. The man fairly exuded confidence, power and virility. Violet did her best not to notice.

"They are playing a waltz," he said. "I have yet to dance with my wife. Would you do me the honor, my lady?"

She started to remind him he had agreed to call her

Violet, but somehow it no longer seemed important. Instead she took his arm, wishing far more that he would stop referring to her as his wife. She would never truly be his and she wasn't the sort to pretend.

Still, she let him lead her onto the dance floor and took her place in front of him. Since he stood nearly a foot taller than she, dancing with him should have been awkward, but from the moment he took her in his arms and the music started, from the instant he swept her into the rhythm of the dance, it was like floating on air.

Round and round the parquet floor he whirled her, keeping perfect rhythm, holding her a little closer than proper, even for a husband. She tried to ignore the warmth of his palm at her waist, the way his long leg wedged between hers with each of his graceful turns. She tried to ignore the way he was looking at her, as if she belonged to him and he couldn't wait to ravish her.

Her breathing quickened. A tendril of heat curled softly in the bottom of her stomach. She forced herself to think of Jeffrey, handsome and fair, blond hair gleaming as he held her hand in the gardens at Griffin Heights and told her he had fallen in love with her.

She tried to imagine she was waltzing with Jeffrey, but when she looked up, it wasn't Jeffrey's face she saw but the solid jaw and beautiful blue eyes of the man she had married.

A man who wanted nothing but the use of her body and her father's armaments factory.

She steeled herself and eased a little away.

"You're a very good dancer," Rule said as the waltz came to a close.

"Am I? I thought it was you."

He smiled. "Perhaps it was the two of us dancing together."

"Perhaps."

"There is a theory that a man and woman who dance well together, make love well together."

Her cheeks colored. "I—I wouldn't know." But an odd sensation filtered into her stomach.

"We are married. Perhaps we should test the theory."

Violet shook her head, though deep down she couldn't deny the tiny thread of interest the notion stirred.

Making love with Rule Dewar. She had been fascinated with the man's incredible good looks and charm from the moment she had met him. If things were different, if there were no strings attached and she and Jeffrey didn't already have an understanding, she might be tempted to try it.

"I hear congratulations are in order."

Violet looked up to see a dark-haired, handsome man nearly as tall as Rule striding toward them.

"They are, indeed. It's good to see you back in Society." Rule smiled down at her. "Violet, this is Benjamin Wyndam, Earl of Nightingale. He's the previous owner of what was formerly Hawksworth Munitions and is now Griffin Manufacturing. The man from whom your father purchased the plant."

"Yes, I remember hearing your name. Lovely to meet you, my lord." Inwardly, Violet smiled, beginning to get the hang of using the ridiculous British titles.

"You, as well, my lady." Nightingale smiled at her softly and she noticed a sadness in his eyes that seemed deep and abiding. "I lost my wife two years ago. I hope you and Rule are as happy as Maryann and I once were."

And clearly he grieved for her still. "I am sorry, my lord. And thank you for your kind wishes." What else could she say? The earl had obviously loved his wife. If only Rule could—

She broke off the thought. Rule wasn't the sort to fall in love. Their marriage was no more than a business arrangement. If she wanted a husband who loved her, she would have to marry Jeffrey.

Violet frowned, disliking the way the thought had come out. She didn't *have to* marry Jeffrey. She wanted to.

It was simply that he was so far away.

Another man walked up just then. He was perhaps forty, beginning to lose his hair and had eyes that seemed to miss nothing. "So this is your lovely bride. Your marriage seems the only interesting bit of gossip I've heard all evening. Your wife is quite a lovely surprise, my lord."

"Thank you," Rule said somewhat stiffly. "Violet, this is Burton Stanfield. Over the years we've had some business dealings together."

"That is correct. And a few weeks back I tendered an offer to buy Griffin Manufacturing. Unfortunately, his lordship turned it down."

A buyer for the company! Exactly what she needed. But Rule had refused the offer. The information nettled, considering how much she wanted to sell. At home, trouble was brewing in the Northern and Southern states, the country fiercely divided over the issue of slavery. Violet had friends on both sides, people she cared about. She didn't want to be in the business of making the weapons that might be used to kill them.

Still, Rule had done a good job managing Griffin so far. He might have had good reason for turning the man down.

Violet focused on Stanfield. "Perhaps your offer wasn't high enough. With the tensions growing between the states in America, there is already increased demand for weapons. I should think that would make Griffin worth a good deal of money."

Burton Stanfield smiled. "A woman with a head for business. How unusual." He turned to Rule. "I believe you have managed to capture yourself a very interesting female."

"Her maiden name is Griffin," Rule explained. "Violet spent a good deal of time with her father at the Boston branch of the business."

"I am also half owner of Griffin," she said sweetly, drawing a frown from Rule.

Stanfield studied her with heightened interest. "Is that so? Then perhaps I can win your support for my cause."

She kept her smile in place. "I'm afraid I would have to discuss the matter with...my husband."

Stanfield cocked an eyebrow. "Indeed. A promise I shall hold you to, my lady."

Rule's hand settled possessively at her waist. "If you will excuse us, there are some other people I would like my wife to meet."

"Of course." Stanfield made a polite bow and stepped out of their way. Leaving the man behind, she let Rule guide her rather forcefully toward a quiet area off the main part of the ballroom.

"It is not considered polite to discuss business matters at affairs such as these."

"Is that so? Or is it merely impolite for a woman to discuss business matters at affairs such as these?"

Rule eyed her darkly. Then a corner of his mouth edged up. "You are not like other women, Violet Dewar. Perhaps that is the reason you intrigue me."

"Do I?"

His blue eyes darkened. "In ways you are yet too innocent to understand." He took her arm and laced it with his. "Come. We'll make a pass round the ballroom. I'll speak to a few more of the guests and then, if you are ready, we'll go home."

Violet breathed a sigh of relief. "I should like that above all things…my lord."

It was the first time she had used his title and Rule grinned, carving the dimples she remembered into his cheeks.

"My lord?" he repeated as if she had finally accepted him as her master. "That has a very nice ring."

She bit back a smile and shook her head. "You are a devil, Rule Dewar." With the devil's own charm.

And the way her stomach lifted when he looked at her the way he did now, as if she were a particularly delectable sweet, put her on guard.

If she weren't extremely careful, she might wind up in the devil's bed.

Rule left Violet in the care of his sisters-in-law and wove his way among the guests. As much as his somewhat tarnished reputation would allow, he wanted to smooth the way for his wife's admittance into the inner sanctum of upper-class British Society.

As he paused here and there to speak to friends and answer questions about his bride and his unexpected marriage, he began to frown at some of the things he was overhearing. Gossip about the reasons for his hasty wedding, implications that his bride had been less than pure at the time they spoke their vows.

He tried to explain about Howard Griffin's illness and the arrangement the man had made to secure his daughter's future, but the more he talked, the more smug smiles and winks he received and the more irritated he became.

It surprised him to feel so protective of Violet when he had never felt that way about a woman before. He hadn't known his mother, who had died giving birth to him. The only females in his family were his frail old aunt Agatha, whom he adored as the mother he never had, and his sisters-in law, whom he greatly respected.

He told himself his protectiveness came simply because Violet was his wife and not because he was so strongly attracted to her, not because he admired her for having the courage to travel all the way to England to confront him.

He watched her laughing at something Reese said. Reese, who rarely joked and hardly ever smiled until he married Elizabeth.

Rule liked it when Violet smiled. He would like it even more if one of those sweet smiles was intended for him.

He watched her until, from the corner of his eye, he caught sight of her cousin, Caroline. He straightened as he realized the girl was in conversation with his best friend, Lucas Barclay. Good God, Caroline Lockhart was as innocent as Violet, and, he noticed for the very first time, far more beautiful than he had realized.

And Luke was eyeing her like a wolf with a fresh piece of meat.

Rule strode toward them. "I see you've met my cousin, Miss Lockhart."

One of Luke's dark eyebrows went up. "Your cousin?"

"My wife's cousin. My cousin by marriage." Rule tried for a smile but it was thin at best.

"Ah, yes. I have yet to meet your lovely bride. Amazing, isn't it? My best friend has a wife and I am the last to know."

Rule sighed. "It's a long story. I realize I owe you an explanation. Perhaps over lunch on the morrow?"

"Oh, indeed. Better late than never." Luke's tight smile softened as he gazed down at the little blonde. "In the meantime, Miss Lockhart has just agreed to partner me in a waltz." He extended his arm. "Shall we, Miss Lockhart?"

She accepted Luke's arm and returned his smile. "I would be delighted."

They started forward but Rule stepped in front of them. "One dance, Luke. That's all."

Luke eyed him darkly. He made a stiff nod of his head. "I shall keep your wishes in mind." But he didn't say he would obey them. Luke was angry that Rule had kept his marriage a secret.

He had a right to be, Rule supposed. The two of them were like brothers.

But then he hadn't told his brothers, either.

He watched the couple on the dance floor, Luke tall and dark, Caroline small, blue-eyed and fair. They made a handsome couple, might even make a good match—except that Luke was the biggest rake in London and fiercely opposed to marriage.

Rule inwardly sighed. Already his duties as husband were starting. He had a responsibility to his wife, but also to her family. He blew out a breath, wishing his first duty wasn't to guard his cousin-in-law against his best friend.

Six

Half an hour passed. Rule decided to make a quick trip through the gaming room, see what sort of fires he might put out there, then collect his wife and go home.

He smiled as he walked down the hall, oddly pleased by the thought. *My wife.* Never once had it occurred to him he might like having a woman belong to him. Still smiling, he had just turned the corner when a lady gowned in scarlet silk appeared in front of him. Evelyn Dreyer, Viscountess St. Ives.

"Good evening, my lady," he said to his former mistress. "You're looking quite splendid tonight." With her pale blond hair and amazing cheekbones, she was a beautiful woman. Rule gazed at her and thought of hair the color of flames and a pert nose dotted with intriguing little freckles.

"I just heard the news," Evelyn said with a viperous smile. "You are married."

"Yes, I am."

"For quite some time, I gather."

"Three years." Though still not officially, since he hadn't yet bedded his bride, but that was none of Evie's business.

Her mouth thinned. Before he realized her intent, her hand snaked out and connected solidly with his cheek.

"You're married," she said. "How dare you!"

Rule rubbed his cheek. "In case you have forgot, my dear, you are also married. In point of fact, your husband is currently standing in the ballroom."

"It is not the same thing."

"Indeed? The viscount might disagree."

"Harold is old and ugly and cannot even function while your wife is…is…"

"Beautiful and desirable?"

Her slender nose went into the air. "I didn't say that."

"You didn't have to marry Harold. You could have married someone else."

Ignoring the statement, she pinned him with a glare. "You should have told me."

"I should have told a lot of people. My apologies, madam." He made her a mocking half bow. "And now, if you will excuse me…"

Evelyn said nothing more, but her cheeks still carried an angry flush, and he could see that ending their affair had disturbed her far more than she had admitted.

It didn't matter.

It wasn't Evelyn Dreyer he wanted in his bed. It was the woman he had married.

A jolt of desire speared through him and his shaft went hard. He wanted Violet Dewar and he meant to have her.

It was only a matter of when.

Violet stepped back into the shadowy alcove indented into this section of the hallway. Her heart was beating, thrumming like a bird trapped in her chest.

She had been on her way to the ladies' retiring room

when she spotted Rule in the corridor in conversation with a woman. She was tall and statuesque with high, carved cheekbones and a lush bosom no man could miss. Her eyes were dark, her lips full and red. She appeared to be several years older than Violet and she was beautiful. Violet couldn't hear the conversation, but clearly the woman was angry.

She took a deep breath. Setting a hand over her heart, she willed it to slow. She knew exactly who the lady was, the only person it could be.

She recalled the most recent conversation she had overheard in the ballroom.

"You don't suppose his marriage has anything to do with his mistress, Lady St. Ives? I heard they parted on very bad terms. Perhaps he married the chit out of spite."

He hadn't, of course. He had married her for money and power, not vengeance.

She thought again of the beautiful Lady St. Ives. Violet wasn't surprised to learn Rule had kept a mistress. Most married men did.

And in truth, as he had said, they were not, in the strictest sense, actually married.

Still, it bothered her. She didn't like to think of him kissing the blonde, doing more than kissing.

I will show you what is more than kissing, he had said, almost as if it were a vow.

She drew in a shuddering breath. *The man is a rogue of the very worst sort,* she reminded herself, but she couldn't get that kiss out of her head.

Checking to be certain the pair no longer stood in the hallway, Violet continued on to the ladies' room. She was on her way back, nearing the alcove she had hidden in before when she heard Rule calling her name, and a little shiver went through her.

"There you are. I've been looking all over."

She thought of the elegant blonde. "Have you? I thought perhaps you were looking for someone else. Lady St. Ives, perhaps?"

He frowned. "So you've heard. I imagined you would, sooner or later."

"Actually, I saw the two of you together in the hall."

He glanced away, released a weary breath. "I won't lie to you, Violet. I'm a man and a man has needs. The affair is over. Has been for some time. I have no interest in Evelyn Dreyer and won't anytime in the future."

She pondered the words, wondered if they were true. "I see."

"I hope you do."

Her eyes widened as he began to ease her backward into the alcove. His arms came around her, drawing her close, and his mouth came down over hers.

It wasn't the same gentle kiss as before. It was a hot, taking ravishment so powerful it made her dizzy. Her fingers curled into the muscles across his wide shoulders. Her mouth parted under his fierce assault and his tongue slid over hers.

Violet made a little mewling sound and simply clung to him, swamped with sensation and completely unable to think. He tasted of brandy and she could smell his spicy cologne. Her body was thrumming, pulsing. Every feminine part of her ached with the need for more of what he offered.

Rule finally ended the kiss, but kept an arm around her as if he knew he had left her weak in the knees.

He reached out and ran a finger down her cheek. "God, I want you."

Violet stood there trembling. "You…you can't keep doing that."

"Kissing you? I'm your husband. I can kiss you whenever I wish, and furthermore, I intend to do it every chance I get."

"But...but..."

"You gave me thirty days to convince you. That is what I am doing—convincing you."

"But I can't just... You can't just... We can't just..."

"Yes, we can. Come along, sweet wife. Let us collect your cousin. It is past time we went home."

Violet swallowed, but she didn't argue. She had mistakenly thought she would be safe from Rule at a very large, well-attended ball.

She had just discovered there was no place she was safe from Rule Dewar.

Violet lay on the mattress staring up at the ice-blue canopy above her head. Guilt rested like a heavy weight on her chest. She shouldn't have been kissing Rule. She was going to marry Jeffrey. She shouldn't have responded the way she did.

Dear God, why had she agreed to Rule's ridiculous arrangement in the first place?

But, of course, at the time it had seemed the best solution, the easiest way out of the marriage. No attorneys, no scandal, just a quiet annulment to which Rule had promised to agree.

She sighed into the quiet of the room, trying not to remember tonight's kiss, the incredible sensations that had burned through her body. Surely it was merely a physical response. If Jeffrey kissed her that way, she would feel exactly the same.

A sound reached her from the hallway outside her bedroom. She jerked upright at the squeak of the silver doorknob turning. Surely Rule wouldn't—

She relaxed as Caroline slipped into the bedroom and told herself she didn't feel a flicker of disappointment.

"We didn't get to talk after the ball," Caroline said, plopping down on the edge of the mattress in her nightgown and pink silk wrapper. Low flames curled over the grate in the hearth, banishing the chill and lighting the room with a soft yellow glow. "Wasn't it simply magnificent?"

Violet scooted back, propping herself up against the headboard. "I suppose it was."

"You suppose? Good heavens, I had a marvelous time. I danced until my slippers were nearly worn out."

"You weren't the one having to pretend to be something you are not."

"Like a wife, you mean?"

"Like Rule's blissful bride."

Caroline wound a lock of long blond hair around the tip of her finger. "I think his family liked you. I don't suppose that truly matters, but still…"

"I wanted them to like me. They are very nice people."

Caroline eyed her with suspicion. "You aren't thinking you might stay married?"

"Of course not." She examined a fold in the satin counterpane. "Rule had a mistress. Did you hear?"

Caroline sighed. "I heard the gossip. Everyone was buzzing about it. She was there, you know."

"I saw them together. Rule says the affair is over, but that doesn't mean he doesn't intend to replace her with someone else. Most married men think nothing of keeping a mistress."

"You are better off with Jeffrey."

"I know."

"Did you meet anyone interesting?" Caroline asked.

"Actually, I did. A potential buyer for the company. A

man named Burton Stanfield. Apparently he made an offer but Rule turned it down."

"Did you ask him why?"

"Not yet, but I intend to. Of course, he couldn't have accepted without my approval even if he had wished."

"Maybe he doesn't want to sell. Maybe he likes running the company."

"Once the marriage is annulled, I become sole owner of Griffin and I can do whatever I want. I don't want to make weapons that could be used in a war to kill my family and friends."

"It's going to come to that, isn't it? We're going to have some sort of revolution?"

"Yes, I feel certain we are. At any rate, Rule has done a good job thus far and I'd like to know his thoughts on Stanfield as a buyer. At the same time, I don't want to alert him to the fact I intend to sell. I'll have to tread carefully."

Caroline grinned. "You can do it. You are good at getting what you want."

It was true, though lately, where Rule was concerned she felt greatly out of her element.

"I met someone interesting tonight, myself," Caroline said.

Violet's interest sharpened. "Did you? Who was it?"

"He is a friend of your...of Rule's. His name is Lucas Barclay."

"Good grief, you can't be serious. People were talking nearly as much about him as they were about Rule. The man is notorious."

In the firelight, Violet caught her cousin's smile. "Luke is a marvelous dancer and unbelievably handsome." She grinned. "And I've never been one to listen to gossip."

"Luke? You call him Luke? You had better be careful,

cousin. What would your grandmother say if she knew you were spending time with a rogue like Barclay?"

"It was only a dance, Vi. And speaking of my grand-mother…I have put off my visit for as long as I dare. Grandmother will begin to worry. I am going to see her tomorrow. She'll want to meet you. Will you go with me?"

"Of course I will."

"She's expecting me to stay for at least the next few weeks."

Violet nodded. "I know you have obligations. But I shall miss you terribly."

"It won't be all that bad. Grandmother lives here in London. We'll be able to see each other often."

But Violet would be alone in the house with Rule. She didn't trust him.

More importantly, she wasn't sure she could trust herself.

Seven

After her late evening at the ball and a restless night of battling her worries and guilt, Violet slept later than she intended.

By the time Mary had helped her into a lace-trimmed russet silk day dress and pulled her hair back into a simple chignon, she was fidgeting to get on with the day. When she reached the top of the staircase, she spotted Caroline pacing nervously in the foyer. As Violet reached the bottom of the stairs, her cousin hurried toward her.

"You didn't forget, did you? My grandmother is expecting us this afternoon for tea. I don't want to disappoint her."

Inwardly, Violet groaned. She hadn't forgotten. Today she was accompanying Caroline to her grandmother's, staying for a brief visit, then leaving her cousin and the older woman to their long-awaited reunion.

"I didn't mean to sleep so long, but I am ready now. We can leave whenever you wish. Will you be staying or coming back here?"

"I want to be certain everything is set. If it is, I'll stay. Tomorrow, I'll send for my things."

Violet glanced around the entry. The house seemed overly quiet, no sounds coming from the drawing room or the study down the hall. Rule wasn't there, she was sure, for she always seemed able to sense his presence.

"Where is his lordship this morning?" she asked Hatfield, his spindly old butler.

"Lord Rule has gone to his office at Griffin. That is where he usually spends most of his day."

"I see." And since she hadn't gotten up early enough to speak to him before he left, she would go directly from Mrs. Lockhart's to the factory.

"Do you wish to leave him a message?"

"Thank you, no. I'll speak to him later." She turned to Caroline. "Let me fetch my shawl and we can be on our way."

Dashing back upstairs, she returned with a warm cashmere wrapper. April in England was often still cold and today was no exception. Hatfield took the shawl from her hand and draped the soft fabric around her shoulders.

Caroline had already donned her cape. A few minutes later, they were on their way to the corner to hire themselves a hansom cab for the ride to Belgravia, where Caroline's grandmother lived.

The early-spring wind was brisk and Violet was glad she was wearing her shawl. Around them, the streets were a noisy throng of pedestrians, merchant vehicles and carriages. A horse-drawn omnibus painted in red and yellow rolled past, several men seated on top while others hung off the sides. Children played along the lanes and young boys sold coal or peddled newspapers.

Eventually they reached Grandmother Lockhart's house, a large brick structure, the exterior well maintained. The interior was neat, as well, if in need of a bit of modernization. Adelaide Lockhart, a kindly older woman with wavy silver hair and Caroline's same blue eyes, seemed perfectly content with the way things were and not the least concerned that the carpets were beginning to fray and the decor was a bit out of fashion.

Money was not the problem. The late Mr. Lockhart, an extremely successful merchant, had done very well for his family, and Caroline's father had continued the tradition, making his own vast fortune in America. Adelaide Lockhart spotted them and her eyes misted at the sight of the granddaughter she hadn't seen in years.

"Oh, my dear, you are so lovely. The same blue eyes as your grandfather, God rest his soul."

"It is wonderful to be here, Grandmother."

Mrs. Lockhart greeted Violet with equal warmth, then they followed the older woman into the drawing room where tea and biscuits were served. Violet had resigned herself that coffee was a treat she would only get in the mornings and was beginning to actually enjoy an occasional cup of tea.

The conversation was lively and warm. There was only one uncomfortable moment, when Caroline's grandmother inquired of Violet's husband.

"I should like very much to meet him," the older woman said. "I am not acquainted with any of the Dewars, but everyone has heard of the Duke of Bransford and his very successful ale-making business." She smiled at Violet. "Perhaps you and your husband might join my granddaughter and me for supper one evening."

Violet shot a nervous glance at Caroline.

"They are just settling in, Grandmother, now that Violet is here in London."

Violet managed to curve her lips. She hated to lie but there was no help for it. "Caroline is right. Now would be a difficult time, but a bit later on my husband and I would be delighted to accept your invitation."

The older woman beamed, obviously pleased that the brother of a duke would be dining in her home. "That would be lovely."

Violet kept her stiff smile in place, lifted her cup and took a sip of tea.

It was nearly three o'clock by the time several pots of the jasmine brew had been consumed and Violet was able to leave the Lockhart residence. Before she could escape, Adelaide Lockhart insisted on lending Violet her carriage for the ride to Griffin Manufacturing on the south side of the Thames.

"That isn't the best part of town, you know," Mrs. Lockhart said. "Are you sure your husband would approve your traveling there unaccompanied?"

Violet swung her shawl around her shoulders. "Rule respects my independence." Which of course was a load of rot. The man had all the earmarks of becoming a demanding, overbearing, overly protective husband.

Not that she intended to give him the chance.

The carriage ride was a long one, through areas that were indeed questionable, but eventually they arrived at a huge brick structure marked by an imposing tower and a sign that read Griffin Manufacturing. A symbol she recognized, the mythical griffin, rose formidably above the sign.

Violet felt a wave of nostalgia and her eyes misted. The symbol was the embodiment of her father, a man with the courage of a lion and the vision of an eagle. Dear God, she missed him. Rarely a day went by she didn't think of him.

With a calming breath, Violet collected herself and sent the memories away. The coachman helped her descend the iron carriage stairs. Lifting her russet silk skirts, she headed for the door marked Office.

A bell rang as she walked into the reception area and a young blond man with a pale complexion and rosy cheeks hurried up to the counter to greet her.

"Good afternoon, madam. May I help you?"

"My name is Violet Dewar. I am here to see…my husband."

The young man's eyes widened. "Of course, my lady." He nervously cleared his throat. "Currently, your husband is in a meeting with his foreman. Please have a seat while I inform him you are here."

"Thank you." She sat down on a long mahogany bench that ran the length of one wall. Beneath her feet, the wooden floor was swept and polished. The office was neat and clean, efficient she would call it, with a desk behind the counter to serve the fresh-faced young secretary and a row of cabinets at the back for filing information.

Through the brick walls, she could hear the familiar pounding, hammering and tinkering that indicated the assembly of the manufactured weapons: pistols of assorted shapes and sizes, and several varieties and various types of muskets.

In Boston, she had enjoyed running the business side of the factory, pretending to be J. A. Haskell and managing sales and accounting. She enjoyed the challenge of working, but there were other types of businesses to run, ones that had nothing to do with Americans killing each other in the war that was sure to come.

The sound of a door opening ended her musings. She rose as Rule stepped out of his private office. For an instant, his tall, masculine beauty stole her breath. With his shirt-sleeves rolled up, revealing his muscular forearms, and his hair a little mussed, he looked capable instead of elegant, a force to be reckoned with, a man in complete control.

She forced herself to breathe normally and smile, then noticed he was frowning. His expression continued to darken as he strode toward her.

"What the devil are you doing here?"

She didn't like his tone. She forced herself to ignore it. "I wanted to speak to you. I overslept and missed you this morning so I came here to see you."

He took her arm, hauled her rather forcefully into his office, and firmly closed the door.

"This is a factory, Violet. Hardly the place for a lady. The building is only a few blocks from the wharf, which means there are ruffians and blacklegs about. How did you get here?"

Her chin went up. She didn't appreciate being questioned like some sort of criminal. "Caroline's grandmother, Adelaide Lockhart, loaned me her carriage. There weren't any problems. I arrived in perfect safety."

"If you wanted to come down here, you should have asked me to give you escort."

She clenched her teeth and told herself to stay calm. "Need I remind you that I have the same right to be here as you?" More so, actually, since they were not truly married and his half ownership could still be revoked.

Rule blew out a breath. He raked a hand through his wavy black hair. "I'm sorry. I just don't want you getting hurt."

"That is kind of you, but as you can see I am fine."

"You wanted to see the plant?"

"I know what a munitions factory looks like. I came to discuss the future of the company. I thought perhaps you might have some thoughts on the subject."

The tension in his shoulders did not ease. Clearly, he didn't like the idea of a woman involving herself in the operation of the business. He escorted her to one of the leather chairs in front of his desk, waited till she took a seat, then sat down in his own chair.

The inner office, she noticed, was as Spartan and efficient as the outer, somewhat of a surprise since his tastes in most things ran to the stylish and expensive.

"So you wish to discuss the future of the company."

"Actually, meeting Mr. Stanfield got me to thinking about it." She tried to appear nonchalant. "He has shown an interest in buying the business and I thought that perhaps selling wouldn't be such a bad idea."

"That is what you think? That selling is a good idea?"

"It's something to think about. There are lots of other business opportunities to explore. Textile manufacturing, railroads…steamship companies are making incredible profits. Why did you refuse Mr. Stanfield's offer?"

"Because I didn't believe your father would wish me to sell and because Burton Stanfield is completely unscrupulous and not the sort with whom I wish to do business."

"I see."

He rose from behind his desk. "I appreciate your taking an interest in this, Violet, but the fact is, when your father chose me as your husband, he entrusted me with the welfare of the company. Making decisions that are right for the business is what I have been doing for the past three years. Now, unless there is more you wish to discuss, why don't I take you home?"

Her mouth thinned. He was dismissing her out of hand, treating her like some prissy, harebrained female. Her father had never done that and she didn't believe he had intended for Rule Dewar to behave that way, either.

She bit back a sardonic smile. Once their marriage was ended, he would certainly be in for a surprise when she informed him of her decision to sell—not that he would suffer for it. He had received some money from her father upon his death, had already earned a small fortune in salary and bonuses, and his severance pay would be equally large.

"If you have nothing more to tell me, then I suppose we might as well leave." Rising from her chair, she allowed him to take her arm and guide her to the door.

Rule sent the Lockhart carriage back to Belgravia and helped her into his own.

"I'll see you have a carriage for your personal use as soon as possible," he said. "I don't want you roaming the streets in search of a cab."

Violet didn't argue. She could use a means of transportation for the remainder of the time she was in London.

Rule took a seat across from her, sinking back into the comfortable velvet squabs, studying her from beneath his black lashes. As the vehicle jerked into motion, she could feel his gaze on her and a little shiver of awareness went through her that Violet purposely ignored.

"So your cousin will be staying with her grandmother?" he asked, his tone casual, though his eyes dipped to the swell of her breasts.

She nodded. "I'm to have the rest of her things sent over in the morning."

He stretched his long legs out in front of him as best he could in the confined space inside the carriage. "I've decided to take a few days off. You have never been to London. As your husband, it would be my pleasure to show you around the city. Would you like that?"

Of course she would! She had never really traveled until now. She would love to see such an exciting city.

Inwardly she sighed, knowing she shouldn't go with him. The less time she spent in his company, the better. On the other hand, she might never be back in England and she would hate to miss the chance to see it.

She met his assessing gaze. "That would be very kind of you."

For the first time Rule smiled. "We'll take a drive round town, perhaps enjoy luncheon in one of the quaint little restaurants in Bond Street. We'll visit the London Museum and, of course, you will have to see the Crystal Palace, perhaps take a ride in Mr. Croxwell's air balloon. Oh, and I shall take you to the opera." He cast her a glance. "You do like opera."

She smiled. "Of course."

He seemed to ponder the notion. "On second thought, I think the theater might be more fun. There is a new play opening at the Royal Pantheon. I keep a box there. How does that sound?"

It sounded wonderful. She loved theater and also the opera. And yet, she hesitated.

Rule's raven brows drew slightly together. "You gave me your word, Violet. All I want is a chance for us to get to know each other."

It didn't seem too much to ask and she *had* agreed.

She gave up a defeated sigh. "All right. I should love to see London and I would particularly enjoy a night at the theater."

Dimples appeared in his cheeks and her stomach lifted alarmingly. She hated that he could do that to her so easily.

"Excellent! I shall make the necessary arrangements. Starting tomorrow, I am going to show you London. Once you see what an extraordinary place it is, you will never wish to leave."

But already she wished to leave. She wanted to see Jeffrey. She wanted to hear his voice and bask in his warm, adoring smile. She wanted him to tell her how much he loved her, make her forget her absurd, unwanted attraction to a man to whom she meant nothing.

Only a little while longer, she told herself. Surely she could manage a bit more time in company with her soon-to-be-former husband.

Violet ignored the little voice that warned she was making another mistake.

Eight

Violet spent all the next day with Rule. As promised, he took her on a drive around the city, putting the top down on the fancy black landau he chose so that they might enjoy the sunshine. The carriage rolled past the elegant mansions in Mayfair and the expensive shops in Bond Street where, as promised, they luncheoned in a charming little French restaurant.

Later in the day, he ordered the coachman to drive them through fashionable Hyde Park where the trees had begun to leaf out and the first spring flowers pushed up through the soil. There wasn't time that day to visit the museum, which was holding an exhibition of Egyptian art, but Rule promised they would see it soon.

The following day he took her to the amazing Crystal Palace.

"Good heavens, I didn't expect anything quite like this."

She had read about the fabulous exhibition hall, of course, but as the carriage rolled toward the vast complex on the hill, a structure three stories high made entirely of glass, she still wasn't quite prepared.

Rule just smiled. "After the Great Exhibition of '51, the palace was moved here, piece by piece, and then re-assembled. Since it reopened, millions of people have come to visit."

As the carriage drew near, Violet surveyed the massive glass domes with awe.

"The designers wanted to make it educational as well as entertaining," Rule said. "The palace houses everything from live giant lizards to a stuffed rhinoceros."

Violet's excitement grew. Whole trees grew inside the glass conservatory, she discovered as they strolled through the interior, and fountains and lakes sparkled everywhere.

Rule played the gentleman as he had done each day, buying her ice cream and a hand-painted fan she had stopped to admire. Though she enjoyed his company more than she wished to admit, she would rather have shared the experience with Jeffrey. Jeffrey was the perfect suitor, always proper, never pressing her for more than she wished to give. Not like Rule, whose hungry gaze left little doubt of his intentions.

They ended the afternoon early, returning to the house in time for Violet to nap then dress for an evening at the theater. She told herself she wasn't excited, but as the hour of their departure drew near, anticipation raced through her veins.

"I wish I knew which gown to wear," she said to Mary, who had laid an emerald-green brocaded silk next to a deep rose taffeta with an overskirt of heavy cream lace. Both were lovely, both cut fashionably low. She told herself not to consider which of the dresses Rule might prefer.

At Mary's suggestion, she chose the emerald-green. "It'll look lovely with yer complexion."

"All right then. Help me, will you, Mary?" She walked to the bed. "Let us see if you are right."

The buxom, brown-haired maid helped her into her undergarments and corset, which cinched her waist to amazingly small proportions, then helped her into a cage crinoline, a petticoat fashioned of stacked metal hoops that made her skirt even fuller than it usually was. The gown came next.

"Gor, milady. I were right, don't ye see? The green goes perfect with yer eyes."

While Mary fastened the buttons at the back of the dress, Violet stood before the tall oval mirror to view the effect. She rarely paid so much attention to her appearance, but tonight was a special occasion. She wanted to look her best.

Then again, though Rule had thus far been well behaved, he had made his intentions clear. He wanted her to remain his wife, and in that regard he was determined. She wondered what pitfalls the evening might hold.

She took a deep breath. Rule would be waiting. She couldn't put it off any longer.

"Have a good time, milady."

"Thank you, Mary. I'm sure I will." Too good a time, she feared. *You need to keep your distance,* she warned herself, but couldn't help a rush of pleasure as she reached the bottom of the staircase and caught the appreciative gleam in Rule's brilliant blue eyes.

"You look beautiful," he said, and he meant it, she could tell.

A hint of color crept into her cheeks. "Thank you"

Rule smiled. "You'll be the loveliest woman at the theater."

She laughed. "Now you are being gallant. The color of my hair is quite unfashionable and I am too short to be elegant, but I am glad you approve."

"Your hair is like fire and you are petite and perfectly formed. Believe me, I definitely approve."

His eyes ran over her and Violet could feel the hunger

he had made little effort to hide. Her heartbeat quickened. In his black evening clothes, a diamond stick pin perfectly positioned in his white cravat, he was impossibly handsome.

Which meant nothing, she told herself. Less than nothing. It was the man inside who was important.

Rule took her emerald-lined, black velvet cloak and draped it around her shoulders, then the butler opened the door and stepped back to let them pass, the hint of a smile on his wrinkled face. Perhaps he wasn't as stodgy as he appeared.

"Good night, Hat," she said just to throw him off balance, which apparently she did, his pale eyes widening as she stepped out onto the porch.

Rule grinned. "You'll give him apoplexy if you smile at him that way too often."

"Don't be silly. Your Mr. Hatfield is quite the proper butler."

Rule just smiled.

They reached the Pantheon Theater, their carriage pulling into line behind a row of similar conveyances moving slowly toward the portico at the entrance. The front of the building was ornately gilded and as they walked in on a length of red velvet carpet that matched the red flocked wallpaper and the carpets inside, she saw that the theater was lavish in the extreme.

The play called *The Mariner* was billed as a rousing adventure, a musical farce where pirates attacked and a damsel in distress was saved by the hero. There was much excitement about the opening, since the playwright's last production had been such a huge success.

"My box is on the second floor," Rule said, guiding her up one of two wide, curving staircases that spiraled up from the right and left sides of the theater. Leading her down the hall, he guided her into one of the velvet-draped boxes that formed the second-floor balcony.

A wide stage rested against the back wall, she saw as they sat down inside the box, and the pit yawned below, lined with rows of seats.

"There is open seating on the third floor," Rule said, "but the boxes provide the best view of the stage."

And a bit of privacy, as well. With the curtain back in place, it was difficult if not impossible to see inside the box, and she wondered if Rule had used that privacy in his seductions. And if he would attempt to do so tonight.

A little thread of heat slipped through her that Violet firmly ignored. He hadn't kissed her again since the night of the ball, though he had vowed that he would. A kiss she could endure, she told herself, but she would allow nothing more.

They chatted pleasantly for a while, until all the seats were filled and the gas lights began to dim.

The action began on the stage and eventually she forgot the tall man beside her and found herself caught up in the excitement of the play. A cardboard ship held captain and crew and, of course, the heroine—the daughter of the wealthy ship owner, a young woman traveling to see her father.

Fake waves moved up and down, making it look like the ship was at sea. A medley of songs were sung and the audience laughed at the players' antics. Near the end of the first act, pirates attacked, firing their cannons at the cardboard ship, sending sparks and smoke into the air.

Violet wasn't sure exactly how the effect was achieved, only that it didn't go exactly the way it was planned.

And that was when the trouble began.

Rule's eyes remained on Violet, watching her as he had all evening, wishing the play was over and they were back in the house, determined that tonight he would kiss her, touch her, continue his seduction.

Damn, he wanted her. Every time she took a breath, her lovely breasts rose enticingly above the bodice of her gown, soft twin mounds ripe for the tasting. Just a glance at the delicate line of her jaw, the sweet curve of her lips, made him hard. He'd been hard off and on since the moment he had watched her gracefully descending the staircase at his house. He was so enchanted, so filled with lust for her he was barely able to watch the play.

And so it took a moment for him to realize that something was wrong, that there was a stirring in the audience, that people were rising from their chairs.

"Rule…?" He heard the note of worry in Violet's voice the instant before he realized that part of the fireworks display used in the pirate attack had gone awry and the stage curtains had caught fire.

He stood up abruptly and gripped her hand. "Hold on to me and whatever happens, don't let go." Quickly, he moved toward the door leading out of the box, taking Violet with him.

On the stage, the flames were moving fast, racing along the walls, catching on to the red-flocked wallpaper, leaping from curtain to curtain, spreading along the sides of the theater toward the people in the pit, who were screaming now and running toward the entrance.

The hallway outside the box was already filled with frightened people, the women's elegant skirts taking up huge amounts of space. Some of them were crying as they were shoved and jerked forward, the men doing their best to make way for them as the crowd surged down the hall.

"Try to stay calm. I'll get us out of here, Violet, I promise you."

She only nodded, her pretty green eyes frightened but

steady as she moved into the massive wave of people pushing and shoving along the corridor. The terrified mass surged forward. Smoke filled the hallway and, through one of the boxes, he saw that the fire had nearly reached the staircase on the opposite side of the theater. There were shouts and then panic as the choking smoke filled patrons' lungs and the flames leaped across the aisle, blazing upward, catching the drapes that enclosed the boxes and licking out into the hall.

A woman fainted, falling beneath the shoving, pressing mob. A man went down on top of her and then another. Rule kept Violet close to his side and her hand clasped tightly in his. Fear for her gnawed at him. He had brought her here, put her life in danger. He would get her out safely, he vowed. No matter what it took.

The crowd surged as one toward the curving staircase, which wasn't nearly wide enough to hold so many people. Flames broke out ahead of them, red-orange and hot. And full-blown panic set in.

A man turned and charged back in the opposite direction, smashing into Violet, knocking her small hand out of Rule's grasp.

"Violet!" He tried to reach her as she was carried backward by the man's momentum, then she disappeared beneath the surging mass of humanity fleeing for their lives.

"Violet!" Terror struck him. She was tiny. She could be crushed to death. Like a man possessed, he shoved against the heavy wall of people, knocking them aside, shouldering his way through the crowd, determined to reach her, terrified she would be trampled beneath the frantic mass.

Using his shoulders, he opened a path, caught a glimpse of emerald silk and shoved his way toward her. He gripped her hand, hauling her to her feet and into his arms.

"Violet, thank God!"

Shaking all over, she clung to him, her hair unpinned and falling free, a curtain of flame that matched the fiery inferno around them, her gown torn and hanging off her shoulder.

Rule steeled himself. "We have to get out of here. Come with me." He couldn't let her see his worry, his fear. He had to get them out of there. In an instant, he made a decision.

"This way!" he shouted above the din of shrieks and screaming people. "Back the way we came!" Choking smoke and flame roared among the boxes on the theater side of the hallway, but if they stayed close to the wall on the opposite side, they might have a chance.

The man who had run back down the hall had disappeared behind a blanket of smoke. Rule knew where he was headed—an exit in the back wall of the building, a narrow, outside staircase that led into the alley. He had noticed it once on his way to the men's room.

The screams and shouts grew louder, more terrified, a sound of horror unlike anything he had ever heard before. From the corner of his eye, he caught sight of a woman whose skirt had caught fire, heard Violet cry out and start to turn toward her.

"Keep going!" he commanded, forcing Violet's head away from the female human torch, knowing it was already too late, dragging Violet forward, toward the wall of heavy black smoke. He could feel her shaking as he urged her down the hall. "There's a door at the other end of the corridor. If we can reach it, we can get out!"

She coughed, glanced back once, then nodded and tightened her hold on his hand. She was trusting him with her life. Rule didn't intend to fail her.

They ran along the hall, Violet's heavy skirt and crinolines making it hard for her to keep up. He wished there was time to get rid of them.

Flames licked out in front of them. "Stay close to the wall!" he shouted, dragging her farther into the smoke, feeling her hesitate only a moment, then follow him into the billowing darkness.

God, he prayed, *please, show me the way.*

But smoke and darkness were all he could see ahead of him. He pulled a handkerchief out of his pocket and handed it to Violet, who pressed it over her nose and mouth. Coughing wildly now, he hauled her forward, his back against the wall so he wouldn't lose his way, afraid her voluminous skirts would catch fire before they could reach the door.

Flames chewed through the ceiling, licked down toward the floor.

"Are we…" She coughed wildly. "Are we going…to die?"

"Not if I can help it." Rule hauled her forward, keeping low, but time was running out. If he was wrong, they would be dead.

The wall seemed endless. No opening in sight. He moved forward as fast as he dared, afraid the floor might give way beneath them. Still no escape in sight. Only more smoke and flames.

Rule cursed violently and pressed forward through the clogging, blinding darkness, Violet's hand gripped in his. He knew how terrified she must be and yet she had not given up.

Neither would he.

"Hang on," he said. "We're almost there." Blinking against the burning in his eyes and praying it was true, he finally saw it—the door to the narrow wooden outside staircase leading down to the alley. Small flames chewed around the edges of the frame, but there was room to get through. He lifted the latch, thanked God it was unlocked and wondered if the man who had run this way had made it to safety. Shoving it open, he tugged Violet forward, gulping in a breath of the fresh night air.

"Come on!"

Violet tried to step through, but her skirt was too wide. She lifted the metal cage, held it up and turned sideways enough to get outside, but as she stepped onto the platform, her green silk skirt caught fire.

"Rule!" She wildly slapped at the flames that ate into the fabric. Rule slammed the door behind them, shed his coat and used it to stamp out the fire.

Satisfied she was safe, he surveyed the steep wooden staircase. "Can you make it?"

"Help me." She turned her back to him, displaying the row of tiny covered buttons she wanted him to unfasten. There wasn't time for that. Grabbing the fabric in his fists, he split the dress in two, drew it up over her head and tossed it aside. Violet unfastened the tabs on the crinoline she wore and Rule helped her step out of it.

He didn't have time to admire the way she looked in her chemise, drawers and stockings. All he could think of was getting her to safety.

Fire licked out the windows now and the door was completely in flames. He went down a few steps ahead of her so he could catch her if she slipped, but she descended the narrow wooden stairs at a steady pace that reminded him she was Howard Griffin's daughter.

The moment they reached the ground, he draped his scorched coat over her shoulders, covering all but her pretty stockinged legs, pulled her into his arms and just held her.

Trembling all over, Violet made a soft sound in her throat, reminding him they were still in danger, and Rule gripped her hand and tugged her forward. They raced down the alley away from the burning building, now engulfed entirely in flames. People rushed past them, a throng of actors and stagehands who were also racing toward safety.

As they reached the street, a big red fire wagon pulled by four galloping white horses roared past them, joined by three more wagons, approaching the burning theater from different directions.

Violet stumbled. Rule caught her before she could fall, scooped her up in his arms and kept running. The building was well beyond saving. Anyone left inside was doomed.

Searching through the chaos of terrified people, some of them weeping, all of them grateful to be alive, Rule scanned the street, hoping to find his carriage, and amazingly, spotted his coachman running toward him.

"I knew ye'd make it. I knew ye wouldn't let yer lady die."

Rule felt a swell of emotion that brought a tightness to his throat. He squeezed his coachman's shoulder. "We need to get her out of here, Bellows. We need to make certain she's all right."

"Don't ye worry, milord, I'll get 'er home." He pointed along the street. "The coach is just down the block. No way to bring it to ye in this crowd. Ye'll need ta follow me."

Rule looked down at Violet. Her face was smudged with soot, her chemise hanging by a single strap. She was shaking so hard he could hear her teeth chattering, barely holding herself together.

He adjusted his coat to cover her a little better. "You're safe now, love. Soon you'll be home."

"I—I'm all right. You don't have to carry me. I—I can walk."

Rule ignored her. He wasn't letting her go until she was

safely inside his carriage. Falling in beside his burly bearded driver, he finally spotted the carriage. Bellows opened the door and Rule settled Violet in the seat.

"Take her home, Bellows."

Violet swung toward him. "What…what about you?"

"I need to see if there is anything I can do to help."

"I'm not…not leaving here without you."

He could see she was determined, and her concern made something expand inside him. "All right, I'll be back as quickly as I can."

By the time he reached the front of the theater, he could see the fire company and the police had already taken control. The injured were being attended and carriages hauled the survivors away. There was nothing left for him to do but pray for the poor souls who had died.

With a last glance at the scene, he turned and strode back to the carriage, anxious to get as far from the Royal Pantheon as possible. He signaled his driver, opened the door and climbed into the dimly lit interior.

Violet was fighting not to cry, he saw, as he settled himself on the seat beside her. "It's all right, love, it's over. Everything's going to be all right."

Violet looked up at him and the tears in her eyes rolled down her cheeks. "People…people died in there. There was a woman, her…her skirt caught fire and then her hair and…and…"

"Hush, sweetheart, don't think about it." Violet didn't protest as he lifted her gently onto his lap. "Just think about how brave you were and how proud I am that you are my wife."

She shook her head. "I wasn't brave. You were brave. I was terrified."

He smoothed back her disheveled copper curls. "That

is what bravery is. Being afraid and still having the courage to do what has to be done. And believe me, I was afraid."

Afraid he would lose her. Afraid his beautiful, courageous little wife would never have the chance to experience life. Afraid he would fail her even worse than he had by leaving her in Boston.

"Those poor, poor people." Burying her face in his shoulder, she began to cry, deep racking sobs that reached straight into his heart.

Rule just held her.

Silently, he thanked God that he had been able to save her.

Nine

Violet didn't remember the carriage ride back to the house or Rule carrying her upstairs to her room. She only remembered him holding her in his lap inside the coach, stroking her hair, telling her she was safe.

She remembered the way he had looked, his handsome face blackened with soot and his evening clothes singed by fire, the smell of smoke and the determination in his eyes as he had led her into the smoke and flames.

She remembered wondering if she had followed him into hell or if he led her down the path to safety. In that moment of uncertainty, she remembered the way he had looked in his office, so capable and in control, and she had placed her life in his hands.

Rule had not failed her.

She looked up at him now, standing next to a silver tray that held a bottle of brandy and two crystal snifters the butler had brought up to her room, watched him pour some of the brandy into the glasses. He strode back to where she sat in the small sitting area in front of the fire and pressed one of the goblets into her trembling hand.

"Drink this. It will steady you."

She did as he asked, allowing the warmth of the liquor to burn down her throat, trusting him now as she hadn't before. She had never tasted brandy. Her father liked whiskey. He had given her a sip now and then and she had grown to enjoy the flavor.

"Drink the rest." He urged the glass back to her lips and she drank the balance, beginning to relax.

Rule left her a moment, walked over to the dresser and poured water from the pitcher into the basin. Before she'd left for the theater, she had given Mary the night off to visit her mother, Violet recalled as she watched Rule dip a clean linen cloth into the bowl and return to where she sat. She felt the soothing wetness as he carefully bathed her face and shoulders, then he returned to the basin to wash his own face and neck.

His coat was gone, still draped round her shoulders. His cravat was missing, his waistcoat tossed over a chair.

"Better?" he asked as he returned to where she sat.

Violet nodded, but all she could think of was the woman in the hall, the flames spreading over her gown, her hair, her awful shrieks of horror. Another memory arose—being pushed away from Rule, stumbling and falling, the crush of a man falling on top of her and then another, pinning her down on the carpet, their weight so heavy she couldn't breathe.

"Could I... Could I have a little more?" She held up her empty glass. Rule refilled it and brought it back to her. Violet's hand shook as she took another sip and then another. The warmth of the liquor soothed her, made her feel languid and warm, dulling some of the awful memories.

"I wonder how many...died tonight." She upended the glass, finishing the drink, wishing she had more, wishing it could make her forget completely.

As if he read her thoughts, Rule poured a little more liquor into her glass. "I don't know. Too many, I'm afraid."

Tears welled, began to slip silently down her cheeks. She felt like a weakling, a coward. What would her father think? Then Rule was there, taking the glass she had emptied, sitting down beside her, pulling her into his arms.

"I'm sorry I took you there. If I could change the way things turned out—"

"It wasn't your fault," she said tearfully, and felt him draw her closer. She leaned against him, seeking his comfort, his protection, her hands slipping up around his neck.

"I was afraid I would lose you," he said, kissing her forehead. "I've never been so frightened in my life."

Violet reached up and cupped his cheek. "You saved my life. If it hadn't been for you...if I had been there with anyone else—" Her voice broke on this last word and Rule silenced her with his lips, a soft, gentle touch that said how sorry he was for what she had suffered.

Violet kissed him back, seeking the solace he brought, desperate to block the awful memories. The kiss went on and on, a gentle tasting that deepened into something more. The liquor erased her reservations, made her think only of him and not the awful tragedy she had witnessed that night. Her body turned languid and warm, began to stir to life.

Need rose inside her, slowly changing the heat of his kiss into a smoldering flame, then burning hotter, brighter, flaming out of control as the fire had that night. He eased his coat off her shoulders and pressed his mouth against her bare skin, kissed the side of her neck and returned to her lips.

Hot, wet kisses followed, an onslaught that buried the awful memories and turned her thoughts to the need building inside her. Easing off the remaining strap of her chemise, he kissed her shoulders, the soft swell of a breast, took the fullness into his mouth. Desire rose, swift and sharp, fierce and demanding, and any thought of stopping him slipped away.

She was alive and grateful for it.

Alive because of him.

His teeth abraded her nipple, which was hard and throbbing, aching as his tongue swirled around it. He suckled and tasted and her skin heated. Her body grew flushed and damp.

She barely noticed when he lifted her into his arms and carried her over to the bed, when he rested her on the deep feather mattress and stripped away the final remnants of her clothes. He was kissing her again when she roused herself, taking each of her breasts into his mouth, sliding his hands over her body, tracing a finger through the tight red curls above her sex. When he parted the moist folds and slipped a finger inside, need unfurled in her belly.

Her heart pounded frantically and her skin felt hot and tight. She arched upward, wanting more of the deep drugging kisses that held her in thrall, the skillful stroking of his hand.

Every part of her pulsed for him, throbbed for him. He left her for a moment and she bit down on her lip to keep from begging him to return. Then the mattress dipped and she felt his heavy weight above her, felt him part her legs and settle himself between her thighs.

"Violet…" he whispered, kissing her softly again.

As he leaned toward her, the muscles across his powerful chest rubbed against her nipples and they stiffened and swelled. His shoulders were wide and muscular and her fingers dug into them, seeking purchase in the storm of pleasure his kisses evoked.

"Easy, love," he whispered as her hips arched upward against the heavy, hard length pressing against her belly.

His hand found her softness once more, dipped inside, stroked her until she cried out his name. He was preparing to take her, she knew, but Violet didn't care. They were married. He had saved her. She wanted this, ached for it.

Rule positioned himself and pressed forward, moving slowly, entering her with exquisite care. He kissed her deeply as he reached her maidenhead and surged beyond, seating himself fully. There was an instant of pain, far less than she would have expected, and even that single moment was fleeting. Soon all she felt was the warm weight of him above her, the thickness of his shaft inside her, the slick glide and the rising pleasure that filled her.

She was so wet and sensitive. Fresh need stirred to life, heated her, aroused her until she couldn't think. With every deep thrust, he impaled her. With each withdrawal, she sobbed for more. Tension built in the depths of her, so thick it felt tangible, pulling her muscles tight, making her stomach contract.

Then it hit her, waves of pleasure so sweet, so powerful she couldn't hold back a cry, sensation so intense her whole body shook with it.

Beneath her hands, the muscles in Rule's shoulders tightened. His throat moved up and down and his head fell back, and she knew he was feeling the same sweet pleasure he had given to her.

His tense muscles finally eased and he relaxed against her. Several seconds passed. Then he kissed the side of her neck, lifted himself away and lay down beside her. Rule eased her into his arms, and bliss stole over her, contentment unlike anything she had known. The warm sensations lingered, gentle now, soothing. It was the last thing she recalled as she drifted off to sleep.

* * *

Rule lay next to his sleeping bride.

His wife.

She was his now. She belonged to him. The knowledge filled him with a powerful sense of triumph. And relief. And a feeling of satisfaction he had never experienced before.

He smoothed back a tendril of tousled copper hair. He hadn't intended to take advantage. She was hurting and vulnerable and several times he had told himself to stop. Then he remembered those moments in the flaming inferno, moments when he'd thought she might die and he would lose her. If he made love to her, she couldn't annul the marriage. She would belong to him. She would be his wife in more than just name, and they could begin to build a future together.

A moment had occurred when he thought of all he would gain. He would keep his half ownership in Griffin, as her father had planned, a company worth a veritable fortune. But it wasn't the money that had driven him.

It was his need for Violet, an urge to claim and protect her and keep her in his life.

And pure, driving lust.

She had almost died tonight. Both of them had almost died. He would never be able to live the superficial, unfulfilled life he had enjoyed before. He wasn't sure exactly what future he wanted, but he had married a woman of incredible courage and beauty and he meant to keep her.

He leaned over and kissed her forehead. She was his now. Her virginity marked the sheets. There was no way she could deny it.

Rule lay back down beside her, hard once more and wishing he could have her again.

It wasn't going to happen. At least not tonight.

Drawing her a little nearer, he closed his eyes and tried not to remember how close he had come to losing her.

Violet awakened to the sound of Mary's voice speaking to her in soft, gentle tones.

"Yer 'usband sent up a nice warm bath, milady. 'Tis nearly noon. Ye wouldn't want the water to be gettin' cold, now would ye?"

Violet struggled to wakefulness and tried to sit up. A hammerlike pounding and a shot of dizziness forced her head back down on the pillow.

"Ye had a very bad night, milady. Ye recall the fire, don't ye? Ye'd best take it nice and slow."

The fire. Dear God, how could she have forgotten?

Images arose, flames licking the curtains, people screaming in terror. A woman engulfed in flames.

Her throat tightened. Violet closed her eyes, fighting to block the memories.

"Are ye all right, milady?" Mary's round face peered down at her. "Should I fetch 'is lordship?"

Violet slowly shook her head, working to control the pounding, the nausea in her throat. "I just need a moment and I'll be all right."

A few seconds later, she made a second attempt to get up, but as she started to rise, she realized she was naked, and fresh memories assailed her. Rule kissing her. Rule making love to her!

Jerking back the covers, she stared down at the proof of her lost virginity, the scarlet stains on the sheets, and anger blocked everything else.

"How dare he!" She pulled the covers up once more, fighting for control. "Hand me my robe."

"But...but what about yer bath?"

Violet looked over at the steaming copper tub, large enough for her to sink into. The scent of violets drifted up from the water. She needed a clear head to face him, needed to wash away the reminders of the terrible fire.

Along with the remnants of his lovemaking.

Clutching the robe in front of her, she took Mary's hand and let the woman lead her over to the tub. Very carefully, she climbed into the water and settled back against the sloping rim.

The water felt wonderful. Her headache was fading, but she ached all over. She remembered falling in the hallway, the crushing weight of the people on top of her, remembered that she couldn't breathe and the instant she was certain she would die.

Then Rule was there, shouldering his way through the crowd, fighting the throng of desperate, screaming people, determined to reach her.

He had saved her last night. Saved her from certain death in the theater.

He had kept her alive.

In return, he had taken her virginity. He had gained what he wanted—the fortune her father had set aside for him as her husband. He had gotten what he had been after from the start.

"Let me help ye, milady. You'll be wantin' to wash ye hair."

Violet didn't argue. She smelled of soot and smoke. And something far more intimate. Rule's musky male scent seemed to stamp his ownership on every part of her body.

Rule. She didn't want to think of him. Didn't want to remember the way he had made her feel. Not yet.

Instead, she concentrated on the bath, accepting Mary's help to wash and rinse her hair, then wrap it in a towel around her head.

"That feels much better." She leaned back against the

rim of the tub. "Thank you, Mary. Now, if you don't mind, I'd like a few moments alone."

"Are ye certain, milady? Yer face is kind of pale. Are ye sure ye'll be all right?"

"I'm fine. If you wouldn't mind coming back a little later, I could use your help getting dressed."

"Of course, milady." Mary backed away, stepped out into the hall and quietly closed the door.

With a weary sigh, Violet settled deeper in the tub and closed her eyes. She had known better than to trust him. And though he had saved her, he had taken advantage of what had happened and betrayed her in the very worst way.

Just as she had betrayed the man who loved her.

Her heart squeezed. Dear God, how would Jeffrey feel when he found out what she had done? Jeffrey would never forgive her. There would be no future for them. She would never have the loving husband she had dreamed of, only years spent with a man who cared only about himself and his own personal gains.

Violet felt like crying. She bit back a sob.

After what she had done, she didn't deserve the solace of tears.

When Mary returned, she was ready to leave the bath, ready to dress and face Rule. She couldn't wait to see the look on his face when she told him she wanted a divorce.

Rule sat behind the desk in his study. A stack of drawings he had brought home from work sat in front of him, illustrations of new weapon designs, changes in some of the rifles and muskets currently being built. He needed to go over each one, decide which improvements he wanted to make, develop ways to implement the necessary changes in order to see them done.

Instead, all he could think of was Violet and what had happened between them last night.

She had suffered a terrible trauma. He shouldn't have made love to her, yet he couldn't truly say he was sorry. It would have happened, sooner or later. He was determined in the matter of making their marriage real.

He shoved back his chair. If she wasn't awake by now, he would awaken her. He was worried about her. He needed to be certain she was all right.

He started for the door just as it opened without the slightest warning. Surprised to see Violet walk into the study and head straight toward him, he began to smile, thinking about last night and wanting her again.

Violet didn't smile back. Her pretty lips compressed, seemed to lack their usual sensuous curves, and slight smudges darkened the skin beneath her leaf-green eyes. She looked tired and well ravished—and utterly beautiful.

She stopped directly in front of him. "How could you? How could you do it?"

He blinked. He had considered she might be a little upset, but noticing the fire in her eyes and the flush in her cheeks, he realized she was furious.

"You could have stopped me, Violet. You wanted me to make love to you. Surely you don't deny it."

Her lips flattened out even more. "I was frightened. I needed your care and concern, not your—your—"

"Lovemaking?" he supplied, though he knew she was thinking of the part of his anatomy that was stirring to life even now.

"You took advantage. You knew the way I felt. You knew I wanted an annulment."

Rule didn't move. The scent of violets drifted up from her hair and he clamped down on a surge of lust, hardly appropriate under the circumstances. "You may have come to London with that intention. It was *my* intention that we stay married. I've never lied about that."

She clamped her hands on her tiny waist and glared up at him. "You wanted to keep your half interest in the company. That is all you've ever cared about."

Rule shook his head. "That isn't true. I may have married you for business reasons in the beginning. Marriages are often forged for purposes other than love. Last night, I simply wanted you. And if you're honest, sweeting, you also wanted me."

Her chin inched up. "After the fire and barely escaping with my life, perhaps I reacted in a manner that I shouldn't have. I may have desired you last night. What I want this morning is a divorce."

Rule's eyes widened. "What?"

"You heard me. You took advantage. You got what you were after. You're half owner of Griffin. Now give me what *I* want."

His chest felt tight. He hadn't expected she would be this distraught. They were well suited. He had hoped she would see that. He only shook his head.

"Why not?"

"Do you understand what it takes to get a divorce?"

She gave him a nasty smile. "Actually, I do. I would need to prove desertion, adultery or cruelty. I believe, after last night, you qualify for all three."

A knot tightened in his stomach. He hadn't meant to be cruel. He had only wanted to make her his wife. "In regard to the first two, there were extenuating circumstances—of which you are aware. And I don't believe I was cruel to you in any way last night. Are you willing to distort the truth that much?"

She shrugged her small shoulders. "I realize your name would be somewhat besmirched, but—"

"*Somewhat besmirched?* My brother is a duke. We are one of the oldest families in England and never has a single Dewar ever divorced."

"You should have thought of that last night."

Rule forced himself under control. He might have taken advantage, but she had wanted him to make love to her, just as he had said.

He raked a hand through his hair. "Perhaps in a way you are right. Perhaps I should have behaved differently last night. But you weren't the only one affected by the fire. People died in that inferno. I was damned glad to be alive and so were you. You're my wife, Violet, and I needed you. I wanted to make love to you. I look at you now and I want to do it again."

Soft pink rose in her cheeks.

"What happened between us last night was good," he said. "Very good. Can you at least admit that much?"

She glanced away. "I—I barely remember last night."

But he could see by the heightened flush in her cheeks that she remembered very well and that the experience had not been unpleasant.

He gentled his voice. "Give us a little more time, sweetheart. That is all I am asking. Stay with me a little while longer, see what it might be like to be my wife. See if perhaps you could be happy."

She studied him with those perceptive green eyes. He could almost see her mind working. Long seconds passed. "I'll think about it," she finally said, and he was surprised by the enormity of his relief.

He made a slight bow of his head. "Thank you."

He watched her turn and walk out of the study, her full

skirts swaying enchantingly, and remembered the extent of her passions, the desire he had only begun to awaken. He would give her a little time, then talk to her again.

Unfortunately when the time came and he went in search of her, he discovered she was gone, and the knot returned to his stomach.

Ten

Violet hurried past the butler into Adelaide Lockhart's three-story brick residence in Belgravia. To her relief the lady of the house was away visiting a sick friend, leaving Caroline at home. Her cousin was making her way down the hall off the entry when she spotted Violet.

"Good grief, look at you! You are pale as a ghost!" Caroline reached out and caught both of Violet's hands. "What on earth has happened?" Even as she spoke, she led Violet down the corridor into the family drawing room and hurriedly closed the sliding doors.

Violet sank down on the burgundy horsehair sofa. Her head had resumed its throbbing and she hadn't eaten since yesterday luncheon.

Caroline eyed her worriedly. "I'll have the butler bring us some tea. And from the look of you, some cakes would not go amiss."

"Thank you," Violet said weakly. Now that her confrontation with Rule was over, her vitality seemed to have fled.

Neither of them spoke more than a few words until the tea cart arrived and the butler had left the room, giving them privacy once more. Caroline poured tea from a silver pot into a pair of porcelain cups and handed one of them to Violet, along with a plate filled with tiny frosted cakes and flaky shortbread biscuits.

"Your hands are shaking. You had better eat something before you get sick."

"I am already sick."

Caroline's head came up. "Dear Lord, what's happened?"

Violet lifted her teacup and managed a careful sip. "Have you… Have you heard about the fire last night? I thought it might be in the morning papers."

"Great heavens, yes. At the Royal Pantheon. Twenty-two people were killed at this morning's count. Some of them crushed in the stampede to get out, some of them burned to death trying to escape the flames. I cannot imagine such horror."

Violet's hands started shaking even harder. She set the teacup down without taking another drink. "We were there. Rule and I. We went to see the play."

"Oh, my God!" Caroline set her cup and saucer on the table in front of the sofa, hurried over to Violet and gathered her into her arms. "Oh, my poor dear cousin. Are you all right? What about Rule? Dear God, tell me neither of you were injured."

Violet shook her head. She took a shaky breath and expelled it. "It was a nightmare, Caroline. I still can't get the horrible images out of my head. Rule… Rule saved my life. Both of us nearly died last night."

"Oh, my poor dear." Caroline kept an arm around her, steadying her a little. "Is that why you came? You wanted to talk about what happened?"

"I wanted to talk about what…what happened after."

Caroline frowned. "After? What do you mean?"

"We were both upset. Rule took care of me, tried to console me. We made love, Carrie. Rule and I made love."

Caroline just stared. "You and Rule, you…you…"

Violet managed a nod. "At the time, it was as if it weren't actually real, as if…as if it were some sort of dream. I was so grateful to Rule for saving me and I was so glad to be alive. Now…well…I'm not a virgin anymore."

Caroline's pale blue eyes widened. "Oh, my."

"Exactly. So you see why I am upset. I can no longer get an annulment, and Jeffrey will never forgive me."

Caroline sat up a little straighter on the sofa. "Dewar took advantage of you. You must have been frantic. You were probably half out of your mind with fear. The man is the cad you have always believed. Good heavens, what are you going to do?"

"I told him I wanted a divorce."

"Oh, my God!"

Violet sighed wearily. "The thing of it is, Carrie, I could have stopped him. I wanted him to kiss me, to touch me. I wanted to feel all of the things he made me feel."

Caroline squeezed her hand. "Was it…was it wonderful, then?"

Violet felt the color creeping into her cheeks. "You've heard the gossip about him. They say women clamor to get into his bed. The man is a practiced lover and, yes, it was wonderful. But he only did it to secure his portion of the company. Making love to me meant nothing to Rule, less than nothing. And I won't let it happen again."

"So you are truly getting a divorce?"

Violet stared down at her lap. "I don't know. It carries a terrible stigma. I would be shunned from Boston Society. People would no longer invite me into their homes."

"And there is the not-so-small problem that after last night, you may be carrying Rule's child."

Violet's head shot up. "Goodness, I hadn't even thought of that." Though strangely enough, the notion of having Rule's baby was not at all unpleasant. "He asked me to give the matter some thought, see if…see if I might reconsider. He wants me to find out if being his wife could possibly make me happy."

Caroline shook her head. "I don't know, Vi. I don't trust him."

"Neither do I."

"Still, you are married—and in more than just name."

"I know."

"And if it was truly wonderful—"

"That doesn't matter."

"I think it would matter to me."

Violet gazed off toward the window. "I have to write to Jeffrey. I can't let him go on planning a future that includes me as his wife."

"Yes, I suppose you are right."

"I'll see it done today." She rose from the sofa, but Caroline tugged her back down.

"You are not leaving here until you have a cup of tea and something to eat."

Violet closed her eyes against a fresh wave of dizziness. Her cousin was right. She had to take care of herself. She had to be strong to find a way out of the awful dilemma in which she found herself.

Time was the answer. She would stay a while longer in London. And while she was there, she would accomplish her second reason for coming. She would inform Rule of her decision.

She would tell him she intended to sell her half of the company.

* * *

Violet hadn't returned by late afternoon. Rule had no idea when she had last eaten and he was beginning to worry she might fall ill. Dammit to hell, so they had made love. That was what married couples did.

And both of them had enjoyed it.

Violet hadn't admitted it, but she hadn't denied it, either. What he needed to do was make love to her again and quite thoroughly. Sooner or later, she would see how good they were together and she would forget this ridiculous notion of getting a divorce.

He sat behind his desk, examining ways he might return to her bed, trying to find a solution to his dilemma, but getting no suitable answers. He glanced up at the sound of a sharp knock at his door, saw Royal walk into the study. There were lines across his forehead that weren't usually there and his jaw looked tight.

"I just heard about the fire at the theater last night. Lily and I have been frantic with worry."

Rule shook his head. "It was bad, I can tell you. Fortunately, Violet and I escaped without physical injury."

The tension left his brother's face and his shoulders relaxed. "You mentioned you planned to take your wife. When we read the paper this morning, we feared the worst."

Rule raked a hand through his hair. "I don't know how I'll ever get the images out of my head. I thought we might die in there. As it turned out, we were among the lucky ones and both of us escaped."

Royal walked over and sat down in a leather chair in front of Rule's desk. "Reese is already returned to Briarwood. I told Lily I would send word to her at home as soon as I was sure you were all right."

"I am fine, but Violet is still a little shaken." That was putting it mildly.

"So it was as bad as the newspapers said."

"Worse. The place was an inferno. It was a miracle we got out." Rule fought a memory of Violet falling beneath the crush in the hallway, the smothering weight of people pinning her to the floor. He pushed back from his desk and stood up. "I believe I need a drink. Would you care to join me?"

Royal shook his head. "I've meetings this afternoon. Brewery business."

"Of course."

"So aside from the two of you nearly dying, how are things going between you?"

Rule poured brandy into a snifter and took a drink. "If you're asking if I've made the marriage real, the answer is yes. Unfortunately, my timing wasn't the best and now my wife wants a divorce."

Royal's golden eyes widened and he sat up straighter in his chair. "Tell me you are jesting."

"I wish I were."

Royal surprised him with a grin. "And for years I've been hearing what a great lover my youngest brother is. Why don't you simply put those skills to use and make her fall in love with you like half the women in London?"

Rule sipped his drink, for a moment actually wondering if it might be possible. But he had betrayed Violet's trust two times already.

"That would hardly be fair, since I am not in love with her."

Royal leaned back in his chair. "But you admit you care for her."

"I care for her a very great deal. But caring for someone and being in love are far different things."

Royal eyed him closely. "I believe there may be hope for you yet, little brother."

"Why is that?"

"Thinking of Violet's needs before your own. That hasn't happened with a woman before."

"I haven't had a wife before."

Royal smiled. "Exactly so."

They talked of more mundane matters for a while, of Royal's plans for expanding the brewery. Finally, he rose from his chair. "I had better get home and tell my wife you and Violet are safe or she will have my head."

"Tell her we appreciate her concern."

"I'll send a note to Reese, as well, in case he hears you were there."

Rule just nodded. As he watched his golden-haired brother disappear out the door, for the first time in his life, Rule envied the man his happy marriage.

For the next two days, Violet declined to join Rule for breakfast or supper, pleading exhaustion and nerves from her ordeal.

In truth, she simply wasn't ready to face him.

Now that her anger had faded, her thoughts kept straying back to the night he had made love to her. She recalled every kiss, every touch. The way it had felt when he had been inside her.

The memories kept popping into her head and every time they did, her body went warm with desire.

Dear God, she had never thought of herself as a passionate sort of woman. Now she wondered. Was it merely that making love had awakened her womanly needs? Or was it something more? Whatever the truth, sooner or later she had to face him. She was his wife and at least for the present that would not change.

And there was the matter of her decision to sell the company—at least the half she retained.

Violet prowled the house all morning, occasionally distracting herself with reading and embroidery, wishing she had something more interesting to do. But Rule had returned to his daily routine of working in the office and he wouldn't be home until late in the afternoon.

Violet sighed. In Boston, every day she had made a trip to the factory, entering by the back door and working for most of the day. Her life was interesting and full, not empty and boring as it was here in London.

Returning to the small private drawing room she favored at the back of the town house, she picked up her embroidery hoop. When boredom set in once more, she napped for a while, just to pass the time.

She was waiting in Rule's study when he got home, reading a gothic novel she had found on a dusty, half-hidden bookshelf.

"So this is where you are." Rule's deep voice held a note of warmth she hadn't expected. "I'm happy to see you are out of hiding at last."

"I wasn't hiding."

"Weren't you?"

She glanced away. "Well, perhaps a little."

"Making love isn't a sin, Violet. It is supposed to bring you pleasure." His gaze ran over her. "Did it?"

She pretended not to understand him. "Did it what?"

"Did my lovemaking bring you pleasure? Because you certainly pleasured me."

Her cheeks began to burn. "I told you, I hardly recall."

Rule strode toward her, dark and tall, and at the moment

a little intimidating. He hauled her up from her chair and straight into his arms, and his mouth came down over hers.

It was a hot, ravishing, entirely thorough kiss and though she told herself to fight it, pleasure washed over her. He nibbled her bottom lip and kissed the corners of her mouth before he lifted his head, breaking the contact.

"Does that help you recall?"

Her cheeks were flaming now. Oh, she remembered, all right. She remembered his kisses, his mouth on her breasts, the feel of his heavy length moving inside her. She remembered the incredible sweep of pleasure, the heart-pounding ecstasy she had felt in those final, blissful moments.

She looked up at Rule and saw that he was remembering, too, and inside her corset, her breasts began to swell.

Violet glanced away. "I need to talk to you. It is a matter of some importance."

"All right. Why don't we sit down? Shall I ring for tea?"

"Not unless you are inclined. I have had tea enough to last me a week."

He chuckled softly. "Coffee, then?"

"No, thank you."

"It doesn't sound as if you enjoyed your day."

"I'll admit I've had more interesting days."

Rule cast her a glance, but made no reply. Taking her hand, he led her over to the sofa in front of the hearth and they sat down on opposite ends. Violet tried not to notice the way he looked at her, his eyes a fathomless blue that should have seemed cold but instead burned with a heat that said how much he wanted her and warned her to be wary.

"So what did you wish to discuss?"

"Business. Besides the annulment I hoped to gain, I came to England for a second reason."

"Which is?"

"I want to sell the company."

He seemed to mull that over. "I recall you mentioned the subject before."

"Since I never thought to consummate our marriage, I thought I would have the right to dispose of it as I saw fit. Obviously the situation has changed. My intention to sell, however, has not."

"I'm afraid I don't understand. Griffin is one of the most successful armaments manufacturing companies in the world."

"True enough and under different circumstances, I wouldn't feel the need. But as you must know, a war is about to break out in my country. I have friends and family on both sides of the slavery issue. I have no wish to build weapons they will use to kill each other."

"You don't believe people should be able to arm themselves for protection?"

"That is not the issue. I traveled to England with a small pocket pistol among my possessions and I assure you I am a very good shot. This is different. I simply don't want to feel responsible for friends and family dying."

Rule raked a hand through his hair. "You're asking me to sell my half, as well?"

"It would make things easier."

"The company makes a good deal of money. Why should I wish to give that up?"

She gave him a sugary smile. "I can't imagine you would give up anything that benefits you personally. That has been your approach since the day we met. So here are your choices. I will sell my half and you will have a new partner to deal with. Or you may buy me out."

"Bloody hell."

"There is no call for that sort of language."

"Dammit, woman!"

She merely lifted an eyebrow and Rule fell silent.

"I'll expect your decision by tomorrow. I would like to hire a solicitor to promote the sale." She rose from the sofa. "Now, if you will excuse me…"

She thought he grumbled something about preferring to bed her than excuse her, but she couldn't be sure.

Lifting her skirts out of the way, Violet swept out of the study. A small smile tugged at her lips. She wasn't sure why it felt so good to leave Rule Dewar with that irritated look on his face.

But it did.

Rule strode into the entry of his brother's recently completed town mansion. Over the years the profits from Royal's successful ale brewing business had helped him rebuild the Bransford fortune, repair Bransford Castle and build an elegant home in London for whenever the family came to the city.

Though they preferred country living and usually made their home at the castle, Royal and Lily and their children were staying in town while Royal worked on the expansion plans for the London location of the brewery.

"Where is he?" Rule asked Rutgers, the longtime family butler.

"His study, my lord."

Rule strode past the gray-haired man and continued down the hall. The study door was open and Rule walked into the comfortable, wood-paneled chamber where a fire burned in the hearth, warming the room against the April chill.

At his appearance, his brother rose from the chair behind the desk. "I haven't seen you this many times in the last two years. What has Violet done now?"

"Violet wants to sell the company—that is what she has done. I can't believe it. She just walks into my study and says she wants to sell and if I don't like it, I can either buy her out or put up with a new partner."

Royal chuckled as he sat back down. "Sounds like you have finally found a woman you can't sway with pretty words and a night in your bed."

Rule just grunted.

"So why don't you sell? Did you not tell me a few months back that you were thinking it might be a good idea?"

"I thought it might be. A couple of people have shown an interest in buying the business. It is worth a great deal of money and there are a lot of opportunities out there right now. Railroads and steamships. Industry of all kinds is growing by leaps and bounds. I thought it might be an interesting challenge to see if I could take the company in a new direction."

"So why don't you do it?"

"Because I am supposed to be the man of the family. I don't want my wife thinking she can just walk in and start making decisions. Her father arranged our marriage because he wanted me to take care of Griffin—and also his daughter."

"She does own half the business. I believe that's what you said."

"She owns half."

"Why does she want to sell?"

"She is worried about the war. She knows there is going to be a conflict in America and she has family and friends on both sides of the issue."

"I can see where she might be concerned."

"So can I."

"So tell her you'll agree to the sale, but you want to keep the partnership intact. Tell her you'll submit a list of investments to be made with the proceeds, and from that list, the two of you must agree on whatever purchases are to be made."

Rule paced over to the fire then turned back. "Interesting notion." And one that would keep the two of them together.

"In that way," Royal continued, "Violet gets what she wants and you get what you want."

He liked the idea. His brother had a head for business, always had. It was a sound suggestion, a fair compromise.

Then again, Violet was a woman. In his experience, women were rarely open to compromise of any sort.

"I appreciate your thoughts," Rule said, walking back toward the desk. "Give my best to Lily and the children."

"Good luck," Royal said.

Rule just nodded as he headed for the door. Where Violet was concerned, the only luck he'd had so far had all been bad.

Eleven

Violet accepted Rule's invitation to supper. He was taking her to a restaurant called the Dove, an exclusive establishment he thought she would enjoy. He promised that if she would join him, he would be willing to discuss the sale of the business.

Violet didn't want to go. The last night she had spent in Rule's company, he had ended up making love to her. Every time she saw him, those memories returned—the scorching kisses, the heated caresses, the feel of his mouth on her breasts.

Even now, as she dabbed a spot of perfume behind each ear and smoothed the front of her aqua silk gown, his image returned and she felt flushed and damp. Worse yet, she wanted him to do it again. The man had a powerful effect on her. It was ridiculous to deny it.

She should have refused his invitation. She should move out of the house and in with Caroline and her grandmother, though she had no idea how she would explain that course of action to Mrs. Lockhart. The simple fact was she was married to Rule Dewar and, as her cousin had pointed out, not merely in name.

She owed Rule a chance, owed it to her father and perhaps even to herself.

She thought of Jeffrey and the life she had wanted but could no longer have. She had written to him as she had vowed and seen the letter posted, but it would be weeks until he received it and she received his reply.

In the meantime, she wanted to sell at least her portion of the business, free her conscience from any part the company might play in the upcoming war. Unfortunately, without Rule's cooperation, it wouldn't be that easy.

Violet wondered if Burton Stanfield, the man she had met at the Wyhurst ball, might still have an interest. She would prefer not to deal with him, since Rule didn't trust him, but she might not have any choice.

She would soon discover her options, she thought as she picked up the reticule that matched her aqua gown and headed downstairs. Rule stood waiting at the bottom, handsome as sin in his black-and-white evening clothes, a perfect complement to his thick raven hair. Memories of his fiery kisses and passionate lovemaking returned, and a flush crept over her skin.

Violet steeled herself against his devastating charm and managed to smile. "Good evening, my lord."

"You look enchanting, my lady." He bowed gallantly over her white gloved hand, pressing his lips against the back.

"I see you are full of flattery, as usual."

He only smiled. "I'm glad you agreed to come."

"Well, I shall have to wait and see if I am glad when I hear what you have to say about the sale."

He kept his smile in place but it didn't look quite as sincere as before. "Come." Lacing her arm with his, he led her toward the door. "Our carriage waits out front."

She allowed him to guide her without saying more. She

wished she didn't have to be on guard every moment she was with him, but he left her no choice.

Rule helped her into the coach and sat down across from her. As the vehicle lurched into motion, Violet fixed her attention outside the carriage on the activity lit by the gas streetlamps and the light spilling out through house windows.

As Rule had promised, London was a fascinating city. The climate here was milder than in Boston, though the air was a little less clean. A dog barked in the distance and a black-and-white mutt ran off into the darkness. She spotted the occasional policeman keeping watch as the coach rumbled on toward St. James, the location of the restaurant Rule had chosen.

They arrived right on time and the footman at the rear of the carriage jumped down and opened the door. Rule climbed out first and helped Violet down, then took her arm and led her into the elegant two-story establishment. A seating area filled with linen-draped tables lit by candlesticks formed the middle of the restaurant, and a row of private booths lined one wall.

"Good evening, my lord." The maître d' approached, smiling, obviously well acquainted with Rule.

"Good evening, Rafael."

The man was very tall and very thin, with curly black hair and a Roman nose. She wondered if his slight Italian accent was real or strictly for the benefit of his patrons. "Your booth is ready, sir. If you will please follow me."

Violet let Rule escort her around the perimeter of the room to a booth draped in heavy red velvet. Once they were inside, Rafael untied the gold sashes and the curtain fell into place, giving them privacy.

Violet's senses went on alert. She had thought in a

public restaurant she wouldn't have to worry. She wasn't prepared for a return to this kind of intimacy. She worried what Rule expected when he had brought her inside the private booth.

"You needn't get that look on your face. I don't plan to ravish you here."

She cast him a glance, arched a copper eyebrow. "Somewhere else, then?"

Rule grinned and his gorgeous dimples appeared. "If I had my way, yes. I've never lied about my desire for you, Violet. Now that we've made love and I know what a passionate little creature you are, that desire has only grown stronger."

She started to rise. "I didn't come here for seduction. If you will excuse me…"

Rule caught her hand. "Take it easy, love. We came to talk business. That hasn't changed."

Violet eased back down in her chair. Rule poured champagne from a bottle in the silver bucket beside the table and handed her a crystal glass.

He lifted his own in toast. "To the future."

It was a toast she could drink to, whatever it might hold, though she would be careful this time not to drink too much. "The future."

They made small talk as the waiter appeared to take their orders, a turbot in lobster sauce for her and roasted veal with pecan dressing for Rule.

The curtains fell into place once more and Rule set his champagne glass down on the table. "You're still determined to sell, I imagine."

"I explained my reasons. They haven't changed."

"All right. Perhaps, as you suggested, we should explore the possibility."

For the next few minutes, he outlined his thoughts, explaining that he had actually examined the possibility of selling several months back but, because of his obligations to her and her father, hadn't really considered it.

"As I told you, I received an offer from Burton Stanfield, but I don't like the way he does business."

"So you said."

"There is another party who may be interested, a man named Charles Whitney. He approached me about it some time back, but I discouraged him. He lives in York but spends a good deal of time in London. I believe he may be in town. I can approach him again, but with the market as strong as it is, I don't think finding a buyer will be a problem."

"Everyone is betting there will be war in America. If there is, there are great profits to be made. We should most certainly get offers."

"But selling only half is much harder."

"Probably," she agreed.

"Then here is what I propose. I'll consider selling my half along with yours on two conditions."

"Which are?"

"First, you agree to keep our partnership intact and we reinvest the proceeds of the sale. I'll put together a list of possible investments. Both of us would have to agree to whatever is purchased."

He went on to relate the potential of various industries including shipping and railways, both of which appealed to Violet greatly.

"I realize it would be somewhat of a compromise on your part, since you might wish to dissolve the business altogether, but that is the first of my terms."

She sat back in her chair, her mind running over his proposal. On the surface, there was nothing untoward about it. They were business partners now and that would continue. Only the nature of the business itself would change.

And the various possibilities intrigued her. "It sounds fair enough."

He actually looked surprised. "You are telling me you will agree?"

"Is there a reason I shouldn't?"

"Not at all. I merely thought… I suppose I thought you might be determined on some other course and not open to compromise."

"I have often found compromise the best way to achieve one's goals."

He smiled faintly. "As have I, Violet. Which brings me to the second condition—the one I deem most important. If you agree, whatever happens, you will have the chance to obtain both of the things for which you came to London."

He was talking about the divorce, a subject she wasn't yet ready to discuss.

"What are you suggesting?"

"I want you to agree to continue our marriage for at least another month."

"That is impossible."

"Why? It's what your father would have wanted. It's what I want. And I think, deep down, you might even want it, too."

If things were different, she might, but there were other considerations. She looked him straight in the face. "Do you love me, Rule?"

His gaze held steady. "I care for you, Violet. I desire you greatly. To tell you the truth, I don't really know what love is. I know I would like for us to stay married. Say you will give us a chance."

Violet glanced away. The last thing she wanted was a

too-handsome husband who didn't love her, a man who had half the women in London vying for his attention.

"There are other women you could marry. Why are you so determined it has to be me?"

He leaned toward her across the table, his features turning dark. "I don't want another woman, dammit. I already have a wife. We spoke vows in front of God. What could it hurt to find out if your father was right?"

Violet closed her eyes. She could almost see Griff's face, his expression stern but loving. She knew what he would want, understood why he had arranged the marriage in the first place.

If only he could have known Jeffrey. She was certain he would have wanted her to marry a man who loved her.

"Violet?"

"What about…about…conjugal rights? You are the sort of man who would expect his wife to abide by her wifely duties."

"I would never force you. I would hope that you would welcome me into your bed as you did before."

She felt the color rising in her cheeks. "And if I did not?"

"Then I suppose I shall have failed in my duties as a husband."

Violet mulled that over. He had promised not to force her. She could say no to his efforts at seduction if she wished. "All right, I'll agree. I suppose whether we divorce now or a month from now doesn't matter."

Rule grinned broadly. "You won't be sorry, sweetheart, I promise."

But she was already sorry. She wished she had stayed in Boston, communicated her wish to end the marriage through her attorney. Now it was too late.

She held out her champagne glass, though it wasn't

completely empty. "If you wouldn't mind, I think I would like a little more to drink."

"Of course." Rule lifted the bottle out of the ice bucket. When his gaze returned to her face, she could see the hunger, the desire he no longer tried to hide. He was thinking about the liquor she had consumed the night of the fire and the hours that they had spent making love.

Violet set the glass back down on the table. "On second thought, I think I've had enough."

Rule made no reply. Violet was grateful when the waiter arrived with their meal.

Twelve

A stiff wind rattled the branches, shaking the budding leaves on the trees. The late-morning temperature was colder than yesterday, but at least the harsh breeze had cleared the air.

Since Rule had resumed his daily routine and long ago left for the office, Violet rambled around the house, wishing she had something to do to wile away the hours that seemed endless since she was used to working.

She was padding toward the entry when she spotted Hatfield carrying a message on a silver salver.

"This just came for you, my lady."

"Thank you, Hat."

His wrinkled face always turned a little pink when she called him that and yet she thought it pleased him. She opened the wax-sealed message and began to read.

Dearest cousin,
There is no easy way to say this. Jeffrey is here in London, arrived on a ship from America only just last night. This morning, he came to Grandmother's

house in search of you. I told him you had gone out but that you would return this afternoon. He is due to arrive at two o'clock. Please—you must be here when he gets back.

Your worried and loving cousin,
Caroline

Oh, dear God, Jeffrey was in London! What on earth could she tell him? How could she possibly explain?

Rushing frantically up the stairs, she called for Mary to help her change. She had no idea what she would say to Jeffrey when she saw him. There was no possible excuse for what she had done.

Her heart squeezed. She had betrayed him, pure and simple.

Violet blinked against the sudden sting of tears. Jeffrey was a good and decent man. They could have been happy together.

She thought of the promise she had made to Rule, that she would give their marriage a chance. Rule had said he wouldn't force her to make love, but neither did he intend for their marriage to be one of convenience.

And deep down, she had begun to anticipate the moment when he would return to her bed.

Now Jeffrey was here, a reminder of all her life would be missing. Unlike Rule, Jeffrey had declared his love for her and vowed to dedicate himself to making her happy. Her heart ached. Once Jeffrey knew the truth, he would turn away from her in disgust. Even if she obtained a divorce, he would not want her.

Shoving away her heartbreak, Violet dressed in a gown of apricot silk, grabbed her white cotton gloves and headed back downstairs. At precisely one o'clock, she boarded the carriage Rule had provided for her and set off for the Lockhart house in Belgravia. She wanted to get there early. She needed to speak to Caroline, ask for her advice.

Thirty minutes before Jeffrey was due, she arrived at the large brick house, her heart squeezing and her thoughts circling round and round in her head. Caroline opened the door before she had reached the top of the wide front porch steps, grabbed her hand and hauled her into the entry.

"Thank God you are here."

"I came early. I was hoping we would have a chance to talk." As they traveled down the hall, arm in arm, she glanced around in search of Mrs. Lockhart. "Where is your grandmother?"

"Upstairs. She has been feeling a bit under the weather. I am sure it is nothing serious, but at the moment, I am grateful she won't be able to come down."

"What did she say when Jeffrey arrived?"

"I told her he was a longtime friend of your family's and mine. She didn't seem to think it untoward that he had stopped by to pay a call."

"I suppose, under different circumstances, it would be completely expected."

Neither of them said more until the butler had securely closed the doors to the family drawing room.

"I still cannot believe it," Caroline said. "Jeffrey in London! What on earth are you going to do?"

Violet felt a lump building in her throat. "I will do what I must. I have to tell Jeffrey the truth. What else can I do?"

Caroline sat down on the sofa, but Violet began to pace back and forth.

"This is dreadful," Caroline said, "simply dreadful."

"I know."

"Jeffrey is going to be crushed."

Violet sat down next to her cousin and fought not to cry. "I wish I could change things, Carrie, but it is far too late for that."

Caroline reached over and caught her hand. "It is never too late. There are always choices to be made. Speaking of which, how are things going with Rule?"

Violet sighed. "He has agreed to sell the company. But he wants our partnership to continue. He wants to reinvest the proceeds into business opportunities on which we both agree."

"That sounds reasonable, I suppose."

"He also wants the two of us to stay married for at least another month."

"What?" Caroline leaped up from the sofa. "But you can't possibly do that!"

Tears welled in Violet's eyes. "You have to understand, Carrie. My marriage to Rule was what my father wanted above all things. Once the annulment was no longer possible, I knew my relationship with Jeffrey was over. It never occurred to me he would come to London."

Caroline sank back down on the sofa. "Oh, dear."

Violet drew a lace-trimmed handkerchief out of her reticule and mopped at the wetness beneath her eyes. "I don't know how I am going to face him."

Caroline squeezed her hand. "None of this is your fault. Your husband abandoned you and then seduced you. Just tell Jeffrey the truth. There is always the chance he will forgive you. After you've talked to him, perhaps you will know what you should do."

Violet looked up. "I just… I wish I had stayed in Boston."

They talked until the chimes on the grandfather clock struck twice, indicating the hour of Jeffrey's arrival. A few minutes later, a soft knock came at the drawing room door.

"Mr. Burnett is returned, miss," the butler said to Caroline. "The American gentleman who was here this morning?"

"Yes, we've been expecting him."

"I've asked him to wait in the formal drawing room."

"Thank you." Caroline gave Violet a reassuring glance, and together they walked out into the hall. Following the butler, they made their way to the formal drawing room, which like most of the house was a little worn but adequate, with dark blue silk draperies and gold velvet sofas. Like most Victorian homes, there seemed to be a little too much of everything to suit Violet.

Caroline hesitated in the doorway. Across the drawing room, Jeffrey stood with his back to the door, his shoulders straight, his golden hair gleaming in the light coming in through the mullioned windows.

"I think it would be better if I waited until the two of you have spoken," Caroline whispered. "If you need me, I'll be just in the other room."

Violet just nodded. Taking a breath for courage, she started across the drawing room. Jeffrey turned at the muffled sound of her footsteps on the carpet, and a wide smile lit his face.

"Violet, dearest." He strode toward her, a handsome man, fair instead of dark like Rule, but attractive all the same. He stopped directly in front of her. She thought that after such a long absence, he might sweep her into his arms, but Jeffrey merely reached for her gloved hand and brought it to his lips.

"It is so good to see you, my dear Violet."

She managed to smile, though her chest was tight and she was fighting to hold back tears. "You as well, Jeffrey." She led him over to the sofa and both of them sat down. "How was your journey?"

"Difficult. But then that is expected when one travels across an ocean."

"I wish...I wish you had written and told me you were coming."

"I would have, but the notion came fairly swiftly once you were gone. A message wouldn't have reached you before my arrival." He unfastened the tiny buttons on her glove, lifted her hand and pressed his lips against her wrist. It was the most intimate gesture he had ever made.

"You look beautiful, Violet. Even more lovely than I remembered."

Violet eased her hand away and rose from the sofa. She walked over to the hearth and slowly turned to face him. "You have come a great distance, Jeffrey, and now that you are here, what I have to say will be a grave disappointment. There is no easy way to tell you this."

She released a shaky breath, hoping her courage would not fail. "I can only begin by saying how sorry I am it happened."

Jeffrey rose, worrying lines digging into his forehead, his golden eyebrows drawn slightly together over his warm brown eyes. "What is it, darling? Surely it can't be that bad."

Violet moistened her lips, which suddenly felt as stiff as the petticoat beneath her skirt. "I am sorry, Jeffrey, but there is not going to be an annulment."

Jeffrey began walking toward her. "What do you mean? Did Dewar refuse to agree?"

"He wants the marriage to stand. He said he was coming to Boston to get me. He said he wanted to make our marriage real. Then...then there was a fire and we were both nearly killed and then...and then..." She straightened. "I slept with him, Jeffrey. He made me his wife. There can be no annulment."

Jeffrey's features turned ashen. He simply stood there staring in disbelief.

"I am sorry," she said. Tears welled in her eyes and spilled over onto her cheeks. Violet wiped them away with the tip of her glove.

Jeffrey seemed to awaken from a trance. He completed the distance between them, reached out and gripped her shoulders. "This isn't your fault. Dewar took advantage. You said you were nearly killed. You must have been terrified. I know the sort of man he is. I heard rumors about him when he was in Boston. Even then, he had a black reputation with women. The man is a practiced seducer."

Violet fought to hold back fresh tears. "It doesn't matter, Jeffrey. We're married. He had a right to consummate the marriage."

"He forced you?"

Violet shook her head. "No," she said softly.

"I'll call him out! I'll kill him—I swear it!" He let go of her and strode over to the window, his chest heaving in and out.

Violet moved toward him, rested a hand gently on his arm. "I am married, Jeffrey. I was when we first met. It wasn't fair to lead you on as I did."

He turned to face her. "The man abandoned you, no matter what he says. You had every right to try to make a life for yourself."

She swallowed past the lump in her throat. "It doesn't matter. Unless something changes, I am Rule's wife and he is my husband. Please try to accept that."

She thought of the divorce she might yet undertake, but it wasn't fair to Jeffrey to hold out that sort of hope.

"I love you, Violet. I meant for us to marry."

"I wasn't in a position to accept an offer of marriage and we both knew it."

"We were planning a life together."

"We spoke of it. I wanted to marry you, Jeffrey, truly I did, but it was already too late."

He caught hold of her hands. "It isn't too late. You don't love Dewar, you love me. Say it, Violet. Tell me you love me."

Her throat tightened. Before she'd left Boston, she could have easily said the words. She didn't understand why she couldn't say them now.

"So much has changed. I care for you, Jeffrey. I always will. For now, let us leave it at that."

Jeffrey drew her toward him. For an instant, she thought he might kiss her, as Rule would surely have done. Instead, he abruptly released her and moved several steps away.

"I am staying at the Parkland Hotel, should you need me."

"I am so sorry, Jeffrey." He had lost so much. Both of them had.

"This isn't over, Violet. You may rely on that."

Violet said nothing. She was still uncertain what the future might hold. Uncertain whether Jeffrey might yet be a part of it.

She watched him storm out of the drawing room. She ached for Jeffrey and the warm, companionable marriage they would have shared. Yet even after seeing him again, she couldn't quite convince herself to proceed with the divorce.

Perhaps in time…

Violet brushed another tear from her cheek. As she walked out of the drawing room and went in search of her cousin, she thought of Rule and what might lie ahead.

For the first time she wondered what her husband would say if he discovered her relationship with Jeffrey.

Thirteen

Rule sat behind the desk in his office at Griffin Manufacturing. In the days after his discussion with Violet about selling the company, he had hired a solicitor who specialized in the sale of businesses and discreetly let it be known that Griffin was for sale. He also mentioned his interest in reinvesting the proceeds.

Two things occurred.

Buyers seemed to be crawling out of the woodwork, and stacks of business proposals flooded into his office.

Steamship lines offered stocks in return for development money, textile manufacturers wanted capital for expansion. There were mining ventures for sale, railway companies planning to crisscross the country with new routes that promised huge returns.

Next to the large stack in front of him sat a smaller stack Luke had brought for him to look at. Since graduating from Oxford, Luke had gone into the trading business. He was a broker of sorts, specializing in the riskiest kinds of investments. They were also the deals that paid the very highest returns.

Luke liked taking risks and he seemed to have a nose for sniffing out opportunities that on the surface appeared to be disastrous. He had made thousands of pounds for his clients—and an even larger sum for himself.

Rule glanced back down at the taller of the stacks. A few appeared to be sound investments. A number were downright swindles. Most fell somewhere in between.

He blew out a breath, wishing he had time to research the proposals more thoroughly, but he was buried in paperwork here in the office. He might have gained his ownership in the company from his marriage to Violet, but he worked as hard as any man in London to make it the success it was today.

He looked up at a knock at the door. His young male secretary, Terence Smythe, stood in the opening.

"Your wife is here, my lord. Shall I show her in?"

Rule frowned. The area around Tooley Street wasn't a very good neighborhood. He had warned Violet about coming down here alone. He sighed. At least now she had a carriage of her own and a footman to accompany her.

"Show her in, Terry."

"Yes, my lord." Young Terence disappeared and Violet appeared in the doorway.

"I was hoping we might speak…if you have the time."

He wondered what was so important it couldn't wait until he got home. But Violet had been acting strangely for the past several days, avoiding him as much as possible, even more skittish than she had been when she had first arrived. He figured it was the promise she had made, her agreement to remain his wife for at least another month.

As far as Rule was concerned, that meant behaving as a wife in every way. He wanted to make love to her and he believed she wanted that, too. He meant to see it done at the first opportunity.

He smiled as she walked toward him. "What is it, love, that has brought you all the way down here?"

"There is something I wish to discuss." Removing her bonnet and tossing it onto an empty chair, she walked behind his desk to where he stood. Her gaze slanted down to the business proposals sitting on top.

She was dressed simply today, in a practical dark brown woolen gown trimmed with ecru lace. She wore her fiery hair in a plain chignon at the nape of her neck and he fought an urge to pull out the pins and run his fingers through it.

"Have you had any luck with the sale?" she asked, eyeing him from beneath a row of burnished lashes. He remembered the way her pretty green eyes had widened in shock as he made love to her and she reached her first release. He remembered the feel of her gloving him so sweetly, and desire flared inside him.

He cleared his throat, banishing the memory. "Actually, we've had a good deal of interest. I think we may receive a formal offer very soon."

She looked back down at the papers. "And these are the business opportunities we'll be considering?"

He nodded, forced his attention away from the luscious curve of her breast. "If I ever get time to go over them. We need to be extremely careful. There is a great deal of money at stake and a good deal of information to examine. Unfortunately, company business has to come first and it is extremely time-consuming."

"I know." She looked up at him. She was standing so close the scent of violets drifted up from her hair—his shaft filled, lengthening and thickening inside his trousers. Tonight he would go to her, take her in his arms and kiss her until she responded as she had the night of the fire.

"I know how busy you are," she said, and he made himself concentrate on her words and not memories of their heated lovemaking. "In fact, that is the reason I came. I wanted to see if I might be able to help."

"Help? In what way?"

She glanced toward the window. Outside, several tall chimney stacks down by the docks blew thick plumes of smoke into the air.

She returned her attention to him. "What is the most recent news on the Boston plant?" she asked, avoiding the question. "Does all seem to be in order?"

"Reports come in by ship every week. Recently, I received news of an upcoming change in management. Apparently Mr. Haskell will be leaving. With the time it takes to receive the news, he will already be gone, replaced by a man named Douglas Shearing. The Boston branch has always been extremely well run. I doubt there will be much of an upset."

"I certainly hope not. Assuming Mr. Shearing is as competent as Mr. Haskell."

"Haskell did an excellent job. It's a shame we'll be losing him."

Violet's smile held an edge of triumph that suddenly made him uneasy. "I am glad you think so. Because, you see, I am J. A. Haskell."

He frowned. "What are you talking about?"

"I am telling you that I have been running the Boston plant for quite some time. I am the one who hired Mr. Shearing to take Haskell's place, since I would be traveling here. So you see I have an interest in making certain that he is as capable as he seemed."

He shook his head. "I don't believe it. How could you possibly handle that sort of job?"

Her smile only broadened. "I helped my father before

he died. After he was gone, I decided I was tired of sitting home grieving, so I went to the office and started to work. About the same time, the real Mr. Haskell fell ill and left the company, and I took over his job. I kept my efforts quiet, but I'm sure any number of people knew. They were simply smart enough to keep silent."

He shook his head. "I would have known. I would have recognized a woman by the correspondence I received."

"You may not wish to believe it, but it's true. And the reason I am here today is to ask you for a job. You see, I am going mad rattling around your house with nothing to do but sew and read."

"You are here for a *job?*" A second wave of disbelief hit him. He was certain his eyebrows must be touching the top of his forehead.

"That is what I said."

"That is impossible."

"And why is that?"

"Aside from the fact that you are a woman, you are also my wife. That is why."

"Your sister-in-law owns a hat shop and she is the wife of a duke. From what I hear, she still works there on occasion."

"A hat shop isn't the same as running a gun manufacturing plant."

"No, thank God, it isn't. Making hats doesn't interest me in the least. Keeping track of sales and inventory, finding ways to increase production, that I find fascinating."

"No."

She set her small hands on her hips. "If you won't hire me, I shall knock on doors all over London until I find someone who will."

"I swear, Violet—"

"There is no need to swear. Simply say yes." She

reached out and caught his hand. Hers was pale and warm, his large and dark. The contact made him hard again.

"If you want me to stay here as your wife, then you can't expect me to sit and do nothing. Please, Rule. You asked me to give you a chance. Now I am asking you to give me that same chance."

He tried to think of an argument that would dissuade her, but she looked so pretty standing in front of him, so incredibly sweet, and under it all he could see her fierce determination.

And it wouldn't be for long. Soon the company would be sold and he would be running other businesses, companies that posed new challenges.

He looked down at the stack of proposals on his desk. "All right, you handle the day-to-day operation, as you did in Boston, and I'll begin looking into the different investments we'll be considering."

"Oh, Rule, thank you!" She surprised him by throwing her arms around his neck and kissing him soundly on the cheek.

Never one to miss an opportunity, Rule set his hands at her waist, lowered his head and very thoroughly kissed her. For an instant she resisted, pressing her small hands against his chest. Rule gentled the kiss but didn't stop, coaxing instead of demanding, tasting and nibbling until she was pliant in his arms.

The kiss changed from warm to scorching hot. His hands found the swell of her bosom, smoothed over the fullness, moved to the tiny buttons closing up the front of her simple woolen dress. He pulled the fabric apart, reached inside and found her breasts.

Violet moaned as he palmed them, gently caressed them. She was wearing a corset today that closed up the front, and he deftly popped the hooks that held the garment together. Her breasts spilled forward and he bent his head and took one into his mouth, tasting creamy skin and a rigid pink nipple.

God, he was so hard. He couldn't remember wanting a woman the way he wanted Violet. He closed his teeth around the stiff tip, laved it with his tongue and felt her tremble. Damn, he had to have her.

He was throbbing, aching to be inside her. He glanced toward the door. His secretary wouldn't interfere no matter what sounds might emerge from inside the office.

"We have to stop," Violet said breathlessly. "We can't possibly—" Rule silenced her with another burning kiss. Soft nibbling kisses followed. Wet, hot, fiery kisses had her squirming against him.

"Rule…please…"

Taking that *please* to mean please continue, he did, gently biting her earlobe, running his tongue over her shoulder blade, pulling the corset open as far as he could, squeezing those luscious breasts, kissing them, wishing there was nothing between them but skin.

They were both still clothed, but he was a man who rarely missed an opportunity and there was no time like the present.

Lifting her up on the desk, he eased her backward, hoisted her skirt and shoved up her petticoats, exposing her drawers and stockings.

"What… What are you doing?"

He didn't stop to answer. He could barely see her face for all the ruffles and fluff, but he didn't care. Settling himself between her legs, he slipped his hand inside the split in her drawers and began to stroke her, felt how wet and hot she was, how ready.

Violet's head fell back on the desk. She moaned and a surge of triumph filled him, along with a hot rush of desire. He was so hard he hurt, his control pushed nearly to the limit.

Not yet, he told himself, though it took a will of iron. Untying the string on her drawers, he slid them down over her hips all the way to her knees, bent and set his mouth against the lovely tuft of copper curls at the entrance to her sex.

"Oh my God!" Violet stiffened for an instant then started to tremble as he caressed her with his mouth and tongue. She made a little whimpering sound and began to come, fierce spasms that had her pressing a hand over her mouth to stifle her cries of pleasure. Rule opened the front of his trousers, found the entrance to her passage and eased himself deep inside.

Pleasure poured through him. And a feeling of rightness unlike anything he could recall. He had meant to take her gently, but when she arched upward, seating him even more deeply, when he realized she was once more nearing release, his control completely snapped.

Deep, pounding strokes carried him higher—long, penetrating thrusts sent them both over the edge. Driving into her again and again, caught in the wild frenzy of release, he hotly spilled his seed.

He wasn't sure how long it was before his taut muscles relaxed. Violet stirred beneath him, rousing him from his languor and reminding him where they were. Using his handkerchief to remove the remnants of their lovemaking, he carefully rearranged her clothes and helped her up from the desk.

Her face was flaming and he thought how charming it was that such a passionate creature could also be so sweet.

She looked up at him from beneath her lashes. "I don't…don't know what to say. I—I cannot believe what just happened."

Rule only smiled. "It's all right. It is perfectly acceptable for a married couple to make love."

"In that…that way? In the middle of the day? In your office with people working right outside?"

He grinned. He couldn't help it. "Anywhere you like, sweetheart."

He was startled when her lovely eyes filled with tears. "Something must be wrong with me. I could have stopped you but I didn't. Women don't behave this way."

Rule eased her into his arms and gently kissed her forehead. "A passionate wife is the most desirable possession a man can have."

"I'm not a possession," she said against his chest.

"No, you're not. You are simply a woman and my wife."

She moved her head back and forth. "You don't understand."

Rule caught her chin, forcing her to look up at him. "What is it I don't understand?"

"We don't… We don't even love each other."

An unexpected tightness filled his chest. "Perhaps not. But we care for each other and we desire each other. Some marriages are based on far less."

Violet made no reply. Moving away from him, she straightened her garments a little more, retrieved her bonnet and pulled it on over her disheveled copper curls.

"Thank you for giving me the job," she said.

He simply nodded. "We'll come to work together in the morning."

Violet made no reply, just opened the door and fled the office.

Rule found himself grinning. His wife was even more responsive than he recalled. And as he had said, mutual desire was a good foundation for a marriage.

He was still grinning when the door swung open anew and a tall blond man he didn't recognize stood in the opening.

"Are you Rule Dewar?"

"I am."

Without another word, the blond man stormed across the office and punched him squarely in the face.

At the sound of the front door slamming, Violet sat up straighter on the sofa. An instant later, Rule appeared in the drawing room doorway. His black hair was mussed, his jacket missing and his white shirt torn. A dark look marred his perfect features and there was a bruise on his cheek.

Violet shot up from the sofa. "Great heavens, what's happened?"

Rule strode toward her, his eyebrows pulled together in a scowl. "Who the bloody hell is Jeffrey Burnett?"

Violet felt the color drain from her face. "Jeffrey? Jeffrey is… He is a friend."

His features tightened. He knuckled his battered cheek and she noticed bruises on his hand, as well. "More than a friend, it would seem. He told me in no uncertain terms that you belonged to him!"

Alarm sent her heartbeat soaring. "I—I knew Jeffrey in Boston. You hadn't come back. Jeffrey and I became friends. He spoke of a marriage between us…after…after I arranged an annulment."

Rule smiled mirthlessly. "But that isn't going to happen now, is it, sweetheart? Certainly not after that little performance that took place in my office this afternoon."

"How dare you!"

"How dare *you!* Acting so high and mighty, making me feel guilty for what happened during the years you were still in Boston. All the time, you were having intimate little rendezvous with *Jeffrey.*"

"We weren't having intimate little rendezvous. We were

friends. Nothing happened, as you well know, since I was a virgin the night you took me."

"But he is here now and you are no longer a virgin, are you, my love? What plans have the two of you made?"

He was fairly seething and for the first time she realized he was also wildly jealous. Why the thought gave her a little jolt of satisfaction, she could not say.

"I haven't made any plans with Jeffrey. In fact, I told him the truth—that our marriage had been consummated and you are truly my husband."

He eyed her with suspicion.

"You fought with Jeffrey?" she asked, though clearly he had.

A smug smile crossed his face. His bottom lip, she noticed, was slightly puffy on one side. "That's right. And if you think I look bad, you ought to see him."

Worry for Jeffrey had her leaping to her feet. "You didn't hurt him!"

He shrugged his wide shoulders. "I boxed at Oxford. I still enjoy the sport with friends. He should have found that out before he threw the first punch."

"Oh, my goodness!" She started for the door, terrified for Jeffrey, but Rule caught her arm.

"Your Jeffrey is fine. I guess it took him a few days to work up his courage after your little tête-à-tête at Caroline's. He was good and mad when he got to the office, but I didn't really hurt him. It isn't his fault the man is in love with you."

She blinked and stared up at Rule. "He told you that?"

"He didn't have to. The question is, are you in love with him?"

She didn't answer right away, and Rule's jaw hardened. "It doesn't matter. You're *my* wife, not his."

"Are you certain he is all right?"

"Not that I much care, but, yes, the man is fine. What I want to know is what his intentions are toward you?"

Violet held her ground. "As I said, I've spoken to him. He knows there can never be anything more between us. You needn't worry about Jeffrey—" Her chin went up. "As long as I needn't worry about you."

"What is that supposed to mean?"

"It means I will remain faithful as long as you do."

A muscle bunched in his cheek. He caught hold of her shoulders. "I am not about to stand for my wife having an affair! Stay away from Jeffrey Burnett!"

Violet just smiled. "*I* am not the sort to be unfaithful."

Rule made no reply. Clearly the statement did not apply to him.

Dear God, why couldn't she have stayed in Boston, proceeded with the annulment and married Jeffrey? She had no doubt of his loyalty, his fidelity. She could trust Jeffrey.

She desired Rule. The night of the fire she had trusted him with her life.

But she didn't dare to trust him with her heart.

Fourteen

The drafty old building that served as a gymnasium was quiet except for the shuffle of feet in the middle of the ring. On Wednesdays Rule and Luke met late in the afternoon for their weekly sparing match. Both had boxed in college and now enjoyed the chance to stay in condition and keep up their skills.

Moving to Luke's right, Rule swung a hard punch that connected with his best friend's jaw. Luke danced backward, just out of reach, and swung a counterpunch that tapped Rule's chin good and hard. Rule stepped in for two quick jabs and a long hard punch that elicited a grunt from his opponent.

Luke raised his hands in defeat. "Enough! You are impossible to best today."

Rule dropped his fists as he walked toward his friend. "Sorry. I didn't mean to get carried away."

Luke reached up and rubbed his jaw, wiggled it back and forth to test the extent of his injury, which wasn't much since they were so evenly matched.

"You may as well tell me what's wrong," Luke said.

"You came in here with a swollen lip and a bruise on your cheek and said it was nothing. Obviously it was something."

Rule blew out a breath. Bare-chested, each wearing only a pair of leggings, they headed for the locker room at the back of the gymnasium.

"A couple of days ago, a fellow showed up at my office. We exchanged a few punches before he got the point that I wasn't about to give my wife to him."

"What?"

Rule opened his locker and pulled out a linen towel. "The reason Violet came to London wasn't to begin our marriage, it was to get an annulment. Apparently, she and this Jeffrey fellow were planning to marry once she was free of her unwanted husband and returned home to Boston."

Luke whistled out a breath.

"Exactly."

"So what did you tell him?"

"I told him he was too late. That Violet was my wife in every way and that wasn't going to change. I advised him in no uncertain terms that he had better go back where he came from."

"You think he will?"

"I don't know. As long as he stays away from Violet, I don't give a bloody damn what he does."

Luke opened his locker and pulled out his own linen towel. "So I guess married life agrees with you."

Rule shrugged his shoulders. "I haven't been married long enough to know."

"But so far you have no complaints."

Rule looked up at him. "Why are you suddenly so inter-ested in marriage?"

Luke just laughed and shook his head. "I'm not. I was just curious is all." They both stripped naked and headed for a row of overhead buckets filled with water. Each of them soaped up then stood beneath a bucket and pulled the metal chain that released the water through a sieve.

Rule shivered against the cold as he rinsed off the soap, but exercising his muscles felt good and the chilly water revived him.

"How does Violet feel about all of this?" Luke asked, returning to their former conversation.

"She's married to me not him. So far, she hasn't complained."

"Well, that has to be good, I guess." Luke towel-dried his thick, dark brown hair. "Are you two going to Severn's ball tonight?"

Rule mopped water from his chest and nodded. "I thought Violet might enjoy it."

"Might take her mind off this Jeffrey chap."

Rule cast his friend a dark glance. "I'll keep her mind off Burnett—have no doubt of that."

Luke just grinned, but Rule was deadly serious. For the past two nights he'd been too angry to go to Violet's bed. They had traveled to work together in the mornings, but spoke only of business during the day. So far Violet had proved as competent as she had claimed, which both irritated and impressed him. She was his wife, dammit. The only duties he wanted her to perform were in his bed!

Tonight and every other night from now on, he vowed, he intended to make love to her. Violet might think she was in love with the American, but Rule believed the passion they shared meant far more than the pallid emotion written about in romantic poetry.

"So I guess I'll see you tonight," Luke said, pulling him away from his thoughts.

"We'll be there."

Rule watched Luke leave and a hint of suspicion crept into his mind. Violet had asked her cousin Caroline to join them. Surely that wasn't the reason Luke had mentioned the ball?

Rule shook his head. He was imagining things. The last thing Luke Barclay wanted was a wife. The American girl was an innocent. Luke had only met her once. He couldn't possibly have an interest.

Still, the suspicion stayed with him all the way home.

Caroline spent hours choosing the perfect gown for the ball that night, a pale blue silk exactly the color of her eyes. The skirt was incredibly full and parted in the front to expose an underskirt of a deeper blue heavily embroidered with roses. The bodice was cut in a *V* at the neckline, modest but low enough to show a hint of her bosom, propped tantalizingly up by her corset.

She hoped Luke would like it.

Caroline turned toward the mirror. Since the night she had first met him at the Wyhurst ball, she had seen Luke three different times. Once at a soiree given by a friend of her grandmother's, once at a house party she and her grandmother had attended and once when she and her maid had "accidentally" stumbled upon him at a small coffee shop just off Bond Street, a meeting he had suggested at the party the night before.

Her heart started thumping at the memory. With his dark hair and deep brown eyes, his hard jaw and that intriguing scar through his eyebrow, the man was dangerously handsome.

He was also a complete and utter rogue, and Caroline knew encouraging him was playing with fire.

A light knock sounded.

"Your friends have arrived, miss." Nell, her ladies' maid, spoke to her through the door.

"Tell them I am coming right down."

"Yes, miss."

Whisking her silk reticule off the dresser, Caroline tugged up her elbow-length white gloves and hurried to the door.

Both Violet and Rule stood at the bottom of the staircase in conversation with her grandmother. Clearly Grandmother was impressed by Rule's good looks and impeccable manners. And it didn't hurt that he was the brother of a duke.

Grandmother looked up as Caroline reached the bottom of the stairs. "There you are, dear heart." She flicked a glance at Rule. "I told you she wouldn't keep you waiting, my lord. My granddaughter is very considerate. It's been a great pleasure having her here for this visit."

"It's been wonderful," Caroline said, meaning it. "I've so enjoyed the chance for us to get to know each other." And during the weeks she had been in London, she had come to like her grandmother very much. There was no set date for her return to Boston. She could stay as long as she liked.

London was so very exciting. She told herself staying had nothing to do with Lucas Barclay.

"If you ladies are ready," Rule said, extending an arm to each of them, "I believe it is time for us to leave. Good night, Mrs. Lockhart." He smiled. "You may trust your granddaughter is in very good hands."

Grandmother blushed like a schoolgirl. "Oh, I am certain of that, my lord."

They made their way out to the carriage and settled themselves inside. It didn't take long to reach the mansion belonging to the Earl of Severn. Golden lights streamed from rows of tall windows, and two liveried footmen raced up to open the carriage door.

One of them, young and blond, helped the women down

and Rule followed. Caroline noticed that his brilliant blue eyes rarely strayed from his wife and even more surprising, Violet's gaze often went in search of his.

It seemed to Caroline that Dewar meant to keep his wife no matter the cost, and though Caroline believed that Jeffrey would have been a more suitable match for her cousin, she was beginning to think there was a chance she was wrong.

As they moved through the reception line into the ballroom, Rule led the women toward a group of his friends, people Caroline had met at the Wyhurst ball or at various affairs she had attended with her grandmother.

Her heartbeat quickened for a moment before she realized Luke was not among them.

"You remember Lord Wellesley," Violet said of tall, elegant Sheridan Knowles, Sherry to his friends.

She dropped into a curtsy. "It is good to see you, my lord."

He bowed slightly. "Miss Lockhart."

"And Lord Nightingale?"

She turned the earl's direction. "A pleasure, my lord."

"The pleasure is mine, Miss Lockhart." Though he smiled and bowed politely, a sadness lingered in his expression.

More of Rule's friends came and went from the circle, including tall, black-haired, incredibly handsome Jonathan Savage, and hard-looking Quentin Garrett, Viscount March. Rule's brother Royal and his lovely blonde wife arrived in the circle.

"Miss Lockhart," the duke said. "I hope you've been enjoying your time in London."

"Very much so, Your Grace." She chatted with the duchess for a while. Then Lord Wellesley asked her to dance. She forced herself not to look for Luke and began to wonder if he had decided not to come.

It was better if he didn't, she knew. The man had no desire to marry and she wasn't ready for marriage yet, either. Still, she was drawn to him.

At the end of the dance, she looked up and spotted him at the edge of the floor, his dark hair mussed as if he had come in out of the wind. When he looked at her, his eyes gleamed with appreciation. His smile held a hint of danger. Her heart took a treacherous leap, and Caroline knew she was in serious trouble.

Strains of a waltz filled the air, along with the chatter of the dozens of guests in the ballroom. Some distance from the dance floor, Violet stood next to Rule and an attractive, mustached man with dark brown silver-streaked hair. Charles Whitney, Rule had said, was interested in buying Griffin Manufacturing. Yesterday Whitney had contacted their solicitor and made a formal offer to purchase the company.

Violet regarded him closely. A man in his early fifties of medium height and build, Whitney possessed an air of confidence that made him seem larger than he actually was.

"My husband tells me you are interested in buying Griffin, Mr. Whitney."

Whitney smiled. "Very interested. I am hoping your husband and I will be able to come to an agreement very soon."

She smiled a bit too brightly. "Howard Griffin was my father. If you buy the company, you will be buying it from both of us."

One of Whitney's silver-flecked eyebrows arched up. "I see."

"I'm afraid my wife is one of a handful of women who are interested in business," Rule said. "I am still growing used to the notion."

"I daresay a woman in the business of making guns is quite a novelty. Can you shoot a pistol as well as build one, my lady?"

"I assure you I can, Mr. Whitney. My father was a very good teacher."

Whitney chuckled. "A woman, then, with whom a man should not trifle."

Violet smiled. There was a hint of amusement in Whitney's voice but no disapproval. She thought that she liked him and hoped that he turned out to be the man who purchased the company her father had built.

They spoke a moment more before Rule led her away. "I had a chance to read Whitney's offer. It was a good one. I'll let you take a look at it in the morning."

"He wants both of the plants? The one here and also the one in Boston?"

Rule nodded. "Apparently his man in America had already done a good bit of research on Griffin in Boston. He's seen the plant in operation, though neither man has reviewed the new designs and that is a condition of the offer. And of course Whitney will want to see our ledgers, take a look at the bottom line."

"He'll like what he sees. Griffin is a very profitable company."

"Whitney owns a number of different companies. He has a reputation for intelligence and honesty."

"On first impression, I like him. Of course, that doesn't always mean much."

"Oh, I don't know, I think you have very good instincts." He grinned. "You married me, didn't you?"

She smiled, though it wasn't the truth. She had married Rule because her father wished it. Her own instincts had led her to Jeffrey.

"Your cousin has returned," Rule said as he spotted Caroline walking toward them. "I need a word with my brother. I won't be long."

Caroline stopped in front of Violet, an anxious look on her face. "Jeffrey is here," she whispered the moment Rule was gone. "At this very moment, he is walking straight toward you."

"Oh, dear Lord." Violet looked over Caroline's shoulder to see Jeffrey's blond head moving through the crowd. Then he was right in front of her.

"Violet, darling." He took her hand and brought it to his lips. "I am so very glad to see you. I've missed you so much." He had a bruise on his chin and dark skin around his left eye.

"You fought with Rule. Are you all right?"

He scoffed. "The man deserved a beating for the way he treated you."

But as Rule had said, clearly Jeffrey had gotten the worst of it. "Rule is my husband, Jeffrey. I tried to tell you that before."

"The man is a blackguard. He took advantage of your innocence."

"We're married. Please, Jeffrey, I beg you. Go back to Boston. Make a life for yourself with someone else." She rested a hand on his arm. "You deserve to be happy, Jeffrey."

"I'm not leaving. Not until I'm certain you're going to be all right."

Violet started to reply when she felt the unmistakable presence of her husband beside her.

"If you're wise, Burnett, you'll take my wife's advice. You're poaching on another man's territory. Unless you wish to continue where we left off the last time—"

"No!" Violet stepped between the two men. She noticed

several heads turn in their direction and lowered her voice. "You are both done with fighting." She fixed her gaze on Jeffrey. "If you will excuse us, Mr. Burnett, I find I am suddenly thirsty." She turned to Rule. "Would you be good enough, my lord, to escort me to the punch bowl?" Her eyes held his, silently demanding he agree.

"I ought to teach him a lesson," Rule grumbled as they walked away.

"You needn't worry about Jeffrey. I told you that before."

He looked down at her and his dark look changed to a slow, seductive smile. "Are you saying I should worry about you instead? I believe that is a very good notion. Tonight when we get home, I vow I shall see to your every need."

Violet's stomach contracted. There was no mistaking his words, or the hot desire burning in his eyes. She steeled herself against a rush of heat she wished she didn't feel and tried not to look forward to the end of the evening.

In the faint glow of the torches, Caroline stood next to Lucas Barclay in the shadows at the edge of the terrace. She knew she shouldn't be out there with no chaperone and especially not with Luke.

His reputation with women was well-known. She had seen the way they watched him whenever he crossed a room. It was said he was ruthless where women were concerned.

And yet he had been nothing but a gentleman with her.

"You shouldn't be out here," he said, his voice low and husky as he removed his coat and draped it around her shoulders.

She looked into the depths of his eyes. "Shall I go back inside?" She didn't want to go, but she wanted him to ask her to stay.

"That isn't what I want and you know it."

She smiled. "I suppose I do."

The edge of his mouth faintly curved. "Are all American women as independent as you and your cousin?"

She gazed up at him in the darkness. "Most men don't like independent women. So most women are afraid to behave that way."

He chuckled, a soft rumble that made her insides soften. "Not you, though. You aren't afraid of anything, are you, Carrie? Not even me."

He had called her that almost from the start, a pet name Violet had used on occasion ever since they were little girls.

"I should be. I have no idea why I'm not." In the moonlight his dark eyes seemed to glitter. She wasn't afraid of him. She was only afraid he wouldn't kiss her. It seemed in that moment she would die if he didn't.

Luke didn't disappoint her. Moving closer, he captured her face between his big hands and settled his mouth over hers. What started as a simple tasting became an exploration. Luke nibbled the corners of her mouth and kissed her softly, and an odd weakness floated out through her limbs. When she parted her lips, his tongue slid inside and she heard him groan.

Luke broke the contact, though she wished he had not. "That was what you wanted, wasn't it?"

She stared up at him. "Yes."

Luke backed away. "Dammit, Caroline, you know the kind of man I am. I don't want marriage—not now, maybe never."

"I'm not ready for marriage, either."

He raked a hand through his hair. "This is madness." But he pulled her back into his arms. Deep drugging kisses followed. Slow, savoring kisses had her pressing herself against him, wanting more.

Luke did not oblige. Instead he broke the kiss, snatched his coat off her shoulders and turned her toward the door. "Go back inside and find your cousin before I do something we'll both regret."

Caroline reached up to touch her kiss-swollen lips. Until she met Luke, it had never occurred to her that desire could be such a powerful force. For the first time, she understood Violet's attraction to Rule Dewar.

She glanced back over her shoulder for a last look at Luke. She could see his tall silhouette in the moonlight, his shoulders still taut.

"Good night," she said softly and disappeared back inside the house. Skirting the ballroom, she headed for the ladies' retiring room to rid herself of any traces of Luke's passionate kisses. But the memories lingered.

She wanted more, she realized. She wanted him to touch her, to strip away her clothes and make love to her, and yet she knew that could not happen. Neither of them were ready for marriage. Perhaps Luke would never want a wife and family, and Caroline wasn't completely certain, either. Her parents' outright cruelty to one another made her doubt the merits of marriage.

It was time to return to Boston. If Violet didn't wish to go home, she would hire another traveling companion and make the journey alone.

Caroline sighed. If she ever did find the courage to wed, she hoped the man she married could stir at least some of the passion she felt in Luke Barclay's arms.

Fifteen

Jeffrey returned to his hotel, the Parkland, and quietly entered his suite. A lamp was burning. A small fire glowed behind the grate in the hearth. He dragged off his coat and tossed it over a chair, then walked directly to the sideboard and poured himself a drink from the bottle of strong Tennessee whiskey he had brought from home.

"While you're at it, pour one for me," came a deep, rusty voice from the shadows.

Jeffrey turned to see J. P. Montgomery—a big, barrel-chested man with curly brown side whiskers—rising from the overstuffed chair in the corner.

Jeffrey poured another drink, walked over and pressed it into J.P.'s blunt fingers. Montgomery hailed from Virginia, just as Jeffrey did. He was dedicated to his homeland, as Jeffrey was, and they had traveled together to London with a mutual desire to help the Southern cause.

"I wish I had good news," Jeffrey said. "I had hoped to gain control of the armaments business through my marriage to Violet. I no longer believe that is possible." He downed a hefty portion of his drink. "Perhaps if I had come sooner, or convinced her not to come to London in the first place…"

But he had believed Violet loved him, as he loved her.

His chest tightened. He had met Violet through mutual friends at a house party in Boston. Though he was born in Virginia, he had moved north ten years earlier to attend Harvard Law School. He had obtained a degree, joined a prominent law firm and eventually lost his Southern accent.

His family was wealthy. He enjoyed the high life in Boston but missed his home and intended, once he married, to return.

He had rarely discussed his background with Violet, who clearly disapproved of slavery, and though she knew he was born in Virginia, he had never told her his family owned one of the largest cotton plantations in the South. It would all work out in due time, he had been sure.

Jeffrey knew the appeal of his blond good looks and charm. And he sincerely loved Violet. He had been certain she would marry him.

Now all of his dreams had come to naught.

"If we want our citizens properly armed, we need weapons," he said, stating the obvious. "To get them, we're going to have to buy the company." He took another swallow of his whiskey. "Violet has convinced Dewar to sell. If we can raise the money—"

"Money's no problem," Montgomery drawled, his accent pronounced. "At least not yet."

"Then we had best make an offer. Are you sure you want to buy the Boston factory, as well? Once this war gets started, there might be problems getting the guns out of the North."

"We don't know how long it's gonna be before things might reach that point. We'll have some time. We'll stockpile as much as we can in the months to come."

"That sounds good. I think we'll do better if our association remains unknown. At the moment, I'm not high on Dewar's list of favorite people."

Montgomery nodded. "I'll hire a man tomorrow to speak to Dewar's solicitor and make a formal offer."

Jeffrey finished his drink. "The sooner the better. Once we're in control, we can go home."

And he could forget Violet Griffin Dewar. At least he hoped he could. It bothered him to think of his sweet Violet defiling herself with a bastard like Dewar. She had been so innocent when they had first met.

One thing was certain. The sweet, genteel young woman he had fallen in love with was going to be hard to forget.

Violet awoke from a languid slumber, sunlight streaming into her bedroom through the windowpanes. When she moved beneath the sheets, her body felt tender, her breasts a little sore.

Hot color flooded her cheeks. As he had promised, Rule had come to her last night, and though part of her had wanted to deny him, they had made passionate love.

She glanced at the clock on the mantel. Dear God, it was nearly noon! She and Rule were supposed to go over the offer Charles Whitney had made. They were going down to the plant to collect the information Whitney needed to review.

Tossing back the covers, Violet pulled on her lavender silk wrapper and hurried over to the bellpull. Mary bustled in to help her bathe and change. Half an hour later, she was dressed and ready to face the day.

Unfortunately, when she arrived downstairs, Rule was already gone.

"He said not to worry, my lady," Hatfield declared. "He said to tell you he would return with the offer and you could go over it together."

Violet sighed. She thought of summoning her carriage and joining Rule at the office, but it was already so late in the day she decided to wait for his return. She glanced at the tall grandfather clock in the entry, knowing how long the hours would seem.

For a while, she walked in the garden, enjoying the brisk spring air and the tiny flowers pushing up through the soil, then she returned to the house and settled into the gothic novel she had been reading.

A sound in the entry she was certain must be Rule urged her to set her book aside and she jumped to her feet. It was Caroline who walked into the drawing room, her expression strangely glum.

"I hope I am not intruding."

"No, of course not."

"I came to tell you I am leaving."

"Leaving!" Violet hurried toward her. "Surely not. I thought… I had hoped you would be staying much longer."

Caroline removed her bonnet and tossed it into a chair. "It is past time I went home, Vi. I booked passage on a ship sailing for Boston next week."

"Are you certain? It is such a long journey. Are you sure you don't want to stay at least a few more weeks?"

"I guess that means you have no interest in returning with me."

"I'm married, dearest. My home is with my husband."

"I know, but you spoke once of divorce. Are you saying that's no longer a possibility?"

She thought of last night and glanced away. "Not…not at this time."

Both of them sat down on the sofa.

Caroline pinned her with a look. "You realize you are falling in love with him."

Her eyes widened. "That is not true. I care for Rule and he cares for me."

"And you want him."

Violet colored faintly. "You are still an innocent. You wouldn't understand."

Caroline's laugh held a faintly bitter ring. "I'm not quite the innocent you believe, Violet. My parents barely know I'm alive. I've had to make my own happiness. I suppose that is the reason I've done things that perhaps I shouldn't."

Violet's eyes widened. "What are you talking about?"

"I'm talking about Lucas Barclay."

"Barclay? But you barely know him."

"Actually, I know him fairly well. We've met on several occasions. Last night I danced with him more often than I should have. Out on the terrace, I kissed him."

"Good Lord, he didn't… He hasn't…"

"I am still a virgin, if that is what you are worried about. But now that I've met Luke, I've begun to understand desire. I wanted Luke to kiss me. I want him to make love to me. That is the reason I am leaving."

"Great heavens, Carrie, Barclay is a dangerous man. He uses women and tosses them away like worn-out shoes. You can't possibly want a man like that."

"Maybe I understand Luke better than other women. Underneath his tough facade, he is as lonely as I am. And he is not as bad as people believe. He knows I am attracted to him. Whenever we're together, desire crackles like sparks between us. He could seduce me if he tried and he knows it."

"Good grief!"

"He hasn't because he doesn't want to hurt me."

"He said that?"

"Of course not. It isn't what a man says, Violet, it's what he does."

Perhaps that was true. Rule didn't love her, but the night of the fire, he had risked his life to save her. And when they made love, he took care of her needs as well as his own. She knew she was risking terrible pain in staying with him and yet she couldn't force herself to leave.

"The problem is that neither of us is ready for marriage," Caroline continued, "and since I no longer trust myself where Luke is concerned, I am going home."

Violet mulled that over. If she had never come to London, she would never have fallen prey to the desire she felt for Rule. She would have had her annulment and married Jeffrey instead.

Then again, she was no longer certain marrying Jeffrey would have made her happy as she had once believed.

Caroline stood up from the sofa. "I had better be going. I have a lot to do before next week. I'll see you before I leave."

Violet walked her to the door. "I am going to miss you."

Caroline leaned over and hugged her. "Me, too."

"Give your family my regards when you get back to Boston."

Caroline nodded, but both of them knew Caroline's family wouldn't really care one way or the other. The weeks her cousin had spent with her grandmother meant more to her than the years she had lived with her parents. Caroline had no brothers or sisters. Her father worked long hours simply to avoid his wife, and her mother was busy with her wealthy friends and her numerous affairs.

Caroline had grown up fast. Perhaps that was the reason she took chances, the reason she wanted to feel passion.

The reason she could so easily succumb to a man like Lucas Barclay.

Violet felt a wave of relief that her cousin would soon be going home.

* * *

The following day, two more offers to purchase Griffin came in. One was from Burton Stanfield, whom Rule had turned down once before. Another came from an American named J. P. Montgomery.

Rule was seated at his desk reviewing the paperwork when Violet walked into his office.

"You wished to see me?" She looked pretty today in a simple gray gown trimmed with heavy white lace. For an instant, he remembered the way she had responded to him last night, moving wildly beneath him and crying out his name.

His shaft stirred to life and inside his trousers he went hard. It was one of the drawbacks of working with a woman he desired.

Inwardly, he smiled. So far the positive aspects had outweighed the negative. Violet was doing a very good job of managing the day-to-day activities of the business, leaving him to the task of finding new opportunities in which they might invest.

And as he rose from his desk, he recalled the afternoon he had made love to her right there on the top—there was always a chance it would happen again.

He cleared his throat and forced his mind to the reason he had called her into his office. "Two new offers came in. One is from Burton Stanfield. You may recall meeting him."

"I also recall you said he was an unscrupulous man of few principles."

"That is what I said."

"What about the other offer?"

"It's from a man named J. P. Montgomery. He's on his way here now." He handed Violet the offer and she perused it carefully.

"This is a bit less than Whitney's."

"True enough, but Montgomery may be willing to pay more. Why don't we see how we feel after we meet him?"

Montgomery arrived at the office a quarter hour later. Rule sent for Violet, who had gone back to work in the office he had provided for her down the hall. She walked in a few seconds behind the potential buyer.

"J. P. Montgomery," the beefy man said, sticking out a meaty hand to Rule, who accepted it.

"Rule Dewar. This is my wife, Violet."

"Ma'am." He tipped his head in her direction. "So what did ya'll think of my offer?"

Rule flicked a glance at Violet, who hadn't missed the man's thick Southern drawl. "Is the offer coming directly from you or will you be purchasing it in some sort of partnership?"

"I'll be the man in charge. I'll have investors, of course, but the buck, so to speak, stops with me."

"I see." Rule invited him to take a seat in the small conference room off the working part of his office, and Montgomery appeared a little surprised when Violet walked in with the men.

"She owns half the business," Rule explained. "She has as much right to the decision making as I do."

"Fine by me," Montgomery said, but he looked a little uneasy. Rule wondered if it was because she was a woman or if it was something else.

For the next few minutes, they went over the offer line by line, and Rule agreed that should they be willing to accept, he would provide company records and access to the plant for Montgomery's inspection.

When the meeting came to a close, the American made his farewells and left the office.

Rule turned to Violet, who had said almost nothing during the interview, which was a surprise to Rule. When it came to business, Violet held her own.

"So what did you think?" he asked.

"The price is lower but the terms are better."

"Montgomery is offering to pay all cash. It doesn't get any better than that."

Violet glanced away. "I know, but…"

He frowned. "But what?"

"But the man is… Montgomery is clearly a Southerner." She looked up, beseeching him with those clear green eyes. "I can't abide slavery, Rule. I haven't come straight out and said that before, but I simply cannot."

Rule released a sigh and sat back in his chair. "I had a feeling it was something like that."

"Mr. Whitney is an Englishman. The English abolished slave ownership nearly ninety years ago. If he agrees not to sell arms to the South, I think we should let him buy Griffin."

"Why haven't you mentioned this before?"

"To be honest, until I met Montgomery, it didn't actually occur to me that a Southerner might wish to buy the company."

"Coming from Boston, I suppose it's only natural your sympathies would lie with the states in the North."

"It isn't just that. I also have family and friends in the South. It is the issue of slavery itself. People owning other people. It simply isn't right. And I keep hoping…there is always the chance that if the North is strong enough, there won't be any war."

"It's possible, I suppose."

"Will you think about it, at least? You said yourself that Whitney's offer is a good one."

"I did, indeed."

And so they left the office together, the matter still unresolved—though Rule had a strong suspicion this was one more time he was going to give his pretty little wife exactly what she wanted.

Rule thought of something else he meant to give her later that evening and he smiled.

The week came to an end and slipped into the next. Violet and Rule had tentatively accepted the offer from Charles Whitney, subject to the review of contracts by their respective solicitors, along with Whitney's satisfaction with the condition of the plant and his examination of the profit ledgers.

The American, Montgomery, had upped his offer, which they had still refused, and the man had huffed angrily out of the office.

Caroline had come to see Violet several times. She had not seen Luke Barclay since their encounter at Severn's ball.

"I want to see him before I leave," Caroline told Violet as they sat together in the drawing room. "I want to tell him goodbye."

"Are you sure that's a good idea?"

"Luke isn't some ogre just waiting for a chance to drag me off to his lair. He has been nothing but kind to me. I was thinking that perhaps Rule could let him know that Grandmother and I will be attending the Whitewoods' soiree."

"Rule? Are you mad? Rule would have a fit if he knew you were planning a meeting with Luke. He feels very protective of you, since you are now his cousin. And he doesn't trust Barclay's intentions where you are concerned."

Caroline grinned. "Oh, I am so glad! I would hate to think this wild attraction I am suffering is not returned."

Violet laughed. "At any rate, I am sure you will figure out a way to let Luke know you will be there."

"Oh, I'm sure I can think of something."

"Since you wish to make your farewells, I gather you are still determined to leave."

"My ship sails two days after the party. I figure that will give me time to finish any last-minute packing." Caroline reached over and caught Violet's hand. "I wish you were coming with me."

"You know I can't. We are selling the business and deciding which companies to invest in with the money from the sale. There is a great deal to be done."

"And in doing it, you are completely in your element. Working suits you, cousin."

Violet smiled. "Clearly I am Howard Griffin's daughter."

Caroline hugged her. "Yes, you are. And I shall miss you dearly."

They talked a few minutes more before Caroline left the house, giving Violet time to change for supper. Her spirits faltered. Her cousin was leaving for America. Violet had few friends in London. At the moment, she and Rule were getting on fairly well. At night, their lovemaking was incredible.

But Violet had no illusions. Rule was a great deal like Lucas Barclay. He hadn't come for her in Boston because he liked the freedom he enjoyed as a single man. She had heard the rumors; she knew there had been other women— quite a number of them.

Her heart squeezed. Sooner or later, Rule would tire of her, just as he had the other women in his life.

Violet steeled herself. She told herself it wasn't impor- tant. She had a life of her own and she meant to make the most of it. Besides, it was 1860, not the Middle Ages. As long as she was discreet, a wife could live as independently as her husband.

Violet just hoped when the time came, she could convince herself to be happy without Rule Dewar.

Sixteen

The night of the Whitewood soiree finally arrived. Violet might have talked Rule into staying at home if it weren't for Caroline. This would probably be their last night together in London. Day after the morrow, they would share a brief parting at the dock before the ship sailed, but it wouldn't be the same.

Tonight she wanted her best friend to enjoy her last evening in London. Caroline would be able to dance a little, to flirt with the young men she attracted and say her farewells to Barclay. Violet wanted to be there in case her cousin needed her when the farewells were over and Caroline's last night in London came to an end.

In a gown of cream silk *poult-de-soie* banded with amber velvet, Violet descended the stairs to where her husband stood waiting, his brilliant blue eyes moving over her in a way that set her heart to pounding.

"You look beautiful, love. But then you always do." He took her hand and pressed it against his lips, and she felt warm all the way to her toes.

"Thank you." She wished her heartbeat would slow,

wished the man didn't have such an effect on her. More and more, her cousin's words had begun to replay in her head. *You're falling in love with him.*

She didn't want to love him. Loving Rule was a path that could only lead to pain. And yet, she wasn't quite sure how to stop this headlong journey to her own destruction.

Reaching into the pocket of his black evening jacket, he pulled out a blue velvet box and flipped open the lid.

"That dress needs diamonds. I saw these in the window of a little shop in Bond Street and I thought you might like them."

Violet stared down at the box, accepting the gift with trembling hands. She pulled the necklace out and held it up to the light of the chandelier in the entry. Clusters of glittering diamonds strung together with a larger diamond cluster in front cascaded over her hand.

Rule took them from her, draped them around her throat and fastened the diamond clasp. "Now we are ready to go."

She moved to the mirror in the entry to admire the gift. The necklace was fabulous and incredibly expensive.

"They're beautiful, Rule. Thank you."

But as she stared at herself in the mirror, she began to wonder if this was the sort of gift he would give to his mistress. A parting gift, perhaps.

Her stomach knotted. She looked into his handsome face. There was no mistaking the heat in his beautiful blue eyes, the hunger. He wanted her still. Relief slipped through her. Not a parting gift. Not yet.

Violet took a deep breath. She would enjoy the time they had together. She wouldn't think what the future might hold.

Summoning a smile, she accepted the arm he offered and let him sweep her out of the house.

The soiree was a glittering affair, a gathering of London's elite. The Whitewoods were related to the Duke of Marmont, which meant everyone who was anyone in London was attending. Standing next to her grandmother, Caroline admired the array of women gowned in elegant silks and satins, a rainbow of colors that sparkled in the gas lamps humming overhead. The men, mostly dressed in black, made an elegant contrast to the jeweled collection of women on their arms.

Standing at her side, Violet conversed with her husband and his friend, darkly handsome Jonathan Savage. Several other men Caroline had met were also there, including the Earl of Nightingale and the duke's friend Sheridan Knowles. All of them were politely friendly, asking her to dance and charming her with anecdotes about their days together on the Oxford sculling team.

"We won the championship that year," Sheridan, Lord Wellesley said. "Showed those chaps at Cambridge a thing or two back then."

Caroline smiled. "I'll bet you still could."

Sheridan laughed. "On a good day, perhaps, and with a bit more time spent on the water."

Next to her, Grandmother seemed to be enjoying herself. "I believe I see a friend," she said, lifting her hand in greeting to a woman across the room. "If you will excuse me, dearest, I should like to say hello."

"Of course, Grandmother."

In a gown of black and silver that set off her upswept silver hair, Adelaide Lockhart crossed the drawing room. As Caroline watched the older woman weave a path through the crowd, her gaze went in search of Luke.

"Is he here?" Violet leaned down to whisper.

Caroline shook her head. "I haven't seen him. I'm not even sure he'll come."

"But he knows you are going to be here."

"He knows."

Violet smiled. "Then I am certain he will come."

Caroline tried not to look hopeful. She hadn't realized saying goodbye to Luke would make her leaving seem so final.

And yet she knew going home was the best thing for everyone. Luke might desire her as she desired him, but marriage for either one of them was out of the question.

Though Luke enjoyed his work as an investment broker and had earned a great deal of wealth, he was still unsettled as to what he really wanted out of life, and Caroline wasn't sure what she wanted, either. She needed time to grow up, time to live a little before she settled down.

She spotted him just then, tall and imposing, drawing the attention of a dozen female admirers as he crossed the elegant room. Violet was busy conversing with the duchess, giving Caroline the perfect opportunity to escape. She caught Luke's eye, then slipped out into the hallway, hoping he would follow.

He did just a few moments later, stopping directly in front of her, his dark eyes roaming over her from head to foot and glinting with appreciation. In her amethyst satin gown trimmed with dozens of tiny seed pearls, she knew she looked good, and Luke's hot gaze assured her it was true.

His gaze came to rest on her face. "Your note said you wished to see me."

"That's right." She glanced down the hall. "Do you suppose there is somewhere private we might speak?"

One of his dark brown eyebrows arched up. "How private would you like to get?"

Caroline just smiled. "What I have to say won't take long."

Luke indicated she should continue down the hall, and Caroline started in that direction. When the corridor neared the back of the house, Luke opened a door and motioned her inside.

Caroline walked into what appeared to be a private library smaller than the main one in another section of the house. Rows of books lined the wall behind a polished oak desk, and a pair of overstuffed sofas faced each other in front of a low-burning fire.

"You seem to know your way around," Caroline said as Luke closed the door. Dear God, he was handsome. Not in the usual sense of pale good looks and golden-blond hair, but in a darker, harder, far more intriguing manner.

"Some years back, Lady Whitewood's cousin and I shared a certain…friendship."

"I see."

"It was a long time ago," he said, walking toward her. Taking hold of her hand, he led her over to one of the sofas and sat down beside her. "So why did you send the note? What was it you wanted to talk to me about?"

She looked into his compelling brown eyes. "I wanted to tell you I am leaving, returning home to Boston. My ship sails day after the morrow."

Luke frowned. "I thought you intended to stay in London for several months."

"I did. But certain things have changed my mind. I feel it is time I went home. I just wanted you to know I have come to value our friendship very much."

Luke's sensual mouth edged up. "It wasn't much of a friendship, Carrie. Perhaps you are too young to realize what we shared was mutual desire."

She glanced down, faint color rising in her cheeks. "I know. That is the reason I am leaving." She looked up at him. "I think of you far too often, Luke. I want things from you I know I cannot have."

His gaze deepened. "I've never known a woman like you, Carrie, such a tantalizing combination of beauty, innocence and independence. You're wise beyond your years, love."

She studied his face, the hard lines and the small scar that bisected his eyebrow. "Do you think…before we say goodbye, that you might kiss me one last time?"

For long moments, he made no move. Reaching out, he ran a finger along her cheek and her stomach fluttered.

"I shouldn't. God knows, I shouldn't." And then he was bending his head, gently capturing her lips. The kiss deepened. Softened. Caroline's heartbeat quickened, began a relentless pounding. She parted her lips and his tongue slid into her mouth. Caroline leaned toward him, curled her fingers around the lapels of his coat.

She meant to end the kiss, she truly did, but she had never felt anything so wonderful, so enticing. She breathed into his mouth and her tongue slid over his and she heard him groan.

She wasn't sure how it happened that she lay beneath him on the sofa, that one of his big hands was inside her bodice and now caressed a breast. She only knew that everywhere he touched her, heat burned inside and she wanted more. She loved the feel of his heavy weight on top of her, pressing her into the sofa, and yet it wasn't enough. She arched upward, urging him on, silently begging him to continue, kissing him and kissing him, completely unwilling to stop.

It was the wild shriek of horror that had both of them bolting upright, their attention swinging toward the door.

A group of people stood in the opening, gaping at the sight in front of them, Caroline's gown disheveled and riding up to her knees, the bodice pulled down and exposing a portion of her breast. At the back of the crowd, her grandmother stared into the library in wide-eyed shock.

As she righted her clothes with trembling hands, someone turned and hurried off down the hall. The others slipped discreetly away, but her grandmother remained.

"Mr. Barclay, what is the meaning of this?"

Caroline swallowed. "It…it isn't what it seems, Grandmother. Luke…Mr. Barclay and I are friends. I was just… just telling him goodbye."

Next to her, Luke stood rigid, his jaw clamped so tight a muscle bunched in his cheek. So far he hadn't said a word.

"What's going on here?" Rule strode through the doorway, Violet hurrying along in his wake. His fierce blue eyes bored into his friend. "Luke, what have you done?"

"This isn't his fault," Caroline defended. "We were only…only saying goodbye."

Violet closed the door, giving the small group a degree of privacy.

Adelaide Lockhart pointed an accusing finger at Luke. "That rogue has compromised my granddaughter. By tomorrow, the gossip will be all over London."

Rule turned to Violet. "Take your cousin out of here."

Caroline's chin went up. "I told you this isn't Luke's fault. I am staying."

Violet cast her a look of sympathy but, knowing her as she did, didn't try to convince her to leave.

Rule returned his attention to Luke. "I warned you, Luke. I told you to stay away from her."

Luke said nothing, but his face looked carved in stone.

"You know what has to happen. There is no help for it now."

Luke's jaw worked, the muscles clenching, moving up and down. "I'll do the right thing. I'll marry her."

Caroline looked at him and her chest squeezed. "Are you mad? You don't want to marry me!"

His gaze locked with hers. "I don't have any choice."

Caroline shot to her feet. "Well, I have a choice! I am not going to marry you! I'm going back to Boston where I belong!"

Something moved across his features. Determination followed close on its heels. "You'll marry me. Even if you leave, the scandal won't end. Your grandmother and your cousin will suffer. Is that what you want?"

"Of course not, but…but neither of us is ready for marriage. We said that, we talked about it."

His mouth curved harshly. "That didn't stop what happened here tonight. And if we hadn't been so rudely interrupted, you would have had a lot more reason to marry me."

Heat rushed into her cheeks. Still she held her ground. "I won't do it! I won't!"

"Is there someone else?" Luke asked. "Someone in Boston?"

"No, of course not."

"Then like it or not, I'm the man you're going to marry."

"Let me talk to her," Violet soothed, hurrying to her side.

"Fine, talk to her," Luke said darkly. "But one way or another, we're getting married. I won't be called an even bigger cad than I've been labeled already."

Luke stormed out of the drawing room and for the first time, tears washed into Caroline's eyes. Through a hazy blur, she saw her grandmother and Rule slip out of the room behind him and quietly close the door.

"Luke doesn't want to marry me," Caroline said. "And I don't want to marry him."

Violet handed her a handkerchief. "Are you certain you feel that way? Whatever you feel for Luke must be very powerful or this wouldn't have happened."

Caroline pressed the handkerchief beneath her eyes.

"Marriage isn't…isn't what either of us wants. It just isn't fair."

"That is what I thought when my father asked me to marry Rule. Sometimes fate takes a hand and things just happen."

Caroline looked up at her. "I have to do it, don't I?"

"You have never been one to hurt others. Your grandmother will suffer and so will Luke. But if you marry him, all of this will eventually disappear."

Caroline wiped the wetness from her cheeks. "We'll hate each other."

"Perhaps not. Desire is a powerful force. At least the two of you have that."

She thought of the kiss that had turned into a blazing inferno neither of them seemed able to control. "Yes…I suppose there is that."

"And you like London. You have a grandmother here who loves you and no real reason to return to Boston."

"No."

"We're both survivors, Carrie, you and I. We'll both make the best of what life hands us. That is our nature."

Caroline released a shaky breath. "You're right. We are both of us resilient. And I shall be resilient in this."

And there was one advantage.

Her curiosity would finally be satisfied. She would finally get to find out what it was like to make love with Lucas Barclay.

Seventeen

"It won't be as bad as all that," Rule said to Luke three days later. "You like the chit and you want her. The rest will fall into place."

With the use of a special license, a hasty wedding had been arranged. Beneath a warm May sun in the garden of Rule's town house, Luke stood next to his best friend, awaiting the arrival of his bride.

He stared down at his feet. "She didn't want to marry me. Half the women in London have tried to trick me into marriage and the one I'm forced to wed doesn't want me."

"Give her a little time to get used to the notion. Court her a little, buy her something expensive. Give her some time and it won't be a problem."

Luke scowled. "I intend to have her tonight. That's the only thing I've got to look forward to in this whole bloody affair."

"She's a virgin, Luke. You can't just take her. You need to court her, seduce her into your bed."

"She'll be my wife," Luke argued. "That gives me certain rights." But what if Rule was correct? Caroline was extremely independent. It was one of the things he admired about her. But she was also naive. Perhaps if he waited, things would go better between them.

He glanced over to where his brother Christopher and his sister-in-law Jocelyn sat in the first row of chairs in front of the arbor. Before they had decided to marry, Christopher had been reluctant. Jocelyn was spoiled and selfish, a hellion of the very worst sort.

Luke had been certain his brother's marriage was doomed to failure.

But Christopher had been patient. And firm where his beautiful bride was concerned. In the end, his patience had paid off and they were happy. Blissfully so. With two young children and plans for another in the future.

Luke turned back to Rule. "Do you love her? Your wife—do you love her?"

Rule glanced away. "My mother died when I was born. Aside from my aunt and my sisters-in-law, whom I care for deeply, my only use for a woman has been in bed. To tell you the truth, Luke, I don't really know what love is."

Luke grunted. "That's what I thought."

"It doesn't mean you can't be happy. Married men have a great deal of latitude…if you know what I mean."

Luke knew exactly what he meant. But somehow the notion of bedding another woman held little appeal. "I suppose."

Rule looked toward the terrace where a silver-haired man wearing spectacles and flowing white robes walked toward them. "The bishop is arrived. I had better go and collect your bride."

Luke clamped his jaw. "Let's just get this done."

As Rule moved toward the terrace to escort her down the aisle, Christopher rose from the chair next to Jocelyn and took his place near the altar as Luke's best man.

"She's a beautiful girl," Chris said. He was as tall as Luke, with the same dark coloring, dark hair and eyes.

"She is that." And smart, Luke thought, undoubtedly the reason she'd had to be practically dragged, kicking and screaming, to the altar. He would make a lousy husband. Any woman with half a brain could see that. Aside from the desire she felt for him, she hadn't wanted him. In fact, she had intended to put four thousand miles between them. Why that bothered him, he could not say.

Luke forced his attention up the aisle. In a gauzy silk gown so pale a blue it looked almost white, her golden hair hidden by a sheer tulle veil, Caroline accepted Rule's arm and waited for the organ music to start. Her grandmother walked over and squeezed her hand and Caroline bent and kissed the older woman's cheek.

The organist rested her fingers on the keyboard. As the first chords began, Caroline turned and looked directly at Luke, and he felt the force of her gaze like a blow to the stomach.

Damn, he didn't like this. Didn't like that when they had been caught together in the library, part of him had been glad. He had been attracted to Caroline Lockhart from the moment he had met her. Not enough to offer marriage, of course, just enough to want her in his bed.

It looked like that was going to happen—sooner or later.

Luke sighed. If he followed his best friend's advice, it wouldn't happen tonight.

As he waited for his bride to join him at the altar, Luke silently cursed.

A deal was struck. Griffin Manufacturing would be sold to Charles Whitney with the provision he would not arm the states in the American South.

Violet was surprised the man had agreed. It took any number of buyers to make a company profitable. If it weren't for the possibility of war looming on the horizon, it wouldn't matter who bought the armaments Griffin made. But Whitney was also opposed to the notion of slavery and, since there were plenty of customers for the high-quality weapons being produced, he agreed to the terms of the sale.

Over the next several days, Whitney's solicitors reviewed the contracts, his experts made a thorough inspection of the factory, and the profits shown in the ledgers were approved.

"And your man in America has given his tentative approval of the Boston facility?" Rule confirmed during a meeting at the office.

"That is correct."

"We'll have to wait for final approval before we close the deal in America, but we should be able to finalize the sale here in London by the end of the week."

"Jolly good," said Whitney, grinning beneath his brown, silver-flecked mustache. "There are several fine points we still need to discuss. Once those are settled, I'll have my solicitor set us up for the final closing, if that meets with your approval."

"It does," Rule agreed.

Whitney turned to Violet. "My lady?"

"My father would approve of a man of your character taking over the business he worked so hard to build."

After the meeting, in anticipation of reinvesting the profits from the sale, Violet took the balance of the day off from work. She carried home the information on the projects Rule wanted her to review and now sat in the drawing room poring over them.

She was engrossed in a proposal for a railway line that connected London to York when the butler's familiar light rap sounded on the door.

"What is it, Hat?" she said as he slid open the heavy wooden panels.

"My lady, your cousin Mrs. Barclay is here to see you."

Mrs. Barclay. It still had an unfamiliar ring. "Please show her in." Violet wasn't certain if she should be excited to see her newly married cousin, or worried about why Caroline might have come.

One look at her cousin's teary expression answered her question.

"Oh, my goodness, what is wrong?"

As she sat down next to Violet on the sofa, Caroline pulled a handkerchief from her reticule and dabbed it beneath her eyes.

"Luke hates me. I told you he would."

"I don't believe that—not for a moment." Violet rose and crossed to the bellpull to ring for tea, which her cousin obviously needed. Before she could reach the cord, she heard the telltale rattle of the tea cart coming down the hallway and smiled.

Hatfield was truly a gem.

"Thank you, Hat." She waited while he pushed the cart over to the sofa then quietly disappeared from the drawing room.

Violet poured tea into two porcelain cups, glad she had finally acquired a taste for the brew that seemed a necessity in the country she now called home, and handed one of the cups to Caroline.

"Now take a nice warm drink and tell me what has happened."

Caroline sipped her tea, her face still pale, and Violet

wondered if perhaps she should have offered her cousin something stronger.

Caroline dragged in a shaky breath and slowly released it. The cup rattled as she set it back down in its saucer. "*Nothing* has happened. That is the problem."

"I'm afraid I don't understand."

"Except for that little kiss at the altar, Luke hasn't touched me. I'm his wife, Violet, but he doesn't want me." She sniffed and fresh tears welled.

"Don't be silly. Of course he wants you. That is how the two of you got into trouble in the first place."

Caroline raised her handkerchief and blew her nose. "Perhaps he is simply too angry—not that he lets it show. He is so polite I can barely stomach it. He has taken me for carriage rides in the park and bought me trinkets in Bond Street, all the while he barely says a word to me. At night, we have supper together, then he escorts me upstairs to my room and leaves."

She ignored the tea that was rapidly growing cold in her cup. "Luke is an extremely virile man, Violet. If he isn't making love to me, he must be spending his nights with another woman."

Violet shook her head. "That doesn't make sense. Luke has a wife he desires—whether you believe it or not. Why would he need another woman?"

Caroline started crying. "I don't know. I wish I did."

Violet set her cup and saucer down on the table next to Caroline's. "Well, there is only one way you are going to find out. You are going to have to ask him."

"What?"

"You heard me. You're going to have to ask him why he doesn't want to make love to you."

Caroline shook her head. "I couldn't do that. I'm too afraid of what he might say."

"You are never afraid of anything. You can do this, Carrie. You have to."

Caroline bit her lip, pondering Violet's words. She stood up from the sofa. "You are right. I shall talk to him tonight after supper—before he goes off to his mistress or whatever it is he does."

"Good for you."

"And if he doesn't tell me the truth, I shall give him a piece of my mind."

"Of course you will."

Squaring her shoulders, Caroline headed for the door. "Wish me luck."

"You don't need luck—you have courage."

Caroline managed a halfhearted smile as she disappeared out the door, and Violet leaned against the back of the sofa. What ill wind had forced Caroline to marry a rogue like Lucas Barclay? Perhaps it was the same ill wind that had whisked Violet into marriage with Rule. Both of their husbands had outrageous reputations and would likely tire of their brides.

Perhaps Caroline was right and Barclay was already involved with another woman.

Violet recalled the night of the soiree when Luke and Caroline had been caught in the library. That same night, she had seen Rule talking to a woman in the hallway outside the main salon. At the time, she hadn't known the identity of the beautiful laughing brunette with the sky-blue eyes.

Later, when Violet had been talking to Lily, she had seen her again.

"Do you know who that woman is?" Violet had asked. "I don't believe I've seen her before."

Lily's gaze followed hers. "Why, that is Juliana Markham, Countess of Fremont, widow of the late earl. Beautiful, isn't she? She is just out of mourning, I gather, and recently arrived from the earl's country estate in Buckinghamshire."

Violet surveyed the statuesque young woman in her mid-twenties. "She is young to be widowed."

"Yes, well, her husband was quite old. An arranged marriage, I'm told, and not a particularly happy one. Perhaps Lady Fremont will find a man more to her liking the second time 'round."

Violet had watched her floating among the ladies and gentlemen like a magnificent butterfly and thought that indeed the young widow was on the prowl.

Now, as she sat in the drawing room remembering the woman with Rule, the two of them laughing together in the hallway, a shiver moved down her spine.

Caroline made it through another supper with Luke, a strained affair with no more than a dozen words spoken. Luke stood up as the meal came to a close and helped Caroline rise from her chair.

She had dressed with special care tonight, in the same pearl-trimmed, amethyst satin gown she had worn the night of the soiree. He had wanted her that night. Perhaps she could make him want her again.

For an instant, Luke's gaze drifted to the swell of her breasts, then jerked away. He cleared his throat.

"I shall leave you to entertain yourself," he said as he ushered her out of the dining room. "I have some paper-work to go over, then I'm going out for a while. If you will excuse me..."

Caroline squared her shoulders. "No. I won't excuse you, Luke. Not tonight."

His eyebrows went up. Then his jaw firmed. "Since when do you tell me what I can and cannot do?"

"*Since when* does a newly married man not wish to claim his husbandly rights? Who is she, Luke? Obviously you are involved with another woman. At least be honest enough to admit it."

His eyes widened. "That is what you think? That I am spending my nights with another woman?"

"Aren't you? I thought you wanted me, Luke. You certainly acted that way the night they found us together. You made it clear you didn't want marriage, but I thought...I thought that at least we shared a...a...mutual attraction."

His gaze darkened to nearly black and his nostrils flared. "There is no other woman."

"What, then? Are you so angry with me for what happened—"

"What happened wasn't your fault. I knew the chance I was taking when we stepped into the library."

Tears welled in her eyes. "But you did it anyway and now we are married. I don't understand why you don't want to make love to me."

For several long moments, Luke just stood there. He seemed to be fighting for control. "You didn't want to marry me. You were forced into it. I was trying to give you some time."

She blinked and the tears in her eyes spilled onto her cheeks. "Truly?"

Instead of answering, Luke bent down and swept her up in his arms. Her satin gown flowed over the sleeve of his coat as he strode toward the staircase. With an urgency that made her breath catch, he climbed the stairs, strode into his bedroom and set her on her feet beside the bed.

"I've never been a fool where women were concerned—

not until you. You think I don't want you? I want you more than I want to breathe."

And then he kissed her. He tunneled his fingers into her hair, knocking loose the pins, and her blond curls tumbled around her shoulders. Cupping her head in his hands, he ravished her mouth, kissing her long and deep.

"Luke," she whispered, opening to him, feeling the slick glide of his tongue and the hot surge of desire she had felt that night in the library.

Luke just kept kissing her, claiming her mouth one way and then another, taking her with his tongue, taking her as if he couldn't get enough.

Long, deep kisses. Short, burning kisses. Wild, wet kisses. She couldn't think, could barely stay on her feet. She hardly noticed when her bodice fell open, baring her breasts. She moaned as he bent his head and his teeth grazed her nipple.

More clothes disappeared. His hands were everywhere, smoothing over her bare skin, molding and caressing her breasts, stroking, gliding, setting her on fire.

"Luke…" she repeated as he lifted her, naked, onto the mattress, then left her to remove his own clothes. Tall and solidly muscled, he strode back to her, the man part of him long and thick and standing high against his flat belly.

"Never believe I don't want you," he said as he came up over her. "I've never wanted anyone the way I want you."

She whimpered as he moved above her and his narrow hips settled between her legs. He claimed her mouth in a slow, lingering kiss that turned deep and hot, then laved and caressed her breasts, driving her mad with need. She could feel his hardness probing for entrance.

"I'll try not to hurt you."

Caroline moistened her kiss-swollen lips. "I don't care if it hurts. I just want this madness to end."

He chuckled softly and kissed her, then his hand found her softness and he began to stroke her. "You're so hot and wet. That means you're ready for me."

She bit her lip and squirmed beneath him, wanting more. His fingers moved inside her and she fought to keep from crying out. She wanted to beg him, weep for what seemed just out of reach.

"Easy, love. We'll get there, I promise."

She felt the thickness of his arousal beginning to ease inside her, stretching her, filling her. And still she wanted more.

"Oh God, Luke, please." Her fingers dug into his powerful shoulders and she arched upward. At the same time, Luke surged forward, seating himself to the hilt. Caroline cried out, and Luke froze.

"Bloody hell." His neck muscles strained with his effort at control. "I'm sorry, love, truly. I tried to go slow but…"

Caroline pressed a finger against his lips. "It's better now. I like the way you feel. I want the rest, Luke, I want it all."

Luke's breathing quickened. He made a growling sound low in his throat and kissed her softly. Then the kiss turned wild and Luke began to move. Each thrust carried her higher, closer to the edge. Her body tightened. It was as if the floodgates opened and there was no stopping the deluge of passion, the onslaught of pleasure. For long seconds, she soared, floated, absorbed the wonder, wished it never had to end.

Luke's muscles tightened as he followed her to release. Seconds later, she felt his lips against her forehead. Lifting himself from above her, he settled on the mattress beside her and eased her into his arms.

"You're my wife now, Carrie. I don't mean to let you doubt it again."

Caroline closed her eyes and nestled against him. Inwardly she smiled. Making love with Luke was so wonderful it almost made up for having to marry him.

Eighteen

Lily insisted on holding a ball for the newly wed couple, a lavish gala at the duke's recently completed town mansion. Violet imagined the duchess wanted to halt the wagging tongues and help smooth the way for the disgraced pair's return to Society.

In a class where marriages were mostly agreed to for the sake of money and power, it was less difficult to forgive two people fortunate enough to make a love match. And though Violet knew the truth, that neither party had wished to wed, by all outward appearances, Caroline and Luke were in love.

And tenderhearted Lily was among those who wanted them to be happy.

Standing beneath the tinkling crystal prisms of an overhead gas chandelier, Violet scoffed. Neither Luke nor Rule was the sort of man to fall in love. And oddly enough Caroline was deeply afraid of the emotion. She had witnessed her parents' unhappy marriage, the shouting and deliberate cruelty, the heart-wrenching abandonment, and Caroline wanted no part of it.

For Violet, marriage and children were something she

had yearned for long before her father died. In her dreams she had wed a man she loved who loved her in return. It wasn't merely desire that held them together.

With Jeffrey, she might have had a chance for that kind of marriage. Now, she was no longer sure Jeffrey's love would have been enough.

The mirrored walls of the ballroom glittered in crystal and gold, reflecting the light of the chandeliers and the ornate gilded sconces. Rule's brother Reese and Reese's wife, Elizabeth, were there, as well as his aunt Agatha, Countess of Tavistock, whom Violet had met for the first time only a few days ago.

She flicked a glance at the small group around her. Silver-haired and frail, Lady Tavistock had begun a conversation with Elizabeth, who looked elegant in sapphire silk, her raven curls gleaming. Caroline was dancing with Luke, and Rule had begun a conversation with Charles Whitney.

The two men started toward the door leading into the hallway, headed for the billiard room. Their voices raised a bit as they discussed the fine points of the upcoming sale, which hadn't yet been settled.

The music swelled, a lovely Viennese waltz. As Rule disappeared out of sight into the hallway, Violet returned her attention to Caroline and Luke, watching as they whirled around the dance floor. She couldn't help noticing the way Luke held his wife, his gaze locked with hers, his hunger barely disguised.

Wishing Rule had asked her to dance, she turned at the sound of masculine footfalls, her heart lifting at the thought that he might have returned. Instead, Jeffrey's rich baritone reached her.

"I need to speak to you, Violet. It's important."

She didn't want to talk to him. She wanted to forget

what they had once meant to each other. But she couldn't ignore him. She had caused him enough pain already.

"We can't speak here."

"I thought we might walk out on the terrace."

His warm brown eyes beseeched her. He had traveled all the way from America to find her. He had loved her, perhaps loved her still. Her heart squeezed. How could she ignore his simple request?

She glanced around the ballroom. Rule was gone. Everyone else was busily conversing. She nodded her agreement and Jeffrey led her the short distance to the French doors, out onto the terrace.

The night was mostly clear, though a bank of clouds lurked in the distant moonlight, promising a later storm. Several stars shone among the few scattered clouds, twinkling in the sky above the guests who had wandered outside the house.

She turned as they reached the balustrade. "What is it, Jeffrey?"

Golden-haired and handsome, he stood in the light of the torches burning at the edge of the garden.

"I can't stop thinking about you, Violet. I can't stop worrying about you. I need to know, dearest, do you love him? Are you happy?"

Violet gently touched his arm. "Oh, Jeffrey, if only it were that simple."

He caught her gloved hand and brought it to his lips. "It could be. If you would just say the word, we could leave England together. We could return to Boston and make a life for ourselves."

"You are saying I should obtain a divorce."

"I suppose you would have to, but it could be done discreetly."

Violet shook her head. "I can't do that, Jeffrey." Even

as she said the words, her heart warned that divorcing Rule might be the only way she would ever have the kind of life she wanted. Rule didn't love her. Sooner or later, he would tire of her.

Emotion tightened her chest. For weeks she had told herself she didn't love him, and because that was so, she could be married to him and still protect her heart. In that moment, looking into Jeffrey's handsome face, she recognized the truth.

Already, she was more than half in love with Rule. And if he grew tired of her, she would suffer heartbreaking pain.

Jeffrey's voice ended her musings. "Are you certain, Violet? Are you sure this is what you want?" The torchlight flickered, lighting his features, and she saw the yearning there.

"I'm certain, Jeffrey. My place is here with my husband." It was a kindly lie for his sake. She wasn't the least bit certain. "I—I had better go back inside before someone comes looking for me."

"Of course." Jeffrey bowed politely, but the bitterness was clear in his tone. "Take care of yourself, dearest."

Violet made no reply, just lifted her lavender skirts and hurried back into the house, grateful to escape.

Rule left the billiard room where he and Charles Whitney had gone in the hopes of a casual game and an easy resolution to the last of the obstacles in closing the sale.

Both had enjoyed the chance to play. Unfortunately, a rather vocal discussion had ensued in regard to the new designs for the small pocket pistol Griffin currently manufactured.

"I am not in favor of the changes you've made," Whitney said. "I don't believe I should have to pay for them."

"As you know, the changes have already been implemented. The new weapons have already been put in production."

Whitney cast him a cool, assessing glance. "Perhaps the problem lies not in the designs, but in the higher offer I heard you received."

It was true. Both Montgomery and Stanfield had increased their offers, but neither Rule nor Violet was interested. As far as they were concerned, a deal had been struck with Whitney and unless something changed, the company would soon be his.

"That isn't the problem," Rule said. "Your offer stands."

The conversation continued with no resolution. Rule finally suggested the sale be postponed until they could reach a suitable agreement on the designs.

Whitney frowned. Then he sighed. "All right, we'll do it your way. I want Griffin, as you well know."

Rule smiled and nodded. "All right, then." The discussion ended and so did the game, and the men walked away friends.

Satisfied that all was well, Rule left the billiard room in search of Violet, surprised to discover how much he had missed her. Every day they were together, she breached his defenses a little more, burrowed a little deeper into his heart.

It was extremely disconcerting.

He knew nothing of loving a woman. In truth, he'd had little use for women over the years. Bedding them was one thing. Enjoying any sort of relationship beyond that had never entered his mind.

But Violet was different.

Special.

He found himself seeking her out at the oddest times for no real reason at all. He wanted her companionship, her friendship. It was a concept that was new to him and one he wasn't certain he approved.

On top of that was the not-so-small matter of his unrelenting desire for her. Unlike the women he had known in the past, making love to Violet only made him want her more. He wasn't sure why, but his physical lust for her seemed to grow instead of fade.

As he strode down the hall, Rule's shoulders tightened. He knew nothing of love and he didn't want to. Even years after his mother's death, his father had not recovered from her loss. The duke had been so deeply in love with Amanda Dewar he had withdrawn into his own personal hell. He had ignored his youngest son, leaving Rule's two brothers and a nanny to raise him.

Loving someone that much was definitely not for him.

Proceeding along the hall toward the ballroom, he had almost reached the entrance when he caught sight of a statuesque brunette with lovely blue eyes approaching from the opposite direction—Juliana Markham, Lady Fremont.

"My lord," she said with a smile that tilted her lush pink lips. "I've been looking for you. I was hoping we might have a word in private."

Uneasiness settled over him. He wasn't quite sure why. "Of course. May I ask in what regard?"

"Your friend, Lucas Barclay, mentioned you are currently in the investment market. I would like to speak to you about some properties acquired by my late husband I think you might find interesting."

"All right."

Rule led her farther down the hall into Royal's study and quietly closed the door. "Would you care for something to drink?" He moved to the sideboard, suddenly feeling the need for a brandy.

"Thank you, no, I am fine."

He lifted the lid off a crystal decanter and poured himself a glass. "You mentioned investments?"

"Yes. Your friend Luke was an associate of my husband's. He made some investment suggestions that paid off handsomely for the earl. Since I am trying to liquidate some of Lord Fremont's assets, Luke mentioned you might be interested in looking at some of the properties that are going to be sold."

"I might be." As Rule took a sip of his drink, Lady Fremont moved closer, so close he caught the scent of her perfume.

Before Violet had arrived in London, he would have pursued the invitation he read in the lady's blue eyes. Tonight, he simply wanted to be out of what could turn into an embarrassing situation.

"I might be interested," he repeated, removing the hand she had rested on his lapel. "But I would have to discuss the matter with my wife."

One of her sleek dark eyebrows went up. "Somehow I got the impression you were a man who made his own decisions."

He ignored the barb. "For the most part, I am. But Violet and I are business partners as well as husband and wife. If you will have your solicitor send the proposals over to my office, I'll be happy to have a look at them."

"Perhaps I should bring them over myself."

Rule set his glass down on the desk. "I don't think that would be a good idea."

"Really?"

"Really."

Her full lips curved seductively. "You intrigue me, my lord. I've seen you watching me—it is not without some interest."

He had to admit he had noticed her. What man wouldn't? But it didn't mean what she thought it did.

"You're a beautiful woman. A man would be a fool not to notice."

"And you are no fool. I'll send the information. Perhaps sometime in the future, we might get together to discuss it. Good night, my lord."

He made a faint bow of his head. "Good night, my lady."

The moment she was gone, Rule released a breath. He couldn't remember a time he had ever turned down such a blatant offer from such a desirable woman.

It bothered him and yet, now that he was married to Violet, he couldn't imagine any other course.

Leaving the study, Rule went in search of his wife.

Violet stood next to Lily in a group that included Elizabeth, Lady Tavistock, Annabelle Greer and her friend, Sabrina Jeffers, the stunning blonde daughter of the Marquess of Wyhurst.

Violet was glad the chatter of so many women made it unnecessary for her to speak. At the moment, her thoughts were still outside the ballroom, her heart twisting as she stood in the corridor outside the duke's study. As she watched Rule and the Countess of Fremont disappear inside and quietly close the door.

Rule had yet to reappear.

Violet thought of what had gone on between Caroline and Lucas Barclay behind closed doors the night of the soiree, and her heart clenched.

Was Rule making love to the gorgeous brunette? Several times during the evening, Violet had noticed the woman tracking his movements around the ballroom. And once she had noticed his gaze fixed on her.

It had been weeks since her arrival. Rule had a reputation for tiring of women easily. He said he was no longer interested in Lady St. Ives and Violet believed him. But the lovely brunette had recently arrived in London. Did she pose a fresh challenge Rule could not resist?

She looked up to see him approaching. He had been gone for some time yet his hair was neatly combed and his clothes looked unruffled. The woman, Lady Fremont, was nowhere to be seen.

Violet swallowed against the tightness in her throat. Perhaps they had merely planned a rendezvous instead of acting on their passions. Perhaps his infidelity was yet to occur.

She managed a serene, unconcerned expression as he reached her side.

"I've been looking for you," he said brusquely. "Come. It's time for us to leave." Though Violet was more than ready to go, there was something in his voice that gave her pause.

"I'll need my cloak."

"The carriage waits out front. I'll retrieve your cloak as we leave."

His expression was hard as he caught her arm and escorted her rather firmly to the door. She had no idea where his dark mood had come from and she really didn't care. She just wanted to go home. Apparently Rule felt the same.

Draping her cloak around her shoulders, he led her to the carriage, helped her climb in, then seated himself on the opposite side.

"We should have bid good-night to our hosts," she said into the darkness lit only by a single brass lamp.

A muscle jerked in his cheek. "We'll send them a note in the morning."

He said no more and neither did she. Her mind was on

the brunette and what might have happened in the study. She was surprised to discover she felt more hurt than angry. If Rule wanted the countess or any other woman, there was only one thing she could do about it.

The word *divorce* slipped into her head.

She didn't want to end their marriage. She wanted Rule to love her.

As she was in love with him.

The realization hit her with the force of a Boston wind. She hadn't understood how deeply she had fallen until tonight...until she had seen him with the brunette.

Her heart twisted hard. Dear God, how could she have let it happen?

But in truth, she had been fascinated by Rule Dewar since she was a girl of sixteen.

Nineteen

A light rain had begun to fall, shrouding the streets in a hazy mist. As the carriage rolled toward home, Violet and Rule rode in silence, the tension thick inside the coach. When they reached the town house, he helped her down and led her up the front porch stairs into the house.

"I'm feeling a little tired," Violet told him, needing to put some distance between them, needing time to think. "I'm going straight to bed."

A muscle tightened in Rule's jaw, making the tiny indentation in his chin more pronounced. "Very well. I have some paperwork to do. Don't wait up for me." Turning, he strode off down the hall to his study.

Clearly, he would not be coming to her bed tonight, which suited Violet just fine.

She wanted to ask him straight out about the brunette, wanted to know if Lady Fremont was the reason for his surly mood, but her pride wouldn't let her. She refused to let him know how much she cared, how much it hurt to think of him with another woman.

Mary was waiting when she reached her bedroom. "Let me help ye, milady."

"Thank you, Mary. I am feeling rather exhausted tonight." A gust of wind rattled the windows and she could hear the rain beating hard against the panes.

"Don't ye worry. I'll have ye in bed in a jiff." Violet thanked God for Mary, who was always so kind and helpful. Several weeks back, Rule had asked if she wanted to choose a maid schooled in managing a lady's toilette, but Violet was perfectly content with Mary.

"Let's get this off ye." Mary helped her out of her gown and caged crinoline. Violet was preparing to remove the rest of her garments, standing in front of the mirror in corset, drawers, garters and stockings, when the door burst open and Rule strode into the bedroom.

"That will be all for tonight, Mary."

The maid's eyes widened at the hard look on his face. "Yes, milord." Scurrying out of the bedroom, she quickly closed the door.

Piqued at Rule's high-handedness, Violet turned a cool stare in his direction and for the first time noticed his dishevelment. His coat, waistcoat and cravat had been removed. His shirt was unbuttoned at the throat, the sleeves rolled up, exposing the muscles in his forearms. His black hair was mussed as if he had run his fingers through it.

His eyes moved over her, burning into her like the blue tip of a flame. They settled on the swell of her breast and though she was still angry at him, her nipples peaked inside her corset.

He crossed his arms over the width of his very solid chest. "So what did your dear friend *Jeffrey* have to say?"

"Jeff—Jeffrey?" There was a squeak in her voice she couldn't quite contain.

His mouth curved harshly. "I gather you two had quite a discussion out on the terrace."

Good grief, she should have known he would find out! Instead of guilt, she thought of the brunette and felt a rush of satisfaction.

"Jeffrey is concerned for my welfare. He wanted to know if I was happy."

Rule moved toward her, stopped right in front of her. "Is that so? Surely that wasn't all. What else did he want?"

She knew she shouldn't tell him, but some evil little demon inside her couldn't resist. "He wanted me to return with him to Boston."

Rule's jaw hardened and a rude sound came from his throat. "You're my wife, Violet. You aren't going anywhere with *Jeffrey.*"

She gasped as his big hands settled on her shoulders and he dragged her hard against him, then his mouth crushed down over hers. For a fleeting instant, she thought of the countess, but his tongue slid into her mouth and desire struck her so hard it made her weak.

"You're mine," he whispered, kissing the side of her neck. His teeth nipped an earlobe. "Mine." His elegant fingers worked the hooks on the front of her corset and her breasts spilled into his hands. Rule squeezed, bent his head and suckled them ruthlessly.

All rational thought disappeared. Scorching need took its place, desire so strong nothing mattered but the touch of his hands, his mouth against her naked flesh. She wanted him, wanted the pleasure only he could give her.

"I told myself to stay away," he said between fiery kisses, "that I was still too angry. But I wanted you too damned much."

His words thrilled her. He wanted her, not the countess.

Her head fell back, giving him access to her throat, and his lips traveled there, burning a path over her skin. She felt his hands in her hair, dislodging the pins, his fingers raking through the heavy copper curls, spreading them around her bare shoulders.

"God, you're beautiful." His mouth returned to her breasts and he suckled and laved the fullness, tugged on her nipples until she moaned in helpless abandon.

"I...want you," she whispered, wishing she could deny the words, knowing they were true. Her hands trembled as she caught the hem of his white lawn shirt and tugged it free of his trousers, slid her fingers underneath to stroke the hard ridges of muscle across his flat stomach. Rule jerked the shirt off over his head and tossed it away, kissed her deeply again.

His hands cupped her bottom and he lifted her, wrapped her legs around his waist. Finding the split in her drawers, he positioned himself at the entrance to her passage and drove himself home.

Violet whimpered. She was wet and ready and on fire.

"This is what I needed," Rule said, carrying her backward until her shoulders came up against the wall. "God, I want you so much." Holding her in place, he began to thrust inside her, deep driving strokes that sent ripples of pleasure through her body. Hard, penetrating thrusts that set her on fire.

The heavy surge and drag of his shaft had her gripping his powerful shoulders, but Violet wanted more. Fingering a flat copper nipple, she bent her head and took the nubbin between her teeth, bit down, and Rule groaned.

Deeper, harder, faster.

Violet clung to him, opened to him, let him give her what she needed.

The pleasure built, a blissful coil of tension that grew to the point of pain. In an instant, she broke free, soaring, soaring, swamped by sweet sensation, crying out his name.

Rule didn't stop. Not until he had brought her to the peak again did he follow her to release.

For long seconds they remained as they were, Violet clinging to Rule's neck, her head slumped on his shoulder.

"Tell me you don't want him," Rule softly demanded. "Say it's me you want and not him."

She looked up at him, surprised at the need she heard in his voice. "I don't want Jeffrey. I want you, Rule." She didn't say the rest. She didn't trust him to know the way she felt, to know how much she loved him.

She was easy prey as it was.

Rule set her on her feet. The rain had lessened but still she could hear it beating against the panes. Wordlessly, he unfastened the rest of the hooks on her corset and helped her remove the balance of her clothes. She thought he would stay, but he didn't.

As she slipped on a white cotton nightgown, he picked up his discarded shirt and walked to the door that joined their two rooms.

"I'll see you in the morning," he said, his blue eyes dark and turbulent.

Violet made no reply. Her own feelings were in turmoil. She was in love with Rule but aside from their mutual passion, she had no idea what he felt for her.

And there was still the unresolved matter of Rule and the beautiful countess. When the time was right, she would confront him, find out the truth.

As Violet slid between the sheets, she listened to the steady patter of the rain and wished for the hundredth time she had never left Boston.

* * *

It was Saturday. The storm had strengthened, grown into a pounding, relentless torrent that suited Rule's mood. He wasn't sure what had happened last night, only that he had been wildly out of control with Violet and he didn't like it.

He released a slow breath. With the storm hanging over the city, he had decided they should work in the house today—he in his study, Violet down the hall in a small drawing room at the back of the house she had appropriated for her use.

He was working on the business proposals he had been studying for the past several weeks, trying to find the best opportunities in which to invest, still not completely satisfied with any of the proposals he had received.

Rising from his desk, he walked over to the fire in the corner, turned his back and let the warmth of the blaze seep into his clothes.

A knock at the door drew his attention. "What is it?" he asked Hatfield, who stood in the opening.

"A note just arrived, my lord." Hat walked over and handed him the message, turned and left the study.

Rule opened and read the note, a little surprised to see Charles Whitney's name scrolled at the bottom.

Several questions have arisen regarding the sale. If it is convenient, I am hoping you will meet me at my hotel this afternoon. Room 112. I'll look for you around two-thirty.

It was already half past eleven. With so little warning, it seemed a bit of an odd request. But while he was in London, Whitney was staying at the Albert in Oxford Street, a hotel not far away. Rule reread the note, wadded it up and tossed it into the fire.

He could use an excuse to get out of the house, away from troubling thoughts of his wife.

When the time came to leave, he called for Hat to have his carriage brought round, then went in search of Violet. She was seated on the sofa in front of the fire, a set of ledgers open on the cushion in front of her. He tried not to think of last night, of how good it had felt to be inside her, how at that very moment, he wanted to shove the ledgers aside, ease her down on the sofa, lift her skirts and take her again.

Noticing his presence in the room, she came to her feet. "What is it?"

"I'm going out for a while. I should be back in a couple of hours."

"In this weather?"

He shrugged. The weather was the least of his worries. "A note arrived earlier from Whitney. He has a couple of questions he wants to ask."

"Do you want me to go with you?"

"There's no need for that. And I could use a bit of fresh air."

"I see."

At the slight lift of her chin, he frowned. "You don't mind, do you?"

"Why should I mind?"

Rule made no reply. He rarely understood the workings of a woman's mind. Turning, he walked out of the cozy drawing room, eager to be out of the house.

Rule stepped down from his carriage in front of the Albert Hotel.

"I shouldn't be long," he told Bellows.

The burly man pulled the brim of his hat down lower

against the unrelenting rain, nodded and climbed back up on the driver's seat.

Rule made his way up the red-carpeted steps into the lobby, all dark wood and mullioned glass windows, and headed for the wide sweeping staircase. A sign at the top of the stairs indicated rooms 100 through 130 to the left so he headed in that direction.

When he arrived at Whitney's suite, he reached up to knock and was surprised to discover the door was un-latched and standing a few inches open. Rule pushed the door open wider and stuck his head inside.

"Whitney? It's Dewar. Are you in here?"

When no answer came, Rule stepped into the room, be-ginning to worry. The minute he walked into the sitting room, he froze. Lying in a pool of blood on the floor in front of the sofa, Charles Whitney stared lifelessly at the ceiling. Blood oozed from a vicious hole in his chest and spread out over his coat.

Rule hurried toward him, knelt and pressed his fingers against the man's neck, hoping to find a pulse. No pulse thrummed beneath his hand, confirming Whitney was dead.

His chest tightened. He liked Charles Whitney.

Rule glanced around. Next to the body lay a small, five-barrel pistol he recognized as one manufactured by Griffin. A single shot was missing from one of the chambers. On the sofa lay a bloody pillow with a fire-singed hole in the center, that had apparently been used to muffle the sound of the shot.

"Step away from the body," a man's hard voice com-manded, coming from the open door. "Make no move toward the weapon."

Rule slowly turned toward the sound of the voice, saw several uniformed policemen standing in the hotel room doorway, all of their attention fixed on him. Rule carefully lifted his hands, outstretched so the police could see he was unarmed.

"My name is Dewar," he said. "I found him this way when I walked into the room."

"How did you get in?" one of them asked, short and bulldog-faced, with a mop of thick brown hair.

"The door was open."

The man approached him cautiously. "That your gun?"

"No." He didn't say it was made by Griffin. He was doing his best to keep the men from jumping to wrong conclusions.

"Ye know him?" a second man asked, this one thin and wiry with small round eyes and a narrow mustache.

"His name is Charles Whitney. We were involved in a business deal together. He sent me a note asking me to meet him here to discuss some of the terms."

The first man glanced down at Rule's hand and he realized Whitney's blood covered his fingers.

"I think you had best come with us, Mr. Dewar," he said.

"I had nothing to do with this. I told you, he was dead when I walked into the room."

"Come along now," said the policeman with the thin mustache, tapping his long wooden truncheon against the palm of his hand. "Ye don't want to give us any trouble or it won't go easy for ye."

The policeman still standing in the doorway stood at attention, clearly ready for trouble.

"How did you happen to come here?" Rule asked, pulling a handkerchief from his pocket and wiping the blood from his hand.

"A fellow came up to me and Officer Pettigru on the

street," the first policeman told him. "Said there was trouble at the hotel. Looks like the man was right."

Rule flicked a glance at the policeman with the thin mustache who appeared to be Pettigru and wondered if the informant was somehow involved in the murder. The timing was certainly good. The police had arrived just minutes after Rule had reached the room, leaving them to assume he was the one who had committed the crime.

As the trio of uniformed men ushered him out of the hotel room, Rule clamped his jaw. As soon as they reached the station, he would send word to Royal. A duke carried a lot of weight. Royal would vouch for his innocence and the mistake would be corrected.

He hoped.

They made their way out through the lobby amid the whispers and stares of several hotel guests. As he was led down the carpeted steps to the street, he spotted Bellows standing next to the carriage looking stunned.

Rule had no time to talk to him as the door to the police wagon opened and he was shoved roughly inside. The wagon jolted into motion and he fell back against the hard wooden seat.

"Take it easy, guv'nor," Pettigru said to him. "We'll get ye there safe and sound and ye can tell yer story to the constable."

Rule leaned back against the scarred wooden seat, hoping the constable was a better listener than the other policemen had been.

Violet lifted her simple gray woolen skirt and hurriedly climbed the steps leading up to police headquarters at 26 Old Jewry. Rule's beefy coachman, Mr. Bellows, moved along close behind.

The station bustled with activity. A surly young man was being charged as a pickpocket and a woman cried in the corner as she received the news her father had been arrested. Trying not to think what sort of news she might receive, Violet approached the long oak counter in the waiting room.

"Excuse me, sir," she said to an overweight man in a dark blue uniform seated at his desk. "Could you please tell me where I might find Lord Rule Dewar? I'm his wife. His coachman says the police wagon brought him here about an hour ago."

Thank God Mr. Bellows had the good sense to follow the wagon when he had seen Rule being dragged from the hotel. Unfortunately, he had no idea why Rule had been brought to the station.

Aside from her concern for her husband's safety, Violet couldn't help wondering if he had gone to the hotel for a rendezvous with Lady Fremont, though why that should result in his arrest she couldn't begin to know.

"I believe your husband is just down the hall, milady. If you'll wait, I'll tell Constable McGregor you're here." The rotund policeman walked off down the corridor, disappeared behind one of the doors and returned a few minutes later.

"The constable says he'd like to see you. If you'll please follow me…"

She flicked a glance at Bellows, who wore a worried expression and stood with his legs splayed and his big hands clasped in front of him. Following the policeman down the hall, she waited while he opened the door, then walked past him into a barren room furnished with only a wooden table and four rickety wooden chairs.

Rule sat in one of them. He shot to his feet the moment he saw her.

"Violet!"

"Sit down, Dewar." The man across from him—stocky build, auburn hair and a rough complexion—rose to face her. "I'm Constable McGregor, my lady. Why don't you have a seat?"

She would rather have remained standing, but she didn't want to aggravate the man before she even found out why Rule was there.

She sat down in the chair he offered and flicked a glance at Rule, whose expression was grim, his black hair mussed and hanging over his forehead. "Why have you brought my husband here?"

Rule shot up once more. "They think I'm a murderer."

Violet's heart jerked and began a rapid pounding.

"I told you to sit down," said McGregor.

Rule slowly complied and the constable turned his attention to her. "I'm afraid there's been a murder. A man named Charles Whitney. Are you familiar with the name?"

Her gaze flew to Rule. Charles Whitney was dead? It seemed impossible. "Why...why, yes, I know him. He is... he was planning to buy the company my husband and I own."

McGregor studied the notes he had written. "Griffin Manufacturing?"

"Yes."

"Your husband was found in Mr. Whitney's room just minutes after the shooting. He was kneeling over the body. There was a gun on the floor at his feet and his hand was covered in blood."

"I didn't kill him," Rule said defensively. "I was trying to help him." There was something in his face... Dear God, he was afraid she wouldn't believe him!

She stiffened her spine. "There, you heard what he said. Mr. Whitney had been shot. My husband was trying to help him."

Rule hadn't done it, she was sure. He simply wasn't the kind of man to commit murder.

"Perhaps. But our investigation has only begun. There is every chance we'll turn up more evidence. When that happens—"

A hard knock interrupted the rest of the constable's words. The door swung open before the policeman had granted permission and Royal Dewar strode into the barren chamber.

"What's going on here?" he demanded. "I'm the Duke of Bransford. I demand to know why my brother is being held against his will."

McGregor rose from his chair. "Your brother was found at the scene of a murder, Your Grace."

Royal's gaze didn't waver. "So his note informed me." He was a good four inches taller than the constable, his manner utterly forbidding. "What possible reason would my brother have to kill the man who was about to buy his company?"

"We don't know why Whitney was murdered—not yet. But we will, I assure you."

Another man walked into the room just then, light blue eyes and a leonine mane of silver hair. "I'm Edward Pinkard. I represent the Dewar family. If you do not have sufficient evidence to file formal charges against his lordship, I would advise you to release him."

McGregor's jaw tightened. Clearly he wasn't ready to let Rule leave. He turned to the duke. "Are you willing to be responsible for this man's conduct until the matter is resolved?"

The duke gave a firm nod of his head. "I am."

McGregor's gaze went to Rule. "All right, you can go. We have no more questions at this time, but I warn you not to leave the city."

"I'll be right here," Rule said darkly. Turning, he made

his way to where Violet stood trembling. He settled a hand at her waist. "Everything is going to be all right. Let's go."

She only nodded. Worry made it hard to speak. Clearly the constable believed Rule was guilty of Charles Whitney's murder.

The small group made its way out to the waiting area. Bellows cast a concerned look at Rule then hurried off to fetch the carriage.

"Thank you for coming," Rule said to his brother.

The duke's jaw looked hard. "I'll follow you back to your house and you can tell me what this is about."

Rule turned to the silver-haired attorney. "I appreciate your help, Edward. If I need anything more, I'll let you know."

Pinkard cast a glance back down the hall. "Let us hope this is the end of it."

Violet's stomach tightened. As they walked out of the police station, she thought of the determined look on Constable McGregor's harsh, ruddy face, and had a very bad feeling this was only the beginning.

Twenty

Rule sat with his brother and Violet in front of the hearth in his study. Every time he looked at his wife, he felt sick to his stomach.

In the past half hour, he had explained in detail everything that had happened: receiving the note from Whitney, finding the door to his room open, walking inside, spotting the man's still-warm body on the floor. He told them how he had knelt and felt for a pulse but found none, how the police had arrived at that very moment.

His brother had believed him, of course. Royal hadn't the slightest doubt of his innocence. But Violet…

Violet didn't know him the way Royal did. There was every chance she would believe the worst of him.

He raked a hand through his already disheveled hair. "They are going to find out the pistol was made by Griffin. It won't take them long."

She slid closer to him on the sofa, her skirt brushing his leg. "You didn't do it. In time, they are certain to discover that, as well."

"I wish it were that simple." He looked over at Royal.

"Whitney and I had an argument in the billiard room at your house last night. It wasn't much, but people noticed. It'll be one more thing for the police to look at."

"Their attention is focused on you," Royal said. "They believe you did it and they're going to do their best to prove it."

Violet's face went a little bit pale. Rule watched as she visibly collected herself. "If that is the case, then there is only one thing to do."

"What's that?" Rule grumbled.

"Find the man who killed Mr. Whitney."

For several long moments, he and Royal just sat there staring.

"She's right," Royal finally said. "We have to find the killer ourselves. That's the only way we'll have absolute proof of your innocence."

"For God's sake, how the bloody hell am I going to find a murderer?"

"We need to start our own investigation," Violet said. "We can begin by finding out if anyone at the hotel saw someone going into Mr. Whitney's room just before the shooting."

"And the note," Rule said, his mind finally coming out of its daze and beginning to focus. "We need to find out if Whitney actually sent it or if someone wanted me in that room at exactly that time."

"Whitney's handwriting must be on some of the documents involved in the sale," Royal said. "We can compare the handwriting on the note—"

"We could—if I hadn't tossed it into the fire."

Royal frowned, drawing his dark blond eyebrows together.

"But the message must have come from Mr. Whitney," Violet said. "Why would anyone wish to blame his murder on you?"

"I wish I knew," Rule said darkly.

"If someone did set you up as the villain," Royal said, "he wasn't working alone. He would have needed someone watching the house to be sure you were going to the meeting. That man would have followed you to the hotel. Whoever did it would need to know exactly when you would be arriving at the Albert."

Violet worked her fingers over a fold in her skirt. "On the other hand, your arrival might have been pure coincidence. Perhaps Whitney had enemies, someone who might have wanted him dead."

"True enough," Royal agreed, flicking Rule a glance. "His death may have had nothing at all to do with you."

"We need help with this," Violet said. "Is there someone we could hire, someone who could assist us in looking into the matter?"

Royal got up from his chair and paced over to the fire. "I know someone...an investigator named Chase Morgan. He's extremely capable. I've used him and so has Reese. I'll send word to his office, tell him you wish to set up a meeting."

Rule nodded. "Thank you."

"In the meantime, I'll talk to Sherry and the rest of the Oarsmen, ask them to dig around, see if they can find out if Whitney had enemies who might have wanted him dead."

"The Oarsmen?" Violet asked.

"My brother's friends from Oxford," Rule explained. "As young men, they rowed together on the Oxford sculling team. They've been friends ever since."

"Sculling? Is that the name for those long, skinny boats?"

"For rowing them, yes," Royal answered. "The boats themselves are called sculls."

"They were champions in their day," Rule added with the slightest hint of a smile.

"Well, I feel better already," Violet said. Some of the color, Rule noticed, had returned to her cheeks. "With everyone helping, it won't be long until this awful affair is over."

Rule looked at his pretty wife, read the determination on her face, and relief filtered through him. She believed he was telling the truth, believed in his innocence.

Until that very moment, he hadn't known how important that was.

The following day Violet joined Rule in his study for a meeting that had been arranged with Chase Morgan. The investigator Royal had recommended was a hard, dark man with angular features. Lean and solid, his appearance made him somewhat menacing.

"Let's go over the facts again," Morgan said. He had commandeered the chair behind Rule's desk, where he took notes with his newly sharpened pencil. "I need to be clear on every detail, starting with the argument you had at the ball at your brother's house the night before."

For a second time, Rule told the investigator what had transpired, down to the smallest detail.

"Where was Whitney's valet when you walked into the hotel room?" Morgan asked. "Shouldn't he have been somewhere about?"

"I would think so," Rule said. "He certainly wasn't there when I got there."

"You said you received a note from Whitney. What happened to it?"

Rule shook his head. "I had no idea it might be important. I tossed it into the fire."

Morgan asked a couple more questions and finally seemed satisfied. Shoving his notes into the leather satchel he had brought with him, he rose from behind Rule's desk.

"This is going to take some time. I'll be in touch if I have any more questions."

"All right." Rule walked the investigator to the front door then returned to the study. Violet was standing beneath one of the gilt-framed hunting scenes hanging on the wall.

"Hiring someone isn't enough," she said. "I don't care how capable he is. We need to continue our own investigation."

Rule shook his head. "Morgan is a professional. My brother is doing everything he can. I'll be digging for information myself, but I don't want you involved."

"What are you talking about? You're my husband. You are under suspicion of murder. I am already involved."

Rule strode toward her, reached out and caught her shoulders. "This was a cold-blooded killing, Violet. Getting involved could be dangerous. I don't want my wife getting hurt."

Violet bit her lip. If she was going to get hurt, odds were it would be Rule, not the killer, who did it. She thought about the countess. At least he hadn't been meeting her at the hotel. She shoved the image of them together far to the back of her mind.

First things first. They needed to solve a murder.

Violet intended to do whatever she could to find the man who killed Charles Whitney and there was nothing Rule could do to stop her.

Violet left Rule in his study and headed down the hall. Remembering Morgan's question about the note had set her to thinking. The note had been destroyed but perhaps they could find the person who had delivered it.

She headed straight for Hat, whose head came up at her approach.

"Is there something you need, my lady?"

"Since there is very little that goes on in this house of which you are not aware, I imagine you have heard about the troubles his lordship is facing."

Hat looked embarrassed. "I may have heard something about it." His shoulders straightened. "His lordship would never commit such a villainous crime."

"I am well aware of that, Mr. Hatfield. Unfortunately, the police are not convinced. Therefore we need to find the man who is guilty."

"How may I be of help, my lady?"

"Do you recall the note that Lord Rule received a little before noon yesterday?"

"Why, yes, my lady."

"Can you describe the man who brought it?"

"'Twas not a man, my lady, but a boy."

"A boy?"

"Indeed. I recall him quite well. You see, two of his fingers were missing from his left hand. He was perhaps eleven or twelve, dressed in coarse brown trousers with a hole in the knee and a shirt that was smudged with soot."

"And two of his fingers were missing."

"That is correct. The way they were scarred, they appeared to have been burned. If I were to venture a guess, I would say he may work as a chimney sweep."

Violet frowned. "Are there not laws to protect a child his age from working in that sort of business?"

"Quite so, my lady. A law was passed some years back making the age for indenture no less than twenty-one, but there are no penalties for breaking it. Most of the master sweeps ignore it."

"I see. Well, I shall need to find the boy's master in order to find the boy."

Hat nodded. "Why don't you ask Mrs. Digby? She is the one in charge of the cleaning and that sort of thing. Perhaps she can be of some assistance."

"Thank you, Hat." Lifting her skirts, she hurried off toward the butler's pantry, where she had last seen the housekeeper.

The broad-hipped woman turned at her approach. She smiled warmly. "Good afternoon, my lady."

"Good afternoon, Mrs. Digby. I am hoping you can help me. I am looking for a boy. I believe he may work as a chimney sweep. Can you give me the name of the man you hire to keep our chimneys clean?" If he wasn't the right man, perhaps he could give her the name of another in the same business.

"The sweep I use is a fellow named Dick Whistler. But there are a couple of others who work in the neighborhood. There is a man named Simon Pratt, though I refuse to hire him. He uses young boys and I don't like the way he treats them."

Violet's interest heightened. She had heard stories of master sweeps who apprenticed young boys and girls and sent them up chimneys that were too hot. Some had been badly burned, some even killed. If the delivery boy was missing two fingers, perhaps Simon Pratt was the man who had abused him.

"Do you know where I might find this Mr. Pratt?"

"I do, but you can't go there, my lady. The neighborhood is quite disreputable."

"I shall keep that in mind." Violet obtained the names and addresses of the two master sweeps who worked in the Mayfair area. Tomorrow, Rule planned to return to the office. Once he was gone, she would pay a call on the two men whose names she had obtained.

Perhaps she would get lucky.

Violet sighed. It seemed she was overdue for a little good luck.

Rule was up early and long gone to work. Violet ordered the carriage brought round, but when she told Mr. Bellows her destination, he insisted she shouldn't go.

"'Tisn't a respectable neighborhood fer a lady to be visitin' by herself."

Violet hesitated. Mrs. Digby had also warned her against the journey and she wasn't a fool. "Perhaps you are right. We shall take Robbie Harkins along with us." Robbie was one of the footmen. She should have thought of him from the start.

Bellows muttered something about how useless the young pup would be if they met trouble, but Violet ignored him. As Robbie walked out to join them, she returned her attention to the coachman.

"Now if you are satisfied, Mr. Bellows, may we proceed to the address I gave you?"

Bellows grumbled but made no more comment. He and the footman exchanged a glance, then he climbed up on the box. The footman helped her aboard the carriage and took his place at the rear.

Simon Pratt's address wasn't as far from Portman Square as she had imagined, just off Great Queen Street in St. Giles. Along the route, there were pockets here and there of impoverished Londoners forced to live with the criminal element. She gave a silent prayer of thanks that she had been born to better circumstances.

It took several stops before Robbie was able to locate the dilapidated two-story wooden building where Simon Pratt lived.

"Are ye sure about this, milady?" Bellows asked as the footman helped her down from the carriage.

"I won't be long. Mr. Harkins, you may come with me."

"Yes, my lady." The young blond footman fell in behind her. He was tall but gangly and pale and not particularly imposing. She stopped and turned. "On second thought, why don't you stay with the carriage? Mr. Bellows, if you would be so kind, perhaps you could come with me."

The beefy driver beamed. "I'd be pleased ta go with ye, milady."

And so it was settled and the two of them made their way up a wooden walkway where grass poked up between warped wooden boards to a door that tilted slightly on its hinges.

Bellows rapped firmly, then stepped back out of the way, and a few minutes later, the door swung open.

A boy, red-haired and no more than seven years old, stood in the opening. "What ye want?"

"I'm looking for Mr. Pratt. Is he here?"

"'E's workin'. 'E won't be home till late."

She tried to see past the child into the house, but it was dark inside, the windows so dirty little sunlight passed through to illuminate the interior.

She smiled at the boy. "What's your name?"

"Me name's Billy Robin."

She kept her smile in place, even as she noticed his ragged clothes and thin, emaciated face. "Is your mother home, Billy?"

"Don't 'ave a mother. No father, neither."

"So Mr. Pratt takes care of you?"

He shrugged his bony shoulders. "I works for 'im."

For the first time she noticed the dirty bandages on his hand and pity slipped through her. "You're injured."

Billy stuck his hands behind his back. "Burnt meself. Mr. Pratt says I'll be fine in a day or two."

She bit her lip, fighting down the anger she felt toward Simon Pratt. "Are there other boys who work for Mr. Pratt, as well?"

He nodded, jiggling strands of grimy red hair. "Girls, too."

"I see. I'm looking for a boy with two fingers missing. Does he work for Mr. Pratt?"

"'E used to."

Her pulse kicked up. "Do you know his name?"

"Danny Tuttle."

She managed another smile. "Do you know where I can find Danny?"

The child shook his head. "I donno, but Tom Dasher's only got part o' 'is arm." As if Tom might serve in Danny's stead.

Violet controlled a shudder, her heart aching for the little boy and the others. Reaching into her reticule, she pulled out a handful of coins and handed them to the child. "Thank you, Billy."

The little boy stared at the coins, then looked up at her and grinned. He tucked the money into the pocket of his ragged trousers and disappeared back inside the house.

Turning, she stepped off of the porch and Mr. Bellows fell in beside her. "Ain't right, is it?"

"No, it isn't."

Several disreputable men watched as they returned to the carriage, but the size of the coachman's thick arms seemed to dissuade them from any evil intent.

They left the neighborhood and headed for the second address on her list. If Danny Tuttle no longer worked for Pratt, perhaps he worked for Dick Whistler. As the carriage rolled toward the second residence, she thought of the children who lived in the ramshackle house and tried to think what she might do to help them.

At the second address, a slightly better cared for brick structure in a less run-down neighborhood, no one was at home.

The front door opened at the house next door and a woman with frizzy blond hair stuck her head through the opening.

"If ye be lookin' for Mr. Whistler, he ain't home. Works till dark. Ye want ta hire him, come back then." The door slammed closed, the sound echoing off the houses across the street.

Violet sighed. "I guess I shall have to return later." Walking next to Mr. Bellows, she returned to the carriage.

"Ain't safe at night, milady."

"I suppose not."

But as soon as possible she would find a way to come back. She needed to find Danny Tuttle. She hoped Dick Whistler could help her.

Pacing back and forth in the drawing room, Rule heard Violet's feminine footfalls approaching down the hall and angrily strode toward the door.

"Where the bloody hell have you been?"

Her chin went up. "You must have a fairly good notion or you wouldn't be so angry."

And angry he was. His jaw felt like steel and his stomach was tied in knots. "I came home early. I had too damned much on my mind to concentrate on work. When I got here, I discovered you were gone."

"I had things to do."

"So I gathered," he said darkly. "When I questioned Hat, he said you were asking about the person who had delivered the note from Whitney. You spoke to Mrs. Digby, as well."

She cocked an eyebrow in his direction. "That's right. I figured if we didn't have the note, perhaps we could find the messenger who brought it."

"And?"

"Mr. Hatfield said it was a boy, not a man. He believed the lad might have been a chimney sweep. Mrs. Digby gave me several addresses, places where I might start my search."

"Tell me you did not go into those neighborhoods by yourself." A murder had been committed, for God's sake. He didn't want his wife getting hurt!

"I did not go there by myself." She gave him a tart little smile. "Mr. Bellows and Mr. Harkins accompanied me."

Rule swore foully. Her eyes widened, since he rarely used that kind of language in front of her. Rule didn't care.

"Dammit, Violet, those places aren't safe for a woman. God's blood, they aren't safe for a man! You could have been attacked or even killed."

"I was perfectly safe with Mr. Bellows and Mr. Harkins. But since you are so concerned, perhaps you will accompany me when I return."

"Return!"

"That is correct. The messenger's name is Danny Tuttle. We need to speak to a master sweep named Whistler, see if Danny works for him or if he knows where we might find him. Since Mr. Whistler works until dark, it would be better if you would go with me."

Rule fought to hang on to his temper. "I swear, Violet—"

"You have already done so, sir."

Rule clamped down on his jaw. "If you were still sixteen, I would put you over my knee and give you a good sound thrashing for putting yourself in danger."

Her smile remained in place. "But I am no longer sixteen. I am a grown woman and your wife."

And he would far rather ravish her than spank her. Though the notion still held a certain appeal.

"You wish to return to the sweep's house tonight?"

"I do. And along the way, there is a related matter I wish to discuss."

Oh, she was a handful. Like no other woman he had ever known. More outspoken, more intelligent and far more determined. He raked a hand through his hair. "What am I going to do with you, sweetheart?"

Her features softened. "For the moment, I hope you will let me help you clear your name."

She was also caring and loyal—and so damned pretty standing there by the window with the sunlight gleaming on her glorious flame-colored hair. A dozen ways he wanted to make love to her popped into his head and he felt himself begin to go hard.

"Well?" she asked, drawing him back to the moment.

If she wished to aid him, he could hardly continue to refuse her. She had already dug up more information than anyone else.

"All right, I could certainly use your assistance, but I want your word you will tell me whatever it is you plan to do. I want you safe, Violet. Promise me you won't go off again on your own."

She smiled, obviously pleased. "If that is your wish, I'll agree. We shall work on this together. Will you take me back to the sweep's house tonight?"

He nodded. "We'll find the Tuttle boy. With luck he'll be able to tell us if Whitney was the man who sent him to deliver the note."

Twenty-One

Seated across from Rule, Violet rode mostly in silence as the carriage pressed on to the house in a court off St. John's Street that belonged to Dick Whistler. Lamps burned in the windows when they arrived. Apparently, he was home.

"We're here," Rule said, leaning over to open the carriage door. "Let's see what we can find out."

She let him help her down from inside the coach and guide her up the dirt path to the porch. The door opened at Rule's light knock and a lean, tired-looking man stood in the opening.

"Are you Dick Whistler?" Rule asked.

"That's me."

"I'm looking for a boy named Danny Tuttle. He's about twelve, maybe thirteen years old. We thought he might work for you."

The man scratched his jaw and shook his head. "Danny's too young to work for me. There's a law against it and I don't break the law."

"Do you know where we can find him?" Violet asked.

"Used to work for Simon Pratt. Lost two fingers because of it. Doesn't sweep chimneys no more. Last I heard, he was doing odd jobs for a fellow named Benny Bates. He's a real sharper, is Bates. Runs a ring of blacklegs and thieves. Danny's not really like that, but I guess he didn't have much other choice. He's alive, but he might not stay that way if he keeps workin' for Bates."

"Do you know where we might find this man Bates?"

"Hangs out at the White Bull Tavern in St. Giles. You might find him there."

"Thank you, Mr. Whistler," Violet said. "I am glad you're concerned about the children's welfare."

He nodded. "Apprenticed young, meself. I know what it's like."

She noticed the scars on his hands as he closed the door and thought of Simon Pratt and little Billy Robin.

"We'll go to the tavern tomorrow," Rule said as they returned to the carriage, "see if we can find Bates."

"All right." Violet settled her skirts around her as the conveyance lurched into motion. "In the meantime, there is a favor I would ask."

One of his winged black eyebrows went up. "Do I dare ask what it is?"

Violet just smiled. "The man Mr. Whistler mentioned… Simon Pratt?"

"What about him?" His voice still rang with a hint of disapproval that she had gone there without him.

"There's a child who lives with him. His name is Billy Robin, a little boy about seven years old. I think there are other young children in the house, as well."

"Go on."

"You heard what Mr. Whistler said. Danny lost two fingers working for Pratt. Little Billy was home because his hands were burned so badly he couldn't work. He was waiting for them to heal." She reached over and touched Rule's arm. "We have to do something, Rule. It's against the law to use children as sweeps. We can't just ignore what that man is doing."

In the glow of the carriage lamp, she caught his nod. "I'll speak to Royal. See if he knows someone who might intervene on their behalf. But they are likely orphans, Violet. They might end up worse off than they are working for Pratt."

"But surely you know a place where they might find shelter, a place where they could find care."

Rule seemed to ponder the notion. "Now that I think on it, I do. Annabelle Greer sponsors a home for orphans. I'll speak to her, see if there might be something she can do to help little Billy and the others."

"Oh, Rule, that would be marvelous! And we are going to find Danny. Once we do, we'll know more about what happened that day at the hotel."

"Let us hope so."

"We'll find the answers we need to prove your innocence," she assured him, and a look came into his eyes she had never seen before.

The next thing she knew, he was leaning across the velvet seat, capturing her lips and kissing her fiercely. Lifting her up, he cradled her in his lap and continued to kiss her.

"I need you," he said, and her heart went out to him. She knew he was worried. He was suspected of murder. He needed to forget for a while and she wanted to give him the chance.

Easing her down on the seat, he made love to her there in the carriage. In the soft glow of the shiny brass lamps, every jolt and sway of the coach heightened the incredible sensations.

"Sweet God," Rule groaned, fighting for control.

The instant she reached her peak, so did he, driving into her until she cried out and shattered a second time. Against her hand, she felt the solid beat of his heart.

Easing himself off her, he reached down and smoothed a strand of her heavy copper hair. "I don't understand it. I can't seem to get enough of you."

Violet's heart took a leap at his words.

A thread of worry followed. There were so many problems ahead of them. Uncertainty about her marriage. The children who needed their help. And the not-so-small matter of solving a murder.

As she straightened her garments, Violet prayed she would find a way through the maze of troubles that lay ahead.

Jeffrey stood in front of the hearth in his suite at the Parkland Hotel, sipping a glass of fine Tennessee whiskey. Seated in a chair across from him, J. P. Montgomery finished reading the article on the front page of the *London Times* and set the paper on the table beside his own whiskey glass.

"Well, it looks like Charles Whitney is out of the running," he drawled.

Jeffrey flicked a glance at the paper he had read before Montgomery arrived. "That it does."

"Bad business…shot like that right there in his hotel room."

"Yes, it is. Apparently the police think they may know who killed him. They are examining the evidence and hoping to make an arrest very soon."

Montgomery studied him over the rim of his glass. "I wonder who did the poor bastard in. Not that I can truly say I'm sorry. With Whitney out of the way, Dewar will have to find another buyer."

Jeffrey took a sip of his drink. "Perhaps he'll take our offer this time."

"Could be. Might be better to find someone else to make the offer. Someone local, maybe. Pretty clear Dewar's sympathies lie with our opponents to the north, though neither he nor his missus ever came right out and said so."

"Having someone else involved might be a good idea." Jeffrey knew Montgomery was right, at least about Violet, though they had rarely discussed the slavery issue. Once or twice she had voiced her opinion, but he had never doubted that after they were married, she would come around to his way of thinking.

He sipped his drink, savoring the taste and the burn. "Whatever we do, we need to take our time. We move too fast, it might put them off."

Montgomery nodded. "Maybe we can find us a partner over here, someone to buy the company and keep our involvement a secret."

"There's a lot of money to be made. Might take us a little time."

"Maybe not. Meanwhile, maybe they'll find out who killed Whitney." Montgomery sipped his drink. "Could work to our advantage."

Jeffrey made no reply.

Whatever happened, they still intended to buy the company. And now that Whitney was dead, things had definitely turned in their favor.

Rule planned to arrive at the White Bull before noon, hoping it might be a good time to catch Benny Bates at the tavern.

"I'm going with you," Violet said as she walked into the study.

Knowing the sort of place it would be, Rule shook his head. "Not this time, sweetheart, but I promise I'll return straightaway with whatever news I discover."

Her pretty green eyes flashed. "We were going to do this together. Take me with you and I'll wait outside in the carriage. If you uncover another clue, I'll be there to help you pursue it."

He knew he shouldn't do it. It was dangerous to get her involved, but it was the middle of the day and the notion of her company pleased him.

He released an exasperated sigh. "Why is it you always seem to get your way?"

Violet grinned. "Because I'm a woman. I shall change and be back in a jiff."

A jiff. She was picking up more and more British slang. Soon she would be talking more like an English lady than an upper-class American.

"Wear something plain," he called after her as she raced up the stairs. "We don't want to draw attention."

And to that end, he had dressed in plain brown trousers, a full-sleeved shirt and a pair of scuffed riding boots. He planned to park the carriage somewhere Bates wouldn't see it, and he didn't intend to be in the area very long.

In a simple gray wool gown, Violet returned faster than he had imagined she would, and they set off for St. Giles. The White Bull took up the bottom floor of a building on the corner, the front painted black with bold white letters announcing its name.

Bellows parked the carriage a block away and Rule descended the narrow iron stairs. He looked up at his coachman. "Make sure she doesn't get into any trouble, will you, Bellows?"

Violet cast Rule an indignant glance through the window, but the burly coachman just grinned. "Aye, milord."

The interior of the tavern was nearly as black as the paint on the walls outside, though once Rule's eyes adjusted to the flickering lamplight, he could see well enough. He strode over to the tavern keep, a fat man wearing a stained white apron, sat down on a wooden stool in front of the bar and ordered a tankard of ale.

For several minutes, he sipped his ale and surveyed his surroundings—the smoky interior, the group of men laughing in the corner, the dark-haired tavern maid serving the customers drinks. As she sashayed past, he caught her arm and pressed a coin into her palm.

"If you have a minute, I wonder if you might help me."

She eyed him up and down and smiled, and he saw that she was young and fairly pretty.

"I'll be happy to help ye, handsome." She rested a slim-fingered hand over his thigh. "What can I do for ye, luv?"

Rule eased her hand away. "I'm looking for a man named Benny Bates. They say he comes in here. Do you know him?"

"Aye, I know Benny—penny-pinchin' blighter that he is." She glanced over her shoulder and Rule followed her gaze to the men in the corner.

"One of those men Bates?"

She jerked a nod. "Short one with the bald head. That's Benny. He does business in here. I'll tell him yer lookin' for him if ye like."

"Actually, I'm looking for a boy named Danny Tuttle. I heard Danny works for him."

The girl's expression changed to suspicion. "What ye want with Danny?"

Rule pulled out a small pouch of coins and set them on the bar in front of her. "Just a few minutes of his time." He shoved the pouch in her direction. "I'd be happy to pay you for making the introduction."

The girl tugged at the front of her low-cut blouse. "You don't look like a copper."

"That's because I'm not."

"Ye'll pay Danny, too?"

"I will."

The tavern maid turned away from him and walked behind the bar. Pulling open a door leading into the rear of the tavern, she disappeared inside the back room. A few minutes later, she returned.

"One of the lads went to fetch him. Bates don't like anyone interfering in his business so Danny'll meet ye out front." She picked up the pouch of coins on the bar.

"If he doesn't show up, I'll be back for my money."

"Danny's the sort to keep his word. He'll be there." The girl returned to her duties as Rule paid for the ale and made his way back out the front door.

The boy was waiting, tall for his age and far too skinny, with tangled brown hair and worn clothes a little too small for his growing size. The minute he spotted Rule, he recognized him and started to run.

"Damnation!" Rule bolted after him, caught him before he reached the end of the block, spun him around and pinned him against the wall. "I'm not going to hurt you. I just want you to answer a couple of questions."

Danny struggled, but he was slightly built and Rule held him easily. "I just want answers, Danny. I'll pay you well for them."

The boy remained stiff with tension, but interest crept into his dark eyes.

"You know who I am, don't you? That's the reason you ran. You delivered a message to my house and then followed me to the Albert Hotel. All I want to know is who paid you to do it."

Danny's bony shoulders tightened. "I don't know nothin'."

"Unless you were in on the murder, this has nothing to do with you. I just need some answers."

Danny's eyes bulged. "Murder? What murder? You think I did murder?"

Rule shook his head. By the stunned look on his face, it was clear the boy knew nothing of the crime.

"Actually, the police think I'm the man who did it. I'm trying to prove I'm not. Now tell me who gave you the note."

Danny nervously chewed his lip. "I…umm… I don't know 'is name. I was runnin' an errand over by the 'otel. Some jackanapes said 'e'd pay me to deliver a message, so I took the job."

"So you delivered the note and then you waited in front of my house. Once you saw me leave, you ran back to the man and told him I was on my way to the hotel. Is that about right?"

Danny nodded. "'E said 'e needed to know if you was coming. After I said you was, 'e paid me and I left." The boy glanced nervously over his shoulder. "Don't tell Bates. 'E'll whup me good just for talkin' to you."

Rule relaxed his grip on the boy's shabby coat. "I'm not telling Bates anything."

Danny darted another furtive glance toward the door but held his ground. "You said you'd pay me."

Rule pulled a gold sovereign out of his pocket and flashed it in the sunlight. The boy's brown eyes widened.

"Tell me what the man looked like."

Danny glanced down at his worn-out shoes, then his gaze snapped back to the coin. "Nothin' special. Not so tall as you, brown hair parted in the middle."

"A gentleman?"

"Nah, just an average-lookin' bloke."

"Any scars, anything that could help us identify him?"

Danny wet his lips.

"They'll hang me, Danny."

The boy blew out a breath. "All right. I noticed 'e had a scar, a thin line what ran from 'is ear along 'is neck down into 'is collar."

Rule made a mental note of that. "Did you see this man go inside the hotel?"

Danny shook his head. "Like I said, I just took me money and run." He stared at the door of the White Bull. "I gotta go. Bates'll be lookin' for me."

"What sort of work do you do for Bates?"

Danny swallowed and glanced away. "I do what 'e tells me. I don't, I don't eat."

Rule could see by the lad's uneasy expression that some of what Bates paid him to do was likely illegal. Sooner or later, Danny would wind up in prison—or worse.

A few weeks ago, concern for the boy wouldn't have entered his mind. Now he couldn't help looking at Danny through Violet's eyes and knowing she would want to help him.

"How would you like a real job, Danny?"

He stared at the sovereign Rule turned over in his fingers. A glimmer of hope sparked in his eyes, then slowly faded. Danny held up his hand, showing the stumps of his two fingers. "These is gone."

"That doesn't make any difference. You get yourself to Tooley Street, on the other side of the river. You'll see a big tower. That's Griffin Manufacturing. My name's Dewar and I own the company. Come tomorrow morning and I'll see you get a job."

Danny's gaunt face broke into a smile so wide something tightened in Rule's chest.

"I'll be there, sir." He started toward the door, so excited he forgot about the money.

"Danny!" Rule flipped the coin into the air, the gold shining as it tumbled end over end toward the boy. Danny caught it easily, stuck it into his pocket, waved and disappeared through the tavern door.

Rule sighed as he started back to the carriage. Danny's information hadn't really helped. Perhaps the man who had paid him to deliver the note had worked for Charles Whitney and Rule's arrival at the hotel at that precise moment had simply been a coincidence.

Rule didn't believe it.

Twenty-Two

Through the open carriage window, Violet watched Rule striding back to the carriage. She had witnessed his brief confrontation with the tall, gangly youth, but it seemed to end without any further trouble.

Rule climbed into the carriage and lounged back against the seat. "Danny didn't know the man. According to his description, the fellow wasn't dressed well enough to have been Whitney himself. As I think on it, Whitney would probably have used someone who worked in the hotel to deliver the message."

"Then you think the man who hired him was the killer?"

"I don't know. He could have been working for someone else."

"But who?"

"That, love, is the question." Rule relayed the rest of his conversation with Danny, including the description of the man with the scar, and Violet was pleased to know Rule had offered him a job.

"The tavern maid said he was the sort who kept his word and she was clearly protective of him. I got the impression it bothered Danny to work for a man like Bates."

Violet smiled at him. "You did a good thing."

"I suppose that remains to be seen."

The carriage rumbled on down the street and when they arrived back home, a note from Chase Morgan was waiting. The investigator wanted to stop by the house that afternoon. Rule sent a footman to confirm the meeting and Morgan arrived at precisely four o'clock.

"I didn't expect to hear from you so quickly," Rule said as Morgan followed him and Violet into the study and they all took a seat.

"After we spoke the last time, I went directly to the hotel. I wanted to see what I might find before the cleaning people came in to put Whitney's room in order."

"And?" Rule asked.

"I didn't find anything useful inside the room. The door was slightly ajar when you got there, so we can figure the murderer probably left it that way. He could have climbed over the railing onto the balcony, but I don't think he did."

Rule frowned. "Really? I assumed that was the way he got in."

"That's what the police believe, as well. By the way, they've ruled out burglary as a motive. Whitney had money in his purse and nothing seemed to be missing from his suite."

"Somehow I never really believed that was it."

"And I spoke to Whitney's valet. He works mornings and evenings. Whitney preferred having the suite to himself in the middle of the day."

"Someone must have kept track of the valet's comings and goings," Rule said.

"I'd say so. When I went to the hotel, I noticed the servants' stairs are located just down the hall from Whitney's room. If you will recall, it rained the night before the murder. I found a set of muddy boot prints leading up the stairs from outside. The imprints lessened as the man walked down the hall, but traces of mud led straight to Whitney's door."

"Good grief," Violet said, "if the killer went in through the door, Mr. Whitney must have let him in. He must have known the man."

"That's one explanation," Morgan said.

"What's another?" Rule asked.

"The killer may have had a key."

Violet and Rule exchanged glances. "The chambermaids would have keys to the rooms," Rule said.

"The killer could have paid one of them for the use of it, or he could have stolen it."

"There were no signs of a struggle," Rule said.

"I think Whitney must have been asleep. The killer walked in, picked up the pillow and shot him through the heart."

Violet suppressed a shiver. "Dear God."

"We need to speak to the hotel manager," Rule said, "see if any keys have been reported missing."

"I'm headed there from here," Morgan said. "Since you were close by, I thought I'd stop and give you a report, see if you'd thought of anything else."

"Actually, we did come up with something." Rule told Morgan about finding Danny and the boy's description of the man with the narrow scar who had paid him to deliver the note. "It wasn't Whitney, but it could have been someone who worked for him."

"Or it could have been the killer," Morgan added. "Anything else?"

"Not so far."

"All right, then, I'll keep you informed." Morgan rose

from his chair and left the study, and Rule walked over and sat down on the sofa next to Violet.

"There are just so many possibilities," she said at his worried expression.

"Unfortunately, there are. And the most logical explanations all point directly to me."

She reached over and took hold of his hand. "We are only just beginning. In time, we'll figure this out."

"*Time*. I'm not sure how much of that we have."

The following afternoon Caroline and Luke arrived at the town house. While Violet took her cousin into the drawing room, Rule led Luke down the hall to his study.

"So how did you hear?" Rule asked as he poured Luke a brandy and one for himself, and they sat down on the deep leather sofa and chair in front of the hearth.

"Royal told Lily, who told her cousin Jocelyn, who told my brother, Chris, who told me."

"Damnation. A man can't have the least amount of privacy in this family."

"It wasn't a secret, Rule. You were taken to police headquarters. The Duke of Bransford arrived to gain your release. Word spread like wildfire after that."

Rule sighed. "Yes, I suppose it would."

"I knew Whitney. He was an honest, forthright man. Who would want to kill him?"

"I wish I knew."

"Maybe it was just a simple robbery that went awry."

"It wasn't a robbery. The police said nothing was stolen."

"Then what was the killer's motive?"

"I've been asking myself that question since the moment I found Whitney dead. Perhaps he had enemies, someone who killed him for personal reasons, I don't know."

"That could be. But if your arriving in that hotel room at that exact time wasn't purely coincidence, then someone wanted you to take the blame."

"That's what I keep thinking."

"And if you're arrested and found guilty, there's a good chance you could hang. Charles Whitney was a powerful man. Being the brother of a duke won't save you."

"I know."

"So who would benefit by getting both you and Whitney out of the way?"

Rule took a sip of his brandy, looking at the question from a slightly different angle than he had before. "I suppose one of the men who wanted to buy the company would be glad to see Whitney gone. We had two other offers. With Whitney dead, we'll be looking for a buyer again."

"Who made the offers?"

"One came from Burton Stanfield, the other from an American named J. P. Montgomery."

"If you were to hang, Violet would become sole owner. You refused their offers. Maybe they think they'd stand a better chance getting a woman to sell them the company."

Rule scoffed. "They might think so. If they do, they don't know my wife." Rule flicked a sideways glance at Luke. "Speaking of wives, how are things going with you and Caroline?"

Luke looked away, his face closing up. "She seems happy enough."

"And you?"

His gaze swung back to Rule. "To my amazement, I discover I like being married. I never thought I would say that, but I do. I just wish…"

"You wish what?"

"I wish I knew how Caroline felt about me." He straightened in his chair. "I'm crazy about her, Rule. God help me, I think I might even be in love with her."

"For God's sake, don't tell her that. Women castrate the men who fall in love with them. You can't afford to give your wife that kind of power over you."

"So you aren't in love with Violet?"

Rule firmly shook his head. "I won't let that happen. I care for her a very great deal and I think she cares for me. Whether or not we love each other isn't important. We enjoy each other. That is more than most married couples can claim."

Luke just shook his head. "I don't know… I feel like I want more. I feel as if something is missing."

Rule said nothing. He was happy the way things were. He didn't want to risk any deeper feelings for Violet or any other woman. "Be glad for what you have, Luke. Just relax and enjoy yourself."

"That is what you're doing? Enjoying yourself?"

"Of course. What's wrong with that?"

"And if you grow tired of Violet?"

Rule shrugged his shoulders. "I'll do what other men do, I suppose."

Luke made no reply. Leaning back in his chair, he took a sip of his drink. "All this talk of women and marriage has made me think of a suspect you might have forgotten."

"And who might that be?"

"Jeffrey Burnett. You said he was in love with Violet. With you out of the way, he might believe he'd have a chance of winning her back."

"Why would he choose Whitney? He doesn't even know the man."

Luke shrugged. "It was just a thought."

Rule couldn't deny Burnett would like nothing more

than to be rid of him. But Jeffery had no connection to Whitney and no motive for wanting him dead.

"I think it's time we joined the ladies," Rule said, rising from his place on the sofa. "What do you say?"

Luke nodded and stood up from his chair. "I wish I knew what Caroline was in there saying to Violet."

Rule slapped him on the back. "My friend, don't even try to guess."

"So, you are happy?" Violet asked, taking a sip of tea.

"Very happy. If I had to pick someone to marry, I couldn't have done better than Luke."

Violet studied her closely. "*If you had to...?* I assume that means you would still prefer to be unfettered, as you were before."

Caroline shrugged her shoulders, moving the puffed sleeves of her crisp peach silk gown. "I wasn't ready for marriage. You know that."

"Not even to Luke?"

For an instant, Caroline glanced away. She took a sip of her tea. "I've seen what happens to marriages, Vi. My parents came to hate each other. As long as I keep things the way they are, I am safe."

"So you're afraid to fall in love with Luke."

Caroline's chin went up. "I'm not afraid of anything. I'm just... I'm happy with the way things are."

"I see...."

"Do you? You're in love with Rule. If things go wrong, you are going to be badly hurt. I don't want to risk that kind of pain."

Violet didn't argue. In a way, Caroline was right. As long as she kept her emotions in check, she was safe. Unfortunately for Violet, it was already too late. She was deeply in love with Rule and if something went wrong, she would be devastated.

"At the moment," she said, "the thing I am most concerned about is proving his innocence."

"That is the reason we came. Is there anything we can do to help?"

Violet set her cup and saucer down on the table. "Just keep your eyes and ears open. If you or Luke learn anything that might aid Rule's case, please let us know."

"You know we will."

The doors slid open just then and the men appeared in the opening. Violet ignored the funny little curl in her stomach that seeing Rule always stirred. Luke was smiling warmly at Caroline and a slight flush rose in her cheeks.

Her cousin might pretend to be immune to her husband, but Violet wasn't so sure.

Inwardly she sighed. She ached to be loved. Caroline feared it.

Violet wondered what the future held in store for the two of them.

It was three days later that a gathering of the Oarsmen was called. Rule met Royal and his friends in a small meeting room at White's.

Royal stood in front of the paned window staring out at the street when Rule walked into the room a few minutes early. His brother turned at the sound of footsteps on the thick Persian carpet.

"I am happy to see you look none the worse for wear. How are you holding up?"

Rule sighed. "All right, I guess. I haven't heard anything more from the police. I'm hoping that is good."

Royal strode toward him. "The others should be here

any minute. Quent's out of town. Only Savage, Night and Sherry are in London, but they've all been nosing around."

"Anything they uncover might be useful."

The brothers made their way over to a polished mahogany table lined with eight matching high-backed chairs upholstered in dark green silk. Gilded gas sconces lined one wall and a chandelier hung from the ceiling.

Royal sat down at the head of the table and Rule took the chair to his left. To Rule's surprise, the first person to arrive was Reese.

"I thought you were at Briarwood," Rule said, smiling at the brother who, with his thick black hair and blue eyes, looked the most like him. He shouldn't have been surprised to see him. The trio stood by each other no matter the circumstance. They were family. That was what mattered.

"I couldn't just sit home while my little brother was being accused of murder," Reese said darkly, taking a seat across from him.

"I haven't been formally charged."

"No, but from what I hear, there's a good chance you will be."

"What have you heard?"

"I stopped by the police station and spoke to Constable McGregor. They know the pistol that killed Whitney was made by Griffin. They say they are pursuing other information."

Rule swore softly. "The maker's mark was on the weapon. I knew it wouldn't take long for them to realize Violet and I own the company. I just hoped they wouldn't figure it out so soon."

"I hear Morgan's on the case," Reese said.

"Yes, and working hard to find the murderer. Yesterday he sent word that one of the chambermaids had quit her job at the Albert the day before the crime. The key to room 112 was not among those she turned in when she left. Morgan believes there's a good chance the killer or someone in his employ paid her handsomely for the key and warned her to leave London. Morgan's trying to find out where she went."

"Anyone in the hotel see anything that day?" Reese asked. "Maybe someone leaving or going into Whitney's room?"

"Not that Morgan has discovered. He thinks the killer came up the back stairs, used the key to get into Whitney's room, murdered him while he was sleeping, then left the way he came in."

Rule looked up as the door opened and tall, dark Jonathan Savage, the black sheep of the group, walked into the meeting room, followed by lanky Sheridan Knowles. Benjamin Wyndam, Earl of Nightingale, arrived, a ruby ring flashing on his right hand.

"Thank you all for coming," Royal said as his friends sat down at the table.

"One never knows when he might be in need of a little help himself," Night said, his reasoning sound as always.

"Just so you all know," Rule said, "I didn't kill Charles Whitney. I went to the Albert in response to a note I received. At the time I believed Whitney had sent it. So far I haven't been able to confirm that one way or another."

"We never believed you killed him," Sherry said, steepling his fingers and looking at Rule down his aristocratic nose. "In fact, we've been digging around, trying to find out who might have had cause to want Whitney dead."

"Tell me you came up with something."

Lounging back in his chair, Savage answered first. "A man named Peter Austin made threats against him. Whitney and Austin were partners in a steamship endeavor that ended badly."

And Savage would know about that, Rule thought, since he had made his fortune in the shipbuilding trade.

"There were problems right from the start," Jonathan continued. "Seams failed in the hull and some of the panels caved in, crushing one of the workers. A crane dropped its load, killing several of the men working below. Things got so bad no one would work on the bloody ship. They said Austin was using inferior goods and the *Aurora* was cursed."

"I think I read something about that in the *Times,*" Sherry said, interest glinting in his bright green eyes.

"Several articles were written about it," Savage added. "Whitney cancelled the project before the ship was ever completed. He said he wouldn't be responsible for any more loss of life. Austin was furious. He called Whitney a superstitious fool. Said he'd make him pay for all he'd lost—one way or another."

"Interesting," Royal said.

"I'll talk to Morgan," said Rule. "See if he can find out where Austin was at the time of the murder or if he wanted Whitney dead badly enough to hire someone to kill him."

"I don't think Whitney deserves any of the blame for what happened with that ship," Night said. "From what I could discover, Charles Whitney was well respected in the business community. I would be inclined to believe Austin did use inferior goods in the construction."

"I'll grant you Whitney was successful and respected," Sherry agreed. "But his personal life was a little more complicated."

"How is that?" Rule asked.

"It seems Charles and his brother, Martin, had a fairly recent falling out. Charles was a widower. Martin was married, but a bit of a rounder. Rumor has it, he and Charles were competing for the affections of the same woman."

"Who was she?" Rule asked.

"The Countess of Fremont."

"Fremont?" Rule's interest sharpened. "I know the countess. I can't say I'm surprised. She seems to be on the prowl."

"When the countess ignored Martin's advances in favor of Charles's," Sherry added, "Martin completely cut off any communication with his brother. But Martin never stopped his pursuit of Lady Fremont."

"So you think Martin might have murdered his brother in a fit of jealousy?"

"Or perhaps in the hope that with Charles out of the way, Lady Fremont would return his advances."

"I saw her taking to Martin a few weeks back," Royal said. "From what I could tell, the man was definitely smitten."

Sherry's mouth faintly curved. "Juliana Markham is one of the most beautiful women in London. Half the men in the city are in love with her."

"And apparently Martin Whitney was one of them," Rule finished. "I appreciate your bringing it to my attention."

"Anything more from anyone?" Royal asked.

"Not at the moment," Night said.

"We'll keep digging," Savage promised.

Rule surveyed the group of Royal's friends who had become his friends, as well. "Thank you all. You have no idea how much I appreciate your help."

The men just nodded and began to rise from their chairs. Reese remained a few minutes after the others had left.

"Elizabeth and I are staying at Holiday House until this is resolved. If you need anything, just let us know. And keep us informed, will you?"

"Of course."

Rule left the club along with his two brothers. Armed

with several new possibilities, he was eager to get home and share them with his wife.

Whitney was a good man, but he had enemies.

Rule wondered if any of them were angry enough to do murder.

Twenty-Three

Violet heard Rule as he walked into the entry. Anxious to discover how the meeting had gone with Royal and his friends, she hurried down the hall to greet him. Rule surprised her by sweeping her into his arms and capturing her lips in a very thorough kiss.

She was weak in the knees and a little short of breath by the time he let her go. "The news was that good?"

He just smiled. "Not really. You just looked so delectable I couldn't resist."

Warmth crept into her cheeks. She thought that she did look good in an apricot silk gown trimmed with lace that set off the copper hue of her hair. Taking her hand, he led her into the drawing room and drew her down beside him on the sofa.

"So what did the men have to say?"

"They found out Whitney had enemies, two in particular, and both of them had reason to want him dead."

Rule went on to tell her about Peter Austin and his disastrous partnership with Whitney, and the threats Austin had made. He also told her that Sheridan had learned Charles had a falling out with his brother over a woman.

"As I think on it," Violet said, "for a man in his early fifties, Charles was an extremely attractive man."

"He was also a widower and wealthy in the extreme."

"So you think his brother was jealous enough of this woman to kill him?"

"I don't know, but that sort of thing has certainly happened before. I plan to speak to the brother and also to Lady Fremont."

Violet's heart jerked. "L-lady Fremont was the woman?"

"That's what Sherry said. I'll know more after I talk to her."

Something tightened in Violet's chest. "You and the countess... The two of you are close enough friends that you believe she will confide in you?"

Faint color rose beneath the strong bones in his cheeks. "We are acquainted. She knew Griffin was for sale and that we planned to acquire new businesses. She told me she planned to sell some of the companies her late husband owned. She thought we might be interested."

"We or *you,* Rule?"

His winged black eyebrows drew slightly together. "What are you saying?"

"I'm not saying anything. You want to talk to her, go ahead. I'm sure she'll be delighted to see you."

His well-formed lips flattened out. "This is my life we are talking about. I need to follow every lead."

"Yes, and it should be interesting to see where this one takes you." Rising from the sofa, she swept out of the drawing room, leaving him staring after her.

Her heart trembled. Had she been right all along? How well did Rule know the beautiful countess? And was this simply an excuse for another rendezvous with the luscious brunette?

Violet had no way of knowing.

She only knew her heart was aching, telling her this was only a sample of how terrible she would feel if Rule wound up in another woman's bed.

After their heated conversation in the drawing room, no more was said about Lady Fremont. In a way, Violet regretted her outburst. Rule was fighting to prove himself innocent of murder. If there was a chance the countess had information, Rule had no choice but to seek her out.

Still, as the evening came to a close, she wasn't certain what she would do if he came to her bed.

She found out soon enough. Her heart lurched when his brisk knock sounded at her door.

She could read his troubled expression, the need for her that always seemed to be there in his beautiful eyes as he stood there in the opening.

"Do you deny me?" he asked, poised at the threshold in his dark blue silk dressing gown.

Her gaze lit on the expanse of chest exposed in the *V* of the robe, the curly black hair, the bands of muscle across his smooth, dark skin. Her body wanted him and her heart could not deny him.

"No…"

Relief drained the tension from his face, and whatever thoughts remained she could not decipher. His strides were long and purposeful as he moved to the bed, bent and kissed her. Shedding his robe, he climbed onto the mattress and she saw that he was fiercely aroused.

As always, their lovemaking was wildly passionate, but this time there was some small part of her that Violet held back. She loved Rule, but she had never really trusted him to be faithful. Knowing he intended to meet with Lady Fremont was enough to put her on guard.

Still, as he cuddled her against his side and they drifted off to sleep, she realized she had come to a decision. At the moment, proving Rule's innocence was all that mattered. She would deal with the rest after the murder investigation was over and Rule was no longer under suspicion.

Rule returned to work at the office. Tomorrow Violet intended to join him. Her wish to sell the business had not changed, nor had her determination not to sell to Montgomery or Burton Stanfield.

Sooner or later, another suitable buyer would appear. In the meantime, they had a company to run and they meant to see it done.

Today there was a call she wished to make. As promised, Rule had spoken to Annabelle Greer in regard to little Billy Robin and the children Simon Pratt was illegally using as chimney sweeps.

Anna had agreed to help them. She was highly respected for her charity work and the mayor himself agreed to lend his support. Yesterday the authorities had intervened and removed the children from Pratt's run-down residence. They were taken to the Blue Haven Orphanage that Annabelle sponsored.

Violet was excited at the prospect of meeting the children and seeing little Billy again. By the time the carriage rolled up in front of the large, two-story brick dwelling that sat on a pleasant street not far from Green Park, she perched anxiously on the seat.

These last few April days were warm and the front door stood open. As Violet departed the coach with the help of a footman, several young faces pressed against the screen, peering out to watch the visitor's arrival. Violet recognized the little red-haired boy inside.

"Hello, Billy." Smiling, she bent down to make herself more his size and spoke through the screen. "I'm Mrs. Dewar. Do you remember me?"

The little boy nodded. "Aye. You came to Mr. Pratt's house lookin' fer Danny."

"That's right."

A broad-hipped, matronly woman with gray-streaked brown hair arrived just then and pushed open the door.

"Do come in, my lady. I'm Eleanor Oldfield. Lady Anna sent word you would be coming by to see the children some time this morning."

Violet stepped out of the brilliant sunlight into the house. As her eyes adjusted, she saw Billy surrounded by five other children near his same age, two girls and three boys.

"Are these the other children who worked for Simon Pratt?"

"Why, yes, my lady." Mrs. Oldfield smiled. "I swear, I have never seen a hungrier brood than this lot."

Mrs. Oldfield said the words with obvious affection and Violet caught the aroma of a rich beef stew coming from the kitchen.

"There's fresh bread in the oven, as well," the woman said. "We'll be eating the noon meal shortly. You are more than welcome to join us."

"Thank you, but no. I just wanted to stop by and see how the girls and boys were faring."

She looked down at the top of Billy's head, reached out and stroked his thick red hair, now shiny and clean. "Do you like it here, Billy?"

He grinned up at her, exposing a missing tooth. "We

gets lots to eat and nobody hits us. And we don't has to sweep chimneys no more."

Her heart squeezed. "That's right, you don't, and you won't ever have to do it again."

She continued talking to Billy and the other children until Mrs. Oldfield called the group in to luncheon. Promising to return, Violet waved to the boys and girls and started down the path to her carriage. She had almost reached it when a man appeared on the sidewalk in front of her.

"'Twas you, weren't it!" He loomed over her, a wiry, long-muscled man with a sallow face and dark brown hair that needed washing and stuck out in places. "Yer the one what stole me sweeps!"

Violet set her jaw. "It's illegal to use children that young and you know it."

He made a rude sound in his throat. "Ye caused me a parcel of trouble and I ain't one to forget. Ye'll pay for this, ye uppity li'l baggage. Or me name ain't Simon Pratt."

Violet ignored the faint chill that ran down her spine. "I'd advise you to leave here this minute, Mr. Pratt. Before I send for the authorities."

One side of his mouth curled. "I kin find meself other sweeps—the city's full of the scrawny little vermin. But nobody steals from Simon Pratt and gets away with it—nobody! Ye remember what I said."

At the murderous look on Pratt's ugly face, Violet shivered.

The coachman's deep familiar voice came from behind her. "I'd advise ye to do what the lady says," Mr. Bellows told him. "Ye don't, ye'll deal with me."

Pratt sneered, but he was smart enough to realize he wouldn't win against a man with arms the size of a stout tree limb.

"I'll be seein' ye," Pratt said grimly and sauntered off as if he owned the street.

"Oh, he is a nasty man," Violet said.

"Aye, that 'e is." Bellows' gaze followed the sweep until he disappeared around the corner. "We'd best be leavin', milady. Ye never know about a man like that."

And so she climbed aboard the carriage and they left the orphanage. Violet considered telling Rule about the incident, but with murder charges hanging over his head, he already had too much on his mind.

Certain today's encounter would be the last she heard from Simon Pratt, she rode in silence back to the town house.

The afternoon waned as Rule sat behind the desk in his office at Griffin. He was finishing up some paperwork so he could leave early to stop by and see Chase Morgan.

He looked up when his secretary's familiar knock came at the door. "What is it, Terry?"

"A boy, my lord. He says his name is Danny Tuttle. Says you promised him a job."

Rule stood up from behind his desk as the skinny youth walked in, a tattered felt hat in his hand.

"So you decided to come after all. I'm a little surprised to see you. You were supposed to be here days ago." For the first time, Rule noticed the purple bruise beneath the boy's eye and a dark smudge on his cheek. "What happened to your face?"

Danny glanced away. "'Twas Bates. 'E said 'e needed me. Said people what worked for 'im didn't leave." Unconsciously he reached up and brushed his cheek. "I finally got away."

Rule rounded the desk. "I'm sorry that happened, Danny."

Worry lined the young boy's face. "Do I still get the

job?" Rule knew if Griffin didn't hire him, he'd have no place to go, no way to take care of himself.

"The job is yours, just as I said."

Relief washed over Danny's thin face. "Thank you, sir. I appreciate this chance. What'll I be doin'?"

"I'm afraid you'll be sweeping again."

The lad's face fell.

"Not chimneys, son. You'll be working with the maintenance crew, sweeping floors and keeping the plant in order. Do a good job, you can work your way up through the ranks of the company."

Relief and hope shone in Danny's dark eyes. "Thank you, sir."

"There's a room upstairs we don't use. You can sleep there until you earn enough to get a place of your own."

Danny twisted the hat in his hands. "I'll do a good job, sir. I promise you won't be sorry."

Rule just nodded. "My secretary will show you where to go. Terry?"

The young blond man appeared in the doorway. "Sir?"

"This is Danny Tuttle. I want you to help him get settled."

"Yes, my lord."

Danny flashed him a last grateful smile and disappeared behind Terry.

Pleased that he had given the boy a chance to better himself, Rule returned to the paperwork on his desk. Tomorrow Violet would be returning to her office down the hall, taking over the duties she had been handling before. Rule hadn't realized how much he had come to depend on her help. Now that she would be back, he could hardly wait for her return.

He glanced at the clock on the wall. Time to leave for his meeting with Morgan. He needed to tell the investigator what he had learned about the enemies Charles Whitney had made.

Half an hour later at the investigator's office in Thread-needle Street, Rule filled Morgan in on the animosity between Charles Whitney and Peter Austin and also the problem between the Whitney brothers over the affections of Lady Fremont.

"I'll find out what I can about Austin," Morgan said, "see if he has an alibi for the afternoon of the murder or if there is anything about him that seems suspicious."

Rule nodded. "I'll speak to Lady Fremont. We're already acquainted. I think I may be able to get her to confide in me about her relationship with the brothers."

"All right. But keep it as quiet as you can. You don't want to be the focus of any extra attention."

"You're right, I don't." Nor did he wish to cause any more problems with Violet in regard to the countess. The last thing he would ever do was embarrass her by openly pursuing another woman.

And he had no desire to experience more of the awful, gut-wrenching moments like the one he had felt as he had walked into her bedroom the night of the argument. The thought of her turning him away had made him feel physically ill.

"I'm glad you stopped by," Morgan was saying, drawing him back to the present. "I've something to report, as well."

"Which is?"

"I found the chambermaid, Molly Deavers. She claims she merely lost the key to Whitney's room. She knew she would be severely reprimanded so she quit, or at least that is her tale."

"And you believe her?"

"No. When I mentioned the man with the scar on his neck, it was clear she knew who he was."

"So you think he paid her for the key."

"That's the way it looks to me."

"Do you think the scarred man is the murderer?"

Morgan leaned back in his chair. "Perhaps. Or perhaps he is merely in the murderer's employ. Either way, there's little question he's involved."

"We need to find him."

"I'm working on it." The investigator rubbed a hand over his lean, hard jaw. "So far no one seems to know who he is or where to find him."

"The scarred man may be the key. If we find him, this could all come to an end."

"It's possible. But in my experience, murder is rarely that simple."

Twenty-Four

Violet walked toward the sound of men's voices in the entry. Spotting them grouped around Hatfield, she recognized the rough-complexioned, auburn-haired policeman who had interrogated Rule at the station, and her heart began to pound.

"I told them his lordship was not at home, my lady," the butler informed her as she approached.

"Thank you, Hat. I'll speak to Constable McGregor." She turned to the policeman. "If you will please follow me."

Leading the three men into a drawing room where they would not be overheard, she waited while Hatfield closed the door.

"I'm sorry, Constable McGregor, but as our butler told you, my husband is not at home."

"When do you expect his return?"

Violet took a breath. She didn't want to lie, but neither did she want them putting Rule under arrest. "What do you want with him?"

"We need him to come down to the station and answer a few more questions."

She pasted on what she hoped looked like a smile. "Perhaps I can be of help."

"Not unless you can tell us about the argument your husband had with Charles Whitney the night before the murder."

Her stomach knotted. Rule had mentioned the incident. He was afraid if the police found out, they would use it as more evidence against him.

"I'm afraid I can't help you. I was otherwise occupied at the time."

"So you admit the two men quarreled."

"I wouldn't know."

"And you won't tell us when your husband will be returning."

"As far as I know, it could be anytime. He went to work this morning. I know he had errands to run on his way home. Perhaps if you come back tomorrow…"

A noise sounded in the hallway. She could just make out the murmur of Hatfield's voice, speaking in low, muffled tones. An instant later, the doors slid open and Rule strode into the drawing room.

"What is going on here?"

The constable drew himself up several inches. He was not a tall man, but was formidable just the same and clearly confident in his job. "As I was telling your wife, we are here to escort you down to the police station. There are a few more questions we'd like to ask."

Rule exchanged a glance with Violet. "Why don't we sit down right here and you can ask your questions now?"

The constable frowned, drawing his heavy auburn eyebrows together. Clearly this was not what he had in mind.

"I suppose that will do…for the present."

The other two policemen sat down. Violet sat next to Rule on the sofa.

Constable McGregor remained standing. "What were you and Charles Whitney arguing about the night before the murder?"

"We were discussing the final terms of the sale. His purchase of the company was about to close and there were a few details left to iron out."

"Whitney believed you wanted out of the sale altogether, isn't that right?"

"He thought that. I assured him he was wrong."

"But you *had* received a higher offer?"

"That is true, but the amount of money wasn't the only consideration. Both Violet and I wanted someone we believed would do a good job running the business. We thought Whitney would be the best man for the job."

"I see." McGregor paced back and forth in front of the sofa. "On the other hand, if you failed to meet the terms already agreed upon, Whitney could have sued you for breach of contract."

"I suppose he could have."

"But if he was dead, the contract was invalid and you would be able to accept more money."

Violet leaped to her feet. "That isn't the way it was. We wanted Mr. Whitney to buy the plant. We wanted to be certain the weapons that Griffin makes would not be sold to the American states in the South."

McGregor eyed her with speculation. "I gather you hail from Boston, my lady."

"That's right."

"You must be a very patriotic person to give up a large chunk of money in favor of your principles." He glanced over at Rule. "Perhaps your husband, being British, is less of a patriot than you."

Violet bit back a reply. The man had his mind made up. There would be no changing it until they found Whitney's killer.

"Have you looked into the possibility that someone else might have wanted Whitney dead?" Rule asked. "His business partner, Peter Austin, for one. Or perhaps his brother, Martin?"

The constable set his jaw. "We know Austin made threats, and we know Martin and Charles had an occasional disagreement. We're looking into it."

"Is there anything else you want to know?"

"Not at the moment."

McGregor motioned to his men, who rose from their seats in the drawing room. Silently they headed for the door. McGregor stopped and turned, fixing Rule with a drilling stare. "I'll be in touch."

As the men filed out of the room, Violet stood up next to Rule. Without a word, she turned and went into his arms.

Jeffrey welcomed J. P. Montgomery and a third man— older, silver-haired and dignified—into his suite at the Parkland Hotel.

"Jeffrey, this here is Marcus Wrigby," Montgomery said in his thick Southern drawl. "He's agreed to come in as a partner in the acquisition of Griffin."

Jeffrey made a slight bow. "It's a pleasure to meet you, Mr. Wrigby."

"You, as well," the older man replied in crisp, upper-class British tones that both Jeffrey and J.P. hoped would help them make the deal.

"With the war comin'," said Montgomery, "ownin' a

percentage of Griffin is going to make you rich. "That is, richer than you are already."

"I take great care in choosing my investments." Wrigby accepted the glass of whiskey Jeffrey handed him. "As you say, Griffin has tremendous potential for growth."

"Speaking of Griffin," Montgomery added, accepting a glass, as well, "have ya seen the latest *Times?*"

Jeffery glanced at the newspaper lying on the table. "I saw it."

"Looks like Dewar's a prime suspect in the murder. Police wouldn't confirm, but that's what the paper's sayin'."

And, Jeffrey thought, if Dewar was arrested and convicted of murder, he would likely be sentenced to hang. Violet would end up a widow. She would be lonely and in need of his protection. With Dewar out of the way, the two of them could be happy, the way they had been before.

"You think he did it?" Montgomery asked.

"The paper said he was the man who found the body," Jeffrey said. "His hand was covered in blood and he was leaning over the murder weapon. They think he wanted Whitney out of the way so he could accept a higher offer for the company."

"Perhaps after thinking on it," the Englishman put in, "he wished to make a larger profit by taking your offer instead."

"I suppose it's possible." But Jeffrey thought that once Dewar had made up his mind, he wouldn't have sold to a Southerner no matter how high the price.

"Make our lives easier, if it turns out he's guilty," Montgomery drawled.

If that happened, they would be dealing with Violet. She would need his comfort and friendship. She had listened to his counsel before; he believed she would do so again.

Or if things progressed as he wished, they might even take up where they had left off. They might even marry.

Jeffrey hoped so. As hard as he tried to forget the woman he had loved, Violet remained solidly in his thoughts.

"How long do you think we should wait before we approach Dewar?" Montgomery asked.

"Another week, maybe." Jeffrey took a sip of his drink. "Time enough for them to start thinking of selling again."

"Then a week from now," Wrigby said, "I shall go in with a very fine offer. With my credentials, there is no reason for them not to accept it."

"Long as you keep us out of it," J.P. drawled, "you'll do just fine."

And in the meantime, they would wait to see if Dewar was arrested. See if he was tried, convicted and hanged.

Jeffrey would quietly wait to find out what the future held in store for him.

Rule went to his club in search of a drink and a few hands of cards, anything to divert his morbid thoughts from visions of hanging. He had seen today's *Times*. The article hadn't said he was guilty of murder but the reporter's speculation certainly leaned in that direction.

Rule had no idea how the paper had discovered his involvement in Whitney's death, but after his trip to the police station and the visit from the constable at his home, he wasn't surprised.

Heading deeper into the elegant, unfettered interior of the club with its comfortable overstuffed chairs, polished mahogany tables and thick Persian carpets, he started toward the card room, then spotted Lucas Barclay lounging back in a chair off by himself, a drink in one hand, his dark eyes staring straight ahead.

Luke glanced up at Rule's approach. "I didn't expect to see you here…not after that article in the paper."

"I figured this might be the one place I could come and not be looked at like a criminal."

"I wouldn't count on it."

Rule glanced round and saw that several members had spotted him and now stood whispering among themselves. Obviously, Luke was right.

He sighed and collapsed into the chair beside his friend. "Perhaps I should just toss myself off the top of a building and save the police the trouble of hanging me."

Luke grunted and took a sip of his drink. "Perhaps I'll join you."

For the first time Rule noticed that his friend was half-foxed. "What's the matter with you?" He held up a hand. "No, don't tell me—whatever it is has something to do with your wife."

"My wife," Luke growled. "I got more attention from my mistress."

"Isn't that the reason men keep them?"

Luke whispered out a breath. "Somehow I thought with Carrie it would be different."

"Oh, really? Why is that?"

"I guess because I love her."

Rule cocked an eyebrow. "I thought we talked about that."

"We did."

"And?"

"Maybe you were right. I should have tried harder to control my feelings. Since the day we married, my wife seems determined to spend less and less time in my company." He looked up. "Except in bed, of course. There she is the veriest hoyden. The woman is nearly as insatiable as I am."

Rule chuckled. "Then stop grumbling. A man can't complain when he's getting satisfied at home."

"Is that so? What about you?"

Rule found himself smiling for the first time in days. "Violet is a passionate little creature. I have no complaints."

"Passion isn't everything."

"As far as I'm concerned, it is."

"That's all you want from Violet, then? Just the use of her body and her response to you in bed."

"I told you before, Luke. The last thing I want is to fall in love."

Luke just grunted and took another long sip of his drink.

When a waiter arrived, Rule ordered a brandy. He had come to the club to escape his troubles. Now, as he looked at the men he'd called friends and read the wariness in their expressions, he understood there was no escape.

Of a sudden, he wished he had stayed home with Violet.

"Anything new on the murder?" Luke asked. "Aside from what I read in the paper."

"Not enough."

"Something I can do to help?"

"Looks like you have enough trouble of your own, but I'll let you know if I think of anything."

Luke sipped his drink, his gaze turning morose again. Setting his glass down a little too hard on the table, he rose from his chair.

"I'm going home. Caroline might not love me but she wants me. I might as well give her what she wants."

Rule made no reply. As the waiter arrived with his drink, he set it aside and headed for the door, thinking for once, Luke had a good idea.

Luke hadn't realized quite how drunk he was until he tried to negotiate the stairs up to his bedroom. He hit the banister once before he reached the top, and even before he reached his door, began to toss off his clothes.

Half-undressed by the time he arrived at the door between their rooms, he didn't bother to knock, just turned the knob and walked in.

In the dim glow of the lamp next to the bed, his gaze shot to Caroline as if she held an invisible chain, which in a way, she did. Wearing the skimpy little French silk nightgown he had bought her, obviously anticipating his arrival, Caroline sat up in bed. "Luke…"

"You were expecting someone else?"

"Of course not." Her delicate blond eyebrows drew together. "You're drunk."

"A little. Do you really care?" He dragged his shirt off over his head, leaving his chest bare, slid his trousers down over his shoeless feet and kicked the garment away, then dragged off his small clothes.

Caroline stared at the heavy arousal riding against his belly. "Well…?" he challenged.

She moistened her lips, which made his erection leap. "No, I don't care if you're a little drunk."

As usual, she wanted satisfaction. The sad truth was, that was all she wanted from him. He strode to the bedside, caught her lovely face between his hands and captured her lips in a rough, burning kiss.

For an instant, he thought she would push him away. Then her arms slid up around his neck and she kissed him back. Luke ravished her mouth, breathing her in, taking her deeply with his tongue, then he turned his attention to her breasts.

They were round and plump, with hard little rose-colored crests he ministered to until they turned diamond hard. She was trembling when he came up over her on the bed and kissed her deeply again. She barely noticed when he eased her onto her stomach, grabbed one of the pillows and stuffed it beneath her hips.

"Luke, what are you...?"

"Just relax." She was wet and ready, he discovered as he positioned himself on his knees behind her, found the entrance to her passage and buried himself to the hilt.

Caroline moaned.

Luke set his jaw and began to move, taking her with deep, heavy strokes that had her arching her hips to accept him even more fully. She cried his name as she reached her peak, and he followed a few moments later.

On a shuddering breath, he withdrew, eased her onto her back and kissed her one last time. Then he left her alone in the bed.

She frowned as he started walking away. "Aren't you staying?"

"You got what you needed from me. From now on that's all you're going to get." Striding toward his room, he walked through the door and slammed it loudly behind him.

If Caroline didn't need his love, he didn't need hers.

Rule was right. All he needed was the use of her luscious little body and her passionate response in bed.

In time he would come to accept the loneliness he had felt before he'd met her, and his life would return to the way it was.

Twenty-Five

~~~~~~~

Time was ticking away. Rule needed to speak to the countess and the urgency of doing so was building. This morning he had sent the lady a message requesting a meeting and asking if he might stop by her house that night.

Lady Fremont had agreed.

Hoping to avoid any further arguments with Violet, he didn't mention where he was going when he left the house, just said he needed a little fresh air and that he would probably stop by his club before he returned. Though after his last visit, he wasn't so sure it was a good idea.

As his carriage rolled toward Fremont House, Rule went over the questions he wished to ask and hoped the lady would be willing to answer them. He gazed out the window as he drew near. Located on a slight rise overlooking Hyde Park, the mansion was a lavish, showy residence that looked more like a castle than a home.

Departing the coach beneath a wide portico out front, he made his way up a stone walkway to the arched, heavy wooden door. A light knock and the butler pulled it open.

"Lord Rule Dewar," he said to the butler. "The countess is expecting me."

"Yes, my lord. If you will please follow me."

The stately black-haired man led him down the hall into a magnificent drawing room. As he walked inside, Juliana Markham, Lady Fremont, rose from her spot on a blue velvet sofa, and the butler closed the tall paneled doors.

Rule strode toward her. "Lady Fremont." He bowed over her hand. "Thank you for seeing me."

She looked as beautiful as he remembered, her hair as raven as his own, her eyes a lighter, softer shade of blue.

"I've been expecting you. I heard the dreadful news that you were under suspicion for Charles's murder—not that I believe you could possibly be guilty. I presumed it wouldn't take long before you found the connection between Charles and me."

"You, Charles and Martin, was it not?"

She strolled over to the silver tray sitting on an ornate sideboard, her elegant blue silk skirts floating out around her. "Would you care for a drink? Brandy, perhaps?"

He didn't want a drink, but he wanted her cooperation and he didn't want to offend her. "Thank you, that would be nice."

She poured him a brandy, and a sherry for herself, walked over and pressed the crystal snifter into his hand. "Why don't we sit down?"

Nodding his consent, he let her lead him over to the sofa and both of them took a seat.

The countess smiled. "Now, what exactly has brought you here to see me?"

"I'll be frank, my lady. I am in need of your help."

"Please…we are friends, are we not? I would rather you call me Juliana."

He managed to smile. "All right...Juliana. As I said, I need your help. I realize my questions are of an intimate nature, but I need to know about your relationship with Charles and Martin Whitney."

One of her sleek dark eyebrows went up, but he didn't think she was truly surprised. "Very well. Charles and I, we were...friends. Close friends...even before my husband died."

"I see."

"I hope you won't judge me. My husband was nearly thirty years my senior and ill a great deal of the time. Charles was a widower, older than I, but so incredibly charming. He was the most vital man I've ever known."

"I liked him very much. And I can hardly judge you, Juliana, when I've had a number of women friends myself."

"Yes, so I've heard."

"So you and Charles were close. What about Martin?"

"I had met Martin several times over the years. But it wasn't until I came to London that he became interested in me."

"And were you also interested in him?"

"No." She delicately sipped her sherry. "Oh, I was polite to him. By then, Charles and I were ready to go our separate ways. My husband had died nearly three years earlier. Once I was out of mourning, I was finally free to explore my options. Charles was the sort of man who understood."

"But not Martin."

"Martin was an arrogant fool. I told him I wasn't interested in him in any way but he wouldn't listen. He was jealous of Charles, though I told him repeatedly it was over."

"Do you think Martin would have gone so far as to kill his brother?"

"I don't know. I don't know Martin well enough to say. As I told you, I was polite to him, mostly because of my fondness for his brother, but I had no interest in him beyond that."

Rule set his unfinished brandy down on the table and rose from the sofa. "Thank you, Juliana, for your honesty. And for your belief in my innocence."

She set her sherry glass aside and stood up, as well, so close he could smell her sweet perfume. She flattened her palms on the lapels of his coat. "I am not interested in Martin Whitney. I am extremely interested in you, Rule."

Alarm bells went off in his head. He caught her delicate wrists as she slid them up around his neck and very carefully removed them. "You are free, Juliana. I am not. Under different circumstances, I assure you I would return your interest."

Those circumstances being the woman to whom he was wed, the lady who at present had captured his wholehearted attention.

Juliana's hands fell to her sides. "Are you certain this is the way you want it?"

Oddly, as lovely as she was, he was extremely certain. "I am."

She stepped back from him and a confident smile curved her lips. "You are yet newly married. In time, perhaps things will change."

It probably would. Surely it would happen as it had with the women he had known before. A strange sense of melancholy settled over him at the thought.

"Thank you again." He made her a last polite bow.

Turning, he found his way to the door, stepped outside and inhaled a breath of the clean night air, glad the task he had set himself was over.

* * *

Leaning back in the seat of her carriage, Violet thought of the house that looked like a castle and closed her eyes against the image of Rule walking inside.

She knew she shouldn't have followed him. No self-respecting wife would lower herself to sneaking about, trying to discover what her husband was doing after he left home.

But Rule was generally forthright in his endeavors and she could tell by his actions this evening he wasn't being forthright tonight. She knew he planned to interview Lady Fremont. She had resigned herself to that. What bothered her was that he had refused to tell her he was going.

The carriage rolled toward their house in Portman Square. She had left Lady Fremont's before he had come out. She was only willing to stoop so low. If he was being intimate with the beautiful countess, she certainly couldn't stop him.

And she still held out hope.

Perhaps he would tell her the truth when he got home, explain that he hadn't wanted to upset her or whatever might have been the reason for his deceit. She prayed that he would.

Once she reached the house, she told herself she should retire upstairs to bed, but instead sat in the drawing room, a book lying open in her lap, an ear cocked toward the entry for the sound of her husband's footfalls.

When she heard his voice in the entry, relief hit her so hard she felt dizzy. He had returned earlier than she had imagined. Rule didn't do anything by half, and Violet believed that if he made love to the beautiful brunette, he wouldn't be interested in some hasty coupling, but would do so well and thoroughly.

The thought made her stomach tighten.

She looked down, tried to concentrate on the book lying open in front of her, to pretend that she was reading, but the words on the pages all ran together. She set the book aside when he spoke to her from the open drawing room door.

"Violet…I thought you would already be in bed."

She rose as he approached, so tall and handsome her insides softened. "I—I wasn't sleepy. I didn't expect you home so soon."

He smiled. "I discovered I would rather be home with my wife than playing cards with my friends."

Her heart kicked up. Perhaps he had gone to the club for a few minutes after his visit. "Did you?"

"I did." He bent his head and kissed her very softly on the lips.

"So that is where you spent the evening. You went to the club but decided not to stay?" She held her breath, praying he would tell her the truth.

Instead, he glanced away, faint color rising beneath the bones in his cheeks. "As I said, I just needed a little fresh air."

A lump formed in her throat. "Yes…that is what you said."

"Shall we go upstairs?"

She couldn't make love to him, not tonight. Not after he had lied about seeing the countess. "If you don't mind, I am feeling a bit under the weather. I thought that I would stay down here and read for a while. I shall be up a little later."

His expression turned to worry. "If you are ill, perhaps you should be in bed."

Just the word *bed* on his beautiful lips stirred her pulse. *Not tonight,* she told herself. Not tonight.

"I would rather stay here. It's a… It is merely a bit of woman trouble. You needn't bother yourself about it."

"I see. All right, if you are certain."

"I'll be fine."

He left her there in the drawing room and headed for the stairs.

Violet sank back down on the sofa.

She didn't bother to pick up her book.

She knew she couldn't read with her eyes so full of tears.

Violet pled illness the following day, staying home from work and away from Rule. On the morning of the next day, she paid a call on Caroline. She didn't intend to tell her cousin about Rule's visit to Lady Fremont or that he had lied about going.

Just seeing her best friend always made her feel better.

Except that when she arrived at the newlyweds' town house, she found her friend in tears.

"Oh, dear," Caroline said from where she curled up in a velvet settee in her bedroom, sniffing and dabbing at her eyes. "I didn't mean for anyone to see me like this."

"The housekeeper said you weren't feeling well. I insisted she let me come up." Violet sat down next to her cousin and put an arm around her. "What is it, dearest? You are crying as if your heart is breaking."

Caroline sobbed. "It is." She sniffed and dabbed her handkerchief against the wetness in her eyes.

"Tell me what is wrong."

Caroline straightened a little. She dragged in a shuddering breath. "It's Luke. He's changing, Violet. He was so sweet and caring and now...now he wants nothing to do with me. The only time I see him is at night when he comes to my bed."

Violet frowned. "Did you ask him what is wrong?"

"I know what is wrong."

"Tell me."

"Luke thinks I don't love him."

Several seconds passed. "I thought that was the way you wanted it."

She swallowed. "That's what I told myself. I tried so hard, but…"

"So you *do* love him."

Caroline looked up, her pale blue eyes magnified by a film of tears. "Of course I love him. I've always loved him. That is the reason I decided to go back to Boston. I was in love with him even then."

Violet felt a sweep of relief. Her cousin deserved to be happy. Perhaps now she would have the chance. "Then I don't see a problem. All you have to do is tell Luke how you feel."

Caroline shook her head. "I couldn't possibly do that."

"Why on earth not?"

"Because I'm afraid of what he'll do if he knows the truth. Men are only interested in making the conquest. Once they know they have you in their power, they aren't interested in you anymore."

It was a difficult point to argue. Even now Violet worried that Rule had grown weary of her, that he was turning his attentions to the beautiful countess.

"Maybe Luke will be different."

"And if he isn't?"

"You are miserable now, are you not?"

Caroline wiped away her tears and nodded. "He looks at me as if I'm someone he barely knows and I feel like I am dying."

Violet reached over and took Caroline's hand. "Tell him, dearest. You fell in love with Luke because he was different from other men. Perhaps in this he will be different, as well."

Caroline looked up and a tear rolled down her cheek. "I don't know…" She shook her head. "I'll give it some thought. Perhaps if the time seems right…"

Violet didn't press her. After all, she had never told Rule the way she felt.

She simply wasn't that brave.

Twenty-Six

⸺⛦⛦⛦⸺

Still feigning illness, Violet stayed home from work the next day then spent all afternoon trying to work up the courage to confront Rule about his meeting with the countess. Before he had left for the office that morning, he had insisted that if she weren't feeling better by the time he got home, he was calling a physician.

It was time to stop pretending, time to discover the truth, but the thought of what he might say tied a hard knot in her stomach.

Violet sighed as she stood at the window in the drawing room. The weather seemed to mirror her dismal mood. A storm had blown in, a torrential downpour that had started late in the afternoon and hadn't let up. Through the rain-spotted panes, she saw Rule's carriage arrive out front, saw him step from the coach into the downpour, his clothes drenched by the time he reached the porch though a footman hovered over him with an umbrella.

She was standing in the hall when he shed his caped overcoat and hat in the entry and handed them to Hatfield. "Have you seen my wife or is she still upstairs in her room?"

She started toward him. Apparently his concern for her had not lessened. Violet felt only a trace of guilt for the deception.

"I am here, my lord."

He turned at the sound of her voice and smiled. "So you are up and about. I hope you are feeling better."

"Much better, thank you. I told you it was nothing to worry about."

She could see the relief in his eyes and it eased some of her fear. Perhaps she was wrong. Perhaps his meeting with Lady Fremont had not been the beginning of an affair.

"I could use a cup of tea," he said to Hat.

"I'll see to it, my lord." Hat disappeared and Rule turned a warm smile in her direction.

"Why don't you join me, sweetheart? A nice hot cup of tea would probably do you good." He hadn't used the endearment lately and her heart lifted a fraction more. It was time, she decided. There was no point in waiting any longer.

She managed to smile. "Tea sounds lovely."

They had just begun to settle themselves in the drawing room when a commotion in the entry put them on alert. Both of them rose as Hatfield appeared in the doorway.

"I am sorry, my lord, but Constable McGregor wishes to speak to you."

Violet didn't miss the tension that seeped into Rule's shoulders. "Bring him in. We'll speak in here."

"I'm afraid that's no longer acceptable." The stocky, auburn-haired policeman sauntered past Hat into the drawing room, followed by two other policemen. "I'm here to arrest you in the Queen's name for the murder of Charles Whitney."

"Dear God." Violet shot to her feet, fighting not to tremble.

"You may come quietly, my lord, or we can force you to come. The choice is yours."

"I'll go to your brother," Violet promised. "I'll tell him what has happened. The duke will know what to do."

Rule stiffly nodded. "I'll come with you," he said to McGregor. "I would like to know, however, why you have decided of a sudden to take this step."

"A man was found dead. You might recall him, a fellow with a jagged scar that ran along the side of his neck."

Rule's face paled.

"He was found in an alley not far from Tooley Street. Not far, my lord, from your place of business."

Rule's jaw firmed. "What does that have to do with me?"

"We spoke to a chambermaid named Molly Deavers. Miss Deavers admitted to selling the key to Charles Whitney's room to a man with a scar on his neck. Whitney is dead and now the man who could have linked you to the murder is also dead—just blocks from where you work."

"You think I killed him? What about Peter Austin or Martin Whitney? Either of them could have murdered Whitney."

"Austin was in Portsmouth at the time of the murder. Martin Whitney was with friends at his club. Several patrons will attest to that."

"Perhaps one of them paid the man with the scar to do it."

The constable ignored him. He gave a nod and the two policemen moved behind Rule in warning. "Time to go."

One of Rule's hands fisted but he didn't resist. Allowing the men to guide him down the hall and out the front door, he stepped into the driving rain.

"I'll bring Royal!" Violet called after him, desperation ringing in her voice. "He'll straighten all of this out."

Rule made no reply, just let them lead him to the door of the police wagon, ducked his head and disappeared inside.

Violet's heart squeezed. Dear God, they hadn't even given him time to get his overcoat.

She whirled toward the butler. "I'll need the carriage readied immediately."

"I have already sent for it, my lady. Mr. Bellows will be out front any moment."

Violet felt the sting of tears. "What would we do without you, Hat?"

The old man's thin cheeks colored. He hurried off to retrieve her cloak and a dry coat for Rule and returned with the items a few minutes later.

"You'll need these." He handed her Rule's coat and draped her woolen cloak around her shoulders.

"Thank you."

The carriage arrived out front in record time. Hurriedly descending the steps, her cloak flapping in the wind as a footman held an umbrella over her head, Violet climbed aboard. An instant later, the conveyance lurched into motion, the wheels rolling over the slick cobbled streets, the horses pounding along at the fastest pace possible in the weather and the traffic.

It seemed to take forever to reach the duke's mansion, though it wasn't that far away. *Royal will know what to do,* she told herself as she stepped down into the rain, repeating the phrase like a mantra.

Violet prayed that it was true.

Neither Royal nor the fancy barrister Mr. Pinkard insisted Rule hire were able to get him released. Late that night he was taken to Newgate and placed in a barren cell on the master's side of the prison, a private accommodation arranged for by Mr. Pinkard.

Violet had heard that the prison had been remodeled

four years earlier to make it more modern, but it remained a cold, drafty, inhumane place not fit to house the rats who lived inside the gray stone walls.

"I don't want you to come down here, Violet," Rule said to her when Royal and Mr. Pinkard stepped out of the cell to give them a few moments alone. "If things go badly, this is not the way I want you to remember me."

"Oh, dear God!" She hurled herself into his arms and clung to him, aching for him, trembling. "Don't even think such a thing. We'll find a solution. We'll find the real killer."

Rule took a shaky breath. "Royal is going to take you home. I want you to stay there, Violet. Better yet, tomorrow I want you to go to the office. Keep yourself busy. Let Morgan and the others do their job." He bent his head and kissed her, softly at first, then fiercely.

"I love you, Rule," she said, unable to stop the words, wishing with all her heart he would say those words to her.

Instead, he kissed her one last time. "Pray for me," was all he said.

The clank of the heavy cell door marked Violet's departure. The sound made Rule's chest squeeze. She had gone to his brother as she had promised, pled with the constable for his freedom, braved the ugliness of Newgate to come to him, to try to give him hope.

She was unlike any woman he had ever known, smarter, sweeter, more courageous. More determined.

And she had said that she loved him.

For an instant, he'd felt light-headed, as if those simple words had thrown him completely off balance. She had said them and he could see that she meant them.

His heart beat dully as he recalled the moment. What man wouldn't want the love of a woman like that?

And yet, Rule did not.

He knew that Violet's love came with a price. That she would want, perhaps even require, his love in return.

But Rule didn't have that sort of love to give. He loved his brothers, his family, but it wasn't the same. Violet craved a man's love, a husband's love, the deep abiding affection of a sort he didn't understand. He had never felt that kind of love and probably never would.

He thought of her sweet face and prayed she could be happy with the depth of his caring, his deep concern for her welfare. He prayed she would be content with his affection and his passions.

A noise in the corridor outside his cell drew his attention, the weeping of a prisoner in another damp enclosure in a different part of the prison. The dismal sound reminded him he was in Newgate. That perhaps his worries about the future wouldn't matter.

Perhaps he would never be able to prove his innocence and he would hang.

If that happened, Violet would be free of him, free to find a man who loved her the way she deserved.

The thought made him sick to his stomach.

Violet couldn't stand another moment of pacing, of wandering through the empty house, a place that echoed with her loneliness and fear. Rule had pressed her to return to work and now as her desperation continued to build, she realized he was right.

Forcing aside her exhaustion from another sleepless night, early the following morning she fashioned her hair in a tight chignon at the nape of her neck, dressed in a sturdy gown of russet wool against the continuing stormy weather, and traveled to her office at Griffin.

Looking pale and shaken, Terence Smythe greeted her at the door as she walked in. "I only just heard, my lady. We are all of us just so angry. How can they believe Lord Rule would murder someone? He is simply not that sort."

She managed a smile. "No, he isn't, Terry. We can only hope and pray that the real killer will be found." *Before it's too late,* she silently added. But in England, prosecutions moved swiftly. Mr. Pinkard had been able to convince the magistrates to give him a little more time to mount a defense, but it wouldn't be long.

Moving down the hallway, she went into the office that belonged to Rule to see what matters of importance might be stacked upon his desk. She picked up the item on top of the stack and saw that it was a formal offer to purchase the company.

The offer had come from Burton Stanfield.

Fury engulfed her. How dare he! With her husband in prison, Stanfield had the temerity to believe she would be forced to accept his offer. Perhaps he was convinced Rule would be convicted of the crime and would no longer pose an obstacle to his acquisition of the business.

Violet held up the several sheets of paper, tore them neatly in two and discarded them in the waste bin.

She looked up as Terry appeared in the open doorway. "Would you like me to bring you the weekly ledgers, my lady?"

"Yes. I'll start on them as soon as I go through his lordship's correspondence."

Terry disappeared then reappeared with the heavy leather-bound volumes, which he placed on a corner of the desk.

"Thank you, Terry."

As the young man left, quietly closing the door, Violet glanced around the office that belonged to her husband,

and a thick lump swelled in her throat. Everything in the office reminded her of Rule. His framed diploma from Oxford, a trophy he had won during his university boxing days, the crystal decanter on the sideboard that held his favorite aged brandy.

There was a portrait of his mother and father, and one of him and his two brothers, painted in the countryside around Bransford Castle when they were little boys. Her eyes misted at what a beautiful child he was. She moved one of the papers on his desk and caught a whiff of his cologne.

Dear God, she was so afraid for him!

And she loved him so much.

She recalled the moment she had finally said the words, no longer able to keep them locked inside. Rule had simply ignored them and her heart had clenched with longing. She told herself it didn't matter. That whatever his feelings for her, nothing could change what she felt for him.

Violet drew in a calming breath, determined not to dwell on what she could not change. Keeping the company running smoothly was what Rule would want.

Turning her attention to the task at hand, she replied to several letters he had received, made decisions on a number of other business matters, then began on the ledgers. But no matter how hard she worked, every so often her mind would wander back to Rule and his dismal cell and her eyes would fill with tears.

Loving someone, she discovered, could be a very painful proposition.

The afternoon began to wane. Outside the window, the rain had stopped but the sky remained overcast and dull. A stiff wind rattled the branches on the trees and they scraped eerily against the panes. She glanced at the clock on the wall, determined to leave in time to stop by the prison before it got dark. She knew Rule wouldn't like it but she simply had to see him, be certain he was all right.

A soft knock sounded, drawing her from her thoughts as she began to straighten the desk. She expected to find Terry but it was the boy she remembered seeing outside the White Bull Tavern who walked in and closed the door.

"Me name's Danny Tuttle, milady. I gotta talk to you. It's important."

She managed to smile. "My husband told me he gave you a job. How can I help you, Danny?"

"I heard about 'is lordship…about 'im gettin' tossed into prison and all. I know 'e didn't kill that man like they say."

Her pulse leaped. She forced herself to remain calm for fear she might frighten him into silence. "Go on, Danny."

"Your 'usband…'e were good to me. I don't want to see 'im hang—not for somethin' 'e didn't do."

Her heart was beating, pounding away inside her chest. "What are you saying, Danny?"

"I lied to 'im, milady, that day outside the White Bull. 'E asked me about the man what paid me to deliver the note. 'E wanted to know what the man looked like. I figured it wouldn't matter so I told 'im about the scar. But I said I didn't know 'im."

"Go on, Danny, please."

"'Is name is Michael Dunnigan. Quick Mike, they call 'im. 'E runs the li'l goes—the lotteries for Benny Bates."

"Bates? That's the man you used to work for?"

"That's 'im."

"The man with the scar—Michael Dunnigan—I'm afraid he is dead. They found him in an alley just a few blocks away."

"I heard."

"What…what do you think happened to him?"

"Bates paid Quick Mike to get the key to one of the rooms at the Albert. Mike sent me to deliver the note to your 'usband. I think whoever 'ired Benny to 'elp 'im set up the murder kilt Mike to keep 'im quiet. Mike were always spoutin' off, ya see, the boastin' sort, 'e was. I think the man kilt 'im and hauled 'is body down 'ere to make it look like your 'usband done it."

Violet moistened her trembling lips, fighting to stay calm. "You don't think Bates did it?"

"Nah. Mike was Benny's friend. Ain't likely 'e woulda kilt 'im. But I think 'e knows who did."

"Thank you, Danny. So very much." Violet hurried out of the office, stopping only long enough to have Terry retrieve her carriage. She had to talk to Chase Morgan, tell him what she had discovered. If anyone could get Bates to talk, it was the hard-edged investigator.

She knew his office was in Threadneedle Street. She had gone there once with Rule. Fortunately, when she arrived unannounced, Morgan was still there, though it appeared he was about to leave.

He opened the door, hat in hand, then paused when he saw her. "My lady, please come in." Stepping back to let her pass, he hung his hat back on the rack, led her out of the waiting area into his private office and quietly closed the door.

"I wish I had something new to report," he said, "but I'm afraid I don't. The duke stopped by yesterday to tell me the police had found the body of the man with the scar and that they had arrested your husband. They haven't been able to discover the man's identity. I've been doing my best to find out, but so far—"

"His name is Michael Dunnigan. He worked for Benny Bates."

Morgan lifted a dark brown eyebrow. "How did you find that out?"

"The boy Danny Tuttle. Rule gave him a job and apparently he felt grateful. He came to see me. He gave me Dunnigan's name but said he didn't think Bates killed him. He thinks Bates was hired by someone to set up the murder and that person killed Dunnigan to ensure his silence."

"Then hauled the body down to Tooley Street to convince the authorities your husband killed him to keep him quiet."

"Yes."

Morgan took her arm and started guiding her toward the door, grabbing his hat off the rack as he passed. "It's getting dark. Will you be able to get home all right?"

"Of course."

He escorted her out to the carriage and helped her inside, obviously eager to be on his way. "Assuming I can find him, I'll talk to Bates tonight. I'll let you know what I find out."

"Thank you." She watched as he walked away, his strides long and filled with purpose.

"Home, my lady?" Bellows asked through the small trapdoor that opened to the interior of the coach.

"Newgate Prison, Mr. Bellows. I need to speak to my husband."

Bellows grumbled something she couldn't quite hear. "Aye, milady," he said on a sigh.

It was dangerous to go there this time of night. She wasn't even certain she could get inside. Still, knowing he couldn't dissuade her, Bellows slapped the reins against the horses' rumps and the carriage rolled off down the street.

Twenty-Seven

~~~~~⟨◦⟩~~~~~

The wind gusted, rocking the carriage. Through the window, the frightening silhouette of Newgate Prison came slowly into view, a giant stone monolith that dominated the rapidly darkening sky.

Mr. Bellows walked Violet to the front gate and for a few extra coins, she persuaded one of the guards to let her into the prison.

"Just the lady," the guard warned when the burly coachman attempted to follow.

"I'll be fine," Violet assured him, praying she truly would be.

Another few coins ensured she was taken to the cell she wished to visit. Newgate was a maze of low-beamed corridors and steep stone staircases, and at night the glow of a few scattered lanterns barely lit the way. As she walked beside the fat, bearded guard, the echo of their footsteps on the uneven stone floor sent an eerie shiver down her spine.

She'd heard stories of what went on in the prison, of malnutrition and disease, cruelty and ravishment of the female prisoners. It occurred to her that if the guard wished to force himself on her, he could drag her into one of the cells and she would be unable to stop him.

The thought made a knot form in her stomach.

Fortunately, the man merely led her along the damp, dim passage to Rule's cell, stuck his heavy metal key in the lock and opened the door.

"I'll be back in 'alf an hour," he said.

"Thank you." She turned at the sound of Rule's voice as he strode toward her.

"Violet! For God's sake, what the bloody hell are you doing here?" His face was lined with fear and disapproval but his arms came hard around her, pressing her fiercely against him.

"I've brought news. I've discovered the identity of the man with the scar. His name was Michael Dunnigan. He worked for Benny Bates."

Rule caught her shoulders. "So Bates *is* involved in this. How did you find out?"

"Danny told me. He said he lied to you before. He said you were good to him and he wanted to help you."

"What else?"

"Danny says someone hired Bates and his ring of thugs to set up the murder. Dunnigan's job was to get hold of the key to Whitney's room. But he wasn't good with secrets. Danny thinks whoever killed Whitney killed Dunnigan to keep him quiet, then made it look like you did it."

Rule turned away, began to pace. "I've got to speak to Morgan, get him to talk to Bates."

"I've already been to see him. He was on his way to find Bates when I left to come here."

Rule returned to her and hauled her back into his arms. "God, Violet." She could feel the tremors racing through his solid, powerful body, the rapid pounding of his heart.

"I know you shouldn't have come," he said. "I know it's dangerous for you to be here, but I'm so glad you came." And then he kissed her, the tenderest, sweetest kiss she could imagine.

"We'll find our way out of this." Tears burned her eyes. "Morgan will help us."

He nodded, held her tightly again. She wanted to say that she loved him, but he wouldn't say it back and it would only make her sad.

Instead, she told him about the offer Burton Stanfield had tendered and how angry she had become.

"The man hasn't the morals of a snake," Rule said.

"Clearly, he still wants the company. You don't think he might be the murderer?"

Rule sighed. "I don't know."

"Perhaps Stanfield believed that with Whitney out of the way and you convicted of the crime, he might be able to convince me to sell."

"It's possible, I suppose. Where a great deal of profit is involved, anything is possible."

That was certainly true and another possibility to discuss with Chase Morgan.

She couldn't believe half an hour had passed when she heard the guard's heavy footfalls coming down the passage.

"It's time for me to go." Swirling her cloak around her shoulders, she kissed him softly one last time. "I'll be back, and don't you dare tell me not to come."

His beautiful mouth curved slightly. She could feel his eyes on her as she crossed to the door.

"Violet?"

There was something in his voice, a faint sound of entreaty. She stopped and turned.

Rule stood just a few feet away, his hands at his sides.

his expression solemn. "Before you leave, there is something I need to tell you."

Fear tightened her chest. Dear God, she was afraid to hear it, terrified of what he might say.

"The night I told you I went to the club, I didn't go there. I went to see Lady Fremont."

Her throat tightened. A dull roaring filled her ears.

"I needed to know about Charles and Martin."

She couldn't form a single word, but her eyes were beginning to burn.

"I didn't stay long," he said. "What she told me wasn't of any real consequence. I left her house and came straight home."

Relief hit her so hard she could barely stay on her feet. "Why…why didn't you tell me?"

"I didn't want you to think there was something going on between us when there wasn't. But I haven't felt right since I came home that night. I'm not good at lying, Violet. I won't do it again."

She ran to him, slid her arms around his neck and just held on to him.

Rule held her tightly.

"Thank you for telling me," she said. "You can't begin to know how much it means."

"I don't ever want to hurt you."

She looked up at him, fighting to hold back tears. "Sometimes the truth is painful. But in the end, it is always better than a lie."

He reached up and ran a finger gently down her cheek. The clank of the key in the lock ended the moment. As the guard opened the door, Rule bent his head and kissed her softly one last time. "Good night, love."

"Good night, Rule." Whirling away from him, tears

blurring her vision, she hurried through the heavy wooden door into the dimly lit passage.

It had taken bouts of terror and fits of panic, but Caroline had finally decided to do it. Tonight, she was going to tell Luke the truth.

As the weeks had passed, more and more she had sensed his need for her love, that perhaps he even loved her in return. She had to tell him the way she felt and pray that his conquest of her heart would not ultimately drive him away.

Luke was late getting home. By the time he arrived, Caroline was a bundle of nerves, pacing up and down the drawing room, the skirt of the pale blue gown she hoped would please him flaring out at every turn. Her heart seemed to throb in a similar nervous rhythm. In the dining room, the table was set with the finest silver and a special dinner prepared—medallions of lamb with mint jelly, one of Luke's favorites.

Her pulse kicked up when she heard him in the entry. She waited until she caught sight of his tall, broad-shouldered frame striding down the hall toward his study.

"Luke?"

"Good evening, Caroline." Not Carrie. She thought that he made an effort not to call her that anymore. "Was there something you wanted?"

"I was wondering…hoping I might have a word with you."

He cast her a glance but his gaze didn't linger, and her heart squeezed. Maybe she had waited too long to tell him. Maybe she was wrong and he didn't really care. Maybe she had already lost him.

He joined her in the drawing room and at the anxious look on her face, turned and slid the doors closed.

"What is it? Has something happened?"

Caroline moistened her lips. "Maybe we should sit down."

His guard came up. She could tell by the tension that settled between his shoulders. "All right."

She headed for the sofa, but Luke moved toward a chair. She caught his hand before he got there. "I was hoping you might sit beside me."

His uneasiness heightened. He followed her to the sofa but sat down on the opposite end. "What is it, Caroline? I have work to do in my study."

Her eyes stung. He was locking her out, doing everything in his power to keep her at a distance.

"There is… There is something I need to tell you. I don't know what you will say when I do. I don't know if it matters to you. I am hoping very much that it does."

Wariness crept into his eyes. "Go on."

"I've been lying to you, Luke. I started lying sometime back and I have…I have continued."

His jaw hardened. "What the hell have you done, Carrie? If you are seeing another man, I swear I'll kill him."

Her eyes filled with tears. "It isn't anything like that. In fact, it is just the opposite. I don't want any other man, Luke. I only want you. I always have."

"We are married. I don't understand."

She rose from the sofa and closed the distance between them, knelt at his feet and took hold of his hand. "I'm in love with you, Luke. I have been since before we were married. That is the reason I wanted to go back to Boston. I didn't want to love you. I was afraid of what would happen if I did." The tears in her eyes spilled over onto her cheeks. "But it was already too late."

For several long moments, Luke just sat there staring. "You love me."

She nodded, tried to smile. "Madly. Desperately. I love

you more than anything in the world." She knuckled away a tear. "And I have missed you so much."

Luke didn't wait, just hauled her to her feet and straight into his arms.

"God, Carrie, I love you so damned much." And then he was kissing her and she was kissing him back and her fears fell away. Luke loved her. And she loved him. Whatever the future held in store, she would deal with it when the time came.

Luke kissed her again, tenderly this time. She could feel his love, his joy, and she melted in his embrace. She was breathless by the time he eased away and a little unsure what to say.

"You…you must be hungry. I had Cook make your favorite supper."

Luke just smiled. "We'll have supper later. Right now I want to show my wife how much I adore her."

She threw her arms around his neck. "Oh, Luke, I love you so much."

Luke kissed her fiercely. "Promise me you will tell me that at least once a week."

"Every day," Caroline promised. "I'll tell you every day for as long as you wish to hear it."

Sweeping her up in his arms, he started for the stairs. "Then prepare yourself to say it for the rest of your life."

As he strode down the hall to his bedroom, the last of her doubts slipped away.

For the first time since that fateful night in the library, Caroline believed that, in marrying Lucas Barclay, she had done exactly the right thing.

Another agonizing day slipped past. Violet stood on the terrace. The wind had cleared the sooty air and stars were visible in the black velvet sky.

Earlier, she had stopped by the prison to see Rule, who had mentioned a visit from Morgan. Rule had told Morgan about the offer from Burton Stanfield and the possibility Stanfield might be the man behind the murders.

So far the investigator hadn't been able to locate Benny Bates. Morgan believed Bates was staying out of sight until the police finished their inquiry into Quick Mike Dunnigan's murder.

They had to find him. Bates was now the key.

The breeze lifted several loose strands of her copper hair and she pulled her light shawl closer around her.

"Excuse me, my lady."

She turned to see Hatfield standing just outside the French doors. "What is it, Hat?"

"I am sorry to disturb you, my lady, but you have a visitor. He says he is a friend." Posture perfectly correct, Hatfield walked over and handed her a card. In raised gold letters was the name *Mr. Jeffrey Burnett.*

Jeffrey. She wondered what could possibly have brought him into the intimacy of her home. "Show him into the drawing room, Hat, if you would."

"Yes, my lady."

Violet took a deep breath. She didn't want to see Jeffrey. She had far too much on her mind. And where Jeffrey was concerned, there was always a nagging feeling of guilt. She had made him promises, or at least there had been expectations between them. She had hurt him and it was something she regretted a very great deal.

With a sigh of resignation, she lifted her skirts, crossed to the French doors and walked back into the house. In the main drawing room, Jeffrey stood up the moment he saw her. His hair gleamed like gold in the lamplight, his fine features were as attractive as ever, and yet she felt not a single stirring inside her.

Jeffrey started toward her. "Violet, darling. I couldn't stay away a moment longer." He reached out and caught both of her hands. "I've been reading the newspapers. I can't imagine what you must be going through."

She eased her hands away. "The police have made a terrible mistake. Rule is innocent. Once that is proven, he'll be released."

"I only know what I've read. I know your husband is in prison. I know you are facing all of this alone. I came here for you, Violet. We were friends before. With all that has happened, I thought you might need a friend now."

His gaze held hers until she glanced away. There was a time she believed she could love him. Now, it surprised her to realize how little she felt for him. "I appreciate your concern, Jeffrey. Truly I do."

"Is there anything you need, dearest? Anything I can do for you?"

"No, Jeffrey, there isn't a thing." She met his gaze more squarely than she had been able to do since his arrival in London. "But maybe there is something I can do for you. You see, as I stand here in front of you, I realize that I did you a grave injustice. You look at me and see the woman you believe you loved, but that isn't the woman I truly am. And I am sorry to say she is someone I never really was."

"What are you talking about? I don't understand."

"I am saying that when you think of me, you think of a naive young woman, sweet and innocent, someone you believed you could mold into the person you wanted her to be. But I am not that person, Jeffrey. I am a strong woman, used to fighting for her beliefs and speaking her own mind."

"You have always been a little outspoken, but—"

"Outspoken? After my father died, for nearly two years I was the person in charge of the Boston branch of Griffin. I worked there under the name J. A. Haskell."

His sleek blond eyebrows came together. "That…that makes no sense. You're a woman, an heiress, why would you wish to work?"

"I liked working, Jeffrey. I liked the independence, the feeling of accomplishment. I still do."

Jeffrey shook his head. "I don't believe any of this. You weren't that way when we were together. Surely you haven't changed that much."

She rested a hand on his arm. "That is the sad part. I was so lonely, so desperate to be loved, I pretended to be someone I was not. For a time, I even fooled myself."

He straightened away from her and a muscle tightened in his jaw. "You've changed because of *him*. They are going to find him guilty, Violet. All the evidence points to your husband as the man who murdered Charles Whitney."

Anger filtered through her. "What possible motive could he have? Charles was going to buy the company."

"That's right. I think Dewar realized he had sold the business too cheap. He and Whitney fought about it. Dewar couldn't break the contract so he killed him. Unfortunately he got caught in the process."

"That isn't true."

"You'll be a widow, Violet. You'll be just as lonely as you were before. What will you do then?"

"I am going to find a way to prove Rule's innocence. But even if they find him guilty and I am widowed, I won't go back to pretending to be someone I am not."

Jeffrey's gaze didn't waver. "What about the company?

You told me how much you wanted to sell it. You shared your feelings with me about the coming war."

"My feelings haven't changed. Whatever happens, I'm going to sell. Sooner or later, we'll find a reputable buyer."

"I see."

"I hope you do, Jeffrey, truly. I hope you understand I have never wished you ill."

The smile he summoned was tight. He made her a very formal bow. "I wish you luck, then. In all of your endeavors." Jeffrey turned and walked away and Violet felt suddenly drained.

She had told Jeffrey the truth. A truth she had only recently discovered. She wasn't the person Jeffrey had loved and she never had been. Now that he understood, he could go on with his life, find the sort of woman he wanted.

Violet released a weary breath. Rule might not love her but at least he knew her for the woman she truly was.

Violet was determined to prove him innocent of murder.

J. P. Montgomery opened the door to his suite at the Hotel Trafalgar, allowing Jeffrey to walk past him into the elegant sitting room. The Trafalgar was two blocks from the Parkland, where Jeffrey was staying, a precaution they had taken to keep their business relationship secret.

"Sorry, I'm late," Jeffrey said as Montgomery returned to his seat in an overstuffed chair. "My call took a little longer than I expected."

"You don't look too happy. Things didn't go the way you planned?"

"You might say that. Whatever happens, Violet isn't coming back to me."

"That's too bad. It would have made things a whole lot easier."

He shook his head. "She made it sound like rejecting me was doing me a favor. Maybe she's right. She's not the woman I thought she was."

Montgomery grunted. "But she still wants to sell."

He nodded. "That's what she says." Jeffrey walked over and poured himself a brandy from the crystal decanter on the sideboard, wishing he had a glass of whiskey instead. He carried it over to the sofa and sat down.

"Maybe it's time Wrigby went in with our offer," Montgomery said.

Jeffrey took a sip of his drink, let the warmth burn down his throat. "I think we should wait until after the trial. Once they hang Dewar, things might go easier."

"Then again," Montgomery drawled, "maybe doing it now would work in our favor. Dewar might want to make sure his little lady is taken care of before he meets his maker."

Jeffrey scoffed. "His *little lady,* as you call her, assured me she is damned well capable of taking care of herself."

Montgomery adjusted his heavy frame against the back of his chair. "I'll talk to Wrigby. Tell him to have the last of the partnership papers drawn up. We'll need to review them and make any changes. We want to be ready when the time comes."

Jeffrey took a swallow of his drink. "I hope it's soon. I hate this damnable country, the damp and cold. This damnable brandy. I can't wait to get back home."

"Boston?"

"Virginia. There's nothing to keep me in the North any longer."

Twenty-Eight

An early-afternoon sun warmed the air as Chase Morgan walked with Royal and Reese Dewar to the door of a run-down brick residence a few blocks away from the White Bull Tavern.

"You sure he's here?" Reese asked. He was ex-military, Chase knew from working with him before, his attitude always focused and capable.

"According to my sources," Morgan said, "Bates is staying with his cousin until all this blows over."

"As I recall, your resources are extremely reliable."

"Extremely," Morgan agreed. He tipped his head toward the side of the house. "You and the duke go round to the alley. He may try to run out the back door."

Both Dewars nodded and quietly headed off toward the alley at the rear of the house. Morgan gave them time to reach their destination before climbing the porch steps and reaching out to try the front door. He turned the knob, found it unlocked, and walked inside as quietly as he could.

The interior was dark and dreary, with dirty fringed throw covers over a sagging sofa, mostly barren floors, and pieces of mud and lint on the single rug in the parlor.

"Bates!" he called out, and heard the grinding of chair legs sliding against the floor, then the sound of running feet. Bates was moving fast toward the kitchen and Morgan jolted into action, careening around the corner as Bates slammed out the back door.

Ignoring the stench of rotting kitchen garbage, Morgan raced after him. Bates made it to the bottom of the stairs before Reese Dewar was on him, crashing into him with bone-jarring force, bringing him facedown in the dirt.

"Take it easy!" Bates shouted. "Yer hurting me!"

"You haven't begun to know hurt yet," the duke warned, blond hair glinting as he strode up beside where his brother pinned the man to the ground.

Bates struggled futiley, twisting his thick body one way and another, his bald head shining. "What do ye want?"

"We want to know who killed Charles Whitney," the duke demanded.

"I don't know nothin' about it."

Reese wrenched one of Bates's arms behind his back and twisted hard. Bates let out a spine-chilling scream.

"Perhaps you might wish to reconsider," the duke said calmly.

"You better tell them," Morgan warned as he joined the group at the bottom of the stairs. "The man on top of you is Major Reese Dewar. To him you're the enemy. He won't think twice about breaking your arm—or worse."

"I told ye, I don't—" Reese wrenched Bates's arm and he let out another scream. "All right, all right, I'll tell ye! But I didn't have nothin' to do with the murder. I don't want any trouble with the police."

"So you didn't kill him," Morgan said. "You just arranged for the murderer to get a key to Whitney's room so he could go in and kill him."

Bates struggled to lift his head. "I didn't know the bloke meant to shoot him. He said he needed to look at some papers Whitney kept in his room."

"Give us his name," the duke pressed.

"He killed Quick Mike. I tell you who he is, he'll kill me, too."

Reese twisted the arm and Bates groaned. "You don't give us the name, I'll kill you myself. I'm not going to let my brother hang for a crime he didn't commit."

Bates wriggled and squirmed, but Reese held him easily. "You're only making this harder."

Finally Bates stopped fighting. He breathed out a sigh of resignation. "All right, I'll tell ye."

Reese eased his hold, allowing Bates to climb to his feet, but he didn't release him.

"Montgomery. That's the blighter's name."

"Montgomery? J. P. Montgomery?" Morgan glanced over at the brothers. "That's the American who tried to buy Griffin."

"I gave ye his name," Bates said, "but all ye got is me word it was him and that ain't enough to convince the magistrates."

"He's right," Reese agreed.

"Perhaps," the duke said. "But with the Tuttle boy confirming Bates's story, we might convince the magistrates there's enough doubt about Rule's guilt to release him into my custody." Royal smiled. "Occasionally, being a duke can actually work in one's favor."

"Be worth a try," Reese agreed.

"I'll go to Griffin and fetch the boy," Royal said. "It's early yet. He should still be at work."

"Even if you succeed in getting your brother released," Morgan warned, "we'll need hard evidence against Montgomery, not just the word of a sharper like Bates."

"We've got to get to Montgomery," the duke said. "We need a way to trap him into exposing himself."

"How do we do that?" Reese asked.

"I don't know yet." Morgan started back to the carriages. "But we'd better think of something."

Violet was seated behind her desk at Griffin when Royal walked into her office. She knew he and Reese had gone with Chase Morgan, hoping to find and confront Benny Bates.

She shot to her feet when she saw him. "Did you find him?"

Royal nodded. "We found him."

"Wh-what happened?"

"Montgomery is our man. I need to talk to Danny Tuttle."

Her eyes widened. "Montgomery killed Whitney?"

"It looks that way."

Her mind went over the information. "Montgomery still wants the company. He's a Southerner. He wants the guns for the South."

"He must want them badly to do murder."

For an instant she thought of poor Mr. Whitney. The war hadn't yet started and the killing had already begun. "What do you need with Danny?"

"Reese is taking Bates to the magistrates. I plan to meet him there. With Danny's help, I think we might be able to stir up enough doubt about Rule's guilt to get him released into my custody."

"Great heavens, I'll fetch him right away." Racing off, she called for Terry and asked him to go down to the factory floor and bring Danny back to her office.

The boy arrived a few minutes later. One look at Royal, so tall and imposing, and his eyes widened in fear.

"Who's that? What's 'e want with me?"

"That's Rule's brother," Violet said gently, "the Duke of Bransford. He needs your help, Danny."

"I need you to talk to the magistrates," Royal explained, "tell them about Bates and Mike Dunnigan. I think with your help, we might be able to get my brother released."

Danny started shaking his head, his posture as straight as the barrel of a gun. "They'll toss me into Newgate. I'll never get outta that place."

"I won't let that happen," Royal said. "I give you my word. You weren't involved in the murder, Danny. You didn't do anything but deliver a message."

The boy swallowed hard.

"Please, Danny," Violet pleaded. "You said you wanted to help." She flicked a glance at Royal, whose wide shoulders and intimidating stance made him look like the powerful duke he was. "His Grace has given you his word. He won't let anything happen to you. And neither will I."

Danny nervously moistened his lips, his eyes darting back and forth between Violet and Royal.

He slowly released a breath. "All right, I'll do it."

Relief filtered through her. "Thank you, Danny." She looked over at Royal. "What about Montgomery?"

"We need more evidence. Don't say anything to anyone until we figure out our next move."

"What if Montgomery begins to realize something is wrong? What if he tries to run?"

"That's why we need to act swiftly."

Violet just nodded. She watched the pair leave the office, her heart going with them. She prayed they would be able to free Rule from prison.

Still, as Royal had said, they had to find more evidence to prove Montgomery's guilt.

Rule wouldn't truly be safe until they did.

* * *

Violet found herself pacing again. She was home from the office, anxiously waiting to see if Royal would be able to get Rule released.

Dear God, she prayed, *let him come home to me.*

With Mary's help, she had changed out of the gown she had worn to work. She considered putting on something feminine and pretty for Rule, her embroidered aqua silk, perhaps, or her apricot taffeta, then decided against it, choosing a simple navy-blue cambric instead.

If the men went after Montgomery, they might need her help—not that they would ever come out and actually ask for it. Still, she wanted to be prepared if she was needed.

On the other hand, there was no reason she couldn't look her best. Sitting impatiently in front of her dressing table, she fidgeted as Mary arranged her copper hair in ringlets at the side of her neck.

"There now, yer all set."

Checking her image in the mirror one last time, satisfied she looked the best she could, she rose from the stool. "Thank you, Mary."

"He'll be home soon—I know it."

"I hope you're right."

But her worry continued to build. As Violet walked out the bedroom and made her way along the hall, Hatfield's voice floated up from in the entry. Hoping Rule had arrived, she hurried toward the stairs, but it was Caroline who swept into the house. Her cousin waved as she spotted Violet on the stairs.

"Oh, I'm so glad to find you at home. I have news! The most wonderful news I wish to share."

"I could use a little good news," Violet said. "Let's go

into the drawing room." Linking arms with her smiling cousin, Violet asked Hat to bring them tea, then led Caroline through the heavy sliding doors, and they settled themselves on the sofa.

"You talked to Luke," Violet guessed.

Caroline grinned. "I did just what you said. I told him I was madly in love with him."

"From the look on your face, Luke was pleased."

"More than pleased. Luke says he's in love with me, too."

Violet leaned over and hugged her. "I'm so happy for you, Carrie. You deserve a man who loves you."

Caroline reached over and squeezed Violet's hand. "So do you, Vi."

Violet glanced away.

"Has there been any news? What is happening with the murder investigation?"

Violet told Caroline that even now the duke and Rule's brother Reese were speaking to the magistrates. She told her cousin about Bates and Danny and that there was reason to believe it was an American named Montgomery who had killed Charles Whitney in order to stop him from purchasing Griffin.

"He wanted the company that badly?"

"He wanted to supply weapons to the Southern states in the event there is a war."

"Oh, dear, it's already beginning."

"I'm still holding hope the matter can be settled without bloodshed."

"What will happen to Rule?"

"Royal believes with this new information he may be able to get Rule out of jail, but we still need evidence against Montgomery."

"How will you get it?"

"That, my dear cousin, is the crux of the problem."

Hat entered with the tea cart just then, ending the conversation. Caroline stayed for a quick cup, said she would say a prayer for Rule's release, and left the town house.

Thinking of Luke and her cousin, Violet returned to the drawing room and sat back down on the sofa. She was happy for Caroline. And for Luke. She was glad they had found each other.

Still, it made her think of Rule and how much she loved him, and though he cared for her, it was unlikely he would ever truly love her in return.

Her heart squeezed. It didn't matter, she told herself. Few people found the sort of love Caroline and Luke had discovered.

And Violet was happy.

Well, almost happy. As happy as a woman could be in a marriage where she was the only one in love.

It wasn't till well after dark that Royal and Reese appeared on the doorstep. When the men walked into the entry, Violet realized Rule was with them—though with his several days' growth of beard and disheveled black hair, he looked more like a pirate than the handsome, sophisticated gentleman she had married.

"Rule!" Lifting her skirts, she raced toward him, and though he was dirty and unkempt and smelling of his days in prison, she rushed straight into his arms.

"Violet…love." He held her tightly against him, his cheek pressed to hers, and the roughness of his beard felt like heaven.

Her eyes filled with tears. "Thank God you are home." Ignoring his brothers, she caught his face between her hands and pulled his mouth down to hers for a very thorough kiss. Rule kissed her back even more thoroughly before he released her.

He grinned, carving those wonderful dimples into his cheeks. "For a homecoming like that, it was almost worth going to prison."

Violet reached up and cradled his face, her heart squeezing with love for him. Now was not the time. She forced her thoughts to the problem at hand.

"Obviously Bates cooperated." She looked over at Royal. "Where's Danny? You didn't let the police take him? You gave him your word."

"Danny's with Morgan," Royal said.

"There won't be any charges filed against him," Rule added. He cast a glance at his brothers. "While you two fill my wife in on what has been going on, I'll go upstairs and get rid of this dirt. I'll be down as quickly as I can."

Hatfield appeared like a specter in the hallway. "A nice hot bath is already on its way, my lord."

"Thank you, Hat." Turning back to Violet, Rule planted a last hard kiss on her mouth, turned and strode up the stairs.

"Let's go into the drawing room, shall we?" Royal offered his arm and she let him escort her. "We'll tell you what's happened and what we are planning to do."

The plan was simple.

They needed evidence against Montgomery, and together they had come up with a way to get it.

"The hard part was getting the police to agree," Reese said, "but in the end, Constable McGregor turned out to be a fair-minded man and he saw the merit of our idea."

"So let me get this straight." Violet shifted on the sofa. "You sent a note to Montgomery supposedly from Bates, demanding five thousand pounds in exchange for his silence in the matter of the murder of Charles Whitney."

"That's right," Royal said. "He's been staying at the Trafalgar Hotel. The note we sent instructs him to bring the money and meet Bates at midnight in the alley behind the White Bull Tavern."

"And you think he'll come?"

"We think he will," Reese said. "Either to pay Bates off or more likely to kill him. Unfortunately for Montgomery, the police will be waiting."

"As well as the three of you," she added, certain Rule and his brothers would want to be there.

Royal nodded. "We'll be there. In the meantime, we have a few things to do to get ready." The men rose from their places in the drawing room. "Tell Rule to meet us at the rendezvous point no later than eleven o'clock."

That didn't give them much time. Violet watched anxiously as the men departed, on their way to arm themselves and make final preparations. She couldn't help being nervous. Montgomery was a killer. One could never tell what might happen with a man like that.

Violet shivered.

Jeffrey rapped on the door to J. P. Montgomery's suite at the Trafalgar. A few moments later, the brawny Southerner pulled it open. His neck cloth was untied and hanging around his thick neck and his jacket was missing, draped over the back of a chair.

"I'm glad you're here," Montgomery said, stepping back to let him pass. "Somethin's come up. We need to talk."

"What's happened? I thought Wrigby was taking the new offer in to Griffin tomorrow."

"Yes, well, that's all well and good." Montgomery

turned his powerful frame around and headed in the direction of his bedroom. "The two of you can handle the details. Just get the offer accepted. As soon as the deal is closed and the company is ours, you can go home."

Trailing Montgomery into the other room, Jeffrey glanced at the bed, where Montgomery's steamer trunk sat open and nearly packed.

"Where are you going?"

"Like I said, somethin's come up. I'm leaving tonight. The *Redoubt* sails with the tide." A fine sheen of perspiration appeared on Montgomery's forehead. His anxiety hung in the air like a heavy perfume.

Jeffrey's senses went on alert. "Why the sudden urgency? What's happened, J.P.?"

The big man stared at Jeffrey for several long moments, then reached into his trouser pocket and pulled out a note. He handed it over to Jeffrey, who read it and looked up.

"This man is trying to extort you. He says he wants five thousand pounds to keep his silence. He is accusing you of killing Charles Whitney."

Montgomery finished folding a shirt and set it in the trunk. "That's right."

"Why would he believe you murdered Whitney?"

Montgomery stopped folding and looked at him hard. "The purchase was set to close. The chance to buy the company would have been lost to us for good. We need arms if we're going to fight. We need that plant and the one in Boston."

Jeffrey struggled to hide his shock. "You...you killed him?"

J.P. shrugged his thick shoulders. "We're going to war, man. A soldier does what he has to."

"We aren't at war yet. There's a chance it won't come

to that. Maybe the North will let us go our separate way. Nothing is certain."

"We have to be prepared."

Jeffrey didn't argue. The deed was done. It couldn't be undone. "So you will just sail for home."

"That's right. You and Wrigby can handle the purchase. You don't really need me."

Jeffrey fought to keep his voice even. "No, I suppose not."

As if the matter were settled, Montgomery folded a last shirt, stacked it on top of the others and closed the lid of the trunk. "Keep me posted, will you?"

"Of course. Smooth sailing, Montgomery."

"You, as well, Burnett."

Jeffrey left the hotel, his stomach tied in knots.

It was one thing to fight a war. Another to commit cold-blooded murder.

And another thing altogether to let an innocent man hang for the crime.

Even if that man was Rule Dewar.

Twenty-Nine

Violet stood in the entry watching her husband descend the sweeping staircase. Dressed in riding breeches, high black boots and a white lawn shirt, Rule shrugged into a jacket as he reached the bottom and hurriedly strode toward her.

"I think I liked you with a beard," she teased.

Rule rubbed his clean-shaven jaw. "I have plans for you later." He grinned wickedly. "I don't want to leave whisker burns on your pretty little thighs."

Violets eyes widened and her cheeks turned scarlet. "Rule Dewar!"

"Sorry." He gave her a devilish grin, not the least repentant.

Violet fought not to smile. "Your brothers said to meet them at eleven o'clock at the rendezvous point. Mr. Bellows has your carriage waiting out in front."

Rule nodded.

"I don't suppose you would consider letting me go with you. I'm a very good shot, you know."

"There will be a small army waiting for Montgomery."

He caught her chin and settled his mouth very softly over hers. "I want you here waiting for me when I get home."

The heat in those blue, blue eyes left no doubt as to his intentions and her heart gave a ragged jerk.

"I'll be waiting," she said breathlessly.

Rule strode off down the hall to retrieve his weapons and disappeared inside his study. Glancing at the clock, Violet fidgeted anxiously.

What if something happened?

Montgomery was a murderer. No matter how many people lay in wait for him, something could go wrong. She couldn't relax until Rule was home and safe.

A book lay open on the sofa in the drawing room, but she was far too nervous to read. She wished she could go with the men, but no amount of arguing was going to make that happen. She started down the hall toward the study to see if there was anything else Rule might need, when she heard the rap of the heavy brass knocker. Hatfield opened the door and surprise rolled through her as Jeffrey walked into the house.

The moment he saw her, he shoved past the butler and strode down the hall, not stopping until he reached her.

"I need to speak to you, Violet. The matter is urgent."

"Jeffrey, I don't know why you are here at this hour of the night but I don't think—"

"It concerns your husband."

Something was wrong. She knew Jeffrey well enough to recognize the worry on his face. "Come into the drawing room." She quickly led him inside, leaving the door open so that Rule could join them. "What is it, Jeffrey?"

He took a deep breath. "I believed your husband was guilty of murder. I thought he had killed Charles Whitney to gain more profit from the sale of the company. Tonight I discovered Dewar is innocent of the crime."

She frowned. "I don't understand. How could you find out something like that?"

"You remember the American, Montgomery, the man who made the offer on your company?"

"Yes, I know him." She didn't say that very soon, if all went as planned, he was going to be arrested for murder.

"We are...we are business associates, Violet."

Her head came up. "Business associates?"

"Montgomery and I...we formed a partnership of sorts in order to purchase Griffin." The news shocked her. Jeffrey was aligned with Montgomery? She glanced toward the door, anxious for Rule to appear.

"You were involved in making the offer?" she asked, but now that she thought of it, she knew Jeffrey was raised in Virginia. The Southern cause was a topic they rarely discussed. "We turned Montgomery's offer down."

"I know. It's all very complicated. But tonight when I stopped by J.P.'s hotel room, I found him packing. He admitted he killed Charles Whitney in order to stop him from buying the company." ·

Her gaze slid back to the doorway. Rule stood stiffly in the doorway, listening to every word.

Her mind spun. "Montgomery killed Whitney."

"That's right."

"But...but why would he try to make it appear as though Rule did it?"

"Perhaps he hoped you would turn to me once your husband was gone. Or maybe he thought you would be more easily convinced to sell than Dewar. It's hard to say for certain."

She looked to the doorway. Rule's jaw was set, his expression hard. The handle of a pistol shoved into the waistband of his riding breeches flashed beneath his coat as he strode into the drawing room. His eyes were dark as they lit on Jeffrey's face.

"You said Montgomery was packing," Rule said, grabbing Jeffrey's attention. "Where is he going?"

"I thought you were in jail."

"Is that why you came here? You thought I was gone and you wanted to see my wife?"

"I came because I don't condone murder, no matter the pretext."

Rule studied Jeffrey's face. "What exactly did Montgomery say?"

"J.P. showed me a note. He was being extorted by a man named Bates who knew about the murder. J.P.'s leaving England tonight, sailing with the tide aboard the *Redoubt*."

"Great heavens." Violet's voice shook.

Rule's jaw clenched. "I've got to stop him."

"You'll need help," Violet said. "You can't possibly go after him alone."

"I'll go with you," Jeffrey offered.

Rule eyed him with suspicion, clearly unwilling to accept the help of a man involved with a murderer. "Someone needs to find my brothers, bring them and the police to the harbor."

"I'll go," Violet said, glad she had worn her simple navy cambric after all.

Rule shook his head. "The area around the White Bull isn't safe for a woman." He turned to Jeffrey. "Your carriage outside?"

"Yes."

"My brothers will be waiting a block north of the White Bull Tavern, an alley near the corner of Childers and Holborn. They'll be there at eleven. Find them, bring them to the *Redoubt*. The harbormaster will know where to find it."

Jeffrey nodded, apparently understanding Rule's reluctance. "If that's what you want."

"You had better leave now," Rule said. "It will take you a while to get there."

Jeffrey flicked Violet a final glance and headed for the door.

The moment he was out of sight, Rule turned in her direction. "Do you trust him to do as he says?"

"Whatever you may think of him, I believe Jeffrey is a man of honor. That he came here tonight should be proof of that."

Rule nodded his reluctant agreement.

"You can't do this alone. I'm going with you."

He shook his head. "Not a chance in hell."

"You need someone with you in case there is trouble. I'm not afraid to use a gun and I am an excellent shot."

"No." He started past her, but Violet caught his arm.

"I'm going to the *Redoubt*. I can either come with you or I can wait until you leave and follow you. Which is it going to be?"

A muscle jerked in his cheek. He released a slow, deep breath. "You are trouble, Violet Dewar. Beautiful trouble, but trouble just the same."

"I assume that means we are going together."

His jaw firmed but he nodded. "Get your wrap and let's go."

Racing upstairs, she tugged open her dresser drawer, pulled out the small pocket pistol she had carried on her journey to England and stuck it into the pocket in the seam of her skirt. If they were going to capture a killer, she needed to be prepared for whatever might occur.

Rule stood impatiently waiting as she draped her shawl around her shoulders and descended the stairs. He caught her arm and hauled her rather forcefully out the door and down the front steps to the carriage.

As she looked up at the small man in the driver's seat, she silently groaned, remembering it was Bellows' night off. They would get no help there. Guiding her up the iron steps into the carriage, Rule told the coachman to head for the harbor, then followed her inside and settled himself on the seat across from her, stretching his long legs out in front of him.

He eyed her darkly. "I don't like being blackmailed, sweetheart."

Violet arched a brow. "And I don't like my husband putting himself in danger with no one to help him."

His hard look softened. He studied her a moment then his lips faintly curved. "You are the most amazing woman."

Amazing enough for him to love? Violet made no reply.

Instead, her thoughts returned to Montgomery and the task of catching a murderer.

And making certain her husband remained a free man.

Thirty

 ⟳⟳⟳

The night was ink-black, no moon to light the way. The Thames was as murky as the sky, marked only by the reflection of a few scattered lamps on the ships bobbing along the quay.

Rule's tension mounted as the carriage pulled up in front of the harbormaster's office. The hour was late enough the office was dark and no one remained inside. Fortunately, the list he hoped to find was posted beside the door, giving the location of every ship in the harbor and their scheduled date of departure.

"Jeffrey was right," Rule told Violet as he climbed back inside the coach. "The *Redoubt* sails with the tide. If Montgomery is planning to leave, he should be aboard by now."

It took another quarter hour to find the space where the *Redoubt* was berthed. A big, three-masted sailing ship with a long, pointed bowsprit and sleekly built hull. Lanterns hung from the rigging and a few crew members roamed the deck, finishing last-minute chores and making ready to leave. Several lamps burned in the main salon and glowed through portholes in the side of the ship. Most of the passengers would be asleep at this hour but apparently a few were still up and about.

"I'm going to speak to the captain," Rule said, "find out if Montgomery is aboard and if he is, get his cabin number and find him."

"Shouldn't you wait for your brothers and the police?"

"There isn't time. The tide is almost up. The ship could be sailing very soon."

"You think the captain will tell you where to find Montgomery?"

"He'll tell me." He smiled darkly. "You know how persuasive I can be." And he was, after all, the brother of a duke. Sometimes a title could come in handy. He leaned over and opened the carriage door.

"If Montgomery finds out you are looking for him, he might try to run," Violet said. "He might find a way to get past you."

Rule hesitated a moment at the truth of her words, then continued out to the street.

"Let me help you," Violet pleaded through the open carriage window. "Surely there is something I can do."

The ship creaked eerily as it rocked against its lines. Rule glanced over at the gangway leading up to the deck. If Montgomery slipped past him, he might escape. Rule couldn't allow that to happen.

"All right, come on." Taking Violet's hand, he helped her down from the carriage. Thank God she wasn't wearing one of those damned metal cages that were all the vogue. "I presume you have brought your pistol."

He knew she wouldn't have left the house without it. Not under the circumstances. Montgomery was a murderer and she had always been proud of her ability to shoot.

She patted the pocket of her skirt. "I have it."

He took her hand and led her into the darkness. "I want you to stay out of sight over here by the gangway. If Montgomery gets past me, he'll have to leave the ship this way. If you see him, fire a shot into the air, then duck back out of sight. I'll hear the shot and come running."

"All right."

"I don't want you taking any chances. Promise me you will stay here where it is safe."

"I'll stay right here and keep watch."

Rule led her to a hiding place among a stack of wooden crates where she wouldn't be seen and yet could watch the gangway. He tucked her safely into the shadows, pulled her shawl a little closer around her shoulders, leaned down and kissed her.

"Remember what I said. Don't take any chances."

She nodded. "Be careful."

Rule's jaw went hard. He couldn't wait to get his hands on J. P. Montgomery. He told himself he wouldn't do anything but hold him until the police arrived, but thinking of the days he had spent in that miserable prison, it would take a will of iron.

Rule stood in the darkness at the bottom of the gangway, waited until the deck was empty, then silently made his way aboard the ship. Lamplight blazed through the portholes in the main salon. He peeked into one of them, searching for Montgomery, but saw no sign of him.

Descending a short ladder, he opened a wooden door and entered the salon, lavishly appointed, paneled in teak and curtained in red velvet. Two men sat in front of a chessboard. One of them looked up as he entered the room.

"I'm looking for the captain," Rule said. "Do you know where I can find him?"

A rusty voice came from behind him. "I'm Captain Hale. How may I help you, sir?"

Rule turned to see a short, stout man with a heavy white beard, pretty much the standard image of a sea captain.

"I'm Lord Rule Dewar. I'm looking for a man named J. P. Montgomery. I believe he's a passenger aboard your ship."

The captain nodded. "Montgomery...yes, I believe he is."

"Can you give me his cabin number so that I may speak to him?"

The captain frowned, his bushy white eyebrows nearly forming a single line. "I'm afraid that information is privileged. Can you tell me what this is about?"

"Montgomery is wanted in connection to a murder. The police should be arriving at any moment. Until they get here, I need to detain Mr. Montgomery."

"I say. This is highly irregular."

"The man is a killer. Do you want that sort among your passengers and crew?"

"No, no, of course not."

"As I said, the police will be arriving any moment. I merely need to be certain Montgomery is here when they get here."

"Dewar, you say? Any relation to the duke?"

"He's my brother."

"I see. Well, all right, then, myself and some of my crew will accompany you to Mr. Montgomery's cabin. We shall see what he has to say about all of this."

He would rather have had a few minutes alone with Montgomery, but perhaps this was for the best. "Very well."

Rule followed Captain Hale out of the salon, up the ladder to the deck, then anxiously waited as he summoned his first officer and two of his crewmen. The group followed Hale below deck down a long corridor lined with cabins.

The captain knocked on a door marked B 66 in brass letters. No one answered.

"Mr. Montgomery? Mr. Montgomery, this is Captain Hale. I'd like a word with you, sir, if you please."

Rule waited tensely for the door to open. When it didn't, an unwelcome tingle began to creep down his spine.

Standing in the darkness smoking a thick cigar, J.P. noticed the captain and another man coming out of the salon. They were joined by the first mate and two other crewmen and the group descended the ladder leading down to the passenger decks.

He tossed his unfinished cigar away and ground his back teeth together. One of the men, taller than the rest, broad-shouldered and handsome, was, he realized, Rule Dewar.

So the bastard had managed to wheedle his way out of prison, had somehow convinced the authorities to release him.

Bates, he thought. So the idiot had done as his note had threatened and gone to the authorities. Now Dewar had discovered his plans and followed him to the ship.

But how?

His stomach lurched, curdled with fury. *Jeffrey!* No one else knew his plans. No one but his partner, Jeffrey Burnett. Livid with himself for trusting the traitor, he turned away from the rail and headed for the gangway. They hadn't caught him yet and with any luck at all, they weren't going to.

Once he was safe, he would deal with Jeffrey Burnett.

Checking to be sure no one saw him, he made his way silently across the deck to the gangway. It swayed as his heavy weight descended toward the bottom, but he saw no sign of anyone following. He had just stepped onto the dock when a woman's voice called out.

"Stop right where you are, Montgomery." He knew that voice. He heard the ominous click of a pistol and caught the faint flash of the barrel in the light of a distant lantern. "If you don't, I'll have to shoot you."

Violet Dewar. He might have laughed if he wasn't so furious. Did she actually think she could stop him?

"Put the gun down, little lady, before you hurt yourself." He started forward, determined to make his escape. The petite woman stepped out of the shadows into the lantern light, her fiery copper hair blazing like a halo around her pretty face.

For an instant, he almost admired her. Then he saw that her pistol was pointed straight at his heart.

"I told you to stay where you were," she said.

His jaw clenched as a fresh round of fury swept through him. "I have places to go and both of us know you're not really going to shoot me."

"My father manufactured guns. He taught me how to shoot and not to be afraid to pull the trigger. This pistol shoots twice, Mr. Montgomery. That's more than enough to kill you where you stand."

She looked small and feminine, holding that little gun in her hand, and not the least bit frightening. "You're a woman, a nurturer. You aren't going to kill me."

He started forward, thought to walk right past her.

Violet pulled the trigger.

Montgomery shrieked and went down. Bleeding profusely, his knee was shattered and no longer able to hold him up. "You little bitch, you shot me!"

"I warned you not to move. And if you don't stay right where you are, I'll shoot you again."

A commotion on deck drew her attention, men running helter-skelter toward the gangway, Rule in the lead.

"Violet!" He raced down the gangway, jolted to a stop when he reached Montgomery and stared at her with wide blue eyes. "You shot him?"

"He was trying to escape."

"I'll probably get gangrene and lose my leg!" Montgomery wailed.

"You thought it was all right for my husband to lose his life," Violet countered.

Rule reached toward her, gently took the gun from her hand. "It's all right, love. I've got it." The minute he took control of the weapon, she started shaking. It was, after all, the first—and hopefully the last—time she'd ever shot someone.

Rule drew her against his side, an arm wrapped protectively around her. The captain stopped next to Montgomery, knelt to attend the man's bleeding leg, but his arrival was lost amid the swarm of men descending on the scene, a group that included Rule's brothers, Jeffrey Burnett and half a dozen policemen.

The duke strode toward them. "Are you two all right?"

Rule shoved Violet's pistol into the pocket of his coat and his hold tightened around her. "My brave little wife captured Whitney's murderer." He cast her a dark look, but his eyes glinted with pride. "I thought I told you to fire a warning shot."

Violet just smiled. "I did. It just happened to go into Mr. Montgomery's leg. You know what a poor shot I am."

Rule's lips twitched. "Yes, sweetheart, that is among the growing number of things I am beginning to know about you."

Violet relaxed against him, his warmth and possessive hold calming the tremors racing through her.

It took a while to straighten out the details of what had occurred, but ultimately the police arrested J. P. Montgomery and hauled him away in the police wagon. Reese and Royal congratulated Rule and Violet on a job well done and departed for their respective homes.

Violet and Rule climbed wearily into their waiting carriage. Rule settled himself on the seat beside her, his arm going around her.

"You were marvelous tonight, sweetheart. I couldn't believe my eyes when I saw you holding that gun on Montgomery."

She gave him an exhausted smile. "The main thing is you are safe. The police will sort all of this out and your innocence will no longer be suspect."

"Thanks in great part to you." He bent his head and very softly kissed her.

Violet slid her arms around his neck and kissed him back. "I love you, Rule." Unable to stop them, the words slipped past her lips. She found herself praying, now that he was safe, he would say them in return.

Instead, he bent his head and tenderly kissed her.

Violet turned away.

"What is it?"

She lifted her head, forced herself to meet his searching gaze. "I need to know, Rule. I love you. I have for a very long time. I need to know if you love me in return."

In the glow of the carriage lamps, he moistened his lips, glanced down and back up, then started to speak.

"Don't lie to me, Rule. I'll know if you do."

Time stretched between them. The air in the carriage seemed to slowly disappear until she began to feel light-headed.

Rule blew out a breath, raked a hand through his heavy black hair. "You are precious to me, Violet. I am unbelievably grateful that you are my wife. I want children with you. I want us to be happy. But *love?* Love isn't something I know how to give."

Her eyes welled and she had to look away.

"You mean everything to me, Violet. I hope you understand."

She only nodded. Her throat was too tight to speak. He cared for her. He desired her. He wanted her to be the mother of his children. It was enough, she told herself— more than most couples shared. But the tears brimmed in her eyes and slid down her cheeks. Violet wiped them away with the tip of her finger.

When they reached the house, she pled a headache and started up the stairs. Rule caught up with her easily. He walked her to the door of her room. Catching her hand, he brought it to his lips and kissed the back.

"The night has been difficult for both of us. We don't have to make love. Just let me sleep beside you. Let me hold you."

She wanted to say no, that she couldn't bear his presence tonight, but when she looked at him there was something in his eyes that made her ache for him and she found herself nodding instead. "All right."

He followed her into the bedroom, sent Mary off to her room and played ladies' maid himself, methodically dispensing with her garments, helping her into a soft cotton nightgown, pulling the pins from her hair then running her bristle brush through it. All the while, his movements remained businesslike, making no attempt at seduction.

Violet was grateful. She needed time to accept the life that lay ahead of her, the knowledge that her husband would never love her the way she had always dreamed.

Once she was properly prepared for sleep, he lifted her into his arms and carried her over to the bed. As she settled beneath the covers, he stripped down to his drawers and joined her. True to his word, he merely lay down and gathered her back against his chest.

Violet felt tears welling. It was ridiculous. Rule was a good husband. He cared for her, worried about her, did his best to comfort her as he was doing now.

A fire burned low in the hearth. Orange flames curled over the grate and bathed the room in a soft golden glow. She could feel the warmth of Rule's body, curled spoon-fashion around her, a muscular arm draped over her hip. Against her back, she felt the rhythmic rise and fall of his breathing.

Her heart swelled with love for him and suddenly lying next to him wasn't enough. She turned onto her back and looked up at him, set a hand against his cheek, roughened by his evening's growth of beard.

"I need you, Rule," she said, knowing it was true, knowing she would never leave him, no matter his feelings for her, no matter that she might not be able to hold him.

Rule bent toward her, settled his lips over hers. "Violet…" he whispered.

The kiss deepened, lengthened, turned fierce. A kiss that went on and on and seemed to have no end, a languid kiss, a torrid kiss, a kiss that stole the very breath from her lungs.

Her nightgown felt too heavy, too much of a barrier between them. She sat up and let him draw it off over her head, waited as he removed the last of his own clothes, the final obstacle between them.

"I need you, too," he said, kissing her again.

She could feel the hard proof of his desire, hot against her thigh, thought that he would come up over her, fill her as she wished him to do, but instead, he lifted her, settled her astride him.

"I want to see you. I want to watch you reach your pleasure."

Her breasts thrust toward him, seemed to swell at his words, her nipples turning kernel hard. Rule reached up and cupped them in his palms, gently squeezed, made them ache and swell. She let her head fall back, giving him better access, feeling the brush of her long copper hair against her hips. His mouth replaced his hands, suckling her, making her tremble at the hot sensations.

His mouth toyed with hers, melding, his tongue fencing, driving her mad with desire for him. His hands gripped her hips, lifting her a little, and positioned her to receive him. He was big and hard, thick and heavy, and she wanted him inside her. She was wet and ready, aching to join with him, her flesh softening, surrounding him, beginning to pulse with need for him.

"Rule…" she whispered, taking more of him, hearing the hiss of his breath as he filled her completely. All the love she felt for him welled inside her. Leaning forward, she rested her hands on his powerful shoulders, her long hair falling forward, forming a curtain around them, enclosing them in the intimate world they shared.

Love for him warmed her insides as the fire warmed their naked flesh.

She began to move and incredible pleasure slid through her. Faint tremors quaked through her limbs. She raised and lowered her hips, taking him deeply, absorbing the pleasure, giving him pleasure, too.

The muscles in Rule's hard body tightened. His hands gripped her hips once more, demanding now, insistent. For several moments, he kept her on the edge, trapped by the building sensations, the feel of their bodies joined as one.

Then he growled her name and thrust deeply and she couldn't hold back any longer.

Release tore through her, pleasure rocked her senses as

she reached her release and an instant later, Rule reached his, his seed spilling hotly inside her.

Long moments passed as she lay slumped against him, felt the brush of his lips against her hair. But no words of love slipped from his lips.

I love you so much, she wanted to tell him, but the words remained locked away. She wasn't sure she would ever say them again.

Her heart hurt, throbbed as if a knife had pierced it, as if it bled inside her chest. She loved him, desired him, welcomed him into her body. She made his house a home and one day she would bear his children.

She meant everything to him, he had said.

But he did not love her.

The tears in her eyes began to slip down her cheeks. Turning away, she stared into the darkness, hoping that Rule would not see.

Thirty-One

At the sound of his butler's voice, Royal looked up from behind the desk in his study. Tomorrow he and his family would be returning to Bransford Castle. Now that the charges had been dropped against Rule, he and Lily could resume the quiet country life they loved.

"What is it, Rutgers?" he asked of the gray-haired man in the doorway.

"Your brother Lord Rule is arrived, Your Grace. He is just—"

"I'm right here," Rule said darkly, stalking past the butler into the study. His cravat was untied, his face unshaven, his black hair in complete disarray. Faint smudges appeared beneath his eyes and worry lines etched his forehead.

"What the bloody hell has happened to you?"

Rule just shook his head. There was something in his eyes, something so haunted and bereft that Royal's chest tightened.

He rose from behind his desk, softening his voice as he walked toward his youngest brother. "Tell me what is wrong."

Rule stared off toward the window. His throat moved up and down. "Violet loves me and I can't love her back."

Royal frowned. "What are you talking about? Why ever not? You've chosen the perfect mate for yourself. Violet is beautiful and giving, loyal and caring, she is—"

"You don't have to list my wife's virtues," Rule said, looking miserable. "You think I don't know them by now? Violet is all of those things and more. She is intelligent and brave and sweet and passionate. She is everything a man could want in a wife."

"Clearly you desire her. When you're with her, you can barely keep your hands off her. And you seem to care for her."

"Of course I care."

"Then what is the problem?"

Emotion flashed in Rule's eyes. "The problem is Violet wants me to love her. I don't think she can ever be happy with a man who isn't capable of love. But I don't know how. I have no idea what the emotion feels like. I haven't the slightest idea what it means to love a woman." Rule sank down on the sofa, dropped his head into his hands.

Royal approached him quietly, feeling some of his brother's pain. "I know you never had a mother. I realize the women you've been involved with in the past weren't the sort who deserved your love. But Violet is your wife."

Rule swallowed. "I know." For an instant, Royal thought he caught a glint of moisture in his brother's blue eyes.

"Perhaps I can help you," Royal said softly, resting a hand on Rule's shoulder. "You want to know what love is? Let me try to explain it, little brother."

Rule just sat there.

"Love is when you think of someone no matter how far away they are. It's when you would rather be with that person than anyone else. It's when the sound of their laughter makes you smile. When you admire them for standing up to you, instead of getting angry. It's when you look at another woman and think how beautiful she is but there isn't a chance you would rather make love to her than the woman in your bed."

Rule was staring as if he tried to process the words.

"Love is when you can't sleep at night unless the person you love is beside you. When you can't imagine a future without her in your life. It's when you look at your wife and feel your chest go tight. When you secretly thank God that He gave her to you. Love is when you feel sick to your stomach because you have hurt her." Royal looked into Rule's haggard face, felt the tension in his shoulders. "Which I have a strong suspicion is the way you are feeling right now."

Rule worked a muscle in his jaw. For several long moments he said nothing. Then he swallowed and rose from the sofa, straightening to his full height. "I love her, don't I?"

Royal just smiled. "Of course you do. I think you have loved her since the day she arrived from America and boldly showed up in your drawing room."

Relief washed over Rule's face, making the dark lines disappear. "I love her." A slow smile curved his lips. "I love Violet Dewar!"

Royal laughed. "I am glad you have finally figured it out. Now that you know, I think you had better tell her."

"Yes… Yes, of course." He started for the door. "I have to go."

Royal followed him down the hall to the entry.

As Rule passed in front of a gilded mirror above the hall table, he caught a glimpse of himself and paused at his dishevel. "I had to get out of the house. I didn't bother with the niceties." He ran a hand over his unshaven beard. "I look like I spent the night in a gutter."

"I don't think Violet will care what you look like."

Rule grinned, a broad flash of white that made him look younger than he had in years. "No, she won't care. She loves me. Thanks to you, I am finally beginning to understand what that means."

Rule hurried out the door, and Royal turned to see Lily approaching, her delicate features radiant at the sight of him. She was pale and beautiful, sweet and giving. He had learned the meaning of love through Lily. And as he had said, he thanked God every day for the gift of her.

"That was Rule, wasn't it?" she said. "He didn't stay very long. What did he want?"

"Just a little brotherly advice." Royal turned toward her. Taking the woman he loved into his arms, he very tenderly kissed her.

Rule couldn't get home fast enough. He felt as if a boulder had been lifted off his chest, as if a ray of sunlight had suddenly descended from heaven to illuminate his way.

He was in love. Insanely in love with his wife.

He couldn't imagine why he'd been unable to see it. How he could not have known.

But then he had never been in love before and he simply hadn't understood.

The carriage ride back to the house seemed to take forever. He couldn't wait to tell Violet he loved her. He couldn't wait to see the look on her beautiful face when he said the words. Fighting to stop a tune from whistling past his lips, he leaned back in the seat of the carriage, silently willing Bellows to drive the horses faster. With so much traffic in the street, it wasn't going to happen.

To pass the time, he began to practice what he would say and was amazed to discover how difficult it was to find the right words. They spun round and round in his head and still kept coming out wrong. He told himself when the time came he would just tell her the way he felt.

He would tell her that he loved her.

Rule just hoped the words still mattered as much to her as they now did to him.

Needing to feel the sunshine on her face, Violet slipped outside into the garden. The peonies were in bloom and she knelt to examine a brilliant yellow blossom the same shade as her embroidered muslin gown.

Reaching out, she pulled an errant weed the gardener had missed and tried not to think of Rule and where he might have gone this morning. After last night's misadventures, she had slept later than she meant to and awakened to find him gone. He wasn't in the house, she discovered, and even Hat didn't know where he had gone.

At least he was safe now. The police finally had the right man under arrest and Rule's life was no longer in danger. Violet took comfort in the fact that she had done her part in proving his innocence. She tried to content herself with that and not dwell on the fact that Rule would never really love her.

She ignored a painful little pang in her heart and tugged on another small weed, then came to her feet at the sound of someone moving about in the garden.

"Well, now ain't ye a pretty sight this mornin'."

Her breath stalled in her throat. She knew that voice, that face. *Simon Pratt.*

Her gaze shot to the French doors, but there was no one in sight. "What…what are you doing here?"

"I come fer ye, girl. Ye took me sweeps. I warned ye. I told ye nobody steals from Simon Pratt."

Her heart raced. Something glinted in the sun and for

the first time she noticed the long curved blade in his bony hand. Violet screamed and bolted for the door, but Pratt was on her before she could make her escape.

"I'd behave myself iffin' I was you. Less ye want a taste of cold steel."

Violet stood silent and trembling, the wiry, sallow-faced man behind her, a sinewy arm wrapped around her neck, holding her against him. Fear churned through her, made her legs feel weak.

Pratt dragged her a few feet backward along the path leading to the back gate, the way he must have come into the garden. Then he stiffened, his hold tightening as someone walked out through the French doors onto the terrace.

Violet bit back a cry. Rule stood tall and imposing in front of the balustrade, his fierce blue gaze riveted on Pratt.

"Let her go." The quiet menace in his voice made her shiver.

"Stay where ye are and don't come any closer," Pratt warned.

Rule's gaze moved to Violet's face and a strange sort of calm settled over her. Rule was there. He wouldn't let Pratt hurt her. Whatever it took, Rule would find a way to keep her safe.

"I said to let her go."

Pratt's laughter was grating and ghoulish. "She took me sweeps. I been outta work ever since."

"You were using children, Pratt. You were breaking the law."

"It were none o' her business." He waved the knife. "I warned her what would happen. Nobody steals from Simon Pratt." His hold tightened around Violet's throat. "Call out and she's dead." Pulling her backward, he edged along the gravel path toward the gate.

Rule followed him step for step, his face a mask of rage. The knife glinted, keeping him at bay.

"What do you want, Pratt?"

The sweep paused. Glancing at his surroundings, he took in the marble fountain, assessed the fine quality of the wrought-iron furniture, the magnificence of the house.

"I come for the woman, since she brung me so much trouble. But ye kin 'ave her if ye pay me price."

"Name it."

"Five hundred quid." He grinned, showing the rotten stubs of his teeth. "She worth that much to ye?"

"She's worth a hundred times that and more."

Her chest tightened. She loved him so much.

"Ye got the five hundred in the house?"

Rule nodded. "I'll get it if you let the lady go."

Pratt just laughed. "I ain't a fool. Keep yer mouth shut, get the money and then I'll let 'er go."

Violet could read Rule's indecision. He didn't want to leave her with Pratt, but she was the only other person besides himself who knew where to find the money.

"I'll be all right," she said, reading his fear for her.

His jaw clenched. "I'll get your money, Pratt, but if you touch her, you die. I'll follow you to the gates of hell and I'll kill you with my own bare hands."

Pratt pointed the tip of the knife against Violet's throat and for an instant, she couldn't breathe.

Rule backed up until he reached the terrace steps then turned and disappeared into the house.

The knife twitched in his hand as they stood there silently waiting. There was a safe in the study behind a gilt-framed painting of horses and hounds. Rule had shown her where to find it and given her the combination. A small rosewood box inside held money for her use should she need it.

It seemed only an instant till Rule ran back into the garden, the rosewood box in his hand. "There's a thousand pounds in this box. Take it and be gone."

The sweep's eyes rounded. "Ye must be bloody in love."

"I am in love, Pratt." He turned to Violet, spoke to her directly. "I'm desperately in love with my wife." He held up the box. "Now let her go before I come over there and beat you bloody senseless."

Violet started to shiver. It was the cruelest of jests to hear Rule say the words that meant so much to her simply to appease Simon Pratt.

She told herself it didn't matter. That Rule was trying to save her.

Pratt just laughed. "Open the lid. Show me what's inside."

Rule did as Pratt demanded, then set the rosewood box on the wrought-iron bench. The sweep dragged Violet over to the box and snatched it up. "Stay where ye are. I'll let 'er go when I get ta the gate."

Rule's hands fisted. As Pratt moved backward, Rule stalked him every inch of the way. When Pratt reached the gate, he shoved Violet forward and she stumbled, gave a little cry of surprise. Rule ran to her, swept her into his arms.

She could feel him shaking, his tall frame trembling as he held her tightly against him.

"Violet..." He glanced behind her, but Pratt had disappeared. Rule didn't seem to care.

"I was so afraid," he said, his hold tightening even more. "God, I love you so much."

Her heart squeezed. He buried his face in her hair and she thought that her heart would surely break in two. *He doesn't mean it,* she told herself. *He's only frightened that Pratt might have hurt you.*

Her throat ached and her eyes filled with tears. If only it were true.

"I love you, Violet," he said softly against her cheek, and he sounded so sincere. She forced herself to ask the question that throbbed in her heart.

"Do you mean it?" she whispered, afraid to look at him, afraid she would see the truth.

Rule drew back so that she could see his face. "You would know if I was lying. You would know."

She swallowed past the lump in her throat. "Yes, I would know."

"I'm not lying, sweetheart. I love you."

Tears rolled down her cheeks.

"It took me a while to figure it out, but now I know the truth. I love you more than my own life."

And then he pulled her back into his arms and she was crying and clinging to him and she could feel Rule's heart beating, feel his love surrounding her.

Something had changed. Maybe it was Pratt's attack. Maybe something else.

Whatever it was, Rule had said he loved her and Violet knew deep in her heart that he was telling the truth.

Rule gently kissed his beautiful wife. His brother had helped him understand what love truly was, but until the moment he had seen Simon Pratt with a knife against Violet's throat, he hadn't known the extent of that love.

If there was any way he could have traded places, been the person beneath the blade, he would have done it. With a flash of clarity, he'd understood that when you loved someone, you would die for them without a moment's hesitation.

He kissed the top of Violet's head and told her again

how much he loved her. Violet cried and clung to him as if she would never let him go, and he had never felt so good, so happy. The world had never felt so right until that moment. Everything made sense in a way it hadn't before. Love was the answer. Love made the difference. It had taken him half a lifetime to see.

And the love of a very special woman.

Rule looked up as Hatfield called to him from the terrace. "The police are here, my lord. I sent for them when I saw what was happening in the garden." Hat's pale lips curved. "Seems they caught a thief just down the block, my lord, uses the name Simon Pratt."

Violet looked at Rule and gave him a watery smile. She wiped tears from her pretty green eyes. "What would we do without Hat?"

Hatfield beamed.

All Rule could think was what would he do without Violet? Bending his head, he very softly kissed her.

"I love you, Violet Dewar."

"I love you, Rule," she said, and he thought now that he understood how important those word were, he could never hear her say them enough.

Epilogue

One month later

Bright golden sunlight slipped through the overhanging trees at the edge of the water. The surface of the Thames glittered as if a mantle of diamonds floated on top. Clustered in groups along the river, the elite of Society were gathered, excited by the prospect of the upcoming race between Royal Dewar, Sheridan Knowles, Dillon St. Michaels, Benjamin Wyndam and Quentin Garrett.

Only Jonathan Savage was missing from the line of competitors, off on some mysterious business he had yet to divulge.

Today the Oarsmen were racing their sleek little one-man sculls in a fierce competition. The winner would receive a trophy in the First Annual Blue Haven Charity Benefit Race. The afternoon's activities and a lavish picnic had been sponsored by Rule and Violet Dewar, and the admittance fees and a percentage of the betting proceeds would be going to Annabelle Greer's charity, the Blue Haven Orphanage.

Standing next to a circle of children she was coming to know and love, Violet gazed at them fondly. Danny Tuttle played catch with little red-haired Billy Robin, who laughed as he caught the ball. A group of his young friends, former sweeps who had been rescued from Simon Pratt, swung mallets as they learned to play croquet.

Since their arrival, the orphanage had expanded, taking more homeless children off the streets and rescuing more young sweeps, pressing hard to stop the abuse of children in the trade.

"Well, you certainly got a good turnout."

Violet turned at the sound of Caroline's voice, saw her approaching in a gown of pale pink muslin and a pretty straw bonnet trimmed with pink silk flowers she had purchased at the Lily Pad, the millinery shop the duchess owned.

Violet smiled. "It's a very good cause. Annabelle is hoping to open another facility as soon as possible. She needs to raise as much money as she can."

"You know Luke and I will be happy to help."

"I know you will." Luke and Caroline were still deeply in love and Violet didn't expect that to change. Both of them had come to realize the rarity of the special bond they shared. Just as Violet and Rule had learned how fortunate they were to have found each other as they had.

Since the day Simon Pratt had threatened Violet's life, Rule had told her he loved her a thousand times. Since that day, their love had deepened, changed and expanded. Rule had said that Violet had taught him the value of a woman. In marrying her, he had said, God had taught him an invaluable lesson about the worth of the female gender.

Violet had come to understand the fierceness of his loyalty and the depth of love he was capable of giving, something Rule himself hadn't known.

"Come on, they're getting ready to start!" Caroline caught Violet's hand and began tugging her toward the edge of the river where the boats were lined up. Rule stood at the starting line, a pistol in his hand.

He winked at Violet and grinned, digging those lovely dimples into his cheeks. He turned back to the racers. "Are you ready?"

The men in the boats shouted a resounding *yes!*

"On your marks." He cocked the pistol. "Get ready. Go!" The roar of the starting gun signaled the beginning of the race and the racers dug in, bending over their oars, rowing hard, using their powerful arms and legs to give them momentum in the sliding seat, each man determined to win.

Standing next to Violet, Caroline smiled as Luke walked up beside her.

"I bet on Royal." Luke slid an arm around his wife's tiny, corsetted waist. "Think he'll win, love?"

"Of course the duke will win," Caroline said passionately. "He's a Dewar, is he not? And he is family."

Luke laughed and so did Violet. The Dewar men were all fine athletes, though Rule's sport was boxing. She looked up just then and spotted her husband walking toward her, tall, dark and impossibly handsome. He bent and brushed a light kiss on her lips, sending a feathery little thrill up her spine.

"Well, they are off. We won't know the winner for a while."

"It really doesn't matter who wins," Violet said as he settled a hand possessively at her waist. "The money they are raising is what is important."

Rule smiled down at her. "Once the sale closes on Griff we should be able to make another hefty contribution."

They had found another buyer for the compan

Englishman named Buckland with a sterling reputation who had agreed to their stringent terms. The agreement stated that should a conflict arise in America, there would be no sale of weapons to those who fought against the abolition of slavery.

Since wars were going on all over the world and there were plenty of other places to sell the excellent rifles and pistols Griffin produced, the buyer had agreed.

Thinking of guns brought to mind the shooting at the dock and she shivered.

Rule looked down at her. "You can't be cold on a day as warm as this. Are you feeling unwell, my love?"

She looked up at him. "I was just thinking of Montgomery."

"He deserved exactly what he got." Justice had been swift and harsh. Losing a leg hadn't kept him from hanging.

Rule ran a finger along her cheek. "I suppose I should see to your shooting lessons." His perfect mouth curved. "Perhaps your aim would improve."

Violet laughed. "I would prefer a different sort of lesson, my lord. And I am available anytime you wish."

His blue eyes glinted with heat. He surveyed the gathering that included Reese and Elizabeth and their two children, as well as Lily, little Katie and Alex. Travis and Annabelle were there, standing next to Caroline's grandmother Adelaide Lockhart and Rule's aunt Agatha, who had proudly wagered a very large sum on her nephew.

"I don't suppose we could leave early," Rule said, looking hopeful.

Violet bit back a smile. "Not today."

Rule sighed.

The breeze stirred a loose tendril of Violet's hair beneath wide-brimmed bonnet and he wrapped the copper strand around the tip of his finger. "Speaking of the Americans, I gather your friend Jeffrey has left England by now."

"He was cleared of any charges. I'm sure he headed home on the first available ship."

"Oddly enough, I wish him well."

Violet's eyes shifted to Rule's as she remembered how Jeffrey had come to warn her of Montgomery's attempt to escape. "So do I."

Rule set his hands on her waist and drew her a little closer. "I wish him good fortune, but I am glad I am the man you married, not him."

Violet reached up and cupped his cheek. "My father was right, you know."

"Your father?"

"Father told me that when the time was right, you would make a very good husband." She looped her arms around his neck and tilted her head back to look at him. "I think he believed we would make each other happy."

"Griff was always right about everything." Rule pressed a soft kiss on her lips. "And you have made me the happiest man on earth."

Violet thought of the father she adored and the wonderful husband he had chosen for her, looked up at the heavens and smiled.

* * * * *

AUTHOR'S NOTE

I hope you enjoyed Rule and Violet's story, the last in the Bride's Trilogy. The series began with Royal and Lily's adventure in *Royal's Bride*. The second book featured Reese and Elizabeth in *Reese's Bride*. All three were great fun to write.

Up next for me is a new contemporary romantic suspense trilogy centered on the handsome Raines brothers. It starts with *Against the Wind,* which begins in Wyoming and tells Jackson's tale, followed by Gabriel's and Devlin's stories, *Against the Fire* and *Against the Law.* I hope you'll watch for them.

In the future, I hope to bring you more from Royal's friends, the Oarsmen. Until that time, happy reading and all best wishes.

Kat